Dark Oak

Book One

Jacob Sannox

For my long-suffering parents and my sons.

Acknowledgements

Mum, Dad and Anna offered so much support throughout this process, so I can't thank them enough.

Thanks to Andy, too. Without the many meetings of the Registry of Unusual Absences in various pubs, I probably never would have got this far.

Thanks to everyone who took a peek at the manuscript and offered their advice!

Map of the World

Also available at www.jacobsannox.com

Chapter One

This is *not* a story about a Dark Lord, though there was one, and his name was Awgren; there were once creatures that could be described as inherently evil, moulded at the time of the Devising; there had been black and white, good and evil, light and dark.

But Awgren was about to die. The woodcutter, however, was not – not yet.

A thousand years had passed since Awgren drove the survivors of mankind from the Old Continent, but although they had started new lives in other lands, they had never given up hope of returning home. Their descendants built their strength in secret, and as the centuries passed, Awgren paid the exiles less heed.

In time, a fire kindled in the dry grass of his complacency, and when Queen Cathryn landed her troops, Awgren found himself outmatched. The armies of mankind marched once more across the wastelands of the Old Continent. The monstrous Creatures of the Devising stood to meet them in a final battle, commanded by Awgren himself. He supplemented his army with enslaved men from the Hinterland, who were forced to fight against their own kind.

Morrick the woodcutter was one such a man.

He had spent the final days of the battle charging up and down the front line, roaring at anyone who took a step backward, hurling those who faltered back into position, and shouting 'hold the line' so many times that the words echoed in the cellars and back rooms of his mind until the day he eventually died.

As the lone regiment of human conscripts amongst the unruly horde of Awgren's Devised, the men of the Hinterland had initially been positioned at the centre of the battle line, but though *they* had fought hard and gained ground, the same could not be said of Awgren's troops on either side of them. The Devised were an undisciplined mob, as likely to turn on their own as to stand against their enemy, and though the Combined People, ruled over by Queen Cathryn and her consort, Lord Lachlan, were far fewer in number, their soldiers were well-armoured, regimented and hardy; their superiority began to tell.

The human cavalry harried Awgren's flanks, throwing the lines of Devised into disarray. So it was that Awgren divided the regiment of the Hinterland and sent the two halves to the flanks, leaving the defence of the centre to his innumerable but unreliable Devised.

Morrick and his fellow pikemen saw off the horsemen, driving the points of their long pikes into any mount that charged them. As sweat dripped from their brows and their muscles began to fatigue, the men quietly hoped their opponents would be victorious; that their liberation was at hand.

Victory for humanity *was* close. Lord Linwood was the most powerful of the queen's lords, and he saw not only the danger to his heavy cavalry on the flanks, but also the new weakness at the centre.

He charged into the Creatures of the Devising and decimated their ranks. Cathryn and Lachlan rallied their people and led the infantry into the chaos at the very heart of Awgren's army. They toiled hard at their blood-work until, finally, Awgren strode to meet the queen and her consort. Together, they struck the Dark Lord down, and the Devised fell back in dismay. Pursued by the queen and her lords, they fled in all directions as they sought escape, trampling all in their way; even their slaves, the menfolk of the Hinterland.

At the exact moment Queen Cathryn's spear pierced Awgren's throat, Morrick was sleeping.

He awoke only when his tent collapsed, and his cot overturned, depositing him in the thick mud. Morrick rolled on to his side as the sound of roaring voices and trampling feet raged around him. His world had been reduced to darkness. He struggled to find his way out from under a press of canvas, crawling and feeling about him for his axe, but to no avail. Finally, he found the edge of the tent, and his head emerged into the dim light before the dawn.

The Creatures of the Devising were rampaging through the camp, snarling, slashing and falling over one another in a ferocious, surging retreat. The stampeding remnants of Awgren's army crushed each other underfoot in their haste to force a path before them, and in their wide, panicked eyes, Morrick saw a glimmer of hope for himself and his people.

They're fleeing, he thought. *It's over. We're free.*

Morrick lumbered to his feet, tottering slightly, and rather than follow his first instinct to warn off the approaching creatures with a roar, he chose instead to gather his weapons and hope not to be jostled or stabbed as the Creatures of the Devising passed him by. They had been unwilling allies for many years, but Morrick and all of the conscripts knew never to trust the Devised; a warning shout might be provocation enough for them to turn on his whole regiment. There was no time for relief at the overthrow of the Dark Lord or his new found freedom, not when Awgren's creatures were bearing down upon his men, utterly without regard for human life.

He searched through the wreckage of his tent and found his wood-axe underneath his smashed cot. He snatched up his leather helm, glad he had slept in his breast and backplate, but left the rest of his possessions where they lay. So armed, Morrick looked about him.

His men were in similar states, either drawing themselves out from collapsed shelters or hurrying out into the open as they rubbed sleep from their weary eyes. Several were wandering aimlessly and looked at risk at being carried off in a tide of Devised. Others were trampled underfoot or cut down by the creatures as they fled.

Having spent less than a second weighing up the risks, Morrick listened to his gut. He hollered above the din of the retreat, holding his wood-axe aloft.

'Men of the Hinterland- Stand to your arms! Form up on me! You there – form up on me!'

The closest of his men paid heed and they in turn shouted out to those further away. In the coming moments, Morrick could pick out some fifteen men in ruddy woollen tunics forcing a path through to where he stood.

'Well done, lads,' he said, looking at each of their faces in turn before guiding them into formation.

'Ranks of three. Keep your weapons drawn. Audric, you're my right-hand marker.'

The men scurried into a block with Audric on the right of the front rank. Only two of them carried their pikes, the rest were either unarmed or carried short swords or daggers. All had followed his advice and slept in armour.

Good, he thought. *Good lads.*

'Right-hand file, face the Devised,' Morrick shouted, and Audric echoed the order, his booming voice carrying across the din. The men obeyed. Morrick moved ahead of the block.

'Prepare to march, advancing to the front. March!' he shouted and was once more echoed by his right-hand marker. Their feet moved as one, and the block began to advance across the face of the Devised towards the front line where the rest of the regiment had been posted. Morrick gripped his axe in both hands, looking all about him, ever watchful. As they moved, feet slipping in the mud and the salt of their sweat stinging their eyes, more stragglers joined them and swelled their numbers. The right-hand file that faced the enemy grew from five to ten men, still three-deep as they sidled onwards. Morrick stood to the lee of the block and picked another steady man.

'You there, Elmick, go to the rear. Keep the men steady there.'

Elmick nodded and bustled into position. Thus satisfied, Morrick addressed his men as they shuffled onwards.

'We force a path through to the front and join the rest of the regiment. Does anyone know what's happened?'

'No, Sergeant.'

Morrick nodded, expecting as much.

'It looks as though the centre has broken. If so, Awgren's army has been divided in two, and even if we aren't killed by the Devised, we'll shortly be surrounded by the Combined People. We must look to strength in numbers and to ourselves now. We must find the rest of the regiment. Courage now and keep your eyes about you; the Devised could turn on us at any time.'

The way was slow and treacherous; they steered a course around an upturned wagon and picked their way between Awgren's fallen beast-riders. Morrick noted broken pikes embedded in some of the mounts. This did not bode well and he clung to the fervent hope that if his regiment had been forced to engage Awgren's own cavalry, that they had come off better and retreated as a unified body; certainly though there were dead men at his feet, there seemed not enough to suggest utter carnage.

From where he marched on the lee side of the block, he was protected from the swarm and could watch as the horde tore onward; their filthy reek hanging in the air, joining the dank odour of the battleground and the smell of rotting flesh that seemed ever present. Mercifully, the rampaging creatures let them be and began to thin out as the block drew near to the rest of the regiment. Morrick was able to see a little better in the direction from which they had flown.

Sure enough, the enemy cavalry were driving the Devised towards them. He could see their banners flying and their helms gleaming red under the rising sun. A sea of horsemen rushed in to fill up the ground between Morrick's side of Awgren's army and the other, now divided and asunder. Far in the distance, Morrick knew, the other half of his regiment was isolated and in a similar predicament.

Where is Awgren?

But of the Dark Lord there was no sign. Of course, Morrick could see very little and concentrating anew, he set about the task of finding the main body of his half of the regiment. It was a great relief to see the ruddy tunics ahead of him nestled under a crown of pikes. They had charged for horse, circled around the drums, facing outwards with the points of their pikes angled to impale any approaching horses. The Devised were still paying his men little heed, but to Morrick's dismay, he saw that the half of the regiment not fending *them* off were under attack. Lord Linwood's cavalry charged towards the pikemen and slashed at their weapons as they tried to force a way through. Seeing the regiment near surrounded, Morrick's men began to curse, sob or fall stone silent as they marched, each according to their constitution.

'Courage now,' he said, the words barely audible as a feeling of dread settled upon him. He could not be certain if he was reassuring the men or himself.

A cry came from the assembled regiment, and Morrick recognised a fellow sergeant standing amongst the conscripts, now just mere yards away from them.

'Prepare to open the line and let them in!' the sergeant cried as he waved, halberd in hand.

It was at this moment that a phalanx of Awgren's Devised, seeing their path to escape narrowing as the two groups of men closed together, set about Morrick's right-hand file with claw, blade and cudgel, trying to force their way through. The uproar of war was renewed with fresh screams, shouts, the shriek of iron upon iron and the sounds of butchery. Skulls smashed, bodies punctured and Morrick's men began to fall.

'Fall back to the regiment! Fall back!' Morrick called, and those of his men not already facing the pikemen began to wheel, stepping backwards towards the opening gap in the line, fighting and dying as they went. Morrick ran towards Elmick who, as the farthest man out, had the longest distance to travel to safety.

He thrust his axe skyward as he reached the boy, checking the downward stroke of a Devised's mace. Morrick threw off the weapon, pulled back his own and drove the head of it into the beast's neck. Boiling blood spurted into his face as the axe stuck fast. The creature contorted as it stood pinned.

Morrick worked the axe free and roared into the faces of his new enemy as he backed away, hewing at any who dared approach his men.

There was no call to fear the threat of the routed Devised for long. The enemy cavalry, heavily armoured and bearing the banners of the Combined People, dashed through the fleeing horde, ploughing them under from the flank as they swept around the bunched pikemen.

His block within the relative safety of the charged pikes, Morrick turned to the south to be sure that the Devised were not doubling back towards them. But as he did so, he was thrown forward by a blow to the back of his head. It sent his brain hurtling against his skull. He grunted once and blacked out before his body slid into the mud.

The feet of Awgren's defeated army stamped him into the mud as it retreated and his face sank into the wet dark as the battle drew to a close.

And so the reign of Awgren failed upon what became known as the Field of the Scarlet Grass. Lord Lachlan and Queen Cathryn carved Awgren's body into many pieces as he lay pierced and defenceless, struck down not merely by spear and blade, but by his own complacency in facing them alone.

Their heavy cavalry, under the command of Lord Linwood, drove the Creatures of the Devising from the field and hemmed in those that survived, to be dealt with when battle was done. Their steadfast warriors fought hard and suffered great loss as they battled those Devised who still stood their ground, amongst them monstrosities ten times the size of a man, but eventually all of Awgren's creations were slain or, in the case of those with the capacity to do so, surrendered, throwing down their arms in realisation of defeat. Thousands of Awgren's creatures turned from overlords to prisoners in the passing of a single hour.

Mankind stood bloodied, but triumphant.

Most of mankind.

Chapter Two

The Hinterland

A small boy found the girls on the banks of the Whiteflow; his mother and her sisters. All three were naked, partially eaten, despoiled and inexpertly hidden with a covering of sand, pebbles and dry brush.

Days later, Rowan found the small boy on the banks of the Whiteflow, dead of exposure. Then she discovered the girls.

The door to the main lodge at the centre of Northall, the Hinterland's largest settlement, burst open, making the overseer and his companions start in their seats at the long table.

'More dead!' she shouted as she stormed towards them.

The overseer should have got to his feet, and the guards should have intervened, but all of them were still reeling from the force of the entrance. As they hesitated, Rowan went for them.

'We have spoken at length, have we not?' she railed. 'We have come to agreements time after time. You gave your word.' Her words rose almost to a howl, her eyes bloodshot from weeping.

The overseer regained some semblance of composure and got to his feet. The guards began to move, but he held up a hand towards them.

'What's happened?'

She reached the table and leant over it as she snarled at him.

'Three girls dead and one wee boy, barely off the breast, and now to go under the ground. Do you know of this?'

He shook his head. The overseer's voice came out at a higher pitch than he would have liked.

'How?'

It was the wrong thing to say and he knew it. She propelled herself back from the table in disgust and pointed at him as she spoke.

'There will be no more of this, I promise you.'

She strode back out of the hall, calling back to them before she went.

'Four dead and by your hand at one remove. The Devised go. All of them. Hear me?'

'I hear you, Rowan, but what would you have me do? My hands are tied!' He sounded feeble as he called after her, but it was of no consequence.

She was already gone.

He sat and turned to the others around the table.

'What do we know of this?'

The council members shook their heads in silence as they sat in thought. One of the guards cleared his throat from the shadows at the side of the hall.

'Beg pardon, Overseer.'

The overseer looked round and saw the guard step forward.

'Beg pardon. Not my place to say, sir. But there was some talk at the barracks this morning.'

The overseer sighed and rubbed his eyes.

'What kind of talk?'

The guard looked nervous and he exchanged a look with one of the others, who was at first reluctant to be seen meeting his gaze.

'Word was that the Devised had been out for sport yesterday, at least; that some slipped out of their camp.'

The overseer shook his head and his fingers massaged his temples. He looked at the faces around the table and he saw how few were looking back.

'What would she have me do? What would each of you have me do? Of course, she's right. We all want them to go. I see in your faces how little you think of me and rightly so, but I am only empowered to echo instructions to my friends as though I am making decisions and giving orders. How am I to remove the Creatures of the Devising except by force? That would be tantamount to rebellion in Awgren's eyes. If he fears loss of control in the Hinterland, he may end the alliance and destroy us,' he said, unaware of Awgren's defeat in the south.

Garrick, perhaps the most respected of the Hinterland councillors, spoke up.

'I for one would rather face death or exile than watch our daughters be raped and killed one by one. Yes, our lands will be forfeit and many of us will fall, but such is the price of war. The Hinterland should have declared for Cathryn years ago.'

The words had no time to hang in the air before another of the councillors spoke.

'And what of our sons and brothers? What of those who have gone to war on Awgren's behalf?'

This time there was indeed a silence. All there knew the answer.

'I believe our sons and brothers would understand our need here. They have already chosen to fight and die for their families – many of them likely *have* died for their families. This Rowan - she may not be swayed by the opinions of old folk and,' he motioned around the table with his hand, 'a gaggle of collaborators such as us," replied Garrick.

The overseer made no outward sign of reacting and Garrick continued.

'Rowan may speak loudest, but she is not the only one who speaks. She gives voice to a common desire across the Hinterland and we all know it, those of us who still trouble ourselves to talk to our people.'

Garrick's words may have been forthright, but he could not bring himself to make eye contact with the overseer who, to his credit, was attending to the older man, seeking to meet his gaze. He gave up and took his turn to speak.

'If she rises up, alone or aided, I will have to act. I would urge each of you to use whatever influence you have to dissuade rash action here. It is my role to oversee the Hinterland in Awgren's stead, but let me reiterate that I do not control the horde penned in that camp. Their captains may imply they are here for our protection, but make no mistake, they are an occupying force. They will not listen to me. Though you may think me a collaborator, make no mistake that Awgren grants me no real authority as his chosen overseer.'

He reached for his goblet and drank of his wine before continuing.

'I see the way you all look at me, as though I have betrayed our people, but somebody needed to stand forward to represent us. I live in constant fear that Awgren will perceive some slight in my actions and unleash the Devised upon us. I have no more love for him than do any of you, but I am all too aware of how we will fare if we stand against him before we are ready.'

'What would you suggest we do then?' asked Acorna, the only female councillor.

'We can do nothing to stop a rebellion from gathering support unless we truly collaborate and root out the perpetrators,' Garrick said, cutting off the overseer's response.

Councillor Cedarick, who had been conscripted himself many years before, had remained quiet and listened, but now he interjected.

'I for one think the time has come for the Hinterland to be rallied and for us to declare against Awgren. The rebellion has been taken to his door, and the queen, with the Lord of the Isles, does battle there. We should be providing what aid we can to the rest of our kind, not sitting on our hands. We should meet with Rowan and plan for war. As a descendant of the thegns, her words carry weight in the Hinterland.'

A light snow fell, and Rowan pulled her cloak about her as she walked. A crowd had gathered outside the main lodge, but she had barged through, ignoring their questions and for the most part they let her go without attempting to waylay her. Her friend, Lara, followed on behind, but Rowan did not mind; they had known each other since childhood, and Lara knew how to handle Rowan's temper. She knew that the flame could not be put out and must be allowed to falter. When she was certain Rowan had calmed, Lara would make her tentative approach.

As Rowan pounded through the village towards home, she was bombarded by memories of Morrick. He had overseen the construction of many of the lodges around her; drawing up plans, felling the trees and joining the toil. He had carved the more ornate adornments, and their shapes summoned his face to mind. She fought hard to dismiss his image, knowing it would lead only to tears and despair that she could not afford.

She turned north as she reached the eastern edge of the village and walked upstream along the Whiteflow towards the forest edge and their homestead. Morrick had, of course, built it himself. Every log was felled by him. Every detail carved into the wood was him. She growled at herself, and looked back over her shoulder southward to where the Devised encampment fouled the river by its mere proximity. She pitied the fish there. If she was one of them, she'd nip at their foul toes if they dared to enter her waters, and if she could do naught else, she would dash herself against some boulder amidst the rapids until her tiny fish brain was addled and useless.

But that's not true is it? They foul your home by their mere proximity in this, the last of the usable lands in a continent razed by Awgren; this beautiful country. Do you fight them? No, you get on with your damn days as best you can and raise hell if they cross the line. Morrick would be ashamed to see how the Devised's behaviour had been allowed to escalate unchecked.

But was Morrick any better? Her husband, strong as he might be, was weak of heart just like every other man and woman of the Hinterland who did not fight all day, every day to overthrow Awgren. Off he went to fight like a good little underling rather than stand his ground.

The tears came, and she checked her pace in an instant. Clasping her mouth and sobbing in shame at how she was thinking of him when he was far from home, force marched into great danger. The polished cherrywood of her wedding band was cold against her lips.

Lara's arm encircled her waist. Rowan shouldered her away and continued charging up the narrow path towards her home, still sobbing as she went. Lara paused, swallowed her hurt and followed on.

She kept pace behind.

The path left the riverside and turned towards the forest. The outer fence came into view and, as always, Rowan was relieved to see her land devoid of Devised. Livestock roamed within the bounds of the fence and crops grew on the forest side of the lodge. The homestead had once been heaving with men seeing to the cattle and tending the crops, while others toiled in Morrick's workshop, but now they had all gone off to fight. Angry as she was and determined not to settle back into routine, Rowan had much work to do while she made her plans. She waited at the gate for Lara, and the two women entered together.

The lodge's shutters were open and secured back against the walls. She frowned and knocked on the door.

'It's Rowan,' she called.

From the other side of the door came the sound of beams being shifted, and before too long, she was granted entry.

'I asked you not to open the shutters while I was away, Mother,' she scolded. 'A Devised can enter through a window as easily as a door.'

'And yet you are happy to allow the boys out to work.' Her mother, Bramble, dismissed her concerns then returned to the baby's cot. Rowan followed and stroked her sleeping daughter's cheek. Bracken stirred and cooed, but did not wake.

'Are the boys working now?' she asked.

Bramble nodded, not turning to look as she shuffled towards the door.

'Aye, I'll head along to see how they're faring.'

The two younger women were left in peace.

Lara took a seat by the empty fireplace and waited for the inevitable. She folded her hands in her lap and watched as Rowan paced the lodge. Minutes passed.

'Eight dead in as many weeks,' she said.

Rowan dropped into her chair, fuming. Lara pulled a fur throw about her against the chill in the air and waited patiently while her friend merely scowled at her in silence for some minutes.

Finally, Rowan spoke.

'Something has to be done.'

Lara nodded and maintained eye contact. She swept a strand of hair back behind her ear and waited.

'Those bastard things need to be eradicated,' said Rowan.

Both women could see many things hanging before them; the faces of their menfolk, the names of their children and the consequences of rebelling, bloody consequences, no doubt.

Finally, Lara leant one cheek against her balled fist, crossed her legs and spoke.

'Out with it then, what are you thinking?' her voice sounded soft and cautious.

Rowan's scowl intensified. She looked away momentarily, but when their eyes met again, her features had softened.

'I think that if we make a move people will die, but that I would rather take that risk than live like this.'

'Under the sway of evil,' said Lara.

'More than that! We facilitate, we collaborate, we reinforce and we tolerate! We, by our inactions are weak, but if that isn't bad enough, we're out there making things worse for those who do have the courage to stand and fight against Awgren,' Rowan shouted.

'I am not going to wait for the day when I find my children's bodies in the fields because some foul thing has got bored and sought fun amongst my own. You want to wait? For that?'

Lara raised an eyebrow.

'I don't want anyone else to die, I know that. But I cannot see a way to avoid death for some of us, one way or the other. If we hunker down and wait for the rebellion to be crushed, we may yet expel the Devised by appealing directly to Awgren through the overseer. Our men may come home and life can go on as it has done. That wouldn't be so bad.'

Lara was about to continue, but Rowan was shaking her head, her eyes fixed intently on Lara's boot. She scratched at the back of her hand with her fingernails.

'I don't think I can live like this anymore. Looking on - It's all we ever do,' Rowan said, quieter now and thoughtful. She looked up and into Lara's eyes. 'Are you good? A good woman?' she asked.

'I'm not sure what that means. I do right by my own. My family are healthy. I work hard. I never wrong anyone if I can help it. Do you not think I am?' said Lara.

'I'm not sure of the answer,' Rowan paused, 'for you or for me. Does a good woman look to her own needs while crimes are perpetrated all around her? Does a good man fight on the wrong side because he fears the consequences?'

'Sometimes a clever woman does. A clever man might,' said Lara.

'If breathing was all that mattered to them,' said Rowan. 'I want my children to become good men, men who toil hard and in good conscience.'

Lara rubbed at one eye. She did not reply.

Rowan leant forward in her chair.

'Cathryn and her people could do as we have done, but they fight and they die because they believe it is right to do so. They could have saved their lands by accepting Awgren centuries ago, as our people did. They could do that now still and carve out a life not filled with war and death.'

Lara smiled.

'I can't give you the answer that you want, Rowan. I like being alive and so do my children. If I could get rid of him and guarantee their safety, I would.' She stood and moved to the cot. She reached in and lifted out the baby. Rowan jumped to her feet and moved to stop her friend, but Lara handed over the child.

'Here. You can have peace, but all I ask is that you dash her head against a rock. Would you do it?'

Rowan cradled the baby in one arm and with the other hand, slapped Lara hard across the face. Her friend fell back and steadied herself against the cot.

'You take my point.'

Rowan breathed heavily and set the baby back in the cot to sleep.

'I'll leave.' said Lara and walked towards the door. Though her cheek throbbed, she made no attempt to cradle her face and through her anger, Rowan began to regret her outburst.

'You don't have to go,' she said.

Lara continued walking.

'You think we should do nothing then?' Rowan asked, making an effort to sound conciliatory.

Lara did not check her pace nor turn as she replied.

'I think we should stay alive.'

She left.

Rowan looked at the closed door for some time, thinking on how she might have handled things differently, but the day was passing quickly; animals needed feeding and crops needing tending. She went out to find her mother to watch the baby so that she could join Callum and Declan.

Rowan's path crossed the shadow of the barn and she could scarce believe that it was still before noon. She tightened her hair back in its bun and set off to find her sons. Her mother was leaning on a wooden fence, watching the boys work.

Rowan padded forward and came to a standstill on the head of her mother's shadow. She ran her eyes over Bramble's form. Neither woman moved for some time whilst the daughter evaluated the mother with a cold regard.

How does she live with herself? Does knowing that I am alive and strong, that I bore her strong grandchildren make life seem worth living as whatever it is we are? Does gentle, hard-working and kind equal good?

Her mind supplied no ready answer and she sighed. Hearing her, Bramble pushed herself up from the fence. She turned, and the spite in Rowan's mind lessened somewhat when she looked upon the familiar features.

'Is she all right?'

'Lara or Bracken?' said Rowan, not really concentrating. Her eyes flitted across the yard to locate Callum and Declan.

'The baby.'

'She's sleeping.'

Bramble nodded.

'That's something. When I heard the shouting, I was sure you'd wake her.'

The criticisms were only implied, but Rowan heard them nonetheless. She said nothing and turned back towards the corral once more. Callum was shoring up the fence on the far side while Declan, the younger of the two, dragged bales of fresh hay towards the stables. Bramble started back towards the house.

'Mother,' the old woman turned, wearing a tired but patient expression, 'what should I do about the dead girls?'

Bramble sighed and shook her head.

'Bide your time and act only when calm. None of us enjoy this, but the generations that came before you stomached it. I stomached it and stomach it still. One day the Hinterland will be free again, and we will unite again with those who fight Awgren now.'

Bramble shrugged and folded her arms tightly across her chest, pulling her shawl taut.

'I'll see to the baby,' she said.

Later on when the moon was up and the air grew ever more chill, Rowan wrapped a fur stole around her shoulders and, carrying a basket, left her mother and children sleeping in the lodge to make her way down to the banks of the Whiteflow. She could hear only her breath and her footsteps on the walk. Even the forest was quiet. The cold air and the hush of early night brought clarity not only to thought, but to sensation. She felt fresh and alive as she hurried with small steps towards the river, ever watchful and listening out for the sound of approaching danger. Before long her feet sank into the sand of the riverbank. Her ankle flexed awkwardly as she made her way to the water's edge, and she cried out. She halted when the bank behind her ran high, offering a little shelter from those who might approach from the south. The land struck out into the straight river there and the water pooled, swirling in the deep crook that had been worn into the earth upstream of the headland. She clambered up the white sand of the incline and peered over to look back towards the Devised encampment though it lay some distance out of sight. She saw nothing and satisfied, she slipped back down to the water and began to step out of her clothes. The water was too cold, but the air was no better and so she braced, breathed steadily and slipped smooth and swift into the Whiteflow. She paused only once the water reached her hips then ducked down to cover her chest and head. Rowan came up shuddering, the cold seeming like a white, dull ache throughout her; so cold she almost felt warmed by the intensity. She floated on her back, looking up at the moon for a time and then returned to the bank, quickly drying herself with blankets from the basket. These she set back inside atop her knife as she dressed. She knew she should hurry back to the lodge, but she was hearing the call of freedom and allowed herself the knowing delusion that she could go wherever she wanted and do as she pleased. Where would she go if she was at leisure to do so? Away, certainly. To Morrick?

She repacked the blankets a little tidier as she thought of him, wishing she could feel his rough hands on her skin; his hot breath on the nape of her neck as he reached round and fondled her breasts – raked his fingers across her stomach. She smiled, thinking of how much that touch conveyed, usually the forerunner of the playful growls at her ear. She thought of the hungry look in his eye as he looked upon her nakedness and then sighed deep, wondering if she'd ever see him again.

Her daydreaming dispelled upon hearing a snort. She started and, crouched prone, she listened. Again she heard the snort and recognised it as that of a horse coming from the direction of the encampment. Hidden from view by the bank, Rowan set down her basket and reached under the blankets for her knife, fearing a Devised rider was concealed from her. She slunk back against the incline and began to inch towards the crest.

She gasped at what she saw; something right out of her memories that she had dismissed as a dream or childhood fantasy. Her eyes could make out the outline of a horse with a foaming white mane that emanated a blue tinge. It stood in the shallows beyond the bluff. The hem of its curtain of hair danced across the surface of the water as it leant forward to drink. Surely it was a trick of the light, but its body seemed translucent, just as it had done when she had seen it before as a child. Rowan relaxed a little and looked around for a rider, reassured somewhat by the lack of saddle upon the animal. There was nobody in sight.

Slow and with obvious movements, she crept up onto the short brown grass and looked down upon the animal as it stood in the rushing water, illumined by the white moonlight. Her heart tripped and she felt the movement rise up her throat. The kelpie raised its head and looked at her, but made no move to bolt. For a time, they stood and regarded one another, then with a snort, the horse trotted upstream and with a thrash of its mane, it hurried into a gallop northwards toward the forest.

Rowan let out a disappointed cry to which the horse paid no heed as it retreated. She watched it go, picked up her basket and set off home. On the way, she pondered the stories her mother told her of the Naiads; the spirits of the waters.

She was still thinking of these tales, warmed by a sense of wonder when she reached the main gate to the farm. Her reverie was interrupted by the sight of a black shape moving along the side of the barn towards the yard.

She stifled a gasp, once more fetched up her knife and, gripping it so tightly it felt as though her knuckles would burst through the skin, she slipped through the gate.

Chapter Three

Deep in the forest north of Rowan's homestead, within the heart of a black oak tree, Riark awoke. There was no sight, hearing or touch as humans would understand it – simply being. He extended his reach to every part of the tree, to the very extremities of the roots and branches. The wind swayed the boughs, and an acorn found its moment to drop. Just as its connection broke, Riark gathered inside it and fell with it. He and the acorn landed on the soft earth in the shade under the canopy, bounced then came to a stop on the mud.

Riark remained with the acorn. To begin with it seemed destined to lie there indeterminately, but one morning a squirrel descended the trunk of the oak, saw the acorn and acquired it for its hoard. Riark would have smiled if he had a mouth, pleased to find a new experience after so many centuries. The squirrel carried him aloft, ran along a branch then leapt to the next tree. On and on the tiny animal darted, jumped and climbed until it happened upon the hollow high up in an ash where it made its store. Thus deposited, Riark determined it was time to move on. He slipped from the acorn into the trunk of the ash, savouring the taste of its sap and the different textures as he coursed through it, towards the ground.

Riark tarried there a while and slumbered until, one day, The First Tree called and Riark paid heed.

At one moment he was in the south of the Impassable Forest and a second later he was inside the First Tree hundreds of miles further north. He waited behind the bark, sensing that he was alone. He took his rest again while he waited for the others.

A vibration stirred him into sentience once again and as awareness dawned, the First Tree changed from a tree to a tree and more. It was time to emerge and Riark gathered his strength and wits.

The bark of the tree began to bow outwards almost imperceptibly then ten rough tentacles began to grow like new branches. Seconds later, the bark between these tendrils also moved outwards and stiff hands forced their way forward, followed by arms. Now a foot formed from the trunk of the tree, then a leg, followed by another foot and yet another leg. These legs walked a long, smooth torso forward and out of the trunk. A taut neck snapped a smooth, carved head out of the First Tree in an awkward nod. The living mannequin stood erect, its head and the tips of its shoulder blades still part of the tree. Riark concentrated and felt the last of his essence leave the tree as he stepped away, yards-long vines resembling hair extended out behind him, finally falling lank against his solid body, hanging down below the wooden imitation of hips. Riark shed the bark and his body gleamed in the bright sunlight like a polished table-top. His limbs flexed as though shaking off an afternoon of inactivity. Features formed into a face, the wood seemingly crafting itself. There were no eyeballs, but the gentle curve of an eye between crested waves of carved eyelids settled into permanent shape. His nose was at first primitive and blocked, but the wood shrank back to give definition. His mane of vines entwined to form a single bunched cat-of-nine-tails that waved and slapped against the back of his thighs. Riark looked up at the sky and raised pupils lifted from the surface of his eyes. He smiled. There was no cavity to his mouth, but the lips curled. Riark, king of the Dryads, had taken avatar.

On the other side of the First Tree, a similar feat was being undertaken by a creature forming from a boulder. Riark exercised his new legs and strolled round, his feet crushing his discarded bark. Wern, king of the Oreads towered above him, some nine feet high, his legs as wide as marble columns and his arms almost forming an arch to the ground. His body formed into the shape of a giant muscular man.

They bowed to one another, but turned sharply at the sound of a laugh emerging from the pool which surrounded the island on which they stood. Samura, queen of the Naiads had arrived. Her ever-flowing waterfall mane rose from the surface and her eyes, blue marbles suspended in a face, translucent and ever-moving, fixed on them in turn.

Riark's vines whipped suddenly around his body, and the surface of the pool was churned up into a succession of waves, flowing outward towards the far bank. Mayri, queen of the Sylphs, took form, constantly dissipating and re-forming, like gathered breaths on a cold morning. On the foreshore of the First Island and in the shallows of the First Waters, the kings and queens of the world called counsel and prepared to understand one another anew.

Riark walked into the pool, forcing his feet down against his buoyancy. He waded out till the waters were around his waist. Samura wrapped shimmering, flowing arms around him and he could feel the water of her body rushing against the solidity of his own. She soaked into him. Wern trudged downwards, his feet taking up great divots each time he lifted them, and when he smashed into the water, even at a slow pace, he drove the water away from him with such force that Riark was nearly lifted with a wave and carried off. Samura steadied him. Wern carried on into the pool even deeper until Riark and Samura could sit upon his shoulders and yet still be half submerged, wrapping their arms around his great stone neck. Mayri took flight and hovered above them. There was not a sound or movement except for the gentle lapping of breaking waves. Then in one quick motion, Wern shrank into the shape of a small stone upon the bed of the pool. Riark's body diminished into nothing but a single-leafed twig, floating on the troubled surface. Samura diffused into the pool and Mayri descended as a mist, hanging above it.

As the hours passed, the kings and queens imitated one another in aesthetic, but new of texture. Trees formed of stone, stones formed of wood, water raised into cloud and clouds fell as rain. Stone began to flow or grow. Air thrust roots into the soil. They were four and they were one, as it had been from the first.

New beings entered the clearing – all of them felt it at once and were still until the newcomers were recognised. Riark approximated a human once more and strode out of the pool not on the island, but on the bank. Five Dryads, all similar in form yet subtly different, stood just outside the treeline.

Riark stood ready and, unseen, the soles of his feet grew downwards into reaching, pulsing roots. These found the roots of his counterparts and as they entwined, Riark heard their thoughts, knew what they knew, and lost himself in them. He heard the whole forest and knew that something was wrong. He turned back to the pool and, sad of heart, for this ceremony would not take place again for many a year, he bowed and left his peers. Riark turned towards the forest and ran towards a silver birch. He dived forward, hands clasped together, and his body disappeared into the trunk.

The dive completed as he sprung forth from another silver birch seven hundred miles to the north, and his body curled into a forward roll before coming to a stop in a steady crouch. His five companions appeared alongside him. They cast out roots and conversed.

Visible through the ranks of trees, men were hacking at the forest with axes. Not just one or two at a time, like on the southern border with what men called the Hinterland, but in tens and twenties. All six of them felt an ash die and heard it crash to the forest floor, each hearing without hearing, its final gasp. Riark surveyed the scene, dismayed. The humans were consuming more trees than they could possibly need to build. He knew consumption was in their nature and that the forest usually sustained its losses, yet the scale of their efforts troubled him.

It was inevitable that, unchecked, these men would unwittingly lop down a Mother Tree, killing the Dryad it had birthed and to which it was still inextricably linked. Perhaps a lone woodcutter could be dissuaded, frightened off or, if necessary, killed, but to stand against such numbers would risk the exposure of his people and, worse, the threat of fire to drive them back. Riark would not risk it, but nor would he allow those who must die to do so without having time to prepare.

He turned to his companions and gave orders that word should be sent to all whose Mother Trees grew in the north.

Riark squatted in the shadow of the canopy and observed the humans work, honouring the passing of each and every tree. He waited for days while his messengers scoured the forests of the world in search of those whose Mother Trees were in jeopardy. His people sometimes wandered afar in forms that were disconnected from the forest for a time, as it had been while he was inside the fallen acorn.

The first of his messengers returned. Nayr's shapely tribute to female human form moved cat-like through the boughs and alighted soundlessly beside her king.

'There are four in this part of the wood,' she whispered, the line of her mouth cracking open and slivers of wood splintering from the new parting as mouth, throat and lungs formed. He saw her chest newly swell.

Riark rested his forehead against hers and for a moment, their grains were as one.

'My thanks. Have they been found?'

'Only two so far. The others are roaming and not at root. The others are looking. Shall we attend the trees?'

Riark nodded, and together the roots beneath their feet moved soundlessly under the forest in search of the Mother Trees, vacant but necessary for the survival of their one-time occupants. Grasping the roots of other trees, the Dryad and his consort listened and felt for the Mother Trees then loosened their grip. Riark led Nayr into the trunk of an elm, and they appeared from another some distance away. The sound of the men's activity had faded a little as they approached the Mother Tree that grew nearest to the felling. She was old, her roots were deep, and her trunk stood far and away taller than her daughters around her feet. Riark stood underneath her foliage, taking pains not to touch her trunk as to do so was to show her a great disrespect.

Riark looked at Nayr admiring the aesthetic of her adopted form, though he had no sexual inclination, nor, in truth, actual gender. She tilted her head when she noticed his gaze and he looked away.

'I will stand watch here until her child can be found. You should join the search.'

Riark spent a few hours in his human form, but, he was curious to note, he felt more restive when he resembled a human and acutely aware of the passage of time. A sensation something akin to glee flooded through him when he noticed he was tapping his foot with impatience. When he could take no more, he took refuge inside the elm through which he had arrived, and as his physicality diffused, it was though a great burden had been lifted from him.

When Riark slept, it was not as he had once done hundreds of years ago. He vaguely remembered the sleep of man. Enshrouded within the body of a tree, it was as though he was a muscle releasing all tension. It was as though a worrying mind relaxed so utterly that it broke free of the biological connection. He felt his consciousness reach the boundaries of his own mind and his individuality disappearing. He lost almost all sense of self and language. His existence was being without thought. He was impetus and growth.

It would be more accurate to say he was woken than to say he awoke. The being that was Riark drew together, mustered and attended to the world without. The men were drawing ever nearer. Riark's eyes formed on the trunk, and he surveyed their approach. There was little time before the Mother Tree would be in peril, he judged.

Somewhere in the system of roots, resonating in the dampness of the soil, a sweeping movement drew Riark's attention. Before he had a chance to examine it further, his curiosity was satisfied.

There was no gradual emergence of the Dryad from the Mother Tree; his kinsman erupted forth; an outthrust shard of timber that broke the surface of the bark as would a leaping dolphin escape the sea. The Dryad slid length first in the grass and then the wood seemed to draw-in towards the middle of the splinter. A humanoid figure drew up from the flowing wood, and Riark sensed the rage, emanating from the Dryad like heat from a fire, so keenly that he was perturbed, sensing that the tree he inhabited might burst into flames. The Dryad's form was much like his own, but its shoulders hunched forward and its hands clenched into fists as it looked on. Riark slipped seamlessly from the elm and approached. Dryads did not startle, but the newcomer whirled in a near approximation. Etched fury marred his face so that the wood cracked along the grain, steamed and knitted together once more. He seemed poised to attack all and any.

Riark raised his hands high, fingers forming rigid claws aiming at the ground. He thrust them downward an inch, but even as the hands halted, the fingers grew downward as quickly as liquid, driving into the soil and lancing forward towards the other Dryad. The newcomer's roots drew back, but Riark's own were faster and grappled with them.

He saw recognition on the newcomer's face and the calmness that arrived with it. The Dryad fell to one knee, looking up at him. He thrust roots into the soil and Riark did the same.

'Your Majesty.' Riark heard the words in his own mind and at once he knew the Dryad's name.

'Ashrider,' he said aloud.

'Your Majesty,' Ashrider said again.

'Rise up, Brother,' said Riark. 'I am here for you and your Mother.'

Ashrider did so.

'It will not be long until the axes are upon me,' he said, the words sorrowful, but cold. Riark sensed that the younger Dryad was prepared to resist. He guessed he had not long died as a human himself, judging from the rage he now displayed. In time, he would lose the ability.

'There are many of them, doing much destruction to the forest,' said Riark.

'Will you help me defend my Mother Tree?' asked Ashrider.

Riark looked in the direction of the men's activity.

'We cannot risk them bringing fire into our nation,' he said quietly.

'They are pests. They devour the forest and threaten my existence. We should drive them back.'

It was an opinion common amongst the younger of his folk, those who were new to the form and still bore the fiery nature that had caused their reawakening as Dryads. Riark had long ago put the loss of the few into some kind of perspective, long ago lost the heat of emotion.

'If we destroy them, many more will come. If more come, it will lead to confrontation. They cannot defeat us in combat, and if they retreat they will return with fire. You understand?'

Ashrider's eyes bore into him as keenly as a woodpecker's worrying of a trunk. Riark sensed that his subject knew the truth of his words, but that his impulse was to stand and fight. Riark feared that confrontation was inevitable and began to ready himself for what would surely come. This young one's animal instincts were yet to fade.

Ashrider could not meet Riark's gaze, and the king's body tensed. The vines of his mane entwined even tighter.

One moment the Dryads were standing quietly under the canopy and the next they burst forth, racing towards the men. Ashrider roared, deep and bestial, unbecoming of his kind, and his limbs powered forward bent on aggression. Riark felt no such emotion as he gave chase. He leapt to the side and disappeared inside the faithful elm, and for a time, Ashrider charged on alone thinking that his king would not intervene.

He drew up on his heels as two beech, standing as pillars ahead of him burst towards one another, shards of bark becoming flying shrapnel as spindly branches wound into a spider's web of wood to bar his way. His momentum was too great and had he been a man, he would certainly have struck the web that was Riark. Instead, he merged into one of the beech, and both Dryads occupied the same tree as their essences flowed down into the deep roots.

'Do not make me.' Riark's intentions echoed in Ashrider's mind. He was horrified, but somehow dismissed the inherent truthfulness of their natural communication. He powered on and sprung once more into human form, running through the wood. The last thought Riark caught before he was left alone in the tree was that Ashrider did not believe his king could truly be capable of such an act.

Riark gave up the chase and set out back towards the Mother Tree. He no longer wanted Ashrider to be able to hear his thoughts if he entered a tree, so he too returned to his human avatar and ran when he was close enough. As he passed the elm, Nayr stepped out of it, but he had no time to consult, and though he had never performed the act in front of another before, he had no time to hesitate. Riark dived deep into the heart of Ashrider's Mother Tree.

Ashrider screamed from away in the forest, feeling the violation even in human form. He threw his head this way and that, then ripped into a nearby silver birch, arriving inside his Mother Tree, having rent a terrible wound in the tree through which he had travelled. Riark felt the distant silver birch's pain and steeled himself against it. Ashrider's essence filled his Mother Tree. Riark battled him, his will stronger and his knowledge infinitely more honed. He had been with this tree before ever Ashrider had died as a human. He had been many trees. He was the forest and he was also its king. He had the mastery and he, Riark, king of the Dryads, used all of it now.

'Calm now or this is the end, Ashrider,' he thought, but the only reply was a sense of frantic, raging instinct. Animal instinct – such displays always perturbed Riark, as he no longer understood them.

'So be it. I am sorry, my brother, but they cannot bring fire to my realm.'

Riark thought of death and he became it. He felt the living pulse of the Mother Tree and turned its sap to poison even as it flowed. He decayed the bark, rotted the wood and caused the branches to break. With that, Ashrider fell silent and diminished. Riark could barely stand the loss, but he remembered how many saplings had died in the shadow of his own Mother Tree's growing branches. He stepped out of what had been the Mother Tree as the last of the life left her. Her trunk split up the middle and her roots hitched up, causing her to ride high. All moisture within her turned to steam, and she toppled against her daughters amidst an ever thickening fog emitting from within her. The wood creaked, cracked and finally sighed.

All was silent – even the axes of the coming men had ceased to chop, disturbed by the sound of Ashrider's frenzied run. Riark allowed his eyes to fade into the surface of his face and unseeing, he stood with his head hanging. He mourned the Mother Tree, and he lamented the passing of Ashrider.

After a time it began to rain, and the moisture soaking into him broke his reverie. He turned to face Nayr, but she was gone.

Riark set out in search of the next Mother Tree in the humans' path.

Chapter Four

The site of the Field of the Scarlet Grass had been farmland in the days before Awgren came to power; insignificant lowlands that stretched out between encircling mountain ranges not far north of Tayne's second city; Brodack.

Over the centuries a tenuous peace had been established between Tayne in the south and two other countries, Crinan and Culrain. The northern borders of Tayne were marked by the river Kenna which flowed southwest from the mountains and the river Marsh which flowed southeast. Crinan was to the northwest of the Kenna and Culrain to the northeast of the Marsh. These three kingdoms flourished and their houses traded across the rivers.

Parties from Crinan traversed the lakes in the north of their country and crossed the Blade Mountains. They established the Hinterland in the bare lands between Crinan and Culrain's northern borders and the forest. The province prospered in its own fashion although it was never considered as more than a frontier between three mountain ranges, most densely populated at the point where the Whiteflow emerged from the Impassable Forest. The trees engulfed the narrowing continent for thousands of miles northward, filling it from west to east. Many considered it impenetrable, so thick were the trees, and so few expeditions ever attempted to cross it. None succeeded.

The nations were strong by sea, and outposts were established to the north of the forest by those who sailed the treacherous coast towards where the air grew bitter, worse even than the climate of the Hinterland.

Sudden war arose from the Wastes which lay to the east of the Hinterland

and the north of Culrain. A cult grew up around a figure known as Awgren, and raids along the border with Culrain led to all-out conflict. King Cormac, the ruler of the largest and strongest of the countries, Culrain, sent his armies north into the Wastes, but none returned; at least none who returned were recognisable. This was the beginning of the time of the Devising, when evil began to spill from the Wastes and march south. The forces left to hold Culrain could not match their foe's numbers, and before a year had passed, the country had fallen under Awgren's command. No living person in Tayne, Culrain, Crinan or the Hinterland had ever seen him, but rumour had it that he stood some twenty-feet tall with the upper body of a man, a featureless face and the tail of a giant snake.

Tayne fortified the border along the Marsh and so in the spirit of mutual defence, armies from Crinan left their own country and reinforced their neighbour's positions, confident that their kin in the Hinterland could prevent Awgren's westward progress, preventing their encirclement.

But in the north the thegns of the Hinterland sent envoys into the Wastes to sue for peace, acutely aware of their proximity to him and their lack of resources.

Battle came to the banks of the Marsh and a long stalemate ensued, but then came the great betrayal.

Creatures of the Devising were given safe passage across the Hinterland on the condition that the lands remained untouched; for the thegns had heard that Culrain had been razed. Awgren's forces swept over the northern defences of Crinan and the country was overrun, as were the few troops posted in reserve along the Kenna.

Ere long, Crinan and northern Tayne too had been razed, and King Abernath of Tayne retreated southward from Brodack while the way was still open. Week after week the few survivors of the Taynish and Crinish armies, along with refugees from Culrain, marched day and night, all the time attacked at the rear.

At the southernmost shore of Tayne, the Arduan Peninsula stretched southwest; a fang of land piercing a churning sea. The approach to the peninsula was known as the Maw; unforgiving rock flanked by high mountain jaws that followed the coasts as the land narrowed towards the point where the mainland joined the peninsula.

Making a fighting retreat, the humans retreated through the Maw until they could see the Maw Keep, with its curtain-wall spanning the gap between the mountains. Here was their last hope for survival, or so Abernath believed. The entire Arduan Peninsula was surrounded by a wall as deep as it was high, a work so great in its undertaking and construction, so driven by paranoia, that it was thought it had taken hundreds of years to complete. The name of whoever had first conceived of it had long been forgotten. This fortress city was simply known as the Folly. Its great gate was dwarfed by spurs of the main wall and the sheer flanks of the mountains. Once the beaten force was inside, the enemy was foiled.

From the Folly, King Abernath and his people hunkered down, looked to their walls and set about recovering. The fleets of Crinan, Tayne and Culrain gradually gathered at the Folly unopposed, as Awgren never took to the seas, inexpert at all things which required skill and craft.

King Abernath sat upon his throne high up in the Maw Keep from where he could only look on helpless as the Devised burned the continent. He set about uniting the remnants of mankind. Though there were some survivors of the royal lines of both Crinan and Culrain, Abernath's claim to their thrones was the greater, as all of the great houses had inter-married to secure peace. However, he appointed lords from among the survivors and tasked them with establishing strong colonies on the continent north of the Impassable Forest and in the islands away to the west. The lords of Culrain abandoned the Folly to make their new home on the rocky, pine-covered mountains of the Isles while the lords of Crinan sailed for the north of the continent.

In the coming months, the Lord of the Isles took up his seat on Long Isle and began to build simple but effective strongholds from the trees that grew there. Gone were the days of quarrying and elaborate architecture. The Islanders, as they became known, lived simply and trained hard in preparation for renewed offences on the old continent. Clans formed on the various islands, led by hunters and warriors.

The Crinish voyage did not fare well and many of their ships foundered on the shoals near to the southernmost bay of the lands north of the forest. So many bodies washed up on that shore that it became known as Strewn Men Bay. The straggling vessels that avoided such a fate learned from their speedier counterparts' mistakes, avoiding the shoals. They made it ashore and established what was to become the strongest province in the lands north of the Impassable Forest. At first the land was named Stragglers' Drift in the mockery of the lords of the Folly, but the Crinish exiles took the name for their own and their highest lord took up his seat in the new city of Stragglers' End. The Stragglers, as the Crinish became known, set about finding resources and unlike the Islanders, they once more quarried and sought for deeper resource so that in time they became strong and the most numerous of the Combined People.

At Oystercatcher Bay on the northwest coast of what had been Crinan, a palisade was constructed and manned so that raiders might land there. The same was achieved in Culrain. Long they were under siege, but well supplied. Yet the Folly was the only true foothold on the Old Continent, which burned far and wide.

Of the lands south of the forest, the Hinterland alone remained unscathed and though the people therein always feared the day when Awgren would renege on his word and the thegns long mused upon the wisdom of their betrayal, it prospered under occupation.

The Combined People started again, readying themselves for a time when they could return.

Many centuries passed and the Combined People triumphed over their new lands, but never did they cease from raiding the coasts of the Old Continent. However, it was only in the time of Queen Cathryn that strength of arms and leadership allowed for ground to be gained.

In her youth, Queen Cathryn was courted by Lord Aldwyn, descended from the houses of both Tayne and Culrain, yet he was injured in battle and could no longer sire children. Despite her affection for him, Queen Cathryn turned him away and wed Lachlan, the Lord of the Isles who was considered the mightiest of all the warriors of the Combined People. He came to live in the Maw Keep, and together they assembled an army at the Folly which, when the time came, burst forth from the Maw Gate to retake Tayne. Lord Lachlan's brother, Hadwyn and his general, Belman, made incursions on the south coast of Culrain and Lord Linwood of Stragglers' End landed with an army on the west coast of Crinan, accompanied by the fearsome heavy cavalry that would later break Awgren's army.

Gradually a hard won victory drew near until upon the plains of Tayne, north of the ruined city of Brodack, the battle of the Field of the Scarlet Grass began. The Combined People trapped Awgren and his grand army then crushed them, as has already been told.

When Morrick awoke, he did not know what had happened to him. He was warm and wrapped in blankets, lying upon a cot. His head ached, and when he reached up, his fingertips touched damp material, bound tightly around his head. Bands of muscle encasing his torso cried out at him as he attempted to push up on his hands to look round. At first, he sagged in compliance, but exerted effort again and turned on the cot. He was in a tent not dissimilar to his own crushed affair, but directly beside him another three cots were crammed together, and another ran across their ends horizontally. Each bore their own wounded man in various states of bandaging and consciousness. Morrick sat and looked for anyone he recognised; he knew every one of them.

At least four of us have survived then.

But where was he?

He tried to call out, but his throat was dry, and he sputtered dust on his first attempt.

'In here,' he called, hoarse but audible.

A hand drew back the tent flap, and a face came into view.

'Back with us, Sergeant?' The man grinned. Morrick felt a little guilty for not remembering the man's name. But then, there was the head wound.

'Just about. Get me off here. What's happening out there?' His whole body seemed to strain in anticipation of the news. He could feel his heart palpitating, whether the sensation was real or imagined.

Were they free?

The man ducked inside, and Morrick was surprised to see him out of his red tunic and, worse, out of armour. The lad caught the look and the frown.

'Uniforms and armour all gone, Sarge,' he said as he shifted the bunk from the end of Morrick's bed.

'Tell me,' said Morrick as he managed to shuffle down to meet him. He sat at the end, his head still swimming. The lad looked back at him. He seemed to be searching for something to say.

'Take a breath and start from the beginning. Where are we?'

'A camp - with what's left of the regiment.'

Morrick struggled to restrain his temper at the boy's inarticulateness.

'You said they took our uniform and armour. Who? Are we prisoners?' he said, softly and slowly. The boy was about to speak, but suddenly Morrick started and looked about him. As quickly as he lost his composure he seemed to regain it. The boy raised both eyebrows, seeming expectant of an explanation.

'It's nothing. Just lost my bloody axe, is all; the one thing I'd managed to keep hold of throughout the whole damn campaign. Last bit of home.' He forced a one-sided smile.

'Oh well, it's gone now. Go on, boy. Tell me.'

The boy squatted and sat at the foot of the other bunk.

'We held off the cavalry, but when their infantry moved up...'

Morrick did not need telling. The long pikes were effective against horses but unwieldy hand-to-hand. Short swords and daggers were all that his men had carried.

'The officers led a charge. All dead. Someone gave the order to surrender and throw down weapons.'

Smart man, thought Morrick. *It's really over then.*

'They rounded us up and had us set up a camp. There's a guarded palisade fencing us in now. That's all I know.'

Morrick nodded.

'How many are left? Who's in command?'

'About fifty.'

'Fifty?' Morrick shot back at him.

The boy nodded. Morrick looked at his feet as anger rose in him. He fought it. A year ago, nigh on a thousand men had been force-marched out of the Hinterland by Awgren's Devised to combat the threat in the south. Cathryn's army had broken out of the Folly, fighting through the wastelands of the Maw and northwards onto the razed plains of Tayne. Morrick had heard word that as Devised forces were drawn away from the coasts to fight the main column, more of the Combined People had landed on the shores of Crinan and Culrain.

'What about the Creatures of the Devising?'

'Hard to say. Most of the Devised were brought down by Linwood's heavy cavalry. Hordes of footmen were trampled or slain. Thousands survived though and, who'd have thought it, one of their generals ordered them to throw down.'

'The Devised surrendered?' asked Morrick.

This was unthinkable. They were mindless and evil to the core, or so he had been taught to believe. They surely had no sense of self-preservation; no higher cognition beyond base animal drives?

'I know it's hard to believe, but I saw it with my own eyes. They're in another camp a short distance from here. The word is that they're suing for peace, offering to work for the queen.'

Morrick simply stared at the boy.

'Cathryn is considering working with the Creatures of the Devising?' he whispered. He felt as though all his hopes had come to nothing, were it true. Liberation was near at hand for the Hinterland. The lords of the Combined People had overthrown Awgren and had an opportunity to cast their light across the lands, banishing evil forever… and the queen was considering this?

'What else can they do? There are thousands of them,' said the boy.

It was a fair question.

Morrick got to his feet.

'That's enough to be going on with. Who's senior in the regiment?'

'You are, Sarge.'

Morrick nodded, but did not look back again as he made for the entrance to the tent.

'Come with me lad, and find something to write on.'

'Yes, Sarge.'

'We're going to take a census. Write our names at the top and meet me outside in five minutes.'

The boy scuttled off, and Morrick followed him out, ducking under the tent flaps. The sun was low in the western sky and puddles of pink cloud stretched out above the horizon. The tents were spread out in a haphazard fashion with the occasional clearing in-between, where campfires blazed and cooking pots hung on their cast iron tripods. There seemed to be no order to the layout. Morrick was still musing on this when the boy reappeared and handed him a piece of parchment. Morrick checked it to remind himself of the boy's name and then smiled up at him.

'Right, Varney, let's muster the men. What's the biggest space available?'

They picked their way over the guide ropes that formed webs across the ground of the narrow, winding passageways between the tents. Once they had found the clearing, Morrick hollered.

'Muster! On me! Muster.'

He turned to Varney.

'Make the rounds and muster the men, Pikeman.'

'Yes, Sarge,' the boy replied and set off at a jog.

Morrick settled on a log next to the clearing's campfire and passed the time of day with the men there whilst the others began to congregate. Soon enough everyone was present, excluding the injured, and Morrick got to his feet.

'All right, listen up. Those of you who know me will be glad to hear, I'm back on my feet; those of you who don't know me... ask the rest if I'm right about that!'

Some muffled laughter rippled around the circle, but not as much as he had expected. Faces ordinarily sullen at musters were looking at him with something approximating kind regard. Little did he know that his attempt to save his men during the final battle had become something of a minor legend with the remains of the regiment.

'So,' Morrick continued, 'what do we know about what's going on? Anyone spoken to someone in charge from the other side?'

A general murmur was the only reply until one man called out,

'Only when they bring the food. And there are a few guards who'll talk around the fence.'

'All right – any of them said anything interesting?'

There were a few snippets of information, but as expected, the rank-and-file of the Combined People's army knew little more of the broader strokes of battle than did those of Awgren's.

'How often do they bring the food and how are you dividing it up?'

Silence.

'I see. Free-for-all?'

Some nods and the murmur again.

Morrick coughed and his hand fell to where the head of his axe should have hung at his belt. He tucked his hair behind his ears instead.

'Listen up. I'm going to be frank with you, lads, and I want a frank reply. Understood?'

Silence.

'Understood?' he called, a little louder looking around the circle of men.

'Yes, Sergeant,' flew back at him.

'I don't know your views, and I don't know your politics, but here are mine. I didn't want to fight in this war, and I'm not proud of our ancestors for granting safe passage to Awgren's army so he could attack Crinan. I've been doing my duty to keep us alive and to keep our families safe. This is a day I've been hoping for my whole life. The rightful queen has won through, and the Creatures of the Devising are rotting or imprisoned. Does anyone feel differently?'

'No!' came from a few of the men whilst others shook their heads.

'Don't be afraid to speak your mind, now,' said Morrick. 'For good or ill, we need the truth.'

Silence again.

'All right then. Well here's how it is. The officers are gone, as are most of our brothers-in-arms; maybe some of your brothers by blood too, as well as fathers, cousins and friends. Maybe sons, the Forest forgive us. Right now, I don't know what the queen plans to do with us. After all we're thought of as turncoats, in some ways worse than the Devised, but I have no desire to become scapegoats for the entire war. We need to show the queen and the lords of the Combined People that we are grateful at being liberated, that we may have collaborated, but we will work to right the wrong. Understood?'

'Understood, Sarge,' they replied, practically in a roar.

Morrick nodded, smiling.

'Well here's how it's going to be. Consider yourself all on duty, but not as was. I'm disbanding the old regiment. I'm taking command and will be seeking an audience with Queen Cathryn and Lord Lachlan tomorrow in an effort to state our case. We will now be known only as the men of the Hinterland. I stand forward as your captain, unless there is some other man you'd prefer?'

Silence.

'Good. Right. Form up ten to a rank facing me. Move.'

The men began to filter into position.

'Varney will be coming down the line taking your name, state of health and where you come from. That will give me a muster roll. As soon as Varney dismisses you, I want anyone with rank to report to me here. We will strike camp and have some order in here. I want the tents in rows with a clear square at the centre. Distribution of food will be organised. Guards will be posted and at dawn, I will speak to the queen or her lords as the captain of an organised people. Everybody on board?'

'Yes, Sergeant,' shouted the now regimented ranks of men.

'Good. Now, those of you who are lying can find me in my tent after Varney dismisses the muster. We'll have it out, away from prying eyes.'

He pointed at another man.

'You there - complete a census of the wounded after providing your own details.'

'Yes, Sergeant.'

Morrick stood with his hands on his hips.

'Let's get about this then, men of the Hinterland. We have fought hard and long and under duress. Today we stand imprisoned and yet more free than we have been in years. We must earn the trust of our captors. We are tough folk from a hardy country. We will win through.'

He breathed in deep before shouting,

'Long live the queen! Crinan! Tayne! Culrain! The Hinterland! Long live the queen! Long live Lord Lachlan!'

He repeated it over and over, urging the men to join in until the cry was taken up and echoed so loud that the sound carried to the ears of the guards, the Creatures of the Devising and the encamped army of the Combined People beyond. Lord Lachlan heard the noise and turned to his wife, Queen Cathryn.

'Can you make that out? What do they call?' he asked, taking her hand.

Cathryn encased his hand in both of hers and listened for a moment, but it was Lord Aldwyn who spoke first.

'They call for you and for the old countries, my lord.'

Lord Linwood of Stragglers' Drift looked up from the campaign desk at which he was writing upon a piece of parchment.

'They do indeed. The sons of the Hinterland are in full voice.'

He pushed back his chair and drew up to his full height. An immense figure of a man; his head was shaved, his face scarred and he still wore his armour of blue steel and brass rivets. His left hand was draped across the pommel of the bastard sword which hung from his belt and the other gripped the handle of the hunting knife that hung from his right – a stark contrast to the simple boiled leather armour worn by Lord Lachlan and the queen, as well as the iron breastplate of Lord Aldwyn.

He barrelled across the command tent and, Lord Aldwyn, a diminutive terrier of a man, stepped back to let him through. Linwood stood just outside and listened, wondering what to make of the call.

'Long live the queen. Crinan. Tayne. Culrain. The Hinterland. Long live the queen. Long live Lord Lachlan,' he said quietly and then repeated it louder so all inside could hear.

Aldwyn came to stand beside him and hear for himself.

'Do you believe their hearts are in it?'

Linwood ducked back inside.

'Who can tell?'

He returned to the campaign desk, and Queen Cathryn left her seat to stand before him, her hands clasped behind her back.

'We would value your opinion, my lord,' she said. She looked on patiently. Linwood did not look up, merely continued writing.

Lachlan stirred in his chair, irritated by the perceived slight, but Cathryn raised a palm to him and he settled again.

'Lord Linwood…' she said once more. He paused and set down his quill. After a second he looked up to meet her gaze then slightly bowed his head. He sighed slightly before speaking.

'The dogs are quick to come to heel now that they consider us masters. Where were they before? Driving pike and sword into our sides? We are all here because of the Hinterland. A small people they may be, but it is their betrayal that cost you…' he pointed to each of the others in turn, 'and yours our homelands and ultimately, our kingdoms. They do not deserve our forgiveness and were it up to me, I would reject any offer of fealty as quickly as we have done that made by the Creatures of the Devising. They are Awgren's folk and have made their choice.'

Lachlan stood.

'We have yet to decide about the Creatures of the Devising,' he said.

Linwood sat back in his chair, his hand wringing the pommel of his sword.

'My lord, the beasts are black of heart and action. They throw down now, I admit, but it is a mystery as to why. We can scarce afford to feed our own, let alone thousands of Devised. Our supply lines do not permit their continued existence. They are forged of evil by evil intent and must be destroyed.'

Lachlan turned to Lord Aldwyn, whose shoulders hunched forward, hitching up his crimson cloak so that it no longer dragged in the mud. His arms were folded defensively across his chest, Lachlan noted.

'I find it hard to disagree with Lord Linwood on this matter. No good can come of working with the Devised.'

'And the regiments from the Hinterland? What would you have us do with them, Lord Aldwyn,' said Cathryn. She took Lachlan by the arm and he sat once more. Now that Linwood was giving his full attention, Aldwyn sat as well, and all attended the royal couple.

'Well, Your Majesty, I believe that the men of the Hinterland were fighting under duress. Their country has done us a great harm, but the men imprisoned yonder had nothing to do with that decision. I doubt they fight because they wanted to do so, Your Majesty. I would hold counsel with their ranking officers and if all is well, send them home.'

Lachlan and Cathryn exchanged a look.

'We are of one mind on this matter,' said Lord Lachlan. 'Linwood?'

Linwood scratched his head, seeming to wince.

'I say they turned the coat once and they will again. Besides, we will need the Hinterland.'

Seeing that all eyes were still upon him, he continued.

'We have an army here that the fields protected within the Folly cannot sustain. If we are to reclaim all of our lands, how will we feed our men as the years progress? Awgren has scorched the farmlands, burned the forests south of the Hinterland and killed the livestock. The Hinterland, remote though it may be, is the only place where crops are still grown and animals still graze. The folk there have forfeited their rights of ownership.'

'Surely we would be as bad as those we have overthrown if we uproot or destroy that people?' Aldwyn insisted. "Whatever wrongs they have done, I would not set them out in the cold so that we can pillage their supplies.'

'Then it is well that it is not your decision,' said Linwood.

Lachlan stroked his jaw, his features mostly shrouded by a full beard.

'The queen and I will consider what has been said. We will contemplate the fates of both the Devised and the people of the Hinterland. Justice will be handed down tomorrow.'

The standing guard woke Morrick at dawn. He ventured out into the new light of morning and took stock. The camp was laid out as he had wished, regimented and ordered into easily traversable lanes. Breakfast was being handed out and unarmed guards patrolled the interior of the palisade, mirroring their armed counterparts on the outside.

Morrick went to clear his bowels, fetched breakfast and then moved towards the main gate set in the south wall of the palisade.

Only then did the shouting begin.

Morrick ran north through the camp towards the sound, wheezing and wrapping his arms around his ribs as he did so. Mud splattered his legs as he went.

At the sight of the smoke he stopped short. The shouts turned into screams. He burst forward into a sprint, forgetting all about his ribs until he reached the palisade. Here many of the men were climbing up one another to try to get a view, but none yet had managed to do so. As the smell of burning flesh reached his nostrils, Morrick knew what was happening. Varney came tripping up to him.

'What...' he began.

'They're burning the Devised. *That* is the smell of a thousand creatures dying by fire.'

So pass the Creatures of the Devising. The land is cleansed once more, thought Morrick, but he did not feel clean. Yesterday morning he would have sworn that none of the Devised were anything but drones and yet they had thrown down their arms in self-preservation; they had offered to work and pay their way. Perhaps some of them were sentient beings that had now been herded up and burned alive. Morrick felt nauseous. He found a tent pole to brace himself against. The hope that had been kindling in his heart began to fade. Foul as the Devised had been, he doubted he could have killed one of them if it stood before him unarmed and surrendering – so what did that say of those who had ordered this act?

Who were Lachlan and Cathryn? What would their reign bring him, his family, his men and the Hinterland? Morrick was barely done thinking this when the main gates of his own camp burst open, and a company of armed infantry marched in. A shout was taken up throughout the camp until it reached the woodcutter's ears.

'Form up on me!' cried Morrick.

'Men of the Hinterland, form up on me!'

The infantry and their spears bore down upon him. Morrick stepped out from the ranks of his men and stood to meet them.

Chapter Five

The figure kept to the shadow of the barn. Rowan stalked forward and crouched beside a fence post that would not have been wide enough to disguise her in daylight. She deliberately softened her breaths so as to make them as quiet as possible and watched. As she did so, straining to make her eyes as wide as possible, she gripped the handle of her knife tight and began to edge along the fence to come up behind the figure.

One of the Devised, she thought. *It's surely slipped out of the camp. Where there's one there'll be more so keep your wits about you.*

The blacker shape within the black shadow darted forward towards the corral, and, bent double, a man-like figure followed the fence towards the stables. Once it was sufficiently far away and she had gathered her courage, Rowan followed on behind, padding as softly as she could. A light snow began to fall. Flakes came to rest then melted upon her hair and her freckled cheeks.

Rowan considered making her way to the house, but decided her best chance was to pick off this creature then double back to search for more. The shape had reached the stable, and she heard one of the horses whinnying as the door was unbolted. Rowan saw the figure disappear, and the door swung slowly closed, but not quite fully.

Rowan rose up and sprinted across the yard. She slowed as she drew near to the stable and listened. Something was moving about inside, talking softly to the horse. She pondered her options. Burst in and take it by surprise? Very risky - she might be outmatched. Almost certainly she would be. Inspiration dawned on her muscles before it reached her mind. Without even thinking, she slammed the stable door and bolted it shut. This done, she spun her back to the stable door and surveyed the ranch. Nobody else was in sight. She ran back to the lodge and eased open the door so as not to wake Bracken.

Her mother, the two boys and the baby were still sleeping soundly. She moved beside the boys' bunk and gently shook both of them.

'Callum, Declan, wake up. Quick now.' She shook harder until they both stirred and looked up at her in dazed alarm.

'There's something locked in the stable. Fetch an axe each and one for me.'

'What are we going to do?' asked Callum, the elder.

'We're going to confront it. You two stay behind me. But first, the axes – go!'

Rowan found Bramble's cot and woke her next, asking her to find a hiding place with the baby. This done, she met the boys at the door. Armed with both knife and hatchet, she led them back to the stable.

'Declan, unbolt the door, and as you swing it open fast, hide behind it. Callum, stay to my left and behind me. Understand?' she asked as they trotted forward.

'Yes, Mother,' said Callum. He sounded eager.

Foolish boy, Rowan thought. *Too keen for action, just like his mother it seems.*

'Declan?'

'Yes, Mother,' he nodded, quieter and shaky. 'I understand.'

The yard was quiet, bar the usual sounds made by the horses locked in the stable and the vague murmur of cattle in the barn. Rowan put her ear to the door, but could hear nothing inside.

'Who's in there?' she ventured. Declan ducked down beside her with his hand on the bolt. Callum stood back and wrung the axe in his hands.

'Who's in there? Answer,' she said.

'What's the correct answer?'

A man's voice.

Rowan frowned and shrank back from the wood momentarily, looking at it as though it was translucent, or perhaps as though it had offended her. She returned to it.

'The truth. Who are you, and what are you doing on my land? Quickly now or me and the men will take the answers by force. Quick about it now,' she rushed the words and cursed herself for sounding less than composed.

There was no reply for a moment then Rowan thought she could hear a sigh.

'My name is Captain Jacob Lynch. I'm looking for food and shelter.'

Once more Rowan shrank back, this time exchanging looks with both boys. Neither of their faces conveyed any answers.

'Captain of what?'

'Captain of the Hope; a trading schooner. Who are you?'

'But the sea is many miles from here!' she protested.

'We foundered on a reef on a scouting expedition up the east coast under orders from Lord Aldwyn. My crew and I made it ashore in the boats, but we're losing men fast and our supplies are gone. Can you help us?'

Rowan tensed.

'A scouting expedition?'

'Aye. When last we were at the Folly, Lord Aldwyn drafted us into the royal fleet to assess Awgren's strength on the east coast.'

'You know of the war?'

'I know it will be ending very soon one way or the other. All forces are committed. The Folly is emptied. The Stragglers and Islanders have landed.'

The words bit at her heart like ice wind on the skin. She felt despair shudder through her, and she looked down at her son thinking that there was every chance he might never see his father again.

'Will we kill him, mother?' hissed Callum. Rowan held up a hand and glared at him.

'Captain Lynch?' she called, hoping the man had not heard her son.

'If I am to let you out, I want your word that you will not harm my family. I think we may be able to aid one another.'

No need for silence this time; Captain Lynch replied without hesitation.

'I was never a man to turn down a business proposal, madam – 'specially if I've little choice. You have my word.'

'Very well,' said Rowan. She backed off and took up a fighting stance, ready to pounce if need be. She nodded towards the left of the stable door, and Callum moved so his back was to the wall, ready to strike from behind if Lynch burst out into an attack.

'Declan, do it.'

Her youngest shot back the bolt and heaved at the door. Callum tensed and readied his swing. The door burst open and revealed only a deeper dark.

'My weapons are sheathed,' said Lynch's disembodied voice from the dark of the stable. Only the vague shape of the horse was visible.

'Come out slow with your hands raised above your head,' said Rowan. 'We'll kill you dead if you don't.'

The silhouette of a man emerged from the darkness with his hands on his head.

He stood just outside the stable door and looked around, seeing only Rowan.

'What happens now, ma'am?' he asked, his voice was gravelly and coarse now he was out in the open and the sound was no longer fettered by passage through wood.

'Stand where you are, sir,' Rowan replied, and she circled behind him. She pressed in close, and her breasts pressed against the wolf pelt that covered his back. She held the knife to his throat.

'I gave you my…' Lynch began and started to shift his weight.

'I accepted it, but I'm cautious. You can understand that, sir. Stay still and no harm will come to you. Callum, disarm him. Captain, if your hands leave your head, your throat will be slit. Do you understand?'

'Nothing has been so clear in my short and deeply unsatisfying life, ma'am.'

Callum approached from the side and hooked the boarding axe from its loop on Lynch's belt. He gave the captain a wide berth as he moved round him to draw a cutlass from its baldric. That done, Callum backed away with the two axes under one arm and pointing the cutlass towards Lynch.

'You missed the knife, son,' said Lynch. 'Look in the boot.'

'Declan. Get it.'

Her youngest reached from his position, crouched by his mother's feet, and after failing to find the weapon in the left boot, withdrew it from the right.

'I am naked and exposed, ma'am. At yer mercy, so to speak,' said Lynch.

'All right, Captain, back in the stable.'

'Beg pardon?'

'Back in the stable you go. We'll lock the bottom door and converse with a barrier between us. Quick about it.' Her voice was stern and Lynch laughed.

'I'm quite put out by all this, but as you would have it, ma'am.'

Rowan drew aside, and Declan scuttled away on his hands and knees. Lynch spun on his heels and, keeping his hands on his head, he backed into the stable. Rowan bent to lock it and, finally satisfied, she turned to her sons.

'Callum, take your brother inside and return with a lantern.'

Declan made no objection, and the two boys broke into a run back towards the house. She was proud they had done so well, but sorry to make them take a part in it at all. She hoped they would sleep for at least some of the rest of the night, but then the thought shocked her. Was she to be so easily lured into believing this man meant them no harm?

Whilst the boys were gone, they stood in darkness facing one another, yet seeing nothing.

'Strong lads?' asked Lynch.

'Aye, strong enough,' replied Rowan.

'You said you could offer aid?' said Lynch.

Rowan folded her arms and rubbed them with her gloved hands. The snow was falling heavier, and she shivered.

'How many on your crew?'

'There were fifty. Thirty-three have made it this far. I knew we didn't have a chance heading south through the scorched lands; the Wastes, Culrain and such. Figured there are men in the Hinterland and women too, begging your pardon? "If hope is to be found," I said to the men, "it'll be in the Hinterland."'

Rowan thought for a moment.

'Hope is not found in abundance here, I must admit, but we could be allies. Most folk in these parts are under Awgren's boot against their own will and good judgement. I will help if I can, though I do ask your assistance in return. I can house your men in the barn, and we have some stores to feed you if you'll work for it.'

'And that's all you ask? We have no more coin than our personal purses contain.'

Rowan laughed. A light turned the corner of the lodge, and she could see Callum running hard towards her with sword in one hand and lantern held high in the other.

'Here you are, Mother.'

'Good lad. Now get inside the lodge, and bar the door. Check the windows are barred too.'

'I should stay with you.'

'Go protect our family. Be the man of the house, eh?'

Callum hesitated, weighing up his duties, then did as he was bid. Rowan watched him disappear out of the reach of the lantern and then turned her attention back to Lynch. He was cloaked in a wolf pelt, but she could see a leather waistcoat underneath. A leather tri-corner hat covered his head and straggles of frozen hair hung down at his jaw. A scraggly beard covered his face and patches of his hair reached right up to the bags under his eyes. He had kind eyes, Rowan thought, predatory eyes, but still kind.

He looks like the kind of man who'd take you by throat then tell you he loves you.

Blood rushed to her cheeks and, grateful for the snow upon them, she forgave herself the thought and persisted.

'We are in the thrall of an overseer here, appointed by Awgren. There's an encampment of Devised by the river. They make sport of us as they see fit, and we dare not rise up as our men are all away fighting in Awgren's army; that same army your people are facing, I have no doubt. They may already be dead.'

Lynch heard the sadness in her voice and leant forward over the door, his heart going out to her. He too knew what it was like to be separated from loved ones, having left a lover back in Eastport and a wife in Brookmouth; children in both.

'What would you have us do?' he asked, his voice soft.

'I do not know.' The words came slow.

'Fight them?' asked Lynch, worried. 'My men are not soldiers, nor naval men. We can fight, though brawl might be a better word for it. We have tough knuckles and can wield either belaying pin or a bar stool, but sword against armour? We can try, but I can't vouch for the outcome.'

Rowan said nothing for a time.

'Perhaps we can talk more on this,' she said, finally.

'Agreed, if you will shelter us before I lose anyone else? They hide in the forest not far from here. And if I can send a few riders south to get word of the campaign?'

'You want horses?'

'As many as you can spare. My men will fetch word of the invasion and of your menfolk, then return,' he said.

Rowan turned her back to him and looked out over the snow-covered outbuildings to the plains stretching west, seaward, the Impassable Forest forming their northern border. The trees stood resolute and unmoved by the white that gathered at their feet and settled upon their brows.

She turned back to Lynch.

'We have an agreement. Fetch your people, and get them into the barn. I'll ready food and what blankets I can provide.'

She took his weapons and his cloak, but let him take the horse. The night was nearly over and the sun threatened to leap up in the east before the crew of the Hope emerged from the treeline to make their way towards the homestead. True to her word, Rowan ushered them inside the barn and, after seeing the horse safely returned to the stable, she returned Captain Lynch's weapons.

'My thanks, ma'am.'

'You were true to your word and so I must act in kind,' she replied. 'There's salted meat, fish and some stew in the lodge; bread too, if some of your people will lend a hand to bring it over?'

It was done with little fuss, and the men devoured the food in mere minutes. She thought them a ragged and inadequate bunch compared with the likes of her husband. In truth, her heart quailed a little at relying on the strength of their arms. She was impressed this band had made it from the coast, given how woefully unsuited they were to scratching a living from the forest. They carried no bows, nor had they managed to construct any. Their weapons were all designed for a single purpose; culling and slashing anyone who boarded the Hope or anyone whose vessel they in turn had decided to board. To a man they were malnourished, lean and with untrimmed beards.

Rowan watched Lynch finish off a piece of bread. He had the eager look of a beggar dining on game prepared in the queen's own kitchens.

'Are any of them ready to work, or do they need to sleep first?' she asked.

Lynch looked up and licked crumbs from the cupped palm of his hand.

'We could all do with sleep, ma'am, but if needs be, I'll set some of them to it, and they can catch up later. What needs doing?'

She was half tempted to take pity on them, tempted also to tell him to call her Rowan. She relented to neither urge.

'We'll need men posted at each extreme of my land to watch for approaching Devised. My boys will direct the rest of them. Can you see to it?' she asked, eyebrows raised expectantly.

Lynch nodded slowly, unsmiling. He thought her presumptuous and that she had the air of one who came from what privilege the Hinterland knew.

'I can that.' He maintained eye contact as he called out to his men.

'All right, lads, about it. Goody's division have first watch. Goody, report to the lodge for instruction.'

Lynch turned back to Rowan.

'What's your boy's name, ma'am, if you please?'

'Callum,' she replied. 'The younger is Declan, and you will take instruction from him too.' She directed her words at Goody. The man nodded and disappeared out of the barn.

'Close the door after you,' she called. Seconds later it was pushed home. She turned her attention back to Lynch.

'Once your men are rested, you can take three of the horses south. They can bear word to my husband, should the opportunity arise to speak with him?'

Lynch nodded.

'And what do you have in mind for us here, aside from working your land, ma'am?' he enquired, his voice low. He leant back against a bale of hay, crossing his legs at the ankle so the tops of his booted feet touched.

Rowan sat down opposite him, ensuring her long skirts covered her legs as she did so.

'I do not know how to proceed for the best. Your presence does not change my position, in many ways. If we overthrow the overseer and the Devised, Awgren may take vengeance on our men in his army.'

'Only if he hears of it,' Lynch replied, and she was taken aback by the severity of his stare when it met her eyes. 'How many creatures are there? How many men loyal to your overseer?'

Rowan's eyes gleamed, and Lynch thought she looked as though she had been waiting for an opportunity to show off her knowledge.

'Sixty-eight beasts with minds, at last count, and ten or so which are nothing but gargantuan animals. Twenty militia guards at the village, but I doubt many would take side with the Devised – even the overseer. He's a collaborator, but not one of them really,' she conceded.

Lynch mused on this and took a swig from his water-skin.

'Two to one. Slightly more. We could maybe do something. I'd need to think on it. Can you get me a map of the area or would you be so kind as to draw me one?'

Before Rowan could reply Lynch shifted position and spoke again.

'I'm not sure you weren't right in the beginning. Any intervention on our part may go very badly for you and the people of this village. And my crew could end up dead. Surely there are other encampments in the Hinterland?'

Rowan glared at him.

'So not a man of his word, after all, Captain. Should I even call you that? A trading tub has a captain, does it? Or are you just a boy, playing at boats?' she snarled. She saw his eyes dim, but was too annoyed to feel any pity, yet though she was resolute in her anger she knew she would regret her words later on. No matter. She would maul him until he cried off from objecting.

'This is what we have to look forward to under the reign of Cathryn?

Puling boys, beggars, thieves and liars? Perhaps I would be better off going to the overseer about your appearance.'

Her voice had raised to such a degree that some of the men heard and Wilson, the Hope's master, drew his cutlass.

Lynch stood, and as soon as she saw him do so, Rowan did the same.

'We are here as your guests and have no desire to do you harm, ma'am. Trading captain I may be and privateer of late, but I take threats no more kindly than does any man. Speak reasonable or speak not, eh?' He leant in closer. 'Do you think we will sleep easier worrying that you or yours may be away to betray us? In our place, would you let that risk stand? Think of your own neck before you threaten mine.'

'You would dictate to me on my own land?' Her fists rammed into the top of her hips. It took everything in her not to lick her lips as her mouth dried out. She tried to rise above the welling bowl of emotion to think, and she could feel a tremor beginning to strum throughout her body as adrenaline flooded into her.

Lynch exchanged a look with the master and sat down.

'Shall we begin again?'

Rowan stood for near a minute, staring down at him.

'Ma'am?'

She gave no reply and then, finally, she sat once more. The master sheathed his cutlass, but moved to the door.

Rowan stared down at her boots, breathing hard.

Lynch took off his tricorn and retied his hair while he waited for his host to regain her composure.

'Let's start with the map. Perhaps you can speak to those you know to be willing to take a stand. See what they are prepared to do?' then as an afterthought, 'What would be the most defensible place in the village?' asked Lynch.

Her eyes turned towards him, and he could see that she was still furious. She looked down again and Lynch felt a sudden intuition that this was her mask, and the lady was struggling to take it off.

'Wilson,' he called, 'tell those not on-duty to sleep, then you do the same. Understood?'

'Aye, Captain,' said Wilson. He was a hard man and in the back of his mind, Lynch wondered whether the old sailor could be entrusted with Rowan's safety if he considered her a threat.

He groaned, and his knees clicked as he stood. Rowan looked up at him, and he extended a hand to help her to her feet. Rowan hesitated then wrapped her fingers round his wrist and allowed him to take her weight as she hauled herself up.

'I'll see what I can find out. Let us both think the matter over and reconvene later in the day. I've work to do in the meantime.'

She did not wait for a reply, and Lynch was left to watch the sway of her hips as she stalked out of the barn. He turned back to his crew, who were settling in to the hay.

'That about proves it lads. They always say you can't outrun your troubles. It's because women are trouble, and they're bloody everywhere.'

He unslung his cutlass and settled into the hay, pulling his tricorn down over his eyes. As he began to grow sleepy, his planning for the coming days gave way to thoughts of Rowan.

The sway of her hips.

Chapter Six

'You have known that this is how it would be from the very beginning!' bellowed Lord Lachlan. The sound was tremendous and without a word, the guards shrank back further into the shadows and even Lord Aldwyn, hardened in battle, jumped.

Lord Linwood remained unmoved however and stood tall before the queen and Lord of the Isles.

'And, with respect, lord, is it not the case that my people are my own to command?'

'They are not your people, Linwood!' Lachlan roared, leaping up from his chair. Cathryn wrapped a hand around his forearm as she stood to join him and though his face shed none of the anger, he straightened a little and much of the tension left his body; he looked less ready to pounce.

Linwood's face showed little emotion, and he set his gaze upon Cathryn, ignoring Lachlan.

'I will do as you command, but I *will* speak my mind, as always, Your Majesty.'

Cathryn nodded, ignoring Lachlan's sigh, so Linwood continued.

'No one questions that your house rules over the Combined People, on that I must be clear. However, it is well known that my own bloodline ties me closer to the throne of Crinan than does yours, and while you must think of your whole realm, my heart speaks to me the loudest not only of my current seat in Stragglers' Drift, but my ancestral homeland.'

'We have *all* fought hard to win back these lands, and none can question my loyalty. Did my heavy cavalry not break through the lines of the enemy and ultimately force them into retreat? Is this not the perfect time for me to seize the throne if I wished it? My men vastly outnumber yours…'

'They are not your men,' Lachlan growled, 'and though you may command them, think not that they have no loyalty for my wife.'

Linwood raised both hands in a pacifying gesture, continuing to engage only with Cathryn.

'I do not wish to cause dissent, but I believe that returning Crinan to its former splendour is the reason I am alive. It is all my line has thought of for a thousand years.'

'You say you wish to return my army home and that Lord Lachlan will lead a force to take control of the Hinterland, leaving but a handful of my people upon the coasts of Crinan. I ask then, for what did my men and I fight?' asked Linwood.

'Allow me to land a force to reinforce our foothold at Oystercatcher Bay and then march for the Hinterland. I can use the territory as a staging ground for ordering Crinan and for sending out parties to ensure the Wastes are cleared of any remaining Devised which may roam the land or lie quiet in their holes. What interest does the Lord of the Isles have in the Hinterland?' Linwood concluded.

Lachlan's mighty chest rose and fell, his eyes boring into Linwood though the lord of Stragglers' Drift remained impassive and continued to shun Lachlan.

'We have discussed this at length,' said Lachlan.

'Yet I was never satisfied,' said Linwood.

'Do you forget that I am of the line of Culrain? That I have a claim to the throne there? Yet I have the wit to see that committing large numbers of troops to hold ground that will be useless for centuries to come, will do nothing but waste men's years and require much exertion when our efforts are needed elsewhere. I go to the Hinterland as the queen believes that my presence will lend significance to our dealings with those who dwell there. If indeed it is true that the Hinterland could supply more than its own people, then of course we will think again on our plans, but with Lord Aldwyn's discovery of the South Continent and the settlement of colonies there, we must think of reinforcing our claim there as well as strengthening what lands we already hold. Is it not true, Aldwyn, that you have encountered new peoples there?'

'It is true, lord. They have thus far been easily subdued, but I cannot say it will be the case for everyone who dwells there. We have not yet ventured far.'

'You see?' said Lachlan. 'While we commit troops to poisoned dirt buried deep under ash, who knows what new enemies could rise up against us?'

'Perhaps the Isles are vulnerable in your absence, Lachlan, but I would not have left the Drift undefended. I can maintain a hold on both the Drift and Crinan.'

Lachlan turned to Cathryn. She said nothing and Lachlan, ever averse to silence at court, spoke again.

'It was your counsel that persuaded us that, having defeated the Devised, we must withdraw *our* armies.' He gripped the arms of the throne and his knuckles whitened. 'Did you not argue that our armies could not be sustained here? Yet, in truth, you believe you could maintain a presence.' He stopped short of the outright accusation forming in his mind.

Cathryn ordered her thoughts and interjected, unwilling to let the argument escalate.

'We must think further on this, my lords. Our armies will march for the Folly in the morning, and we will return to this matter when we are back behind the Maw Gate.'

Lachlan, still seething, stared at Linwood. His brow was lined with furrows, and a weaker man would have wilted under the power of his anger.

'Leave us now, and make your preparations,' he said.

'Your command, my lord,' said Aldwyn, and he was about to depart alongside Linwood when the queen bade him stay.

The three of them remained in silence for a moment until the queen's aide, Ailsa, stepped back into the lamplight.

'Lord Linwood has returned to his camp, Your Majesty,' she said and stepped back into the night.

Lachlan let out a great sigh and let his head fall back against his throne.

'That man,' he said. 'Save us.'

Cathryn rested a hand on her husband's briefly then returned it to the arm of her chair.

'What think you of Lord Linwood's proposal?' she asked Aldwyn.

Lord Aldwyn settled back at his campaign desk.

'It concerns me. The man thinks too much of himself. I fear he may have imperial ambitions.'

Lachlan grunted and nodded.

'A thousand years of unification and still he thinks of us as separate nations. I understand affection for the land; I was and always will be a man of the Isles, but if he thinks I don't care about Culrain, he's wrong. Yet Culrain died before the memories of my grandfather's grandfather. No man alive can say what it was to be of Culrain. Surely, I know that my ancestors sat upon the throne there in Lacranza, but what of it? The names and the places are but fairy stories. I care a great deal more about our true homes and the living than preserving the legacy of the dead.'

'And yet we do owe the dead our allegiance.' Cathryn chided, gently, but enough to once more redden her husband's cheeks. 'It is our duty to reclaim these lands.'

There was an uncomfortable silence that Aldwyn felt compelled to disperse.

'If I may speak plainly, I do consider the man a serious threat to the security of your realm, Your Majesty. Linwood has the strength to invade the Isles or the South Continent, even if he cannot hope to breach the Folly walls. It would not be wise to antagonise him, and yet granting him all he desires may embolden him. Perhaps there is a way to reward him and yet not compromise your own position?'

Cathryn nodded and once more clasped Lachlan's hand, perceiving and soothing his lingering embarrassment.

'I will have my people make enquiries amongst Linwood's men and report back to you with my findings, if it pleases you both?' said Aldwyn.

'Your discretion would be appreciated as much as the effort,' said Lachlan and, bowing to them both, Lord Aldwyn took his leave.

As was their custom, the queen and Lord of the Isles led the armies in a column back to the Folly, and by the time their people had departed there was nothing left upon the battle site but the remains of two palisades. One stood intact, encircling a now abandoned camp and the other was a jaw of broken, blackened teeth surrounding a heaped, cancerous mound of charred flesh and melted armour. The foul stench accompanied them on the march, as did the memory of the act.

Cathryn felt as though the victory had gained them little and judged by her husband's unusually quiet demeanour that he too was troubled. Here was the aftermath of a thousand years of patience, toil and strife. Here was the product of decades of battle and the loss of thousands. And what had they won?

Nothing but a grisly mound of dead enemies and an empty land, she thought.

Without turning towards him, she spoke to Lachlan while she rode.

'If naught else, we have gained vengeance for our people and eradicated the one source of true evil in this world.'

To her surprise, Lachlan laughed.

'Think back on what you just said,' he said when the guffaws had subsided. She watched him, and he smiled back at her. She felt relief at the sight.

'Vengeance achieved and true evil is vanquished. If naught else. *If naught else?*' he laughed again. 'What else is there? We've achieved nearly all there is to achieve.'

Cathryn smiled.

'I suppose that is true,' she said, 'but then why is my mood so black?'

They rode on in silence for a time, the sound of hooves and breathing a little way off behind them. The tramping of feet. The clanking of armour.

'I was expecting to be jubilant, I admit,' said Lachlan, 'but the taste of victory is foul. I regret the burning back there. Regret it bitterly, truth be told, I argue with myself over the wrongs and rights of it.'

'We could not sustain them.'

Lachlan sighed.

'Sustain. That word again. I begin to wonder if *we* rule at all.'

'I do not follow,' she said.

'Well, does a queen stand in thrall to a word? Everything is about what we can and cannot sustain, of late.'

Cathryn smiled.

'I see. True enough. We perhaps did not think beyond Awgren bleeding at our feet.'

Lachlan inflated his cheeks and forced the air out in a whistle.

'Awgren was, at least, easy to understand. Now he's gone, I'm more vexed by that stone giant from the north. Save us from the heirs to the old countries.'

'Aldwyn is not so bad,' said Cathryn, but cautiously.

Lachlan cleared his throat and adjusted his hold of the reins.

'No. At least he says little, and what he does say comes out softer, but who knows what the man is thinking?' He shook his head. 'Perhaps I'm being unfair.'

'You are,' said Cathryn. There was silence between them.

'He seems shrewd,' Lachlan conceded, but the silence returned, and, as was his wont when ill at ease, he filled it.

'We've had clear purpose for years and now, what? Do we expect things to sail on smoothly? It isn't in man's nature. Someone will come for us, be it from without or within, but likely both. I fear it will be Linwood and so something must be done about him.' He sighed. It wearied him to think so cynically, and Cathryn felt pity for him. She was capable of remaining detached where her husband felt every blow, every slight. His was a carefully trained, reluctant paranoia. For Cathryn, it was second nature.

'Do you have something specific in mind?' she asked.

He halted his horse, and Cathryn held up her hand. The gesture was seen, and her generals echoed the command. The column, near a mile long, ground to a halt like the conclusion of a landslide.

Lachlan dismounted and moved to the side of Cathryn's mount. He cupped the calf of Queen Cathryn's leg in his hand. Her skin was cold and soft to his touch. She looked down at him, still gripping the reins.

'Truly? You want to know my mind?' he asked.

She nodded, already feeling tired at the prospect of hand-holding him through whatever this revelation would involve.

'I do have something in mind – returning to the Isles with you, finding somewhere quiet that we can call home. No halls, no laws and no duties. We have achieved all we hoped. Let others squabble over the spoils.'

Cathryn nodded in acknowledgement.

'We're holding up the column, my love.'

He stared at her long after she looked away, his cheeks growing red. He nodded to himself then regained his mount.

'March on,' he hollered. His horse trotted on, and Cathryn dug her spurs into the flank of her own.

'Do you fear something specific of Linwood?' she tried again.

There was only the sound of their progress as the hooves squelched in the mud and the deep, low rumble of the army that followed on behind. Lachlan struggled for mastery of his temper, and only when calm enough did he remind himself of his duty to her and allow himself to speak.

'I am concerned that Linwood means to try to sunder the realm and assert his own claim to royalty. All this time, we've trained for war, we've had a common purpose and whilst we've forged ever stronger ties between the Isles and the Folly, he's been all but autonomous in the Drift. We've planned and schemed to take our revenge on Awgren, but every so often, Linwood says something which makes me wonder about his intentions. Am I alone in this?' he asked, turning to his wife.

Cathryn kept her eyes dead ahead.

'You are astute.' She said nothing more and together they trotted on.

The weeks passed slowly as the column survived only on eked-out rations. As they marched south, the weather grew warmer and the skies became an ever more striking blue. In time, the smell of salt air entered their noses and all knew the journey was nearly over.

Ere long, the column drew near to the narrowing passage of the Maw, and they came under the chill shadow between the mountains. Soon Cathryn spied the Maw Gate opening in the high wall of the Maw Keep, which towered above them, proud and unbreakable.

Over the course of the day the armies of the Combined People returned inside the walls. When all had entered, the Maw Gate stood open for the first time in a thousand years, under guard, but open nonetheless.

The sun settled down in the west, nestling itself into the ocean, and Aldwyn turned away from the window. His chambers were illumined by candles, and though the moon was full and he liked to look upon it, he closed the shutters over the windows against the night. Despite his furs, he shivered. Was it really possible to become accustomed to heat so quickly? It had been but a few years since he settled in the New Brodack colony on the north shore of the South Continent, but already he missed the warmer climes.

He settled into his chair by the fireside and took long draughts from his freshly mulled wine, staring into the flames while he thought on what was to come. He was ashamed to admit to himself that in Linwood's presence he sometimes felt cowed by the man's relentless, battering-ram of a personality. Yet after all he had learned on the march, he would have to choose whether to stand beside him or against him.

In truth it would not be a difficult choice, for he cared little for rebuilding the old countries and, after living away from the Folly, even his childhood home reminded him of woes he had ventured far in the world to avoid. He had discovered a whole new continent in the attempt.

He thought of his halls far away in New Brodack and yearned to return there. The colony was prospering under his watch; there was hard work to be done there and trouble with the natives, but his men were subduing them gradually.

He longed for the new wide flat lands with their little rivers and tall grass as Lachlan must long for his own home. The Isles were small, beautiful and there too, life was hard, but good. Did Linwood feel the same for Stragglers' Drift? Aldwyn thought not. He had never visited the north of the Impassable Forest, but even the place names made him shudder; Strewn Man Bay, where the survivors of the Crinish fleet washed up after it was dashed upon the rocks in a storm; Stragglers' End, Linwood's seat and Forlorn Watch, the largest port in the north. The people seemed cold and joyless to him. And, to Aldwyn, it seemed as though the Drift was nothing but a temporary residence in the mind of the Stragglers – a place to quarry, mine, multiply and breed horses; a place to forge steel and gather strength. It was a bleak place in which to recover a people's breath before returning to battle.

'My lord,' said a voice through the oak door.

Aldwyn came back to reality in an instant.

'Enter.'

The door opened just enough for his manservant's face to appear in the candlelight.

'The queen, my lord.'

Aldwyn shrugged off the furs and stood.

'Please show her in, Harcourt.'

'Yes, my lord.' Harcourt pushed the door gently open and stood to attention against it as Cathryn swept into the room. She nodded at him.

'You may leave us,' she said and closed the door behind him herself, much to Harcourt's surprise.

Aldwyn bowed his head and moved to greet her. She wrapped her arms around him, and he kissed her on the cheek.

'The Lord of the Isles sleeps?'

'More than he does anything else, these days. He is struck down by melancholy much of the time.' She dropped into a chair by the fire. She looked towards his goblet of wine and raised her eyebrows, smiling.

'Wine?' asked Aldwyn.

'Oh, I'm sure we can do better than that.'

He smiled, went in search of something stronger and found a bottle of Elaris whisky from the cabinet under the window.

'A little taste of the Isles?' He brandished the bottle, which had travelled all the way from the Butterfly Isle, at her and she nodded. She took the drink without water and finished her glass in one gulp. Aldwyn refilled it.

'Gods, Wyn. How are you sober? Wine? Are you going soft on me?' She immediately regretted her poor choice of words and gestured apology with her hands.

Aldwyn, the only person who would recognise the slip, let it pass. He settled into his own chair and lifted his original goblet.

'Please don't call me that, Cathryn.'

'Ah, but it vexes you so, and I do like to see an angry flush upon your cheeks.'

Aldwyn looked at the door without thinking, and Queen Cathryn perceived his worries.

'It's thick oak,' she said and sipped at the whisky, closing her eyes and dismissing his fear with a wave of her hand.

'I wish this was all over,' she said.

Aldwyn sat back in his chair and regarded her.

'Have I something on my face?' she said, and he returned her smile.

'Nothing, but the beauty you were born with.'

She laughed.

'Does that work with the native girls in your new home?'

'Would it bother you if it did?' he asked and she raised an eyebrow.

'They'd soon know it and so would you. Ask Awgren how I respond to a slight.' She drained her whisky and poured another. She sipped from it, closed her eyes and savoured the taste.

'I have some tidings of Linwood,' said Aldwyn.

Silence hung in the air between them.

'Go on. Let's hear it.'

'I sent people I trust amongst his men; soldiers, whores and men with bottles to share. It seems that even now there is a great work being undertaken in the north. Not all knew of it, but it seems that Linwood has set about constructing a road to allow passage between his lands in the Drift and the old countries. It will take many years to complete, no doubt, but it seems he has already made some progress and there are new settlements springing up within the forest unknown to us. Or so I assume?'

Cathryn's laughter took the lord by surprise and he frowned at her.

'Cathryn?' he pressed. She drank once more and he could see that familiar wildness kindling in her eyes.

'Lachlan would like nothing more than for us to escape to the Isles, or so he says. For my part, I think he truly longs for ranging about in the mountains chasing after stags and sleeping under the stars. Yet were it not a sign of weakness to allow Linwood to forge ahead with his plans, inviting wider designs, perhaps I would have it so. If his words were sweeter and his footsteps towards the thrones were softer, perhaps he would already have gained his wish.'

She fixed her eyes on Aldwyn's, and he felt unable to look away. She smiled.

'But there is always duty and so I suppose it could never be.' She sighed. 'And now I must consider that if I do not cede to Linwood's wishes, I must make an enemy of him and contest yet another opponent for these lands.'

'It may be so,' said Aldwyn.

'What do you want, Lord Aldwyn?' she asked him, after a time.

Hearing her refer to him so formally in private had exactly the effect she had intended. He was not a vain man, but to hear someone to whom he was so close, refer to him as 'Lord' without a hint of irony, caused him to muster his thought for a worthy answer – thinking how a lord should answer, rather than just a man. But before answering he checked himself, aware that she was playing him.

'For myself or for the people?'

She grinned and sipped her whisky.

'Both.'

Aldwyn pushed back his chair and opened the shutters to the outside so that the cold air flooded in alongside the moonlight, reviving him.

'I am content in the colonies. I press our claim here only to honour the dead and to secure the land against newcomers who might seize it. The world is bigger than we know; the discovery of the South Continent shows that. And did not Awgren spring up from nowhere? Who knows what the future may hold. Evil is gone for now, but may take on new forms.'

'Evil incarnate, maybe,' she replied, shaking her head. 'But both my husband and I see some in Linwood. Evil can perhaps spring from reckless determination and rash action.'

She drained her glass and waved it at him.

'Are you sure? You know how it hits you…' he said quietly.

She glared at him.

'Nonsense. Your queen commands it.'

He sighed and refilled her glass. The bottle was haemorrhaging fast, it seemed. She drank deep of her glass again, stifled a cough then continued.

'If he is extending his territory into the forest and wants to be able to march his forces into Crinan, who is to say that he will stop there?'

'He may not,' said Aldwyn.

'Reading him as I do, I believe that there is a very real chance that Linwood aims to claim the crown of Crinan himself and disband the Combined People. I would say that is the least of his ambitions.'

Cathryn went to join Aldwyn at the window and rested a hand on his shoulder.

'You have not told me what you want.'

Aldwyn turned to look at her and took her hand in his.

'There is what I want and what I can have. What I can have is a life in New Brodack away from memories here. There is hope there for me and new lands to explore. I am more whole than I have been in years. I would return home and leave matters here to others in your service.'

Cathryn drew back from his touch, and he could see she was a little unsteady on her feet.

'I will think on this tonight and speak to Lachlan tomorrow morning. We shall see if there is some middle ground that might satisfy all, without leading us into new conflict. There has been no war between mankind these thousand years past, and I would not have that change in the years of my reign.'

Aldwyn almost warned her against telling Lachlan they had met, but had been scolded for it many times before in the early years of her marriage, before he had taken to the sea to escape her. Even then she had always been true to her word, kept their liaisons secret and not jeopardised his standing with the Lord of the Isles.

He remained silent and watched her as she thought. Her skin was less taut than it had been, but her eyes were still as young as ever. He felt almost overwhelmed by the sight and the scent of her; it pained him. He looked down into his wine, cursing his misfortunes.

'Lachlan spoke of running away whilst we rode,' she whispered, not looking at him.

'Oh?'

She nodded then went on.

'I love him. He can be so bullish, courageous and strong at times, but he is a deeply flawed man. When I am with him now, I often feel like his mother rather than his lover.' She snorted.

'This seems to be a recurring theme, doesn't it, Wyn?' She smiled. Aldwyn could see she was well on her way to drunk. He decided to placate rather than engage.

'It can be hardly as bad as what passed between us?' he asked.

She shook her head.

'No. I exaggerate. All is as well as marriage ever leaves it, I suppose. We actually share a bed, unlike many royal husbands and wives.'

She continued to grin at him with something of a ghoulish aspect and Aldwyn began to feel a little revolted. She had a salacious look in her eye, and the thought of her as a sexual animal only brought the arrow of pain nearer the mark. She saw his discomfort and her smile faded.

'I do not mean to hurt you. You know how I feel for you, even now. If I hadn't been forced to choose duty over the heart…,' she whispered once more and again drained her glass.

Aldwyn sighed. Were they really to have this conversation again?

'This is an old path, well-worn and long abandoned for other roads. Let's not speak of it, you chose who you chose, for reasons we both know. You have princelings and princesses. You continued your name. Your house goes on. You are lucky to have found a man you can tolerate and even love. Many a marriage is not so blessed,' he scolded her, but his voice was soft and kind.

She did not meet his gaze.

'I do still love you. I'll always love you.'

He nodded.

'I know. And I am grateful to be near you for this time that we have, but, in truth, I will be glad to be parted as well. You understand.'

'I understand,' she said. The words were slightly slurred. He hoped she would return to her own apartments soon.

'Besides, it is not often that a spurned man's attempts to escape his hurt lead to the discovery of a whole new continent.' He laughed.

The expression on her face was bitter, but gradually softened as she saw that he was trying to lighten her mood.

She slapped the stone sill under the window in a hearty gesture more reminiscent of a farmer in a tavern at the end of the night rather than the action of a queen. His heart fluttered a little, seeing her off her guard. He softened towards her and tucked a strand of hair behind her ear.

She addressed him once more before taking her leave.

'I thank you once again for your honesty, my lord. We will address the situation on the morrow.'

When she was gone Aldwyn gathered up his furs once more and returned to the fire, turning her glass in half circles. It was no use trying to stop thinking on the old hurts and the confusions ahead, so he escaped them by finding his bed. Many a man is kept awake by his troubles, but Aldwyn had long made his peace with his lot in life and fell asleep in minutes.

The following morning, Linwood and Aldwyn were summoned to the throne room of the Maw Keep. Lachlan and Cathryn were dressed in their most formal garb. The two lords advanced upon the dais and knelt before their rulers.

Lachlan reached out and took Cathryn's hand. Together, they stood.

'My lords,' said Lachlan, 'the queen and I have come to a decision. The Combined People came together because we were forced from these lands centuries ago. Though my blood flows from Culrain, the truth is that my kin have found their true home in the Isles. Lord Aldwyn has made inroads into the South Continent. Linwood, your people have prospered in Stragglers' Drift. Yet together we have combined our strengths and bent our will on gaining vengeance and retaking our ancestral homes. It stands now before us once more under our rule. But how best to go about taming it?'

'The queen and I believe that now our purpose is done, we should do right by the descendants of the great houses of the old countries.'

Now the queen spoke.

'Lord Linwood, I hereby decree that Stragglers' Drift and the territory that was once Crinan are now duchies of the realm. We are prepared to allow you to govern these lands as you see fit. Arise now, Lord Linwood, Duke of Crinan and Stragglers' Drift.'

Lord Linwood seemed unaffected, his face giving away nothing. He stood and bowed his head. He seemed about to speak, but Cathryn stepped forward and addressed Aldwyn.

'Lord Aldwyn. I hereby decree that the Hinterland and the territory that was once Culrain are now duchies of the realm. Arise now, Lord Aldwyn, Duke of Culrain and the Hinterland.'

Aldwyn almost let his mouth hang, but was too conscious of Linwood's presence to show weakness. Cathryn knew how he longed to return to the south and yet she tied him to these lands? His thoughts raced as he got to his feet and bowed, realisation dawning. His new charge in the Hinterland would put him directly between Linwood's lands in the north and Crinan. She had placed him in the path of confrontation should Linwood continue with his plans for a road.

'I am honoured, Your Majesty,' he said. Both the lord and queen nodded towards him in acceptance of his appreciation. They turned to Linwood.

There was a moment's silence. Linwood kept his eyes lowered, his chest heaving.

'My thanks.' He spoke slowly and deliberately. Aldwyn shot him a concerned look and then, unable to contain himself, practically barked at Cathryn.

'Your Majesty, what of the forest that lies between Stragglers' Drift and the Hinterland?'

'The Impassable Forest will stand as a lasting monument to our reign. I name it a royal hunting ground and it shall be protected in our name, as will old Tayne.' She returned to her throne, and Lachlan spoke, even though Linwood continued to stare at the floor.

'The queen and I will grant you both powers to govern your own lands. Renewing them will be challenging, and we leave it to you both to decide how you go about it. Lord Linwood, you will be able to supply Crinan by sea and, as the Hinterland is self-sustaining, Lord Aldwyn will be able to offer aid from his surplus, I am sure.'

The Lord of the Isles went on, detailing their powers and though Aldwyn took most of it in, he tried to catch Cathryn's gaze, trying to convey his dismay. But her resolve was relentless; she ignored his attempts, and eventually he paid full heed to Lachlan. Aldwyn knew he had been out-manoeuvred and felt betrayed by her; he had confided in her and she had used him against her enemy. He realised that the lord had addressed him again.

'Apologies. My lord?'

'The folk of the Hinterland. What say you of their fate?'

At this Linwood's head snapped round and he could feel the bigger, stronger man glaring at him. He had given little thought to the subject, but the duke's reaction immediately provoked a response from him.

'Both Culrain and the Hinterland will be lands that embrace forgiveness and justice. I will formally pardon them, if it pleases you?'

Lachlan smiled.

'May your lands be blessed, my friend.'

Linwood coughed.

'I thank you for your generosity, my lord, Your Majesty. By your leave, I will away and make my plans,' he said.

Lachlan frowned and, despairing at Linwood's lack of reaction, he sighed and said,

'Away then.'

Linwood turned on his heel and marched out of the room, his armour clanking and his sword swinging at his side.

Aldwyn stood silent.

'Would you ask anything more of us?' said Lachlan.

Aldwyn clenched and unclenched his fists, trying to control his breathing.

'What of the South Continent?'

'Your cousin will rule in your stead,' said Lachlan.

He stepped down from the dais and grasped Aldwyn by the shoulders.

'I am sorry to tear you away from your new home, Aldwyn. I am sure you can guess our concerns. We have little imperial ambition, but we cannot allow this continent to fall under Linwood's sway when it is so lately freed from a long endured tyranny. Will you be our iron-clad fist here?'

Aldwyn shot Cathryn a withering look.

'I am yours to command,' he said and bowed.

Chapter Seven

The dungeons of the Folly were unremarkable; stone floors, no sunlight, musty air and filth. There were no beds, and Morrick had been sat on his haunches, in conversation with a group of men, when the doors were flung open and the light from the passage outside spilled into the cell. A large man in armour stepped into the doorway.

'Is Captain Morrick still alive?' the man bellowed, and the sound echoed terribly around the dungeon causing many of the prisoners to duck and wince.

'He is,' announced a voice nearer the door. Morrick gathered his wits and stood up on stiff, complaining legs.

'I am,' he called out above the various replies.

'Come forward,' the man ordered and turned away. Morrick picked his way to the door, his bare feet slipping on excrement as he moved. He shielded his eyes against the light as he crossed the threshold, and the door clanged closed behind him. Two guards seized him then half-carried and half-propelled him down the passage and up steps until they stood outside in a courtyard.

Morrick's eyes could not adjust to the light, and he kept them tightly shut even as he enjoyed the sun on his skin. The men kept tight hold of him as he stood waiting. His heart beat fast as fear grew in him that he was about to be executed – possibly burned alive like the rest of Awgren's army.

Perhaps I deserve it, he thought.

'Do you know who I am, Captain?' came the big man's voice.

'No, sir.'

'No, Your Grace,' said the voice. 'I am Lord Linwood, Duke of Stragglers' Drift and of Crinan.

The words were grand and Morrick could think only how pompous and how dangerous this man sounded. He had heard the name, of course, but knew little that did not come from talk around a campfire whilst the war had still been on.

'Your Grace.'

'The Hinterland has been created a duchy of the realm under Lord Aldwyn of Culrain. The duke, in his wisdom, intends to pardon your people for facilitating the defeat of mine.'

Linwood's eyes blazed, but he continued.

'But for now, you are prisoners of the realm and as it was my own cavalry who defeated your regiment, I will deal with you as I see fit. You may go free to see your family again, Captain Morrick, but wherever you go in the realm of the Combined People, all shall know what you are; a turncoat, a denizen of Awgren and one who stood on the side of evil against better men striving for the light.'

Morrick was about to protest, but with a flick of his hand Linwood instructed the men either side of him.

The guards hauled the woodcutter to his feet, and his aching muscles screamed. Morrick grunted in protest as they dragged him forward towards a wooden building from which smoke streamed.

One of the guards kicked his feet from under him, and they drove him back onto the grass. Morrick cried out again.

'Your Grace, please have mercy. I have a wife and sons.'

Linwood stood above him brandishing a red hot poker. Morrick could not help himself; he screamed, realising suddenly what was coming. Lord Linwood dropped to his knees, laid the poker across Morrick's face and drove it downwards. The pain was immense. The poker hissed against his flesh and a burnt odour filled his nose when he drew in desperate gasps of air between screams. Morrick struggled as his cheek melted under the heat until Linwood drew the poker away. Morrick breathed heavy and fast, feeling as though he would pass out but relieved it was over, but

Linwood turned the poker in a different direction and the pain struck up again as the Duke of Crinan branded the side of Morrick's face with a scorched 'T'. 'T' for traitor, he would come to realise.

Morrick screamed and screamed until finally and, so sweetly, he passed out.

Linwood got to his feet and handed the poker back to the blacksmith.

'Take him back to the dungeons and bring up the next man,' he said to the guards.

When next Morrick opened his eyes he was back in the dungeons. The cell was dark, but the reek, the damp and the sobbing gave away his location.

The skin on his face was tight and when he raised his fingers to it he could feel wet pus and crisp, sharp edges. He drew his fingers back as his stomach began to churn, and he was suddenly, violently sick. On all fours, he panted and spat, then crawled back a little to lie against the wet stone wall.

'Steady now lads,' he called to reassure them though he was far from steady himself, but his voice broke, and his words did no good for those who could hear him..

'They promise us we will go home. Just hold on and we'll be free,' Morrick continued.

He was ever-weary in the dungeons, where there was no light. The oppressive darkness made him feel drowsy and depressed.

He thought the pain would keep him awake, but before long his eyelids grew heavy, and he found relief in the nothingness of sleep; a nothingness that scared him when he woke. It bothered him how easily he had forgotten both his woes and his loved ones in order to rest, but that was not all. Sleep was a dark, empty cave in which the walls were always at an uncertain distance and one could never be sure of the nature of the company. The nothingness told him of what it felt like before he was born and how he would feel again after his death.

As time went on, he lost all sense of it, and with only the cold stone floor to lie upon, the hours passed uncomfortably as he worried for the health of his men. How long before their raw wounds began to claim lives in these filthy lodgings?

Morrick was awoken some time later by the door to the dungeon opening. He winced, shielding his eyes against the light with his hand. Armoured men flooded into the dungeon with flaming torches and began helping people to their feet rather than dragging them away. He too was hauled up, and he filed out of the dungeon then up once more to the yard.

A lordly man was waiting there with a small retinue. Morrick guessed this was Lord Aldwyn. The captain of the Hinterland rubbed his eyes as he emerged into the sunlight and steeled himself, ready to put on his best performance.

'Men of the Hinterland, form up for inspection!' he shouted.

He had half expected some of them to look around bleary-eyed, in pain and far from at one with their senses, but to his relief his men formed ranks out of pure instinct. He ignored his own pain, straightened his back and strode along the front rank then in one fluid motion, turned his back to it and stood to attention. He gathered his breath then issued his best sergeant's bellow.

'The men of the Hinterland are ready for inspection and to serve, Your Grace.'

Hoping, he clasped his hands behind his back and stared above the heads of the retinue to the top of a stone wall above the smithy's thatched roof.

Lord Aldwyn stepped in front of him and took him by the chin, turning his head to the side. Morrick allowed the motion.

'It is true then.' Aldwyn sighed.

'I am Lord Aldwyn. I am newly appointed Duke of Culrain and the Hinterland. I am led to believe you have all already been informed. Your name?' he asked of Morrick.

Morrick kept his eyes up and snapped back the reply.

'Morrick, Your Grace. Captain of the men of the Hinterland who were conscripted cruelly and against their will, Your Grace. Ready to serve in the name of Queen Cathryn and Lord Lachlan, Your Grace.'

Aldwyn smiled.

'Look at me.'

Morrick did as he was instructed. His lank, greasy hair fell in front of his eyes so he was looking at the duke as though through bars of a cell.

'I am sorry for what Lord Linwood has done to you and your men. You will forever bear the mark of Awgren physically now, as well as in your hearts. Tell me truly and speak plain, Morrick. Will you and your men serve me faithfully?'

Morrick could not keep the smile from his face.

'We will gladly serve you, though in truth none of us wants anything more than to return to our homes and our families. We never wanted to march to war, but we are yours to command, sir. Telling you truly, telling you plain - if you'd let us run home, we'd prefer it.'

'I empathise on that score, believe me,' said Aldwyn. 'Very well. Danyar…' he beckoned for one of his retinue.

'Danyar is one of my generals, and he is co-ordinating my people for the sailing to the Hinterland. Answer his questions and he will see that we find suitable accommodation for you and your men. When we march, you will have fresh arms and armour.' Aldwyn turned and walked away. Morrick considered calling after him, asking what had become of their own armour and if they could perhaps have it back, but thought maybe silence was more appropriate. He determined that, given the chance at an opportune moment, he would ask General Danyar.

However, there was more on his mind, and as Aldwyn disappeared into a side street, Morrick excused himself to run after him.

The people of the Folly gave way as Aldwyn and his retinue pounded the streets towards Linwood's quarters. Aldwyn kept his eyes to the ground, trusting in the efficiency of the men in front of him to clear a path.

He realised someone was speaking.

'What?' he snapped, annoyed that his thoughts were disrupted; he was far from certain how to deal with Linwood.

'What will you do, Your Grace?' asked Morrick as he jogged to keep up.

Aldwyn shook his head. He wanted to forget that Linwood had acted at all. He wanted to return to his quarters. He wanted to speak to Cathryn to tell her she had betrayed him. He wanted to kill her. He wanted to run.

The thought of confronting Linwood interrupted all else; the image of the bigger man's broken face barking in his. In the brief moment of every blink, when the world went dark, he imagined a similarly fast strike from the Duke of the Drift – a strike that Aldwyn was too slow to defend. He imagined himself responding, landing ineffectual punches as Linwood laughed.

He wanted to turn to the captain and say 'I don't know, but it cannot stand.'

But he was feeling himself begin to shake as adrenaline was deployed into his bloodstream, and he halted, driving his face into Morrick's so that their noses touched, and he could smell the suppurating flesh where the brand had lain.

'Who are you to presume to chase me down like a coursed hare?' he roared. He expected Morrick to fall back, but instead the other man's eyebrows knitted and he took one step back after a heartbeat then bowed his head momentarily.

'Not my intention, Your Grace. Apologies,' he said. 'But if it is true that we are now your people, surely Lord Linwood had undermined you. If my men are to follow you, do you want it to be out of duty, out of fealty or do you want men who follow you because they believe in you?'

Morrick could hear the tremor in his own voice, and for a time both men, shaking and doing all in their power to emanate strength, locked eyes. It felt as though the moment would strain and break, so Morrick decided to release the tension. He held a hand to his heart and once more bowed his head.

'Forgive me, Your Grace.'

Aldwyn stood up straight and looked about him to gauge his men's reaction. He shook his head and Morrick thought he had regretted his own behaviour – a positive sign.

'Walk with me, Captain,' said Aldwyn.

His retinue moved off again, but the haste was gone from their steps. Aldwyn turned the situation over in his head. This upstart Captain was right, but the love of his people was of less concern than how allowing Linwood to hurt them would be perceived by the Duke of the Drift. Cathryn, he knew, had carefully positioned his lands between Linwood's. If Aldwyn showed any weakness now, he was inviting an invasion of the Hinterland and the hastening escalation of the situation on this whole continent. Aldwyn sighed and once more his feet began to pound faster and faster. He would have to act and he knew it.

Once more they turned into a side street, and the entire retinue halted, this time of their own accord, for the way was blocked by a column of men marching across the road ahead of them. Morrick recognised the colours and the bright steel of their armour as the same worn by the men who had held him down and branded him; Linwood's men.

'They're heading for the harbour,' said Aldwyn. He stormed on towards the troops and called out.

'Who commands here? Where is the duke?'

A mounted officer called out as he trotted by.

'Lord Linwood and his household have put to sea, Your Grace. Can I serve?'

'No. Thank you and safe travels, sir.'

The officer nodded acknowledgement and rejoined the column as it made its way through the stone streets, the sun glinting on the soldiers' armour.

Aldwyn turned back to his men, shaking his head.

'Take a good look at those faces. Before long we will be facing them across a battlefield, I do not doubt it.'

He rubbed his temples. Morrick puzzled as to what he meant about the battlefield, but there was no time to ask, as Aldwyn was instructing the senior man in his company.

'We should make similar arrangements and with haste. We sail for Oystercatcher Bay and from there we march on the Hinterland in the name of the queen. See that it is done. Dismissed.'

Aldwyn's men set off for their own quarters in the Folly, but Morrick stayed as the duke attempted to gather his thoughts.

'Are not Linwood's men and your own, also the queen's?' asked Morrick, leaning back against the stone wall and folding his arms across his chest.

Aldwyn's look tore into him from beneath dark brows, but Morrick decided to hold his ground. He was cautious of appearing overly co-operative and deferential given his people's reputation for collaboration. Excessive fawning after turning sides would surely sow the seeds of doubt over his loyalty. Standing his ground would serve him better in the end, even if it went against all of his instincts.

Morrick held the duke's gaze, hoping that his face appeared placid, and waited for Aldwyn to answer. Every second seemed to last longer than the last.

The column tailed off and once more the people of the Folly milled about in the streets, but giving the duke, resplendent in fine clothes, and the filthy prisoner, a wide berth. Aldwyn's anger seemed to dissipate, and Morrick thought the younger man looked worn, as though he was being whittled away. Still, he waited.

Finally Aldwyn straightened up.

'Let's go up to the battlements and watch his fleet depart,' he said. 'Come with me.'

The inner wall of the Folly dropped abruptly into a chasm that fell a hundred feet to rocks below. It could only be spanned by walkways lain across the gap whenever they were required and stowed on the inner wall when not. Aldwyn walked across one of these narrow platforms without a second thought, but for the first time in his long years, Morrick found himself at height and fear seized him. He froze on the inner wall, and it was only when Aldwyn looked back that he stepped cautiously forward. He looked down at his feet as he moved and either side of him the rocks far below seemed to rise up towards him at an alarming rate then drop again just as fast. Dizziness overcame him and he stumbled to one side, but just before he could fall, someone grabbed his arm and propelled him to the other side.

Aldwyn smiled.

'The height?'

'Seems so,' Morrick nodded.

The immensely tall outer wall was some 30ft wide with high, crenelated battlements towering another 20ft above the top. Ladders led up to stone platforms just wide enough for a single man to stand with a bow, yet not so wide that they could even sidle past one another to return the way they had come. Any attacker who somehow managed to get over the crenulations would be an unmissable target from the outer wall below, with their only chance being to drop onto the ledge and file round, fighting off defenders, until they reached a ladder down, lest they take a considerable fall.

Hatches were set into the top of the wall, giving access to the armouries and barracks below, but even the off-duty Folly guards passed the time around campfires, playing dice and talking up in the sunshine.

Armed with the fresh knowledge of Morrick's fear, Aldwyn led him across the wall and up one of the ladders to the battlements. Morrick paused, breathing heavy and feeling his heart beating faster.

This is ridiculous, he thought. *I have the courage to face down hundreds of armoured horse, armed only with a pike, but I cannot face a ladder and a fine view?*

He mustered his courage, knowing that he had an opportunity to prove himself to the duke and grabbed hold of a rung just above head height. He began to climb, and his body shook.

Morrick had learned from his experience of crossing the chasm between the inner and outer walls. As he ascended, he kept his eyes focused resolutely on the rungs dead ahead of him. After what seemed like hours, he reached the top and, finding a metal rail set into the floor on the platform, he hauled himself up.

The wind hit him harder than he would have believed possible. He wrapped an arm around the parapet and swung his body so that his chest pressed against the lee side of the stone. His forearm bore the brunt of the wind on the other side and Morrick could feel the cold biting at his skin. He took a moment then straightened up and gradually brought his arm back in. For a moment he stood unsupported, but from the corner of his eye he could see the ground far below through the gap of the crenel. He staggered. His hand found a rail running around the inside of the stone at chest height and he gripped it so tight that his knuckles turned white.

'Well done,' said Aldwyn, off to his right. 'It's no easy thing facing down your fears, and this is quite a height.'

As if to validate his point, Aldwyn too seemed momentarily a little off-balance and steadied himself on the rail sunk into the next rise in the stone. He stepped out from shelter and looked down and south towards the sea and Morrick, reluctantly, did the same.

The wall dropped down over one hundred feet on the outer side, and as it continued southward along the coast, it curved out towards the west, sloping down with the hillside so that Morrick could see over it and down into the Folly.

The inner and outer walls skirted the entire peninsula. Concentric walls stood at some distance apart between the Maw Keep and the plains below, staggered down the hillside with houses, keeps and other buildings in-between. Smaller castles and keeps stood on the plains, some miles distant and hundreds of feet below. Morrick looked out across farmlands and smaller towns, still all contained within the great wall of the Folly. At the southern tip of the peninsula, Morrick could just make out the bowl of the harbour, some two miles across and encircled by the sea wall, except for the entrance to a wide canal, barred by an iron gate. A succession of gates blocked the passage of the canal for a mile out to sea. The canal itself was a blue artery between tall stone walls set wide enough apart that a ship could pass between them to the final Sea-Gate.

Morrick could see tens of vessels at anchor in the harbour and a line of more ships already at sea sailing westward towards the open ocean. One vessel was approaching the inner harbour gate, which was slowly beginning to rise.

Morrick forgot his fear as he looked out across the sea for the first time in his life. The blue seemed to stretch on endlessly to the west, but his view to the east was blocked by the towering keep behind him. To the south he could see the long unwavering line of the horizon and his heart seemed to double in awe. The sun was beginning to sink in the west, and a pink light tinged the clouds there. Morrick gripped harder on the rail, feeling as though the vastness of the world might reach out and pluck him from the wall.

Aldwyn watched the older man and smiled, turning back to watch Linwood's ships. They would bear away west until they had cleared Cape Tendril, then take the passage northward between the west coast and Gannet Island, an isolated tower of granite where once a lighthouse had been manned and a quarry maintained. Aldwyn considered that even now, somewhere beneath their feet, some part of Gannet Island probably made up part of the outer curtain wall.

'Tell me about yourself,' he said, still looking out to sea.

Morrick steadied himself.

'What do you wish to know, Your Grace?'

Aldwyn snorted.

'I'm not fond of that address. There is very little grace about me. Who are you? How come you to be here?'

Morrick yelped as the wind picked up and looked at Aldwyn, eyes imploring.

'Could we have this conversation at a less challenging height?'

The duke conceded and, slowly, they returned down the ladder to the top of the outer wall.

Aldwyn surprised Morrick by sitting cross-legged atop the outer wall. The duke patted the floor beside him. When Morrick had settled, Aldwyn spoke.

'So how does a man end up a soldier in the service of Awgren?'

Morrick rubbed his eyes, resting his elbows on his crossed legs. He sighed and paused for a long time. He sounded exhausted by the effort of thinking of an answer.

'As you would imagine, my lord. An army marched into the Hinterland out of the Wastes and informed the overseer in my village that those who did not fight would be killed and if any man did not go, the entire village would be razed.'

Aldwyn's expression suggested a mockery of weighing up the choice.

'Awgren made a compelling argument,' he said when he saw Morrick was not amused, holding up a hand to pacify the woodcutter.

'Indeed. We had little choice. Our people had long been drilled with the pike and the overseer had promoted me sergeant not five months before Awgren's call-to-arms. All our men, no matter their occupation, were trained for the day we would be called upon. Part of Awgren's price for our continued existence being tolerated.'

'What was your occupation?'

Morrick laughed gently, but Aldwyn heard no amusement in the sound.

'My wife and I have a farm on the edge of the Impassable Forest, not far from the Whiteflow. We're descended from the thegns of the Hinterland and so relatively well off. We sustain ourselves for the most part, but my wife is the farmer, even employs people from the village. I work with wood. They call me a woodcutter, but it's a little more than that,' he said, finally stopping rubbing his eyes and giving Aldwyn a weak smile. The duke thought perhaps Morrick was being too humble and so pressed him to explain.

'I felled trees, sculpted logs and supplied not only Awgren, but the rest of the Hinterland too, with wood for construction; firewood too. I fell, I sell, I carve and I build. Wood is my life,' he shrugged then went on: 'and here I am, in a country with no woods, let alone a forest, in a city of stone upon a bloody mountain.' He shook his head.

'And you have a wife back in the Hinterland?'

'Aye, Rowan. Two sons, Callum and Declan. Too young to fight, thank the Forest. A baby, by now, though I haven't met her and don't know her name. Sure she's a girl though.'

Morrick returned to rubbing his eyes. Aldwyn rested his back against the wall, watching the sergeant. His conviction that he had made the right decision not to punish these people was strengthening. He was about to ask how the Hinterland was governed under Awgren, but Morrick looked up suddenly and spoke firmly, as though it had been an effort to begin and he was determined to get to the end of the sentence.

'Is there any word from my homeland? Are the Devised defeated there too? Was it invaded?'

Guilt stabbed at Aldwyn when he heard the earnest fear behind the words, despite Morrick's efforts to appear stoic. This man had managed to put aside his own concerns in order to meet his obligations to both his men and his new lord.

'No, Captain. Awgren committed the bulk of his forces to meet the Combined People on the fields of Tayne. What has come of the provincial forces is as of yet unclear. I am entrusted with clearing Culrain and the Hinterland, while Linwood will claim Crinan. I believe the Lord of the Isles will deal with Tayne. As for penetrating the Wastes, there has been little talk of it. None in fact.' He stopped himself and apologised.

'I'm wandering, forgive me. There has been no word from the Hinterland as of yet. I cannot reassure you about the fate of your family nor the family of any of your men, but we will sail for Oystercatcher Bay as soon as is practicable. We will march on the Hinterland and, together, we will see.'

Morrick nodded and cast his eyes down to the floor.

'Captain, who governs the Hinterland now the thegns are gone? Under Awgren, I mean.'

'Each village had an overseer appointed by Awgren - mere puppets for the most part, although we never allowed his people to know we could see that. A council of elders advises each overseer. Each village has a garrison of Devised to keep order and to keep the overseer making the correct decisions,' said Morrick.

'And militarily? Who commands your forces?'

Morrick laughed. Aldwyn thought it a bitter sound from this generally affable man.

'Those men you saw in the square yonder. That is what remains of the menfolk of the Hinterland. Of the thousand who came, less than fifty have survived.'

'Hardy soldiers indeed, to have done so. Do not think I have not heard tales of the daring sergeant who so valiantly strove to save his men after Lachlan and Cathryn struck Awgren down.'

Morrick's head snapped round.

'Is that how it happened?'

Aldwyn regaled him with the tale and Morrick listened intently, absorbing as much detail as he could. His men were hungry for information so that they could make sense of their ultimate defeat. For a time after Aldwyn finished, there was silence, but the duke eventually broke it.

'Morrick, I should like to name you as one of my captains and commander of the forces that will be stationed in the Hinterland. Until we arrive in your homeland, I consider you to be the leader of your people. You will speak for them.'

The offer should have set his mind a frenzy, he should have struggled for words or been overjoyed, but Morrick barely seemed to react. He was simply too tired.

'There are so few of us left that the role scarce seems to matter, my lord. But I will serve in whatever capacity you deem fitting in the hope that the Hinterland may recover.'

Aldwyn, and thus Morrick, began readying for departure. When the day came, Aldwyn set his captains about the long task of departing through the sea canal. His own ship had the men of the Hinterland aboard and was scheduled to leave last of all.

Finally the time came to depart and Aldwyn strongly considered slipping away, but duty dictated that he call upon the royal couple before setting sail and so he set about it. He saddled a horse himself and rode across the Arduan Peninsula, up the hillside towards the Maw Keep which housed the royal quarters and the throne room.

Men-at-arms opened the great oak doors to the throne room. It was open to the north, the ceiling supported by stone columns. The thrones at the end of the room were vacant and for a time, Aldwyn waited dutifully in the centre of the room as the doors were closed behind him. Some minutes passed and he grew restive, beginning to pace. He came to a halt beside a column and rested against it. From here on the second highest floor of the Maw Keep's barbican, Aldwyn looked north across the rocky barrens of the Maw beyond, now devoid of the siege forces that had been maintained there for so many centuries, harried by archers and engines of war that now stood idle in the mountain strongholds.

A door opened at the far end of the hall, and Aldwyn hurried back to the centre of the room. Lachlan and Cathryn, hand in hand, walked towards him.

'So, the time has come, my friend,' said Lachlan. The words were meant kindly enough and sounded so, but as Aldwyn drew near, he perceived dislike in the lord's eyes. He suspected the Lord of the Isles knew more of his relationship with Cathryn than had ever been acknowledged, but to give the man credit, Lachlan had always remembered his duty and kept his composure. Besides, they were brothers-in-arms and, Aldwyn hoped, Lachlan knew him as a man of honour.

'It has indeed, Lord Lachlan.' Aldwyn forced a smile and bowed his head. He turned to the queen.

'I must ask your permission to depart for the Hinterland, Your Majesty,' he said and felt his insides tremble as her blue eyes locked with his. The rest of the room seemed to fall away until the Lord of the Isles clearing his throat broke the reverie.

Cathryn smiled.

'We ask much of you, Lord Aldwyn. Defend our interests in the Hinterland and protect the forest. Clear Culrain and rule our lands as you see fit. You will always find friendship in Tayne and, I know I speak for both of us when I say, you will always find friendship in this room.'

'I am honoured, Your Majesty.'

He bowed to Lachlan.

'I will send word both when I reach Oystercatcher Bay and when we take the Hinterland. I have word of Devised forces in the area, but anticipate little resistance. I will push on into the Wastes and Culrain when appropriate.'

Lachlan offered his hand and Aldwyn accepted it, each man grasping the other's tight.

Aldwyn gently kissed Cathryn's and she allowed herself a small smile.

'I hope to see you both again,' said Aldwyn. 'By your leave, I will depart.'

That evening a host of men hauled Aldwyn's ship, the Nightingale, along the sea canal, and it sailed out onto the open ocean.

Word was given for the Sea-Gate to be secured and, for the first time since the defeat of Awgren, the queen gave orders to bar the Maw Gate from the inside.

The Folly stood secure against outsiders - assuming of course, that all outsiders had truly departed.

Chapter Eight

In her dream the white mane thrashed, disappearing amidst the flying flecks of foam from the river that ran so high only the horse's head and neck were visible.

Rowan lay flat on the bank, her fingers grasping the overhang and watching as the waters steadily rose towards her. She felt calm as the waters seemed to pour up out of the river as though some deeper chasm beneath its bed had given passage to a deeper source. The snow-covered plains disappeared and the waters continued to rise.

The horse's head thrashed, dipped under the surface and came up once more. Rowan cried out as the horse began to scream in a voice that seemed more than animal, more than human. It was every voice, and she heard it within and without.

Rowan covered her ears with her hands and scrunched her eyes closed as the Whiteflow washed over the lip of the bank and pooled around her. The water rushed into her mouth. Now her throat was the river. She opened her eyes but the pressure of the river against them was too much and she closed them once again. She could not even cough and with her limbs splayed, her body careered downstream. Rowan gave up hope, but her heart beat ever faster.

Her fingers brushed against something and stuck fast, followed by her palms. Her arm wrenched as she was dragged forward, and she reached forward with her other hand, but she was moving too quickly. The oncoming water forced the arm down to her side and her chin towards her chest. Then her head was above the water and she was coughing up fluid. Her hand was stuck to the white horse's flank, her arm arching over its back as it galloped upstream, high in the water – so impossibly high that she knew there was no way its hooves could be reaching the riverbed. She hauled herself onto its back as they drew near to where the Whiteflow disappeared into the forest and as the darkness under the trees swallowed them, Rowan awoke.

Declan and Bramble, who was cradling the baby, were sitting at the main table eating a breakfast of trout, dark bread and ale.

Rowan sat up and wrapped her blanket around her shoulders. The fire was going, but still she shivered.

'Good morning,' she said, yawning. 'Where's Callum?'

'Look who finally joins us.' Bramble smiled. She laid the sleeping baby in the cradle and set about fetching Rowan some food before answering.

'Callum went out early this morning. He told Declan he was going to gather acorns from the Forest to feed the pigs.'

Rowan shot to her feet.

'Alone? Mother!'

Bramble held up her hand, shaking her head.

'Captain Lynch went with him.'

Rowan relaxed a little immediately, but this frightened her in another way. She slipped on her boots.

'I'm going to wash, if you are all right with these two for a little longer?'

Her mother nodded, not looking away from cutting a hunk of cheese. She handed it to Rowan silently then returned to Declan's side. She tousled the boy's long hair.

The light snows of the last few days had melted away and the ground lay bare and brown on the path to the river side. She looked about for Lynch's men as she left the ranch, but they all appeared to be sleeping in the barn, out of sight in the daytime as had been agreed – except for those on watch of course, but those too were not visible. She was about to turn her attention to reaching the river when a movement caught her eye, and she turned to look back towards the town. Two people were coming up the path – women, judging from what she thought was a swish of skirt around the height of their ankles. Momentarily torn between curiosity and the need to relieve her bladder, she elected to return to the farm to use the privy instead of the river. She ran to the barn and called through the door that someone was coming and returned to the path to greet her visitors. By the time she had reached the gate, she could recognise Lara helping Acorna, one of the elders, along the path from the village.

Seeing her friend renewed her sense of guilt about the previous night, but she was also relieved to see her. When her face became visible as she moved towards them, Lara instantly recognised the smile on her lips as genuine and her own hard feelings ebbed somewhat. They met a hundred yards from the gate and Rowan curtsied slightly to Acorna, though she kept her arms folded against the cold. She smiled at Lara, perhaps a little nervously, but Lara smiled back, and the two women embraced.

'What brings the two of you out to see us this morning? Are you looking for my mother, Acorna?' Rowan asked, knowing full well the two elder women had been friends for many long years.

Acorna shook her head.

'I've come to see her more than my fair share this last month. Time she dragged her woe-begotten carcass down to see me. Her turn.' She gave a wicked smile and Rowan laughed.

'We've come to talk about what happened with the overseer. How to proceed,' said Lara, softly.

She felt a strong urge to look back over her shoulder to see if Lynch was returning, but she resisted, unwilling to show that anything was amiss as of yet. But what was the alternative?

'I was about to bathe. Mother let me sleep late. Walk with me?'

The Whiteflow was running high, renewed by the melted snows, but not as high as her dream suggested. The white horse was nowhere to be seen. She laid a fur over the pebbles and knelt down to splash water into her face. Lara took up Rowan's jug and helped her rinse her hair while Acorna sat patiently on a nearby rock.

'It's not a new quandary, Rowan - nothing that countless men and women before you haven't considered. My sons are in the war. Lara's brother and husband too. Many, many people have searched for an answer to the Hinterland's predicament, and do you know what the answer has always been?' asked Acorna.

Rowan closed her eyes, bracing against the cold of the Whiteflow as Lara poured it over the back of her head. She gasped when it was over.

'To do nothing. To collaborate.'

'Collaborating is *not* doing nothing. It's a course of action we have chosen generation after generation to fend off certain reprisal. It is bile in my mouth as much as it is yours, but it has been necessary.'

Rowan sat back on her haunches as Lara began drying her hair.

'You all believe that if we make a stand here, our men will die,' she said, looking down at the pebbles.

'Yes, we do,' said Lara, lifting away the towel and crouching to look her friend in the eye.

'Well answer me this, Acorna,' said Rowan, 'why did we not stand and fight when Awgren's army came and took our men away? Why did the old thegns not resist when Crinan, Tayne and Culrain fought until they had no other choice but retreat?'

For a while both Rowan and Lara looked up at Acorna as though they were small children at their mother's knee.

'Because the thegns knew we could not withstand Awgren and that Crinan would not send aid. They had to look to themselves and, since that first betrayal, the Hinterland has always chosen survival over honour,' said Acorna.

Lara nodded to herself, but Rowan shook her head.

'You think anything but a victory is futile then?'

Nobody said anything, but all heard an answer in the silence.

Rowan gathered her things, her temper once again flaring, and Lara sighed in exasperation before blurting.

'The overseer is considering taking measures to stop your talk.'

Rowan set down the basket, withdrawing her brush and setting to work on her hair.

'I see.' Nothing for a while then, 'At least someone in the Hinterland is prepared to get his hands dirty in the name of a cause, but then, that victory is assured. We like those kind of odds in these parts.'

She continued to brush while Acorna explained the conversation that had taken place after Rowan had burst into the main lodge.

'You felt strongly enough to betray the Council's confidence in order to warn me,' Rowan remarked.

'I have no desire to see your family harmed, Rowan. The overseer is largely powerless, but he does have the ear of the Devised commander. His position is only as secure as the stability and the productivity. Your talk is making him worry. He's asked us all to try to dissuade you from rash action. I'm not going to do that, but I wish to make it very clear what will happen.'

'Tell her,' said Lara.

'You may well be able to raise rebellion. We might kill the Devised, but even if we are successful, Awgren will send a force to find out why he has had no messengers after a while. We may not be able to defeat all of them and if not, word of the rebellion will reach Awgren. The men will be executed. Even if we utterly defeat them, Awgren will send a larger force and all will die.'

'Perhaps that is what should happen. Perhaps we should do our part and die as the Crinish died; as they died in Culrain. Perhaps the scattered remains of our people should flee in boats to the Drift and to the Isles, warmed by the knowledge that our sacrifices have bought back our souls!' said Rowan, her voice rising.

'Wise up, girl. Touch the nettle. Feel the sting. Nobody here will make that choice. So can you ignore your conscience or are we going to make a bloody mess of one kind or another?' snapped Acorna.

Rowan was on her feet and striding towards the old woman before she had even thought about it.

'What if things are about to change? What if I told you that Awgren is about to fall? How would that affect your reckonings? What if before the year is out, Lord Lachlan and Queen Cathryn march into the Hinterland and hang the overseer from the willow yonder so that the maggots from his rotting body fall to feed the fish?' She spat the words, rather than roaring them and Acorna glared at her as she wiped spittle from her cheek.

'Is this how you give thanks for a warning, girl? What would your mother say to see her friend thus defiled?' Acorna shook her head in disgust.

'Lay off her, Rowan. Are you planning on tearing the head off everyone who hears you out and doesn't merely echo back your opinion?'

Rowan turned away, breathing hard and staring off towards the forest, from where the Whiteflow churned out of the darkness to split the bare earth.

'I apologise. To both of you.' She turned and settled on the pebbles, ignoring the discomfort. 'But I am not talking idly now or just in anger. I need to know this conversation will go no further. Can I have your assurance?' She looked to Acorna and Lara in turn, but even their nods did not immediately set her mind at ease.

They waited for her to speak but it was not until a change came over her face, a brightening, that she spoke again. When she did, she sounded almost excited at her realisation.

'When did we last receive an envoy from the Wastes?' she asked. 'When were the Devised last reinforced?'

Now it was Acorna's turn to sound interested.

'It has been some time. Months. Another reason why the overseer is nervous. I think he is worrying what will come when something eventually does.'

Rowan leant forward on her knees, grinning. She was certain now that she would be able to make her point.

'What if I told you I had word from the Folly? Word that Awgren's attention is very likely elsewhere?'

'By the shade of the Forest, Rowan!' Lara screeched, almost playfully. 'What do you know? Stop batting us from paw to paw. Make the kill!'

Rowan broke. Acorna and Lara gobbled up her words, unblinking and often covering mouths with hands. She told them of Lynch and his crew. She told them of the fleet and the invasion. She told them that if Awgren's defeat was not imminent then she believed that at the very least this was to be the largest invasion the Combined People had ever attempted, a thousand years in the making.

When she was done, the reactions varied as quickly as the seconds passed.

Jubilation gave way to despair which gave way to hope before it was dashed by worries.

'I don't know what to think,' said Acorna. 'If they defeat Awgren? Our people stand in his army!'

'Do we want them to win or lose?' laughed Lara, raking her hair back with her fingers in exasperation.

'I should be getting back to the farm. Mother will be worrying,' said Rowan. 'And Captain Lynch may have returned with Callum by now.'

Lara shot her a curious look at that, but Rowan merely frowned and ignored her, setting off back towards her home. Lara helped Acorna up, and they hurried after her.

'What does the Captain want to do?' called Acorna.

Rowan said nothing, but upped her pace.

'Rowan?' called Lara.

Once more she ignored the question.

The three of them arrived back at the gate, all looking around eagerly, but nothing was out of place. Declan was seeing to the horses whilst Callum threw acorns to the pigs.

'Are we coming in to talk further?' asked Lara, clearly anxious.

Rowan slipped through and closed the gate behind her.

'I think it best we speak to the Council. All of us. And Captain Lynch. Can you gather the Council without the overseer knowing and come back after dark?'

'I think…' began Acorna, but Rowan cut her off.

'Not just the Council, all the councils; as many of the elders from the nearby villages as can be mustered.'

'That'll be no mean feat, Rowan,' warned Lara, 'sneaking people in and out with messages.'

Rowan grinned.

'Collaborating just got a little more complicated, didn't it?'

She set off to begin her day's work.

She waited until dusk before waking Lynch. He had, after all, gone out early to look after her oldest boy, and she thought she owed him a little uninterrupted sleep before the elders arrived. She was enjoying the last warmth of the sun as she crossed to the barn when all hell broke loose.

Two spindly-fingered hands snarled around her neck as though they were trying to grasp a wet fish. They squeezed tight as they found purchase, and she was snatched backwards off of her feet. Her head smashed back to the ground, and a slavering face appeared above her, teeth bared and drooling. Its saliva oozed across her open mouth as she gasped for breath. Its eyes widened as it ground its teeth, pouring all of its strength into wringing her neck. Cries and calls filled the air. She could feel the thumping of feet beside her, and she realised with horror that she hadn't asked her mother to bar the door behind her. All of the children were still inside the lodge.

She heard her mother scream.

Rowan's consciousness began to fade even as her lungs screamed out at her, but as her vision began to fade, there was a blur of movement above her, and a booted foot crunched into the creature's face, obliterating its teeth and raining blood all over her.

She was momentarily relieved until the kick followed through and the perpetrator's backside landed hard on her face. She screamed out, and as the offending person rolled off, she clutched at her head, feeling as though her skull was crushed. Pain radiated from her nose and under her eyes, which were filling with tears. Rowan wiped them away with her forearm and pushed up onto her elbows, lying on her front as the sounds of battle raged. Lynch was clambering to his feet, one hand pressed against the base of his spine and thrusting his cutlass forward defensively with the other. All manner of Devised were climbing over the wall and pouring through the now broken gate. The door to the lodge stood open and even seeing the back of a sailor disappearing inside did not reassure her.

Rowan ignored her pain as the steady flow of blood from her nose soaked the front of her shirt. She grabbed the defeated creature's cudgel and tried to burst into a sprint, the soles of her feet scuttering in the dust before finding purchase. Before she had gone ten paces she collided with the bosun, but the big man never even so much as checked his pace; Rowan bounced right off him and fell heavily to the ground. Her head began to spin and the last she saw was Lynch standing over her, facing off against three approaching creatures.

She became aware again a few minutes later, once more with a body lying across her face. She pushed with everything she had, and the man rolled off, his face coming into view. It was Lynch. His right eye was gone and a gash reached down to his chin, severing his lips. She initially thought he was dead, but then saw he was sputtering droplets of blood.

Screams, shouts and sounds of weapon impacts still filled the air, but as she sat up, it became apparent that Lynch's men had been reinforced by people from the village. Old men, women and boys were brawling all around her farm buildings, armed with the most unlikely of things. Even the overseer could be seen wielding a pitchfork against a huge foul-looking Creature of the Devising. Rowan would have laughed at the sight, feeling a little swell of pride in the man, if she were not hellbent on finding her children. She once more snatched up the cudgel and made for the lodge and this time she made it, as the fighting had moved off towards the barn.

The lodge was empty save for the cradle. Bracing herself against the door frame, her heart near stopped at the sight of her baby daughter, Bracken, quiet within it. She hurled herself across the room, crying out in relief. Only when her hands wrapped around the baby did the tears start.

Rowan found herself laughing and weeping all at once – the baby had slept through it all so far. But where was her mother? Where were the boys?

Rowan clutched the baby to her chest and paused, not knowing whether to hide the baby or go out and fight, unsure as to which was the more dangerous course and, in all honesty, whether she should be trying to stay safe or help the villagers. The altercation in this very room with Lara the previous night came to mind and her resolve hardened.

Rowan carried the baby across the room and tucked her underneath Declan's bunk. She ran to the door and barred it, then climbed out of the window and pushed the shutters closed behind her.

'CALLUM!' she shouted at the top of her lungs. 'DECLAN!'

She skirted the lodge and ran towards the continuing fight over by the corral, her feet falling between bodies and once, sickeningly, onto an old man's skull. It crunched beneath her. She fell to her knees and vomited.

So this was rebellion? Suddenly Rowan felt very foolish indeed, but then she saw her mother lying in the dirt across the yard, staring dead-eyed back at her. Rowan could not move; she just stared back into those lifeless eyes, on the brink of a scream that would never come. She strove to dismiss her grief, knowing that above all else, she must find the boys. Rowan found her feet and ran on, roaring and raising the cudgel above her head.

She took a manlike thing by surprise and felled it with a single blow, driven by ferocity beyond even her own expectations.

'Mother!'

She whirled at the shout, relieved to see Callum charging towards her. He was drenched in blood, crying so hard that his eyes were red-rimmed. He was carrying an equally bloody cutlass. Rowan, in that moment, thought she had never seen a sight so horrific as her baby at war. He looked so like his father that it took her breath away.

I wish you were here, Morrick. Why aren't you here?

'Where's Declan?' she screamed, clasping Callum to her chest. He fought her off, pushing her away.

'I haven't seen him. Let go!' he screeched. Unthinking, she had seized his hair and was repeatedly screaming the question at him.

Garrick ran towards them from the south fence of the ranch, shouting. Despite his age, he was carrying a huge broadsword and carrying it well.

'The rest of them are coming up from the village,' he shouted. He panted as he drew close.

'We need to get into the forest,' said a familiar voice. Rowan turned and saw Lynch, held up by two of his people, his face a mess of gore and his words slurred.

'Run?' said Rowan.

'Survive,' said Lynch.

Wilson wiped blood from his cutlass.

'About it then, lads. You heard the captain. To the forest!'

It only took a few seconds for what remained of Lynch's crew to respond. They gathered up the walking wounded, some of their crewmates borne across shoulders on sheer adrenaline.

Rowan grabbed Acorna as she shuffled by, her lower arm dripping blood slightly faster than the gash in her head. She was weaving as she went and a young boy steadied her.

'What about the people in the village? What about the wounded?'

Acorna's eyes were afire when they locked with Rowan's.

'This is what you wanted girl. Those who fall behind… '

The old woman abandoned her.

Rowan grabbed Callum by the shoulders.

'Get your sister from under Declan's bunk. Go!'

She darted this way and that, searching amongst the bodies trying to find Declan.

'Has anybody seen my son?' she called, but those who remained were so busy trying to escape that few heeded her and less replied.

'Callum went into the lodge!' said Garrick as he led the last of the villagers on. 'Come on, Rowan. There's no time.'

'Declan!' Rowan screamed in reply. 'Declan!'

She continued to search, growing ever more desperate. She could hear more Creatures of the Devising coming up from the south.

'I'm here.' His voice was quiet, strained and beyond fear. Rowan spun on her heels and grasped her youngest to her. She called for Callum to hurry.

By the time Callum had fetched the baby, Rowan felt her heart was near to bursting. She looked to the north and saw her people had cleared the north wall and were well on their way to the forest. To the south, she could hear the drums of the remainder of the Devised contingent coming from the village. Drums and screams.

Lara, she thought. She hadn't seen her during the fight or lying on the ground.

She started to walk them north, but realised to her horror that they would almost certainly be overtaken in the open. Instead, she made for the gate and hurried her sons eastward towards the river, hoping that the signs of flight to the north would hold greater attraction than just a few tracks east.

She panted as she ran, her hands pushing on the backs of her boys, trying to drive them on so they could reach the river and hopefully cross it before wheeling north and heading into the forest.

But then she heard hoarse shouts and shrieks on their tail and, looking back over her shoulder, she saw the vanguard bearing down on her. Only a few doglike beasts had come after them, but, Rowan thought, one or two would be enough to slaughter her kin.

Morrick, she thought. She wanted him so desperately then and hoped beyond hope that he would burst out from behind a boulder, battle-worn but healthy, wielding his great axe. But Morrick wasn't hiding nearby. He hadn't deserted and found his way home to protect his family. He had gone off like a whipped dog, just like the rest of them.

'Please,' she breathed as she ran, and the tears began to flow.

'Run, boys. Run!'

It was dark by the time they reached the river and only the moonlight glinting on the water told her they had arrived. She did not stop to think, she pushed the boys in where it was deepest amidst the rapids, Callum still clutching his sister. She dived in after them and went under.

Rowan was so out of breath, that she immediately and instinctively breathed deep of the water. She came up spluttering and coughing, grasping this way and that to secure her children to her.

Morrick, she thought, but then for the first time, *Morrick be damned. We're alone.*

They clung together, Callum holding the baby overhead while Rowan and Declan kicked furiously, trying to keep him afloat. Time after time, one of them would go under and all the time, the baby screamed and cried. Rowan feared for the time when the crying would stop, but there was little time to think. She held her breath when she needed, she breathed deep when she could. She cast her gaze about, looking for some root to clasp to haul them ashore. It had surely only been minutes when the four of them were swept into the very same bowl, carved out by the river into a deep pool, where Rowan had been washing when she had first seen the horse.

The current pushed them up against the bank where it was too steep to climb, and Rowan knew it was the end – their strength would soon give out and unable to fight against the current, one by one her sons and daughter would slip beneath the water.

Then she heard the animals coming up the river bank from the south where their encampment was located. Bracken cried on and Rowan knew that the sound would attract their enemies.

Rowan reached out and took her daughter, forcing Bracken's mouth against her bosom, trying to stifle the sound but not the breath. She could hear Devised moving closer and, in despair, Rowan bit down so hard on her lower lip that her teeth went straight through.

Blood dripped into the water. Bracken cried ever louder.

She pushed her daughter below the surface of the water. Callum yelped, but Rowan gritted her teeth and drove her face towards him so aggressively, intent on her business, that the boy fell silent.

The snarls of the dog creatures drew nearer. Rowan shook, her head down, one arm wrapped around Declan, Callum's arm wrapped around her own waist. She could not see the baby, but could feel her body going limp in her arms. She pulled Bracken close to her in an embrace as she drowned her.

All was silent and the creatures passed them by, but still her family was forced up against the bank. Rowan felt nothing, numbing herself against all thought and feeling.

Suddenly the current seemed to abate. She looked up and before them was the white stallion, standing immovable in the water.

Declan cried out and then again, 'Mother!'

She felt her sons pulling away from her and as a cloud moved aside from the moon, she could see shimmering figures standing tall in the water as though it was far shallower than she knew it to be. They had taken hold of her sons.

'No! NO!' she screamed, but then she saw the water people bear her sons away and help them up onto the white horse.

Another drew up in front of her, blue marble eyes hanging suspended in a head formed from the whipping, circular motions in the foam. She felt hands raise her arms and the body of her daughter above the surface. Rowan looked down for the first time upon Bracken's dead features, her little eyes looking up at the moon. Rowan screamed into the night, not caring about beasts, her sons or anything else at all except her forsaken, sacrificed child who had died so that some of her offspring might live. The figure held her tight in an embrace that Rowan was incapable of escaping. She too was held high in the water and the Naiads pushed her up onto the white stallion's back. She righted herself atop it and the one who had helped her bowed its head. Rowan was near insensible and did not respond. She closed her eyes tight again as she cried and so, when the Naiad darted for her, she did not see it coming. The next she knew, her daughter had been plucked from her arms. Rowan's eyes shot open and she grasped for Bracken's corpse, but already the Naiad was mid-stream amidst the rapids, seeming to wade unperturbed by the current.

Then, turning to face Rowan once more and still cradling the baby, it sank into the waters. Rowan screamed and tried to dismount, but her legs were stuck fast to the side of the horse. Another Naiad motioned with its hand and the stallion reared up before galloping upstream towards the forest. Rowan closed her eyes and wrapped her arms tight around Declan and Callum.

She was not aware of the passage of time during that wild ride. The stallion galloped for the forest, glowing white in the moonlight as it carried its tormented, unwilling riders, passed the spot where they had jumped in, way beyond the homestead and into the complete darkness of the trees.

Rowan could no longer think on her daughter. No longer think of the future. She held tight to her sons and cursed her husband for a coward, blaming him for all that had befallen them as though it had all been part of his devising.

Finally, after what seemed like an unending ride, the stallion slowed and wheeled out of the river and into the trees. It wove its unseen path in the dark, and the riders cried out as branches scratched at their skin until Rowan heard voices ahead of them.

'Something's coming!' said a low, deep voice.

'Take it down,' said another.

A slicing, wet sound filled Rowan's ears and she cried out as she was thrown forward and off the stallion, landing on her sons as they sprawled in the grass. The stallion melted away into water upon the grass, though none saw it go, and the family would later marvel at the creature's disappearance.

'It's Callum!' called her son. 'Callum, Declan and Rowan.'

His voice was desperate and she hoped beyond hope these were not Devised who had waylaid them even as she sobbed, helpless in the long grass.

'Rowan, ma'am?' It was Lynch's voice above her. She clawed out for him, finding his leg.

She clambered up him, wrapping her arms around his chest and sobbing uncontrollably into his shirt, seeing only her baby daughter disappearing into the ice-cold waters of the Whiteflow.

Lynch shrugged off his helper and steadied himself well enough to support her, one hand gently stroking the nape of her neck.

Rebellion had come to the Hinterland.

Chapter Nine

Lachlan, the Lord of the Isles, was gone.

Some commanders view their troops as toy soldiers. Some commanders know each of their people by name. Some officers will send their men to die without a second thought, whilst others will send them, but will be racked with guilt for months, even years afterwards. Queen Cathryn, descended of old from the rulers of Tayne, did not consider herself a commander at all. Her people were commodities, but not in such a way that they did not matter to her. After all, gold was a commodity, as was salt, and only a fool would throw those away; after all, they had intrinsic value.

Only a bigger fool would name each grain of salt or recognise an individual gold coin. So it was with Cathryn and her soldiers. She valued them, but she did not come to know them. A few days after the Folly had been sealed, as she passed the oak doors to the throne room, she paid no particular attention to the identity of the men who wore her colours guarding the door.

A gaggle of stern-faced soldiers, advisors and administrators were huddled around the dais. A few of them dared to meet her eye as she traversed the hall and mounted the steps.

'Where is he?'

Her volume was low, her voice was calm, but those who looked into Queen Cathryn's eyes saw a steely determination barring the escape of a wild fury. Those who did not look were more than aware of what they would have seen, had they dared.

The queen had been defied and by her husband. She had allowed Lachlan appear to be her equal only out of clemency for his own dignity, yet he was full aware she was the true power, and this was how he repaid her?

'What news of the Lord of the Isles?' she asked again.

Several of them exchanged looks, as if asking who should go first. Their voices rose in a clamour, but a particular voice defied the rest and persisted.

'I have an account of the Lord of the Isles' movements, Your Majesty,' said a short woman clad in leather armour which bore the crest of Long Isle. Cathryn thumped down into her throne, crossed her legs under her long dress and waved a hand imperiously.

'Deliver your report...' she paused, realising that though the woman was familiar, she did not remember her name. 'Remind me of your name?'

She did not intend to snap, but the frustration was in her voice none the less. The woman was unflappable and charged into her report.

'Mary of the Long Isle. Captain of your husband's household guard, Your Majesty.'

She did not wait to be acknowledged, though Cathryn did nod as she recognised the name.

'Lord Lachlan dismissed his personal guard shortly before sunset. I have no reports of his activities until much later in the night when the Lord of the Isles, cloaked and bearing a pack, attended by his brother Hadwyn and Lord Belman, began to pass south through the various gates all the way to the harbour. He was either recognised or displayed his seal to ensure co-operation.'

Cathryn began to repeatedly stab downward on the arm of her throne with the outstretched nail of her forefinger. She glared at Mary's feet as the woman went on with some minor details, and then held up her hand.

'Enough. My thanks. So my husband has taken a boat?'

The Folly's castellan stood forward from the crowd and bowed his head.

'The Sea-Gate never rose, Your Majesty, but the watchmen on the south wall report that a schooner that rode at anchor some way out to sea at dusk was gone when the sun came up.'

'You believe he went to sea, Lord Castellan?' said Cathryn, ceasing her assault on the arm of her throne and looking the man in the eye. Here was yet another whose name escaped her despite spending her entire life in the Folly.

Lord Castellan Oisin shook his head.

'It is a possibility and perhaps the most likely possibility. There remains the hope that the Lord of the Isles is somewhere in the Folly,' he said.

Unsaid was the presumption that Lachlan was off on an errand of his own choosing. The queen's aide, Ailsa, had been awakened by Lachlan's personal guard when finally they had grown concerned that Lachlan had not returned. The initial search had been on the basis that the Lord of the Isles was simply taking the air, and after the searches were fruitless, that perhaps some harm, accidental or deliberate, had befallen him. Then tongues had begun to wag and reports of his movements had flooded in to the various watch commanders around the Arduan Peninsula. The inescapable conclusion all had reached was that Lachlan had taken off without consulting the queen or leaving word of his intentions.

All felt the weight of this conclusion. All knew they were not just in the presence of a wife whose husband had humiliated her, but a queen who had been belittled by her lower-born consort. Each stood forward and either confirmed or added to the reports from Mary and Oisin, but kept their own findings succinct.

Eventually all had spoken except one man – Lachlan's squire, Rennan. As the noon bell rang out and echoed across the Maw, Rennan coughed loudly and stepped forward to interrupt more of the castellan's postulations.

He coughed again as the last chime of the noon bell rang out and stepped forward, shoulders back but a tremor shaking his whole body.

'You have something to say, Rennan?' asked Cathryn, fearing what was to come, for Lachlan kept as close a counsel with the squire as did she with Ailsa. Perhaps not quite as close, she thought, looking over the man's figure.

'I…beg pardon, Your Majesty. I had orders.'

A collective sigh seemed to fill the throne room, and Cathryn resisted angry tears, blinking once, slow and resolute, as she faced the open north wall and the shadows of the mountains stretching away from the Maw Keep.

'Orders from the Lord of the Isles, I take it.' She did not turn back to him.

'From the Lord of the Isles, Your Majesty. I did not intend to obstruct your will, Your Majesty.' His voice was in vibrato.

She stood suddenly and advanced on the open wall, leaning against a pillar. All stood silent as they awaited her instructions. When finally she did address them, she had forced a narrow, thin smile onto her features, the effect of which was far from comforting and did little to suggest either happiness or mirth. The castellan actually shivered.

'My lords, tend to your duties and leave us to our business. I can trust to your discretion, people of Tayne?'

'Of course, Your Majesty,' said the castellan and shepherded the others out, leaving the boy Rennan quaking before the dais.

Cathryn regarded him as he watched the floor, wringing his hands behind his back and took pity.

'Come see the view,' she said softly and after a moment's hesitation, Rennan moved beside her.

'See the world we have conquered?' She waved her hand as though to underline the vista of barren rock and the scorched lands beyond.

'Yes, Your Majesty.' He was too afraid to converse casually with anyone, let alone the queen, whom, he was afeared, would consider him a traitor.

Her fingertips grasped his upper arm and his wide eyes were caught in the net of her regard. He shifted uncomfortably.

'Tell me then.' She smiled and this time, it was genuine. She felt no pity for this boy and did indeed consider him a traitor of a sort, but she looked at this commodity as though he was a badly invested coin that might return to the purse, but not bring friends. He was salt upon rotting meat. It was the fault of neither the coin nor the salt and she knew how quickly she could dispatch him if she wished. In not wishing to do so, she benefited from knowing she could show restraint and by convincing herself of her inherent goodness. She nodded encouragingly with an open expression and Rennan seemed to take heart.

'Lord Lachlan told me not to speak until noon today,' he said, searching her impassive face for a reaction. When he saw nothing, he went on.

'The Lord of the Isles has decided that Lord Linwood is not to be trusted and intends to travel the Drift to confirm his suspicions and rally what support he can find.'

'Alone, or as good as,' said Cathryn. It was not a question.

'He has taken his brother and Lord Belman, Your Majesty. He said to commit troops was to weaken areas that need defending. That this was his task alone. He said...forgive me, Your Majesty...it does not feel appropriate for me to repeat his words.'

Cathryn's lip curled upwards on one side and raised an eyebrow. Rennan shivered.

'Oh? Tell all. I've not tossed you on top of the Maw Gate yet, have I?' That snake smile once more, anticipating a barb. Rennan gave up all hope. He learned helplessness.

'The lord's words were that the queen would understand why he had to go. That she would see the wisdom in risking few on a thankless task. Understand that should he fall, the cost to the realm and to the queen would be but three men, who once stood amongst thousands.'

Cathryn ground her teeth. Pain lanced up and down her teeth from the pressure. She released it.

'You may leave.'

Rennan released his breath audibly. Cathryn thought he might even have fallen back if he wasn't so desperately working to maintain some semblance of courtly behaviour.

'I did not mean to be disloyal, Your Majesty.'

Cathryn continued to look out over the Maw, thinking for the hundredth time how ridiculous it was that the throne room looked out across such deprivation when the lush fields of the Arduan Peninsula and the spectacular, outstretched sea lay away to the south. She determined that when her business was wrapped up in the Maw Keep, that she would move to apartments on the south wall.

So, Lachlan was indeed off on a jaunt and to what end? To vanquish Lord Linwood and then what? To clear the Wastes? To quest into the heart of the enemy's stronghold? To strike at the belly of the beast? All noble ideas on a storybook page, but Cathryn lived in the real world. She landed a punch on the stone pillar, grazing the skin on her knuckles and splitting the skin in-between. Blood began to spread across the surface and she splayed then curled her fingers to lessen the sensation.

You've known for some time that he wanted to go – that ruling was too much for him. Is this really a surprise?

But even with the expectation, Cathryn *was* surprised. Though they had never been close or perhaps more accurately, as close as she was to Aldwyn, they had forged a strong bond over the decades. The love-making was regular and far from perfunctory. She believed she had always done her utmost to make Lachlan her equal. Didn't that say it all? She knew that he was *not* her equal, after all. Lachlan was a distant cousin and Lord of the Isles with an inferior claim to both the thrones of Tayne and Culrain. He was considered by many in the Isles as the strongest, bravest warrior and the canniest commander. He was thought to be fair and just by his men – Cathryn had made her enquiries after the accident which left Aldwyn incapable of carrying out one particular kingly duty.

'Your Majesty?'

Not having heard anyone approach, the queen mouthed a silent yelp. Her aide, Ailsa, made her apologies. She was dressed in boiled leather armour and her long chestnut hair was tied in a long ponytail. By the look of her eyes, she had been crying hard. Cathryn breathed out hard, she patted her heart with an open palm.

'You scared me,' she laughed, but then saw that the girl was in distress.

'Ailsa? Your eyes.'

Her aide clucked her tongue against the back of her teeth, turning her head away and looking down to the floor.

'And I thought I had washed away all signs. 'Tis nothing, Your Majesty. Shall we dispense with our session today?' Ailsa held out Cathryn's weapon; the bastard sword was encased in plain brown leather with no ornamentation, as was the custom of the Combined People.

The queen snatched the sword up and partially drew it, then rehoused and returned the blade.

'I'm well versed in sword play,' she sighed. 'Less acquainted with dealing with headstrong, idiot men struck down by a malady of the spirit.'

She walked to the open wall and, carefully, sat with her legs dangling. Between her and the ground there was nothing but air. Ailsa was more wary and moved slowly up behind her, her soft-leather boots near silent on the stone. She crouched then dropped down next to the queen.

'I've heard many rumours,' she said.

Cathryn made no reply and, after a time simply looking at the profile of her crestfallen face, Ailsa too turned her gaze to the great vista before them. A sea eagle soared over the Maw Gate below and Cathryn's eyes traced its progress through the air.

'Lachlan has taken his leave of us,' she remarked, ostensibly unmoved. Ailsa knew better.

'For why?'

Cathryn actually laughed and lay back on the cold stone, her legs still dangling over the edge.

'The reason he gives or the reason I think to be true?'

'Both, if it pleases you.'

Ailsa's head swayed suddenly as the wind rocked her and she shuffled back until she could lean back against a pillar, feeling relatively safe.

'He's off on a…quest.' She laughed again. 'What a ridiculous notion. And so distinctly Lachlan, don't you think?'

'Mmm.'

'Mmm?' Cathryn propped herself up on her elbows.

'I'd hear more before I pass judgement,' Ailsa replied. 'He is your husband and my lord, after all. He's done much for the Combined People, has he not?'

Cathryn blew air between her pursed lips.

'If ever I made a poor judgment it was in thinking my husband was fit to rule beside me. He is well-loved, he fights like a mad bear and, in truth, I love him well enough, but lordship over his house and his lands has done little to prepare him for higher responsibility. Ever he strives for peace in his own life. Ever he looks for meaning where there is none.'

At this, Ailsa frowned.

'I do not follow, Cathryn.'

Cathryn lay back down and closed her eyes.

'There is no meaning to any of this. We strive for domination over all. We have no concept at all of what we should ever do if all existence fell under our sway. Our ancestors claimed mastery over the old lands and built the kingdoms in wealth, knowledge and creativity, but did they ever think they had enough? The lust for improvement cannot be sated and neither can the desire to control one's environment. Look at this monstrosity we now inhabit? Did it ever occur to whoever first considered fortifying this peninsula that it would only need fortifying if it were fortified? Who attacks a field? A farmer, perhaps, in a manner of speaking; or a bird. Not soldiers.'

'A field might be invaded and so be fenced in,' ventured Ailsa, thinking that Cathryn perhaps recognised malady in her husband because of a darkness upon her own heart, even if she did not acknowledge it.

'A fenced-in field becomes a courtyard or a garden. It loses its essence. No, these monuments and cities and fortresses serve only as does a mound of gold that would serve better invested or in a vault.' She laid one forearm across her eyes as though she was staving off a pain therein.

'Lachlan knows it better than most, but it is not the duty of a king to ever acknowledge that all his endeavours and all notion of a realm are nothing but arrogance and power on the march. A king cannot admit that true happiness might be found in dividing his kingdom into equal patches of dirt and letting everyone get on with their own lives. The strongest families rose to the top of the pile and we battled on down through the centuries, increasing our lot, glorifying our needless deeds and creating strife in a world that, without us, would be at peace. I pity these scorched lands because of our return.'

Her chest heaved and Ailsa moved to comfort her then thought better of it as the queen continued.

'The damnable truth is that he's right. I see in his eyes how he wishes to simply revel in the sunlight and ride through the grass; spend time on the beach simply watching the waves. Instead, I have trapped him in a cage of pomposity. And worse, my ancestors have set us all upon this accursed course for vengeance to the exclusion of all else; a course that has led us to being a better people than we were and yet by achieving its goal, are we about to undo all we have achieved?'

'We have lived by meagre means, driven by necessity. Save for Linwood's folk, we no longer build great stone fortresses or monstrous cathedrals taking their aim at non-existent gods in a barren sky. We have become a people honed for war and driven to survive – a hard and effective people. Yet when we lay down our swords after training, we live simpler and truer than did our ancestors.

'When I see Lachlan standing upon the Folly battlements, I see him upon the palisade at Halflight Hold on Long Isle, looking out at the sea. He yearns for home, wishing he could spend less time being king and more time being Lachlan.'

She sighed.

'And do you wish you could spend more time being Cathryn?'

She blew air between her lips once again.

'Who is Cathryn? Who was Cathryn? Now I am queen, but before I was a princess - I was never just a girl. From the day I was born, I was an empty vessel that must be filled with responsibility, decorum, strength and dedication.

'I have no choice where or how I live. I'm not sure I've ever even had one. My life and the life of the realm are as one.'

She turned her head to look at Ailsa.

'Being queen means serving a life sentence in a prison with bars made up of duty, rank, wealth, politics and tradition. The bars are unyielding.'

Cathryn eased herself up to sit on her haunches, looking back out at the old continents.

'What do you think it means to be queen? What gives me the right to control the destiny of all who follow me, Ailsa?'

Ailsa was unable to break eye contact and her brow furrowed more with every passing second as her forehead tightened.

'Well?' said Cathryn.

'…man is a brute beast.' Ailsa whispered. Though safe enough in a familiar confidence with the queen, she felt on unsteady ground.

'I don't understand,' said Cathryn, when Ailsa said no more.

'Man is a brute beast - a predator. The strong establish dominance and the weak follow. Those who become strong challenge the dominant and topple them. The topplers become toppled. It goes ever on and there is no purpose to it.'

'I understand all you say of your life. A queen is the child of a line of predators, handed domination and forced to oversee it. A simple girl like me has more freedom than you. I am free to squire or whore or shovel shit. You are queen, no matter what you desire. You watch over us and we don't care why. We only know that you do. The *way* we are ruled is as much a part of life as are the forests, the mountains or the sea - unquestionable. We have no choice but to fight when we are told, but I believe that we fight all the harder because you represent a realm that looks after its own and does not allow injustice to go unpunished. We came for Awgren and you brought him down hard. I saw it with my own eyes.'

A smile crept onto Ailsa's face and her intense eyes twinkled at the memory of the woman before her dancing a brief, sweet dance with Awgren.

'And,' she went on, 'you have won out. You have secured our borders. And now, if you so wish it, we might all have peace. You and Lachlan may go to the Isles and walk the beaches together knowing the darkness is gone.'

Frost covered Cathryn's heart at the suggestion as she felt the pain of something that would never be. She imagined walking along a sunset beach with her bare feet in the ice-cold shallows and her fingers interlaced with those, not of Lachlan, but Aldwyn – yet another man she had loved who had once escaped the Folly to be free of his duties and the pain they bestowed.

'Perhaps Lachlan has more courage than me in throwing it all away.'

But Ailsa shook her head.

'Think not that he has thrown it away, Your Majesty. Lachlan will return and perhaps he will return renewed if he finds what he is looking for. But I do not think it courageous to throw away inherited responsibility. Usurpers and dominators and dictators those of your rank may be, Your Majesty, but at heart we all know that you lead a dangerous life full of splendour, but little freedom and less joy. We pay homage to your sacrifice in following you. Not every man or woman could lead as you do or has desire to, otherwise why would we not frequently attempt to rise and cast you down? I am more than capable of fighting you and hurling you down upon the Maw Gate even now. Your power is nothing if not bestowed by those who tolerate your arrogance because they would not truly possess it themselves.'

Cathryn's mouth fell open and yet saw the truth of it. Ailsa's cheeks began to glow the colour of summer berries, but Cathryn laughed.

'Well, I did ask.'

'What will you do, Your Majesty?' asked Ailsa, making an effort to show diffidence in her gestures as she stood, clasping her hands behind her back.

Cathryn reached out a hand and Ailsa helped her to her feet. The queen crossed the room and settled into her throne, back straight and face impassive.

'The lord will root out our enemies and ensure the safety of the Combined People. The queen will ensure the security of the Folly and oversee the old countries from her seat high above the Maw Gate.'

Ailsa bowed her head then ventured,

'And what will Cathryn do?'

Cathryn smiled, thinking of her youth when as a princess she had sneaked away to wander the moonlit beaches outside the Folly wall, listening for mermaid song. It made her chuckle.

'Who is Cathryn? I have yet to meet her,' she replied. 'Send word for the admirals. I want reports from all points of the realm.'

Sometime later, the queen left her throne room and, a little after that, the guards at her door were stood down.

'I relieve you,' said one of the replacements.

'I stand relieved,' said one of the guards ending his shift. Both men visibly relaxed while their partners went through the same ritual.

'Much been happening?'

'High folk in and out all day. Generals, councillors, admirals…you name it. Much news of the Lord of the Isles about the place?'

The replacement shook his head.

'Not much new. He's definitely gone though. Who knows where?'

The original guards started to walk off down the hall.

'Hey there,' called one of the replacements. 'Where did you fellows spring from?'

The men halted.

'How do you mean?' said one of them without turning.

'I've been stationed at the Maw Keep some ten years. Never seen you before…'

The man still did not turn.

'Came in from the Isles. Queen is adding to her household guard,' he said, finally looking back over his shoulder.

'I'm off. Need to shit then eat.'

His replacement said nothing.

Once out of sight, the relieved guards exchanged looks and resisted the temptation to start whispering to one another. Instead they traversed the many passages of the Maw Keep, descending steps whenever they came to them. They descended below the levels lit by sunlight, but moved onwards without taking up one of the torches suspended every so often along the passage walls though more carefully with hands outstretched.

Finally they reached the cellars and yet continued downward, around stores and barrels.

In the deepest dark of the Maw Keep's cellars, the men-at-arms knocked upon a heavy door in a particular way. It opened slightly and, their identities verified, they slipped into the even deeper dark where Linwood's hidden regiments bided their time.

Chapter Ten

'What's he at?'

'Who?'

The quartermaster, bracing the ship's wheel with most of his bodyweight, nodded in the direction of the figure standing on the forecastle.

The master huffed, wringing his hands behind his back.

'Him? Who knows, but wish the old bugger would stow himself below.'

'Aye,' the quartermaster grunted.

Desolation, a three-masted frigate, was running north-east under topsails and mainsails. The master looked up and, weighing up the strength of the wind, decided that it would be premature to lay on the topgallants.

'Suppose he wants to be first to spy land,' said the master.

'If I was him, I'd be tucked up in me hammock with an empty bottle, snoring so loud they'd hear us ashore before we saw any of 'em,' said the quartermaster. The master made no reply.

Desolation pitched and rolled, but Linwood kept his feet, bracing himself against the rail that curved forward towards the bowsprit. He was less concerned with sighting land than simply taking the air and admiring the vastness of the ocean. After all, they would happen upon land when it happened, and no amount of scouring the horizon would make it happen any sooner – in Linwood's experience, it would take all the longer for it.

He was out of armour, which was not his custom, and he felt somewhat jaunty in spirit. The voyage thus far had been reasonably uneventful. A few of the men had died of various ailments, but for the most part the crew and the soldiers packed tightly below remained alive and well, if not in good spirits.

They had put down a number of troops at the southern side of Oystercatcher Bay, which belonged to Crinan. He had left instructions for a small camp to be made up near to the natural harbour, but decided not to leave many men. Aldwyn was sure to commit far greater numbers, but Linwood felt that he was obliged to establish a token foothold until he could return in strength. He had felt similarly about the Folly. So it was that with a garrison in Crinan, not far from the border of the Hinterland and a regiment hidden within the great stronghold of the Taynish, Linwood had once more put to sea and was heading northwards to Stragglers' Drift, the barren lands to the north of the Impassable Forest.

The grey peaked waves somehow reminded him of the martial advance of men, with blades rising and falling in unison with the rise and fall of shields. Unexpected panic began to stir in him as he made this connection, conjuring some deep fear or trauma, but he continued to hold the rail, controlled his breathing and made an effort to accustom himself to the sensation then dismiss it. He was a great believer in willing down bodily sensation with the power of sheer determination.

The bleak waters, thrashing in every direction, seemed to put everything in perspective. He was but one man, insignificant in the greater scheme of things. The ocean might snatch him to its bed and though many of his own kind would feel the effect, in a few short decades, his name would be forgotten; that was why Crinan had to live on. Though the old country was nothing more than wasteland for now, it was far from insignificant. Of all the land masses known to the Combined People, Linwood was now duke of perhaps the majority. Was it not right then that he could rule his own destiny and no longer bend the knee to the neighbouring country's ruling line? Lachlan and Cathryn had done well in throwing down Awgren, but now the dust was settling, and it was time to decide how the future was to unfold. Crinan would rise again and would certainly not kneel to the likes of the Taynish monarchy.

What did they know of life in Stragglers' Drift? Lachlan's ancestors had landed in the Isles and though they were smaller than Stragglers' Drift, they were wild, rugged, beautiful and fertile. He envied their existence on those shards thrust far out in the western ocean.

Linwood's ancestors had been blown off course, and many ships had been wrecked in the uncharted waters. His own sire from those times had crawled on hands and knees from the surf at Strewn Men Bay before collapsing on the beach amongst the dead, dying and simply exhausted. No glorious arrival at their new home for the Crinish – they arrived to the north of the Impassable Forest as humble as a man can be. They had fought hard to carve a life there in that land of stone and unforgiving soil, whipping winds and rain-drenched fields. Linwood's people had laboured hard to quarry stone to build Stragglers' End. It was no Folly, but it served.

In time his people began to prosper, though they dressed in no finery and their skin grew rough and calloused from hard work. They battled the land for crops and harangued the livestock into surviving. As it was with all the Combined People, they readied for war and forgot all other concerns. Linwood could wander the Whoreswood in his homeland without naming a single tree, shrub or indigenous animal. There were trees for building, trees for ships and trees for firewood. There were plants for cooking, plants for healing. Animals were prey, companionship or livestock. They had their general names, but all study of flora and fauna was forgotten, except where it served the arts of war. The Stragglers perfected the fighting arts and their small folk mined and quarried. They learned to forge steel.

Linwood turned away from the ocean, nodded to the master and headed below to his cabin. It had been the captain's, but Linwood had ejected the wisp of a man simply by appearing on the gangplank before ever they had set sail.

Linwood settled at the captain's desk and reached into the bottom drawer from which he withdrew a bottle of brandy. He stretched out a map of the whole continent and considered his next move, drinking deeply from the bottle as he did so. His people in Crinan would begin to establish a foothold and he would reinforce the position as needs dictated. They would also spy on Aldwyn in the Hinterland. Those in the Folly? On the allotted day, they would take up arms as instructed. His cuckoo eggs, Linwood thought and smiled.

Linwood tapped the Impassable Forest with his forefinger. Here was his great challenge to Lachlan and Cathryn's rule. He would hasten construction of the road now that the war was done. Dominion of the forest, the Stragglers' and Crinan would make an invasion of the Hinterland a mere formality.

Aldwyn could be cowed, he had no doubt, but should the duke prove more stubborn than expected, Linwood knew in his heart that he was prepared to crush the man and those who stood by him.

After a solid hour of contemplating coming conquests, Linwood drained his bottle of its contents. He immediately felt his head begin to swim disproportionate to the movement of the Desolation. He stood, faltered and braced himself against the desk.

'Damn it,' he said.

Linwood tripped his way across the cabin and managed to clamber up into his cot. He let the brandy set to work on quieting his mind and in a short while, he slumbered, sleeping dreamlessly and unconcerned.

As Linwood slept, Desolation passed by a scattering of small islands and drew in to Strewn Men Bay. The captain ordered that she be hove to and, with her sails set so that near all motion was checked, the great ship waited in the bay.

Linwood stalled till the next morning to make an appearance, when his head was clear. Eager to exercise his arms, he rowed ashore himself. As the small boat ploughed towards the beach, several horsemen came to receive it and waited at the foreshore.

'Lord Linwood,' called his cousin, Lucas, who dismounted while Linwood's men hauled the boat high up the beach, to the dunes where the sand martins made their nests.

'Lucas,' said Linwood, then immediately, 'What news?'

Lucas extended his hand, and Linwood gripped it for a moment then threw off the proffered hand as though he were disgusted by the touch.

'How goes the road?'

Lucas frowned and spoke slowly.

'We have made good progress for months, Cousin, but in recent days there have been mysterious deaths amongst the trees.'

'Deaths?'

'Aye, deaths and some disappearances. Men working on the outreaches are found pulverised, smashed or dismembered. Much force, my lord. Very unpleasant deaths, I imagine.'

What death is pleasant? thought Linwood.

'Have you apprehended the perpetrators?' said Linwood. He walked up the beach towards the horses with his woollen breeches sticking to his legs and slowing his progress. He paid no heed to the sensation and mounted the steed that had been brought for him.

He turned back to the men in the boat.

'Tell your captain to send the troops ashore. When the fleet arrives, he should signal them to do the same.'

He turned back to Lucas who started shaking his head.

'We have caught no one, my lord, but from…'

'Not we, Lucas, you. Do not spread the blame for your own lack of capability in this matter.'

'No, Cousin,' said Lucas, 'there is more, but I fear you will laugh and think me a fool.'

Linwood's look seemed to persuade the younger man that this was already the case and so, faltering, but persistent, Lucas told what he had heard.

'Creatures in the woods?' said Linwood.

'I know it is madness, but such is the talk amongst the men.'

'I have little time for the gossiping of foot soldiers, Lucas. But let us visit the road and see for ourselves.' He spurred his horse onward.

Lucas, who had been looking forward to ale and meat at Stragglers' End, followed on reluctantly.

The coast road ran around Strewn Men Bay higher and higher with the cliffs. The skies were filled with circling gulls that nested on the unseen faces of the cliffs below. To the south, the churning ocean stretched off as far as the eye could see to the line where the dark clouds met the surface of the water.

To the north, the land sloped gently downwards to fields of sedge grass, broken by harsh rocky ridges and, off in the far distance, settlements and patches of woodland. The Eye Teeth mountain range loomed ahead of them in the east and beyond them, the Impassable Forest. It stretched away towards the old countries for hundreds of miles then finally gave way to the plains between Oystercatcher Bay and the Hinterland, upon which, thought Linwood, Aldwyn was likely marching even now.

The forest had ever vexed him, at first because its impassable enormity meant the invasion of the Devised-controlled old countries would have to come by sea, and now that Awgren was gone, because it stood between him and Crinan. Of course, the plentiful trees had made for a strong fleet and provided hunting grounds which had stirred Lachlan to envy when he had visited years before. Linwood had enjoyed that visit.

In moments of great change, sometimes the reality of a predicament can ease off and fade into the background workings of one's mind, only to suddenly be hauled forward to send one reeling. This happened to Linwood now as he rode along the coast road, with the mountains and the forest dominating more and more of the horizon. It was unlikely that Lachlan would visit and hunt again on good terms. Had Linwood not sown the seeds of war throughout the continent? He cast aside all feeling of regret, reminding himself that he worked towards a greater purpose now; such machinations as alliance or friendship were insignificant in comparison to building a realm that might continue for a thousand years or more.

Just as the Eye Teeth foothills were rising, Linwood's men came upon a fork in the road where one branch split away to the north and, after days upon it, Linwood saw the labour camps.

Ranks of campaign tents were headed up by crude wooden lodges where the officers messed. Linwood could see men drilling at arms in spaces between the tents and, further off, horse-drawn carts were hauling felled trees northwards to the great lumber piles. The air was filled with the sound of saws and axe-strokes, both from beside the lumber piles where logs were being hewn into logs and planks, but also from scores of unseen workers in the forest itself.

'There is no shortage of timber,' Linwood remarked, mostly to himself as he slowed his horse. Lucas anticipated his next question.

'We have been reinforcing the most vulnerable parts of the coast, Sire. Palisades are soon to be constructed around all key settlements.'

Linwood nodded, but made no reply. He spurred his mount on, and the party turned east again, heading along the new road towards a gap in the treeline, forty-foot wide, which delved deep into the forest. It was from this gap that the carts bearing felled trees were appearing, and the sound of work came from that direction.

Linwood could not suppress a grin – his plans were advancing. He was swept up in visions of his fortified holds, villages in the forest and a proud road stretching all the way to the Hinterland, where Aldwyn would soon pay homage. The grin faded as, away in the grass to his right, nine graves came into view, marked in the Straggler's fashion by a single black flag which billowed over the plot.

When they had reached the edge of the forest, Linwood tied his horse's rein to a makeshift rail by one of the lodges, and asked for the location of the commandant. It became apparent that Lady Isobel had led a company to reinforce the next encampment.

'Reinforce?' asked Linwood of the man who now passed him up a wineskin.

'Aye, m'lord. Yonder on the road.'

'Is this a battleground, boy?' huffed Linwood, finishing the wine without passing it to his companions then dropping the skin back into the man's hands.

'M'lord. No, m'lord, but men are dying. Lady Isobel has ordered defensive positions be set up amongst the trees – archers and the like. None work alone now.'

Linwood frowned and turned to Lucas.

'How long is the road as things stand?'

'A hundred miles in total. There are way-camps every five miles.'

'Well, gentleman, I have a long ride ahead of me. Lucas, you stay here and wait for word.'

Linwood rode on along the dim road with his great sword at his side. The trees closed about him, and he was swallowed by the forest. He slowed the horse to a canter as he progressed, his senses tuned and, he looked all about him as he rode, wary of any threat.

Guarded as he may have been, Linwood reached the first encampment without incident, and there he found Lady Isobel. Although courteous, Linwood thought she looked harassed by his presence, judging from the redness of her cheeks and the quick rate at which the words fell from her mouth. He decided he had no time for the pleasantries of calming the woman and, tired from his travels, he made his needs known.

'See that my mount is tended,' he said to a nearby man, scarce casting a glance to see to whom he was giving instruction. 'The Lady Isobel and I will be in the command tent, where she will be giving me a briefing on her plans and their progress.' He shot her a marked look and, as intended, the lady felt the comments were as much instruction to her as information for others.

'I need meat and wine,' called Linwood as he trudged in the direction of the command tent.

The brute force of the work was being carried out not far away. Although the road disappeared into the forest, Linwood could see scores of men working to widen the existing path. They were not hacking down trees, but working away at the root with tools, scraping away the earth to expose the great roots then taking these apart with axes. An intimidating oak stood tall, proud and wide, but its feet had been hewn from under it. Linwood watched as two teams of horses were urged on and ropes sprung up behind them, secured to the tree. Harried by lashing strokes of whips, these powerful horses hauled, fighting for every step with their hooves digging trenches in the mud. They reached a point of tension where they seemed able to move no further, then suddenly with a creaking and endless, snapping cracks the great oak began to tumble forward. Its branches crunched into the earth and a whoosh of rustling leaves culminated with a heavy, ground-shaking thump. The teams of horses were detached and teams of workers began shaping the tree and removing branches while still more men forged ahead and began work on the roots of yet another oak.

Linwood felt emboldened by such progress and mastery over all of nature's contrivances. The building of the road would be long, hard work, but in completing it, he would be creating a unified continent.

Inside the command tent there was little light and so he set about opening up the canvas at either end before spreading out maps across Lady Isobel's desk.

She arrived moments later, and Linwood thought she must have splashed water on her face as she appeared a little more composed. She settled in to the chair at her desk.

'Little has changed from the original plans other than slight alterations in the course of the road where terrain demanded it. The first stretch will, when complete, emerge by the shore of the Black Lake. A settlement has been established there by advance parties, and work on the second leg has also begun. They have cut some thirty miles southeast towards the plains on the east coast, though I have authorised a few changes there.' Isobel looked up and met Linwood's eyes, confident in her decision but nervous of his reaction.

'Rather than cut straight across and leave camps in the open, away from resources, I chose to extend the route around the eastern treeline of the forest, with settlements at intervals. These are better positioned to make use of the forest for water, food and timber.'

Linwood nodded and, encouraged, Isobel went on.

'This stretch of the road is also under construction. We have scouted no further into the southern half of the forest, but there will be no more shortcuts. We have the mountain range to contend with if we go straight through, so I suggest we create a coast road opening out on the northernmost part of the Hinterland.'

Linwood looked to the roof.

'On the northeast side of the Whiteflow?'

'Exactly,' Isobel enthused. 'That's all there is to tell. Progress on the first section of the route has been well advanced in your absence, Cousin.'

Linwood cast his eye across the maps, nodding.

'I'm impressed.'

Silence and more scouring of the maps. Plates of meat and two bottles of red wine were brought in by a serving boy and Linwood began to gulp thirstily before speaking again.

'Well done.' Linwood laid a heavy hand on Isobel's shoulder and she could not suppress a grin. He laughed in response and pulled up a chair beside her.

'Your name will be remembered for centuries for this feat, Isobel.'

She blushed slightly, obviously much relieved at the praise. In her glee, she forgot entirely all problems the project faced.

'You've not mentioned anything about the deaths amongst the workers,' he prompted and at once the flush returned. Linwood determined that he should play his cousin at cards sometime if ever he should be short of coin.

'For the... ' she gasped. 'Of course. Those who died were mostly scouts or those assessing the strength of the trees ahead. It started just a few days ago. They were always alone, always isolated and found dead with never a sound having been heard. They were strangled, beaten, crushed...it goes on.'

'I have sent out patrols and, as you can see, no man now works alone and I have troops nearby.'

'Who do you suspect is the agent of these crimes?' asked Linwood.

Isobel's blush deepened.

'I have no evidence to suggest a culprit, but the men speak of the spirits of the trees visiting them in their dreams and more than one has broken off work hysterical, insisting he has seen faces upon the bark of a trunk or figures flitting in the darkness,' she admitted.

Linwood shook his head.

'No more of that nonsense. True or not, spying something unpleasant is no reason to be shirking labour. Have these men flogged and returned to the front. Understood?'

'Flogged?' asked Isobel, her eyes widening slightly against her better judgement. When she received no response to the extent that not an inch did his head move, she let the matter lie.

'What do you make of such rumours?' Linwood asked, softly and between gulps of wine.

'I've heard the tales just as you have, but nothing has been seen of Dryads in living memory. But then none have ever delved so deep into the forest before. And what would we do if some foe decided to pull down our homes and flatten our towns?' she said, her tone cautious.

Linwood sighed. It sounded, of course, like nonsense to him, but though he might be a practical man and hard-headed, he also considered himself to be a pragmatist and open-minded. The Creatures of the Devising and the nature of Awgren himself was enough evidence to suggest that not all that walked the world took on the skin of man.

He took little time to decide on a course of action and the ferocity of his words and the speed of his decisiveness shocked Isobel when he spoke.

'I'll ride out and see if these Dryads will parley with me, if indeed this is what they are. I'll check my horse is well looked after, if you'll arrange somewhere for me to sleep. Send more food and more wine. Thank you, Cousin.' He stood up fast and left the tent before she had time to question him.

Linwood was gone, and Lady Isobel paused for a moment, considering that the briefing had not gone as badly as she had feared. She folded up the maps, put Linwood's orders in motion and returned to supervising the work.

Chapter Eleven

Over several days, countless soldiers disembarked at Strewn Men Bay, but it was not until after dark, by which time most of Linwood's troops had marched inland, that the last of the boats came ashore. It cut across the bay, not towards the open beaches further west, but to the base of the cliffs.

Three men leapt out into the surf, but rather than pull the boat up on the bank, they pushed it back into the waves.

Lord Lachlan led the way up the narrow pebble beach, keeping low. The three figures ducked down under a bank near the foot of the towering cliffs above them where the seabirds nested. They sat there panting for a time, recovering both their strength and their breath.

Lachlan's brother, Hadwyn, raised his head above the level of the bank and, after taking stock, ducked down once more.

'Palisades run west along the length of the beach,' he said.

'Linwood grows paranoid in his old age,' said Belman.

Lachlan said nothing. Something akin to glee was rampaging inside him, and he felt almost light-hearted, desiring to rampage over the crest of the bank and stalk along the palisade, reaving and fighting his way. But in the back of his mind he heard Cathryn's voice reminding him that though the men on guard here might be aiding Linwood in fortifying Lachlan's own lands against him, they were but vassals, not willingly complicit in the attempt. Were he in their place, he would almost certainly be taking the same course of action. Something chimed in his mind as soon as he thought this, and it took a moment to realise that the folk of the Hinterland used much the same excuses for fighting under Awgren. So then, either these men under Linwood were innocent and so were the men of the Hinterland or both were guilty and should be likewise condemned.

The call of a gull brought him back into the moment and he took his turn to look above the bank.

There seemed to be no obvious defences eastward along the foot of the cliff.

Lachlan closed his eyes and tried to remember the geography of the place from the rough drawn maps which had occasionally passed his desk. Lachlan had been to hunt in the Drift many times, but the particulars of this part of his realm were a mystery to him. However, only a blind man could miss that away to the east, if one looked down the length of the cliffs, the vague silhouettes of moonlit mountains stood tall. Lachlan knew these were the Eye Teeth and that the Impassable Forest lay beyond. If Linwood was building a road, he would no doubt start the work north of the mountains, where the terrain was more forgiving.

'There is not much of consequence along the coast and only quarries in the mountains. See yonder peaks there?' he pointed then went on, 'Come, follow. We'll head inland towards Stragglers' End to gather word of Linwood's plans.'

Lachlan adjusted the pack on his shoulders and clambered out over the bank, hurrying to the foot of the cliffs. He waited there on the gathered sea-wrack and gull droppings till the others arrived. Once together, he set off east towards the palisade and after a pause Hadwyn followed. A few more seconds and Belman followed on behind.

The cliff line hunkered, delved, rose and plummeted as they walked beside it. They placed their feet carefully upon the treacherous stones which were ever eager to call out their presence by shifting and scraping against one another beneath their boots. Before long the cliffs tapered down to sea level. Lachlan's company reached a collection of huge boulders, and he wondered if they had tumbled down from a now forgotten cliff or been hurled up from the depths of the ocean by some angry sea-god.

He led the party into the cover of the boulders and soon realised it was as he had suspected; Linwood's palisade protected only against massed forces. Where the cliffs began to rise and the terrain grew obstinate in the face of invasion, the palisade faltered and, peering into the night gloom, Lachlan thought he could make out its end nearby - that and the sound of hushed voices.

He was about to turn to tell the others when a shriek of laughter pealed up ahead. All three men shrank down low without a thought and, with a nod of his head, just visible in the moonlight, Lachlan made it clear he intended to strike away north through the boulder field. His hope was to find undefended open ground on the other side.

The lord and his men took great pains in getting off the beach without detection, for they had no desire to be identified as those who had newly come ashore. As such, the going was slow for the first hour, but after that the beach gave way to rising grasslands and their passing was no longer betrayed by the ground underfoot. They kept themselves in a staggered formation so that they appeared less a body of men and an easier feature to miss as they traversed the landscape.

In his mind's eye, Lachlan relived riding across these grasslands towards Straggler's End, the strongest castle in the Drift. Cathryn had not been with him then, and, in truth, he had been glad of the escape. Now though, she was ever calling him from the back of his mind, and as Lachlan trudged onward, exhilarated by the chill of the night air and the utter scope to go wherever and do whatever he wanted, he was only ever a few steps ahead of the guilt that stalked behind him.

They came to a copse and searched between the trees for both people and animals. Satisfied they would be safe for the night, they made camp; a crude affair consisting of bedrolls and blankets. They talked of a fire, but given that the night was cold, but bearable and, as of yet, they were still to shake the feeling of vulnerability, they decided it would be better to forgo the extra warmth. So it was that the three men laid down a blanket apiece, wrapped themselves in their cloaks and lay down under another blanket, close together like children tucked up in the same bed. For a while, there was naught but the sound of breathing, but all were too excited to sleep, and it was but minutes before low voices broke the quiet under the birch trees.

Belman squirrelled in his pack and drew out three dry biscuits he had retrieved from the schooner's stores. He passed them out, and they ate as they talked, careful to make each morsel last as long as was possible. Lachlan passed a water-skin when they were done.

He lay back and looked up at the stars, framed as they were by the spindly branches of the birch, where branches reached too far and tapered.

'Lachlan,' whispered Hadwyn.

'Aye, I'm awake,' Lachlan replied.

'You expect much trouble on the road?'

Lachlan interlocked his fingers above his heart, his arms above the cocoon of his blanket. He sighed. After considering for a while, he replied.

'I think not. Linwood is harsh in his justice and his sheriffs are notorious, so I fear little from robbers or vagabonds.'

Hadwyn laughed.

'What's funny?' asked Lachlan.

'I have a little trouble imagining Lachlan, Lord of the Isles who I saw throw down Awgren with my very eyes, troubled by robbers or vagabonds even if they arrived by the thousands, and he was caught unarmed whilst about his ablutions!'

Belman snorted and Lachlan hissed for him to be quiet. Hadwyn continued,

'Lawbreakers *are* of little concern, but what of his standing army?'

'We shall see,' said Lachlan. 'He had men defending palisades at the beach. It makes sense that he has closed his borders – the man is scheming, after all and he's always been paranoid. I expect the keeps and towns will also be guarded, but to what extent and what measures he has in place, who can say? I would think that while we are in open country or woodland, we should be safe enough.'

'Have you decided how to proceed?' asked Hadwyn.

'We'll look over the maps in the morning and talk it over. Head to a smaller settlement and see what the locals have to say for themselves.' He yawned. 'Come now. Let's sleep.'

The blanket below him was initially accommodating to his form, but as the night wore on, and he began to feel the chill in his bones, Lachlan could feel sticks and protrusions both real and imagined jabbing into his side. He became fully awake before dawn and not wishing to waste any time, he set about searching for roots, fungi, nuts and other such eatables.

It did not take long to strike lucky. A collection of ceps grew around the mounting roots of birch trees at the centre of the copse. Lachlan set about gathering them up into his hood and took them back to his bedroll, where he left them before going off in search again. He could find little else and when he heard a yawn, he returned to the camp. Hadwyn was stirring, and he gave his brother a gentle kick in the ribs, grinning as he did so.

'Sleeping the day away?'

Hadwyn raised his head, saw it was still dark and closed his eyes once more.

'Tell me you're just up to relieve your bladder, Brother.'

'Nonsense. We've beaten the sun up, and we must keep our advantage. I can hear water nearby. Get Belman awake while I refill the skins,' said Lachlan.

Hadwyn was up and eyeing the mushrooms when Lachlan returned, though he had not dared to steal one. They went through the pile now that the sun was rising and discarded those infested with insects – a disappointing majority. Those they did eat were smoky and reminiscent of chestnut. Each man carried a little salted meat and they shared a little out from Hadwyn's pack, Lachlan pairing a sliver of mushroom with a sliver of meat as he ate. The others jested at his particular way of eating, but he ignored them and kept at it till his lot was consumed. That done he set about rolling up his blankets and brought out the map. While the others were readying their packs, he walked out of the copse and made a reckoning of his location judging from the position of the sun, taking into account their landing point and the rough direction he thought they had walked in.

Hadwyn and Belman soon joined him. He brandished the map and once Hadwyn had it spread out between his hands, he jabbed at a settlement with one finger.

'Redbranch. It is a few days travel to the northeast and lies between Stragglers' End and the forest.'

'Have you been there before?' asked Belman, but Lachlan shook his head. He gripped the straps of his pack, hooking his thumbs under the material and set off north at a fair pace. Hadwyn and Belman exchanged a look, despairing of their lord's energy and set off to catch up.

The miles passed easily enough, and before too long they felt comfortable enough to walk together – three somewhat desperate-looking figures, each cloaked and with packs, each with a bow slung across his back and sword at the hip. Cathryn usually encouraged Lachlan to have his beard trimmed, but the Lord of the Isles was off the leash, and the hair about his face grew shaggy and unkempt.

Aside from the beach palisade, little seemed changed in Stragglers' Drift, and Lachlan felt at his ease, confident that if challenged even his true identity would bring him little issues.

'After all,' said Hadwyn when Lachlan mentioned it, 'If Linwood is making plans to move against you, he would be a fool to disseminate them amongst his people whilst open trade and co-operation is in place. People talk.'

'And how would they recognise you anyway?' said Belman.

They came upon a dirt road, but stayed out of sight amongst the brush while a convoy of carts passed by. Each one was heavily laden with timber.

'What do you make of that?' asked Belman.

Hadwyn and Lachlan said nothing, thinking that, given Aldwyn's intelligence about the road, it was damn obvious what was happening. Belman spoke again before the pause became conspicuous.

'I'd wager Linwood has begun his road and these are bearing away the trees he is felling!' he whispered excitedly.

'Doubtless. Good thinking,' said Lachlan. Hadwyn failed to conceal a small smile. Belman had other strengths and did not deserve to be openly mocked.

The carts passed on.

The company drew close to Redbranch before noon and skirted around the outlying farms westward until they came upon the road which led into the village from the direction of Straggler's End. Lachlan reasoned that, if they so wished, they could pass themselves off as soldiers heading towards the forest from the capital. After some discussion, they decided on the course that had been mentioned first and was secretly most desired by all – finding a tavern.

Their plans went awry before ever they set foot in Redbranch. Though the place was small and a cynical mind might even refer to it as inconsequential, there was a standing guard on the gate. Hadwyn was sure he had seen a patrol of another two guards just disappearing around one of the houses on the perimeter of the village.

'It is what it is,' was all Lachlan would say, but he adjusted his sword belt all the same. He reminded himself yet again that these were not denizens of Awgren he was approaching, that these were his own people. The thought did nothing to quell the mounting tension and rising levels of adrenaline in his blood. He recognised this and did what he could to collect himself, taking long cold breaths of the morning air.

A man and two women passed along the road between the guards before Lachlan's party did so; the man in and the women out. The guards nodded recognition and exchanged a few words with each of them, which Lachlan found simultaneously encouraging and disheartening. The guards seemed informal enough that simple conversation and wit might allow his company to traverse any questioning thrown their way, yet they were familiar with the villagers and therefore the doings of the village, like as not. Lachlan feared his story might not stand up to scrutiny. Nevertheless they walked on. Their previous effort to seem casual, talking amongst themselves, ceased as each man imagined how the situation might unfold. Lachlan was picturing a conversation turning increasingly desperate. Hadwyn pictured them brassing it out, demanding entry and the men giving way. Belman seemed to have bypassed all charm and guile and was dreaming of staving the men's heads in with the butts of their own polearms, a dreamy little smile curling the corners of his cracked lips. It went unnoticed as they approached the guards.

'Good morning,' called Lachlan.

'Good morning,' replied one, quite cheerily. Another took aim at a pebble on the dust road and booted it off into the dry grass nearby.

'What of the day so far then?' said Lachlan. His voice was exuberant and his manner quite overbearing, but not unpleasantly. This was the varnished manner of a man who is used to getting exactly what he wants, who has never met another who can stand in his way, yet has not let it go to his head.

While Lachlan passed the time of day with the guards, Hadwyn looked them over surreptitiously. They wore scant, soft leather armour and hoods. Each was armed with a polearm, seemingly of their own devising or, at the very least, made crudely and locally. Here there was none of the splendour of Linwood's standing army and so Hadwyn judged the men to be local folk recruited into makeshift militia roles. He thought it diligent of Linwood to have such a force in place, and it was certainly more than Lachlan had organised in the Isles. He found himself nodding slightly in approval, before once more heeding Lachlan's efforts to ingratiate himself.

'You folk aren't from around here then,' said one of the militiamen.

'Oh? So obvious?' replied Lachlan, his tone light, but Hadwyn could tell it was forced. He hoped it wasn't so obvious to the militia.

'Aye. Twang in your tongue. Hear it, Ralph?' he turned to his colleague.

'No, Corporal,' said Ralph. He had picked up his polearm and was doing his best to look attentive.

'Barely aware he's alive, that one,' whispered the corporal as an aside, then, 'Go back to sleep, Ralph, eh?'

Ralph grumbled, but not audibly, and the corporal ignored him.

'What was your name again?' asked Lachlan of the corporal.

'John. And yours?'

'Cadby,' lied Lachlan.

'Where you from then?' asked John.

'Family are from the Isles, but we're posted at Straggler's End.'

'Or were,' added Hadwyn.

Hadwyn was relieved when the man just seemed to weigh up the information, nodding.

'Were? What brings you to Redbranch?' he asked, seeming to remember he did actually have a job to do.

'Seen the timber carts?' asked Hadwyn quickly, before either of his companions could reply.

The corporal nodded.

'Not bloody blind, am I?'

'Suppose not,' said Hadwyn. 'Sorry.' He made an effort to look cowed.

'Forget it,' said the corporal. His cheeks had reddened somewhat, and he had straightened his posture a little. 'So you're off to help with the road, are you? What do you do?'

'Shouldn't really say,' said Lachlan. 'Said too much as it is.'

The corporal frowned and pulled at his right ear lobe. Hadwyn judged that the man was feeling slighted and, given that he'd applied for office, it seemed likely that he appreciated feeling in control. Hadwyn decided to feed the man what he needed.

'…but we'd appreciate anything a man could tell about how the scouts are being treated on the road build.' He winked.

John smiled, but it turned to a frown as he realised he had little to tell.

'Not heard much about that. All I see is the carts and the logs.' He looked back over his shoulder. 'They're due to start building a stronger palisade around this place next week. Lady Isobel's aide came and scouted us out a month or so ago.'

Lachlan knew the name and thought he could recall a face from his last visit to the Drift.

'If things don't work out in the forest, we'll be looking for work. You need men for the militia?' asked Hadwyn.

'We can fight,' said Belman, folding his arms in such a way that his biceps bulged. John flicked his gaze to him, and the big man's presence seemed to unsettle him somewhat; perhaps feeling, thought Hadwyn, that with such a trio in the militia, his own standing might be diminished.

Judging they had risked all that was wise with the corporal, Lachlan steered the conversation towards accommodation and found the name of a boarding house not far off. Lachlan made a point of addressing him as 'Corporal' when he thanked him and took the time to shake his hand.

They moved off into Redbranch, but suddenly Hadwyn turned on his heel.

'Say, Corporal, it's not my place to say, but…did you hear the fleet returned?' he asked, his voice hushed.

John leant on his polearm.

'Oh?' He sounded eager. Hadwyn turned his back to him and whispered to Lachlan.

'Should we say?'

Lachlan looked over Hadwyn's shoulder at the corporal's open expression. The man locked eyes with him, and the Lord of the Isles frowned, drawing out the moment as long as he felt he could.

'Meet us at the boarding house after your shift,' he said, and when the corporal returned his nod, he turned and set off into Redbranch.

'Did they do it?' called Ralph.

Lachlan stopped walking.

'Who?' he said, without looking back.

'Lachlan and Cathryn,' said Ralph.

Lachlan, Hadwyn and Belman all smiled.

They soon secured a room at the boarding house, and as the afternoon wore on, the bar filled with more and more villagers, many of them members of the militia who had abandoned their posts to hear from the strangers.

Lachlan finally admitted that the three of them had returned from the wars, and, after much ale was bought for them and many meals were consumed, it had become quite apparent that the people of the Drift were still very much still for Cathryn, no matter how they felt about Linwood.

Amidst the hustle, the laughter and the singing, Hadwyn drew back to a quiet corner and watched his brother joining in. It had been many a year since he had seen him smile and talk so freely. It gladdened Hadwyn's heart to see it.

'All well?' Belman sat down beside him. Hadwyn nodded.

'Thinking,' he replied.

'Thinking on what?' said Belman. 'Are you not encouraged?'

Hadwyn snorted a little laugh and smiled,

'Encouraged, certainly. They love Linwood well enough, but Lachlan and Cathryn? They seem to be more than rulers to these people, something more akin to legends.'

'I thought the same,' said Belman, quaffing from his tankard then setting it down upon the table.

They set off west towards the forest the next day, but as soon as they were out of sight of the village, they turned south and once more circled around Redbranch. They found the road and began the walk towards Linwood's keep at Stragglers' End, for there, they had agreed, was where they would hear all they needed about his intentions.

They spent their days on the road, talking and dodging into cover whenever anybody approached. At night they camped out and dug out well-ventilated fire pits that would burn hot and give off little smoke. They set snares early in the evening and hunted when they could, bagging the odd rabbit or game bird and even, on one unusual evening, a badger. The meat was foreign and made Lachlan feel nauseous. He determined not to try badger again unless in dire need. The next morning they stepped off the road and walked cross-country towards Stragglers' End, not wishing to arrive openly at the main gate.

Before nightfall they had arrived at the Whoreswood, a tract of woodland that surrounded much of the southern side of Stragglers' End, growing right up to the outer wall of the town. There were discreet doors in the walls through which the residents could pass quietly from the town into the wood, to where the eponymous whores plied their trade amongst the ash trees, their caravans drawn up in secluded dells. If ever there was a sacred place in the Drift, thought Lachlan, this was Linwood's notion of it – a place where men put aside quarrels and worshipped the sister goddesses of open legs and soft tits, where hips and plump rumps were gripped as tight during the fucking as was any pew or holy book during the throes of prayer.

Chapter Twelve

Morrick had spent enough time on the ocean to never wish to see it, let alone sail on it, ever again. Many of his men found their sea legs and were even put to good use about Lord Aldwyn's flagship, but Morrick found that his entire nature changed upon the water. Gone was the powerful woodcutter, descendant of thegns. Gone was the fearsome sergeant who steadied the line, inspired his men and held his ground against terrible enemies. That man was replaced by a limp bag of skin that could scarce clamber out of its hammock without emptying his stomach all over the deck. The vomiting was violent to the extent that, days before, Morrick had eventually given up on food. He was starving, exhausted and many aboard felt that he would die.

After a few days, the thought of the damage to his reputation weighed steadily heavier on his mind and, churning insides or no, Morrick determined that the next morning when the watch was called he would be up and amongst them.

The remainder of the week was torturous, but he set himself the task of keeping his men busy and, at all cost, avoided looking up enough to realise that he was not standing on some sort of wooden platform built above dry land. When it was time to rest, he would eat little and trade his food for grog, which he would guzzle down fast, hoping for the welcome, steady oblivion of unconsciousness.

During one watch, not long after sun up, Lord Aldwyn summoned him to the great cabin. The duke wanted to learn all he could, concerning the terrain between Oystercatcher Bay and the Hinterland.

'Beg pardon, m'lord but I've never journeyed out of the Hinterland save southward to war. Best I can tell is common accepted thought where I'm from - follow the southern treeline of the Impassable Forest and we'll reach home.'

'And can you tell me nothing about what to expect on the road?'

Morrick shook his head.

'I'm afraid not – as I say, I've never been out of the Hinterland. The route skirts a mountainous area to the south, but other than that, I can tell you little. I hear tell it's much the same as the Hinterland, but cannot be sure.'

Aldwyn nodded.

'Very well. What of the Hinterland? What can I expect to find there?'

So Morrick told him all he knew of the villages, the overseers and the Devised numbers. He drew maps of his own village and the terrain surrounding it. When they were done, Lord Aldwyn sat for a while staring at the newly drawn map and pondered.

'What would you advise?' he eventually said, looking up at Morrick. The sergeant stuck out his lower lip, mulling over the courses of action. The ship lurched to port and he yelped, clutching the edge of the table. Aldwyn smiled as Morrick blushed.

'Heights and seas. Quite the month for you.' He laughed. Morrick mumbled an apology.

'My answer is that it depends on how you intend to proceed. How many troops are you thinking of committing? Are you stationing any at Oystercatcher Bay or sending any to Culrain? Can I speak frankly?' asked Morrick.

Aldwyn sat back in his chair, interlacing his fingers over his gut, seemingly amused.

'Go ahead.'

Morrick had been voicing his opinions on how to proceed for a short while when a knock came at the door.

'Enter.'

The ship's master entered and doffed his cap.

'Beg pardon, m'lord, but the captain sends his respects and to tell you that we've sighted land.'

'Very good. Please thank him for me and tell him I'll be on deck directly.'
He turned to Morrick as he stood.

'Wait here. Let's see how good a navigator our captain is…'

He ducked low as he moved below decks and hurried up the steps to the
fresh sea air.

The Nightingale had been sailing northeast and, if the captain's reckoning
was correct, they should be drawing close to Oystercatcher Bay. Sure enough
the shape of the coast line was that of the west coast of Crinan, running north
to the southern headland of the bay which was still a day's sail away. From here
on out, he had agreed with the captain, they would sail parallel with the coast.

Aldwyn mused that landfall could not have come too soon. They were
running low on supplies and any inclement weather or delay could well have
been devastating. He returned to his cabin and informed Morrick that they
had but a day before he would once again have his feet on an unswaying
surface. Morrick could not hide a grin.

Aldwyn fetched a bottle of wine and poured out two glasses. He passed
one to Morrick, took a sip and said,

'Allocation of resources is to be of primary importance. I have two main
concerns to consider; firstly I must be confident that the troops left at
Oystercatcher Bay were sufficient to defend against attacks from Linwood's
men both by sea or from any he has put down there on the way home.
Secondly I must commit enough men to secure the Hinterland, without
overstretching supplies.'

Morrick nodded.

'Surely the latter is simple enough. Depending on the rate you march us,
we can be there in seven to fourteen days, I'd say. Might take a little longer in
the foothills, but from what I hear, the land is not so barren there and there
should be good forage. Once in the Hinterland itself, there are both cattle and
crops, if you can pay for them.'

Aldwyn almost laughed. Had he been of a mind to walk in and take all he
wanted, there was nothing the Hinterland could do to stop him. They
survived only by his mercy, but once again his estimation of Morrick
increased for trying to ensure fair treatment for his people.

'I hope that it is so. Lord Linwood landed his people in Oystercatcher Bay not long after the invasion began in the south and drew the attention of Awgren's main army. He had orders to secure the bay, so with any luck he will have sent scouts into the hills and made best use of whatever manpower has to make the area sustainable. We will know soon enough, but either way, our people will need to be ready to both march and fight before ere long.' He sipped again from his glass.

'How does it feel to be heading home, Morrick?'

Morrick blew air between pursed lips.

'I'm frightened what I will find. Unless things have changed there has been no word of the Hinterland since Awgren died. Who knows if the Creatures of the Devising have heard? Part of me hopes they have not and that all remains as it was when I left. If they have somehow learned of his fall, will they have reacted out of spite, vengeance or malice? Will they throw down arms as they did in the south?' Morrick shook his head.

'I have an image of my wife, Rowan, and our children burning atop a heap of the dead,' he said quietly and closed his eyes, drinking up what was left of his wine. When he opened them again Aldwyn was regarding him with a softness in his eyes and his brow furrowed.

'I pray for the safety of your family and swear to you, I will do all I can to keep them safe. You can assist in telling me all there is to know about the Devised forces in the area.'

The Nightingale rounded the southern headland of Oystercatcher Bay ahead a column of some twenty ships. The waters were misty and the light fading, but some hours after entering the bay and yet still distant from shore, a shout went up from the crow's nest.

Aldwyn was called on deck and he found the captain glassing the horizon from the prow of the ship.

'What news?' asked the lord.

The captain handed him his telescope.

'A ship sighted in the bay, still hull-down.'

'Like as not it'll be one of Lord Linwood's,' Aldwyn replied. 'Maintain course.'

In due course though, it became apparent that the vessel was of the design employed in Stragglers' Drift. It also became apparent that the ship was not alone. More and more ships were sighted sailing variously north-to-south and south-to-north across the mouth of the bay.

'What do you make of it?' asked Aldwyn of the captain when they had identified a sixth vessel.

'Has all the hallmarks of a blockade,' said the captain. 'We'll know soon enough when we draw nearer.'

The next morning one of the vessels, surely having sighted the Nightingale approaching from the west, changed course towards her.

A brazen move, thought Morrick, if this was indeed a blockade, given that the Nightingale headed up an entire fleet whilst this vessel would be alone until the next passed by. As such there was little to fear and the Nightingale crashed on under full sail to meet her.

'Heave to!' ordered the captain and the sailors set about checking the Nightingale's progress. Linwood's ship bore the word 'Heron' lettered upon her stern, and bobbed a little way off as her crew put out a small boat. From the ship's rail Lord Aldwyn, the captain and Morrick could see a man sitting in the stern-sheets, dressed in the custom of Linwood's naval officers.

'Good morrow, sir,' called down the captain of the Nightingale. 'To what do we owe the pleasure?'

'Captain Marchment of the Heron, sir, out to meet the fleet from the Folly. Who commands here?'

'Captain Silas Unwin of the flagship commands the vessel and Lord Aldwyn, the fleet,' Captain Unwin shouted back, and at this Aldwyn made himself known.

'What news of Oystercatcher Bay, Captain?' he continued.

'Perhaps I might come aboard, my lord?' Marchment replied.

The captain met with Aldwyn in the great cabin and together they toasted the victory of the Combined People. Morrick paced the deck waiting for the outcome, staring out at the Heron and her crew, who often turned their gaze in his direction. It made him uncomfortable to know that the man who had branded his men was dominating the waters so close to his home and feared what Lord Aldwyn's talk would reveal. When finally the lord did emerge, his reddened cheeks and scowl did little to reassure him. Captain Marchment departed with few words, and the Heron moved off as soon as he was aboard, back in the direction she had come towards the south coast of the bay, in the lee of the headland.

Aldwyn summoned both the captain and Morrick to him.

'Lord Linwood has left orders that no man shall place his feet on Crinish soil. He contests that the entire coast of Oystercatcher Bay falls within the borders of Crinan. In his 'kindness', Captain Marchment informs me that Linwood has given leave for my troops to land at the extreme north of the bay and set up a small camp there within the palisade. He suggests I march directly towards the Hinterland as a large presence will not be tolerated. I am then directed to remove my fleet forthwith.'

'Insolence of the man!' barked the captain. 'These waters belong to the Combined People, not him alone.'

'Indeed,' nodded Aldwyn, 'and though I will respect his wishes about where we land, the fleet will remain within the bay. Captain, see to it that the fleet knows where we land. Morrick, ready your men. We will disembark before tomorrow night if the wind favours us. You are both dismissed.'

So it was that Aldwyn's fleet traversed the blockade heading northeast and eventually hove-to not far from the north coast of the bay. Morrick's spirits rose considerably when he saw the outlying arm of the Impassable Forest not far from the beach, but they fell again when from the boat carrying him ashore, he saw Linwood's troops waiting for them on the sand.

It took all night to bring ashore the army which Aldwyn planned to march to the Hinterland. He left orders for the fleet to remain as long as supplies dictated and when the point of deprivation was approaching, to set sail west for the Isles in order for to resupply. His was the last boat to return to the fleet and once ashore he wasted no time in getting off the beach and away from Linwood's people, whose invitations of hospitality he politely declined through intermediaries. He gave orders for his force to move out and, mounted upon a dappled grey mare, Lord Aldwyn led the men of the Folly on their march eastward to the Hinterland.

Every step was an education for every man of the party.

They left the coast behind and the land sloped upwards as they went. The Impassable Forest grew ever thicker to the north, and they remained within sight of it at all times. Aldwyn sent riders to scout the way ahead and hunters into the forest to bolster their supplies. By night they camped openly, but posted watches for none knew if there would still be Devised forces. However, the march was largely uneventful, and they reached the foothills of the Blade Mountains on the afternoon of the fourth day after setting out. Here it was true that the devastation caused by Awgren had not been maintained to the same degree as the rest of the continent, and Aldwyn's troops marched across grass-covered slopes, occasionally spying birds or rabbits. Aldwyn gifted Morrick a mount, and they spent many hours riding together, talking of their homes and lives. Morrick told of how dearly he missed Rowan, even her temper. How he looked forward to days of once more building and crafting instead of marshalling and killing. The more he talked of it, the more painful his desire to set foot once more within the fences of his homestead.

He determined that after greeting his family and making love to his wife, he would sit for a time by the Whiteflow washing away the last months and looking up at the stars. The possibility that the Devised had overrun the place and killed them all was very real, but he forced these thoughts away, recognising that worrying would achieve nothing. Instead, Morrick chose to hope.

Aldwyn listened to these hopes and fears, all the time trying to glean what knowledge he could from the various stories of the Hinterland. He desired to understand the people and pondered how he would move forward in ruling this new dominion of the Combined People that now sat, possibly, on a hostile border. To begin with he did not speak of Linwood or his fears for the future, but after hours of conversation, he began to trust more in his new servant and spoke more freely. Morrick seemed more shocked than had any of his own people in whom he had confided and his reaction, in turn, shocked

Aldwyn. After all, Morrick was from a people of betrayers – surely deception and malice were no stranger to him? He even voiced this thought to his new friend, though the words clearly caused some offence.

Morrick was sullen and silent for a time, but then spoke of how every man and woman he knew thought of Lachlan and Cathryn as akin to the knights of old who sallied forth on quests regardless of personal cost and likelihood of success. He had done his duty in fighting the Combined People, but he had ardently hoped for the defeat that eventually came to Awgren. To hear that there was already discord amongst these long-worshipped saviours was very sad, Morrick said, before sinking once more into sullen silence. Aldwyn thought on this for a time and made a quiet apology as they rode onwards towards the rising peaks of the Blade Mountains.

The column found the terrain offered little impediment, and little rivers running down from the mountains or out of the forest kept them well watered. In some ways the calm of the march was a welcome relief, and Aldwyn even began to think that if this was to be any indicator of life in the Hinterland, things might not be so bad after all.

He would build settlements in the foothills of the Blade Mountains and beacons in the passes, watching Linwood's borders. He would nurture the people of the Hinterland and bring them in to the fold and, in time, begin to visit his ancestral home of Culrain to set about reclaiming it. Let Linwood have Stragglers' Drift and Crinan – even try to break the Combined People if he liked, but Tayne, Culrain, the Isles and the Hinterland would stand in alliance as long as Aldwyn was alive, he decided. His diminishing anger about his new charge led to increasing admiration for Queen Cathryn.

He thought of her much when the conversation ebbed with Morrick or his aides. At night the weather was not so cold that he felt he needed a tent and instead, he slept fully clothed between layers of blankets, looking up at the constellations wheeling overhead and thinking on what life would have been like if he had been her consort in Lachlan's place; if he was lying beside Cathryn on a soft mattress, far south in the Folly. These were old thoughts and dreams, long accepted as mere fantasy, but they did not cause him much anguish. Instead they offered him comfort to a degree. He knew full well that

Cathryn loved him and due to their separate lives, he knew that would never grow weary or burdensome. Though he would later admonish himself for what he labelled a childish thought, that night he did consider himself the knight errant, questing for justice and holding the love of his lady in his heart, free from the necessity of proximity. Thinking of this, Aldwyn closed his eyes and slept, while Morrick, not far away, thought of Rowan and how in the next few days, he hoped to see her again and wondered what Rowan had called their child.

Morrick woke early the next morning and set about fishing a creek he had spied the previous evening. He caught a trout and, after gathering up some dry grass and firewood brought in from the forest edge, he borrowed a small pan to fry it. The meal was near ready when he heard the thunder of hooves as a rider passed him by, heading from the east and the direction of his home. He thought little of it, as the riders often returned but there was something of the rider's speed that worried him. However there was nothing he could do in the short term and finished his task so that whatever the day might bring, he would at least have breakfasted. If the past year had taught Morrick anything it was that one should eat on the road whenever one can, for it is not always so easy a task to keep oneself sustained.

He was licking grease from his fingers, his belly relatively full, when one of his men approached him at a run. The brand upon his cheek looked raw and had melted his right eye shut.

'Captain! The Hinterland is burning! Lord Aldwyn is seeking you.'

Morrick cursed, jumping up so quick he dropped the pan and spilled his water skin. He ran back to the camp, and as soon as he was within earshot he began hollering orders.

'Men of the Hinterland, strike camp and muster on me! To arms – your homes are burning! Move it!'

Tents were already coming down and armour being strapped on when Aldwyn's mare galloped up. Morrick finished buckling on his belt and took his axe in hand as the lord brought the mare to a standstill in front of him.

'You've heard?' he said. Aldwyn was in full armour, his sword at his side.

'Aye, my lord. We march immediately.' It was not a question, but Aldwyn could forgive the man his need to take action.

'The rest of the men are arming as we speak. Form up at the head of the column – you will lead us in, Captain.' He reared the mare.

The column crested a hill with Lord Aldwyn and Morrick at its head. They checked their pace for only a moment as they saw the smoke for the first time. A small village was directly ahead, already a blackened wreck with livestock bloodied and scattered across the grasslands.

'Onward. At the double!' hollered Aldwyn. He turned to Morrick.

'Ride ahead with me?'

One of the aides behind them piped up an objection, but Aldwyn hushed him with a wave of his hand.

'Take command and lead the men on,' he shouted back to the aide.

He spurred on his horse and Morrick did the same. The two men bore down on the village flanked at some extreme by the outriding scouts.

They saw the first of the bodies between the houses and the first survivor not long afterwards. A woman carrying a baby saw their approach, screamed and ran towards the forest paying no heed to their attire. Morrick, new to riding, tried to head after her but flustered the horse. Aldwyn was quicker off the mark and soon overtook her.

'Fear not!' he called. 'I am Lord Aldwyn, sent by Queen Cathryn of the Combined People.'

The words made no difference and the woman ran on, darting around him. Morrick saw her stumble as he managed to ride after and slowed the horse. On his feet, he ran to her.

'Lady, he speaks the truth. I'm from Northall!'

When it became clear that running was futile, the two men eventually managed to calm her and also those who, hearing her cries, came out of hiding. Reassured they were no longer under attack, one man agreed to talk to Morrick, admitting to having known his father.

'I have sorry news for you, Brother. Your wife attempted to raise rebellion, but was betrayed by a woman of the village. This Lara told the Devised of Awgren's defeat and they rampaged across the Hinterland burning all settlements.'

Morrick's chest heaved, and he spluttered then he dropped to his knees and vomited. But the man took him by the shoulder.

'From what I hear, she lives still. Many of the leaders fled into the Forest and have yet to be caught.'

Morrick retched again, wishing he had not eaten the trout after all. He was overcome with panic and shrugged off Lord Aldwyn when he attempted to offer comfort, telling him that they would advance on the Whiteflow with all speed.

By now the first of the riders had caught up, and Aldwyn sought out the captains.

'We march to battle now,' he told them. 'Be ever watchful.'

He found Morrick already mounted, but called for him to dismount.

'We must be ready to fight now. It is no time to be riding on many miles ahead of our charges. You must be patient…many of your men will already have found loved ones dead,' he said, but Morrick shook his head.

'Fuck you and fuck the men,' roared Morrick. 'I didn't come this far to abandon my family in the dying minutes of hope.'

Aldwyn drew his sword and for a moment, Morrick was convinced the duke would attack. He bared his teeth and grabbed for his axe.

'Let me do this, my lord,' he pleaded, tears streaming down his cheeks.

Aldwyn's eyes burned into him and Morrick dropped his gaze. He was about to apologise and fall into line, when the lord spoke up.

'Go. I will grant you this freedom, but speak like that to me again and I will rip you limb from limb.'

Morrick dropped his gaze once more.

'Apologies, my lord, I am ever grateful for your mercy and am at your service. But my wife. My children…'

Aldwyn sheathed his sword.

'Go. Good luck, Captain. May you find your people safe and well. I will bring the folk of the Hinterland on at your heels.'

Morrick rode onwards and reached Northall within the hour and found it intact. Devised swarmed about the village and the heads of many villagers stood erected on pikes at the village edge.

He heard the Devised roar as they sighted him, but he spurred his horse on and rode for his home. He saw the smoke before ever he reached it, but with little thought he rode on towards the forest.

Rowan, he thought. *Rowan.*

Chapter Thirteen

The forest swallowed Morrick whole and, in an instant he was thrown from the ever-changing present to the timeless shade under the boughs. But this was no opportunity for staking a homecoming or for nostalgia.

His mare raced onwards, head down and ears pinned to its head, the scent of the creatures behind riddling its equine mind in ways that no study or reason could explain. Morrick bounded down and up, ever more up in the saddle until finally after just a few seconds he was hurled off the beast, and it disappeared amongst the trees.

He crashed down amongst the roots, crying out as a gnarl of knot impacted near the column of his spine. He moaned and churned in the undergrowth even as he tried to stand and flee. Ere long he heard the sounds of battle underway behind him; Lord Aldwyn's soldiers had charged to meet the Devised.

Morrick cursed as he found his feet and stumbled onwards, stooping to clutch his fallen axe, gathering speed as the pain subsided a little. His breathing was hard, fast and ragged as he tore onwards. Spindly outstretched branches scratched at his face and arching roots tripped him into stumbling, but he dashed onwards thinking only of escape and finding Rowan, certain that she would have left him some sort of sign.

The sound of weapons ringing against iron faded as he raced onwards, but he only stopped to catch his breath when it was all he could do.

He arrived in a small clearing ringed with tall ash trees and fell to his knees, bracing himself with his hands. His body heaved and wretched as he tried to bring all his faculties back under his control. In time he gathered himself and found his feet once more. The leaves gently rustled and he could hear birds, but these were the only sounds now aside from the intermittent buzz of insect wings.

'Well then,' he said to nobody at all.

He looked around him, adjusted his belt and then sat. He had no notion at all what to do for the best; he knew only that somewhere within these woods, Rowan, Callum, Declan and his baby were fleeing. The thoughts stirred him and he yearned to be on his feet, on the move, hunting them down. But how? To where would the refugees flee?

Morrick could not think of where he would go in their position, let alone what his wife would do.

Many miles to the west, the forest delved down into a gorge that had been cut into the earth over a thousand years by the unceasing artistry of a creek. At the edge of this gorge the trees came to an end and the refugees came to a crossroads. Garrick had assumed the role of both leader and guide, though in truth he had not much more experience of the forest than did any of the other villagers and certainly less than the sailors who had passed through its outskirts only once on the journey from the east coast. Captain Lynch's wound had begun to fester and, to Rowan's horror, his men had burned out the infected flesh. His face was covered with a damp offcut from a shirt as he lay on a makeshift gurney constructed from fallen boughs and as they travelled on, even the injured men took turns in dragging him along. Callum still wore the cutlass at his belt as he walked alongside Garrick. Declan walked with the sailors, one hand on Lynch's carriage.

A straggle of refugees followed on behind and at the very rear, walked Rowan. Her arms were crossed about her bosom, fingertips digging into the meagre flesh above her ribs so that her nailbeds whitened and her knuckles ached. Her hair hung lank in her face, long fallen from its bun; she stared down at her feet as she walked, mindlessly traversing all obstacles. She was so concentrated that she did not notice the line ahead of her halt, and she nearly walked into Acorna.

Garrick stood with his thumbs tucked into his belt, staring down into the gorge. He clucked his tongue and shook his head.

Callum looked down too and then to the north upstream and to the south.

'What now?' he asked when it was clear from the silence that Garrick had no idea anyway.

'We make camp,' said Garrick. 'Two of us go north, two go south. Try to find a way across.'

'And then what?' said Wilson.

'And then cross it,' replied Garrick, not meeting the other man's gaze. There had been a tension growing between the two leaders of the respective groups, at least while Lynch was incapacitated.

'To what end?' said Wilson. He sat down on a rock. 'We have yet to decide where we are going.'

'We've been through this, Wilson. What other choice do we have? We cannot remain in the Hinterland. Our choices are north through the Forest or west to the coast. We can only hope that the Combined People will accept us there.'

Wilson grumbled something and clearly Lynch overheard him.

Though he kept his one eye shut, he spoke up.

'Make camp for now. We'll think more on this matter.'

Lynch's men drew him under a bower and then dispersed, some to help fetch firewood, others to look for food. Rowan sat a little way off, her back up against a tree. After a time, Acorna brought her some water, but knew from experience it was best to leave it at that.

As the evening approached, Rowan sat alone thinking of Bracken, of her little body being carried beneath the waters of the Whiteflow by the Naiads. Her eyelids grew heavy, but every time she began to doze, she started awake again as images of the white horse filled her dreaming mind. Eventually she grew so tired that she did drift off for longer, but a hand on her shoulder woke her again and she yelped a little high-pitched squeak.

It was full dark now and the features of the face looking down at her were merely hinted at by the far-off firelight. The face seemed grim and terrible so that Rowan drew back against the tree.

'Easy there…' Lynch's voice soothed and she recognised him then, breathing out a great gust of relief. He kneeled down and then fell back to sitting. He shuffled over so that his body was nearer to her.

'I'm sorry to wake you, Rowan.' He reached out and his rough fingertips grazed the ice-cold back of her hand. She flinched, but did not shake it off. She said nothing.

'They've scouted the gorge. There's a crossing some four miles to the north and to the south, the forest gives way to the foothills north of the Blade Mountains. A few of my men ventured out and they say the land there is not scorched, that we can make it into the passes and cross into Crinan – make for the Folly.'

Rowan looked up at him, an eyebrow raised slightly.

He recognised the look and nodded.

'Aye, I know. It's too far and there would be nothing to sustain us on the road. That and we'd like as not run into Devised forces before our own.' He began to stroke the back of her palm.

'Others wish to strike out north and head for Stragglers' Drift.'

Before she could object, he continued.

'I know; it's hundreds of miles. Walking would become a lifetime's work, but at least we'd have a chance of sustaining ourselves.'

Rowan stared at him unblinking then eventually croaked, her voice being dry,

'And you?'

Lynch sighed and looked back at his men over his shoulder.

'We lost a lot of people in the forest on the way to the Hinterland and we'd lose more heading north, no doubt. But travelling south would be folly, if you'll forgive the pun.' She did not laugh and he blushed, feeling foolish.

'I'm inclined to head towards Oystercatcher Bay. There was a plan to land behind the palisade there, and there's a very good chance that there is a substantial camp now. If we can reach lands held by the Combined People then we are saved, at least for the time being. It is this course of action I intend to recommend. Garrick seems to agree, though he says he has no clear idea where your people will go from there.'

Rowan was not interested in discussing the future of her people, nor was she particularly interested in discussing anything. She nodded and looked over to where Callum and Declan were sleeping beside Acorna. They had many days hence stopped approaching her, knowing full well that tears came more readily than words. Just looking at them caused a pain in her chest and her breath to shorten. She heard Bracken's laugh from somewhere in the back of her mind and she snorted back tears, but they threatened to come again immediately.

Lynch's fingers grasped her hand, and he grunted as he moved to crouch over her. He hooked his arm under hers, wrapping it around her and held her tight to him. She let the sobs come, shaking her entire body as they did so. She buried her face in his chest then pulled back with a cry as she did so, immediately imagining how she had forced Bracken's face against her own torso as the waters threatened to carry her whole family away. He held her tighter and the scent of his sweat filled her nose, almost floral and under other circumstances, pleasing. She collapsed into him as he tried to soothe her. Though she felt hard of heart, it was difficult not to be comforted by his presence and she wondered briefly what Morrick would think if he could see her. Somewhere in her heart she knew that he would understand that she was grieving and in pain, probably be grateful to the Taynish sea captain.

But in her present state, she hoped he would be jealous, hoping that wherever he was, Morrick would somehow know that another man's hands were on her; that he'd *feel* it. She stretched upwards and planted a kiss on his neck with her dry, cracked lips. He froze where he was and she did it again.

'Ma'am?' he whispered.

She whispered into his neck.

'Do you understand why I did what I did to my baby?' she whispered.

'I do ma'am. Tragedy it is, but your sons owe you their lives.' He tried to pull back, but she held him.

'And do you think my husband will understand?'

He faltered.

'I do ma'am. He will understand that, but not this…you are grieving, Rowan.'

She held him still, but made no move to kiss him again or to speak. After a time, feeling his breath on her brow, she pushed him gently away.

He was confused and returned to his seat beside her, looking about to see if anyone had witnessed what had passed between them. All were sleeping or otherwise engaged and his shoulders relaxed a little. He sighed and probed his wound with his fingers lightly, dabbing at it. They jerked back quickly at a flash of pain.

'I'll leave you to rest, Rowan. We can talk more about what to do afterwards…I figured with your family not yet whole…' he instantly regretted his choice of words, 'that is to say, with your husband still off at war, you might be less inclined to flee to the Isles than are many of those who travel with us.'

She practically growled back at him.

'I have no husband.'

'Rowan…'

'I married a good, strong man, but am wed to a coward, a collaborator and a traitor to the rightful cause,' she said, 'a man who should have been looking after his family, not off trying to kill better men - such as you.'

She closed her eyes and made a token attempt at rolling away, though she barely turned except for her head. Lynch remained for a while, sitting back on his haunches and bracing himself against the trunk of the tree.

'Where will you go, Rowan?'

'Does it matter?' she said without opening her eyes.

'What of your sons?' he said and she could hear disappointment in his voice.

Tears threatened again and she said nothing.

Lynch planted a hand on her shoulder – she appreciated the weight of it – then he went back to his men.

Callum woke her in the morning with a handful of fruit and a water skin. She came to with a scowl on her face, but when she saw the concern in his eyes she softened a little as her heart stirred. She had been so filled with remorse about Bracken she'd forgotten that there were two babies she had managed to save in the river. She drew up her knees and Callum dropped the berries into her pooled skirt. He offered a weak smile and walked away.

'Callum…' Rowan called and he came back to her. She cupped his hand in both of hers.

'Thank you for all you've done. You've become a man in the last few days. I appreciate all you've done, but your sister…'

She stopped as his mouth dropped open a little and his lip began to quiver. He tensed it, trying to remain composed. Rowan dropped his hand and held both of hers up palms outward.

Over the next few days, Rowan forced herself to push thoughts of Bracken from the forefront of her mind, but with little success. The more she tried not to think of her little lungs filling with water, the more the images intruded.

She wondered what Morrick was doing away in the south. Whatever dangers he was facing, she knew that he did not carry the burden, nor would he ever carry the burden of knowing that he had murdered one of their children. She imagined Morrick in the river, snatching Bracken from her arms and saying to her, 'We have to do this to save the family, Rowan,' and then pushing the baby under the water while she screamed.

Anger flashed and her heart rate leaped, hating him momentarily. A lie though she knew it was, the manufactured malice towards Morrick felt easier than loathing herself. So whenever an image of the killing intruded, she placed Morrick in her role.

She took to walking hand in hand with Declan. She would have done the same for Callum, but her eldest insisted on leading the group with Garrick.

They walked south along the creek until they cleared the forest. The company then turned west, following the line of the forest towards Oystercatcher Bay. Lynch started walking for himself, though from the tension in his face it was clear that he was still in extreme pain. For the most part he was intact, but a strip of material torn from a shirt covered his lost left eye. He took to walking on the other side of Rowan from Declan and when they made camp, the two of them stayed up talking.

Lynch talked of all the lands he had visited, including his home at the Folly and of Stragglers' Drift, but it was his tales of the Isles that inspired her most. She began to think that maybe she would like to settle there, building a cottage between the mountains and the bright water of the western sea.

Whilst they were still two days from the bay, though they did not know it, Lynch first took Rowan's hand as they walked, much to the disapproval of Acorna and others who knew her from her village.

Morrick stumbled on as the days passed. At one point he tripped on a rock and blundered into a tree. He did not realise for an hour that in doing so he had punctured his water skin. By morning he was without food and water.

Morrick reached a deep gorge and, with dismay, realised that there was no way across. He sat on the edge with his legs hanging over then lay back looking up through the canopy at the grey sky.

He thought about what Rowan would have done if she made it to the forest, but came to no clear answer. She could not know that the invasion had been a success, so where would she think to go to find refuge. Only the forest was safe and untouched by Awgren. The more he thought about safety, the more conversations he remembered about what they would do if the Devised forces ever turned against them.

We strike out north into the forest, carrying only what we need to keep us alive. Once we get far enough away, we start a life there.

But how would he ever find them in a forest so vast, where it was so easy to lose one's sense of direction *even if* one knew in which direction one needed to be heading? He shook his head and stumbled north along the edge of the gorge thinking that all was lost and that there was little chance he would ever see his family again. What else was there to do but try to find them though? Everything he had ever done was to keep them safe or to ensure that they would all be together.

Before the light began to fade, he gathered firewood together and used a broad piece of branch as a spade to dig out a fire-pit. He dug down first in one place then another, just inches away, so that the hole curved down to meet the first as a vent. He set about lighting the kindling by rubbing dry wood together and eventually got a fire going. There was nothing to eat and he determined that stumbling on was getting him nowhere but to the afterlife, if there was one. The next morning, he decided, he would get down to the creek and fish. Possibly he could set snares and traps for rabbits – forage for fruit, nuts and mushrooms.

Morrick unrolled his blankets beside the fire and curled up, shouldering at the unyielding ground below him, as one might a pillow, to give himself more comfort. He lay by the firelight with the heat just bearable on his face and tried again to think what Rowan would do.

She was impetuous, fiery, driven and so determined to succeed in everything that she attempted. They had talked of rebelling and she had been all for it, but he had placated her, reminding her that the few who had been caught attempting to start a rebellion had suffered rough justice at the hands of the overseers and their Devised commanders. They would have to make do until the time was right.

He had stuck to this line of reasoning even when the Devised came to recruit him and when last they had spoken, he had promised her it would all be all right, that they would survive; that they would be together again. This promise echoed in his ears and he knew that come what may, if he had to wander in the dark forest for the rest of his days, he would never give up looking for his wife, two sons and the baby he had never had a chance to meet.

Morrick lapsed into sleep. Eyes formed in the branch above him though it was so narrow it could not possibly conceal an entire face. They regarded Morrick with cold interest then travelled together, maintaining their relative position to one another until they were at crouching height on the trunk. They blinked their bark eyelids and stared. Riark looked over Morrick's attire and recognised a military uniform similar, but not identical, to that worn by those who hacked into the forest in the north. This one carried not only a small boarding axe at his waist, but a great axe such as those the Dryad had seen hacking at the trunk of many a tree in the north.

The Dryad emerged from the tree and stood as close to the trunk as was possible until the shards of bark dropped from its polished heartwood flesh. It then crept closer and peered into the man's face. The hair on the man's head was longer and he had grown yet more across his face, but the Dryad knew him. This was the man who felled so many trees in the south and directed others to do so; the man who planted new trees to replace what he felled and left offerings in the woods.

The Dryad loomed in closer, for he had no breath to wake the sleeping man. The soft, clammy features of the dirty face awoke something akin to nausea in the Dryad and he drew back. He dissipated back into the tree and flowed out through the roots, seeking westward to where he had heard the call of others. The woodcutter's people had left the forest, but still he wished to watch their progress and learn what he could.

Less than thirty miles apart, Rowan and Morrick slept soundly.

Chapter Fourteen

Even after a thousand years Riark was still learning what it meant to be Dryad. He stormed through the heart of the forest in a form which he found increasingly hard to leave. The more his thought was bent upon the interlopers, the more he came to resemble them. Initially he posited that this effect was due to an exertion of his will, as, after all, much of his life since he had become a Dryad was to do with mental intent or desire of the soul, rather than physical cause and effect. However, he now believed it be a form of defence.

For the first time in his long existence, Dryads were dying in considerable numbers - so many Mother Trees had been felled since he had executed Ashrider.

Riark stood tall and proud in the shape of a man, the wooden flesh of his body grew and wrapped around him as it does around an old oak, thickening the trunk. This time, however, the wood formed into an approximation of armour. He was disgusted by this approximation of man's work and with a thought the wooden armour merged once more with his torso and reappeared as soft brown bark.

Mount Greenwood stood in the heart of the forest. No man had ever set foot upon its slopes, but it was the tallest mountain on the continent and was clearly visible from both the Hinterland and the seas to the east and west. He was the first king of the Dryads to take a home at all, but he didn't build it nor did he feel that he was betraying his nature in forming it.

Mount Greenwood was not made of rock. He had begun the work when he was but a sapling, experimenting with growing his Mother Tree, faster than nature would usually allow. He had wrapped himself, round and around the trunk, extending the branches and thrusting roots down broader and deeper than had been attempted before. When the limits of the growth of the tree had been extended and the roots extended thick and broad from centuries of burrowing, he directed them upwards and out into the open air, arcing upward and inward until they took on the shape of a mountain, a thrusting peak scratching at the sky like an eagle's talon. He dwelt within the roots to sculpt them or direct them as an artist would a brush. He dwelt within his Mother Tree and looked up at the construct from below, assessing if he had allowed enough breaks in the sinew to allow light through.

Riark approached the root wall of his home and passed through it. By now the up thrust roots were as thick as any tree and did not open to the light for a hundred foot, but any Dryad could walk through them. Inside, he marched up a spiralling root towards the upper branches of his Mother Tree, and once there, took his seat nestled in a crook of the elm. As soon as he touched the bark, a calmness settled in him. He waited for the others to arrive.

As the week passed he sat and listened to the reports from all over the forest as his subjects arrived, emerging through the ends of roots or walking in through the main wall.

He heard of the continued efforts to build the road in the north, of the refugees in the south and of the woodcutter who had been found sleeping, alone, amongst the trees. Riark knew him well and pondered his presence after such a long absence.

Nayr was the third to arrive. She was stern and stiff in her movements, all cat-like grace, all femininity seemed gone.

'Riark,' she said, bowing low. Riark noted with interest that she too had chosen the human form and there was the hint of an armoured breastplate upon her.

He sank into the trunk of his Mother Tree and emerged on the ground beside her. They entwined roots and he knew her mind.

'They make further incursions,'she said to him.

Night was closing in, and she looked up into the underside of the mountain and out at the stars that gleamed, lending the scene an eldritch quality.

'Some sixty of our kind have been destroyed in the forest. They now draw deeper into the forest and our losses will number even greater day by day. The elder amongst us have accepted their loss but with so many human losses in the war against Awgren, we have many new folk. They retain many of their former instincts and want to fight to survive. We have not been able to prevent all killing. The forces there are taking note and deploying troops.'

'But as of yet no burning.' Riark mused. 'Troops without fire are nothing to be feared.'

'No burning,' she agreed, 'but the work on the road is well underway and they have begun separate stretches in four other locations. I hear tell also, that camps in the clearings are being gradually turned into permanent dwellings. It is my belief that we will cede much of our territory as they expand, that the forest will be first split and then diminish into separate woods as the centuries pass.'

Riark settled back against the tree and drew nutrients up from the ground. They replenished him, and he closed his eyes. They dissipated into his face, ceasing all vision.

'I have reports from the south also. Weeks ago, a party of sailors travelled through the woods. They re-entered with people fleeing from the Hinterland. The Naiads assisted a few of their number; the family of the woodcutter in those parts,' he said.

'The woodcutter?' asked Nayr, frowning, though without his eyes Riark did not see.

'I hear distaste in your voice.'

'He was a hewer of trees.'

'As is a cuckoo. As is the beaver. Not all are as equipped to live in harmony as are we. He respects the forest and takes only what is needed. He replants saplings to sustain the woods near his home. Have you seen his works?'

Riark's eyes reappeared, and Nayr shivered, an entirely affected response but one learned and ingrained during human life that she had yet to shrug off. She realised she had done it and would have blushed if she had capillaries in her cherry-wood cheeks.

'His works? You mean the mutilation of our trees into cutlery, buildings and statues?' she snapped.

Riark raised a fern eyebrow.

'Look about you, Nayr. Is not Mount Greenwood a mutilation under that definition?'

'It is,' she said without a moment's hesitation, which disquieted the king. He felt her fingers melded into his torso and understood her intimately.

'You think this a travesty of our power?' he said, quietly.

'We do not build. Mount Greenwood is a human affectation.'

'This is nothing more than artistry of growth, Nayr,' he said, but still in tune with her, he knew that she did not consider it to be so.

He separated from her and disappeared into his Mother Tree, reappearing on the soil in the Bower of the King.

'This is the strongest forest in the world. There are glorified woods, pretty little things away in the Stragglers, but those to the south were eradicated by Awgren. He was wise enough not to contend with us and we have had peace. But now we are infested.'

Nayr stood, balling her hands on her hips.

'Perhaps we should no longer stop our people fighting back?'

Riark shook his head.

'It may come to that, but as it seems that banners are being staked in the ground, it is time we did the same for the forest. I will meet with their leader in the north and their queen in the south. I will state our terms, mark our borders and establish a basis for peace.'

'And if they do not accept your terms?'

'We will do as all good farmers must. We will eradicate the pests that invade our crops.' He paused and beckoned to her.

'Come.'

Somewhere outside a wolf howled, but they both ignored the sound. Nayr walked down to join Riark in the bower. She reached out and became one with him again. He was filled with an urgent sense of danger and fear of change. He focused on the need to grow and change, revealed his belief in caution, but also his decision that stronger measures may become necessary. They wrangled back and forth with their opinions for a day or so, and by the time they had done, they had taken root and the two of them had taken on the look of a young tree, limbs stretched over one another's backs. They drew apart and Riark nodded to her.

'I will go first to meet their leader in the north, this…' he struggled, as did all older Dryads, with remembering individual names, but he recalled that the lord in the north was named after the woods. '…this child of the linden dell. We must show him the immutable power of the forest.'

Lord Linwood continued his long ride into the forest flanked by Lady Isobel. He wore full steel armour and a great helm. A shield hung over his back. His great-sword swung at his hip, and he sat upright in his saddle, despite the agony it caused his compressed vertebrae – a complaint he had dismissed ever since he gained it on the Field of the Scarlet Grass, facing down one of Awgren's larger creations. He wore no cloak or cape, for he believed it too cumbersome in a fight, and so he ignored the cold as best he could. Lady Isobel was similarly attired, with her hair tied back into a long, thick plait. She too carried a great sword and shield bearing the emblem of her house – a river running across a green background. The two of them were an image of all the splendour of warfare that now remained among the Combined People.

Their horses reared as something ahead of them burst from the ground, sending up a shower of soil, chalk and rock. Lady Isobel cried out as she expertly wheeled her horse, bringing it back under control. Linwood's reared up, kicking out forward with its hooves, but then righted itself.

Before them stood a diminutive, hunched man clothed in a hood and cloak of dark green leaves and vines. His face was not visible and he supported himself on staff of yew.

'Who passes in the forest?' The voice rumbled and cracked as though it came up from deep underground, splitting roots as it emerged. The man did not raise his head.

Linwood had taken fright quite badly, finding the appearance not only unexpected but eerie in its entire; a moment in which confidence was shattered by violence in a matter of seconds.

'I am Lord Linwood of Stragglers' End, Duke of Stragglers' Drift and Crinan. Who bars my way?' said Linwood, entirely forgetting Lady Isobel. She drew up alongside him, hand on the hilt of her sword.

'And the architect of the forest's destruction?' said the figure.

Linwood steadied his horse, gripping its flanks with his thighs and loosening his hands, ready to take up arms.

'Who bars my way?' he said, forceful but moderate in volume.

'This is not your way, child Linwood,' creaked the figure and Linwood was reminded of an old tree swaying in a high wind.

'This is not a way at all. There are no ways in the forest for the likes of man.'

'I will not ask again,' said Linwood, drawing his sword.

The figure raised his staff and thrust it back down into the earth with a terrible force. Less than a heartbeat later, and roots threw themselves up out of the ground, grasping Linwood's sword and holding it in place in his hand. Another tendril swatted Lady Isobel's hand away then hovered at the hip height, its tip swaying back and forth like a cobra.

'You do not make demands nor do you command here, child of the linden dell,' said the figure. It drew itself up, the hunch disappearing, and the hood and cloak fell away to leaves upon the grass. Beneath, Riark stood unguarded, his polished wooden flesh not far akin in aesthetic from a dummy Linwood had once slashed at in training using the very sword he held now. Riark's features formed on his blank face, monstrous and terrible. His cold, blank eyes snatched at Linwood's gaze and held it. Plates of wooden armour formed from Riark's flesh, piling layer upon layer of breast and backplate, vambrace, gauntlet and pauldron, coif and helm. His long vines coursed out from under it and a beard of moss stretched down to his waist. He grew in stature until he stood a full eight-foot in height, and only then did a tall, spindly crown of mahogany burst forth from his head, shooting splinters down upon the cowed lord.

Linwood gulped and felt his own shoulders shaking. His mouth dried up and his lips shrank back, curling under his teeth. He licked his lips and gasped when he tried to speak. Isobel's horse backed up then turned to flee. This time, she was not successful in checking it. Linwood's mount bucked, reared and galloped back the way it had come. Still gripping his sword tight, Linwood was plucked from the saddle and cast down upon the grass without his weapon.

Riark bore down upon him, forcing one terrible foot into his breastplate. When he spoke, the words were a roar so loud that Linwood heard his ears bang. Sap sprayed across his face and momentarily blinded him until he could wipe it away on his sleeve.

'I am Riark, king of the Dryads, and the forests are my realm, child of the linden dell. You would well to remember it. Draw off your people and leave my borders.'

Linwood said nothing, grasping for some retort and pondering how to take down such a creature. It seemed the stories his men told were not as fanciful as he had first supposed.

Riark leant in ever closer, rage splintering his face and scalding steam hissed from the cracks. Knots grew, shattered and reformed. Linwood looked into the nothing of his polished eyes and could not move.

'When your men have left our borders, seek for me again, child of the linden dell. My people will be watching. We will discuss terms for your road; perhaps a route; perhaps nothing. But we will discuss what favours I am prepared to grant your kind; you will no longer take without asking leave.'

Riark decided to leave the man a little pride and did not force an answer. He pushed down with the foot and to his credit, Linwood did not cry out as his ribs fractured. Riark drew off a few paces, and some twenty Dryads, differing in the details of appearance but all terrible, all magnificent echoes of trees from some nightmare, stalked forward and planted their roots beside Riark.

'We are the forest. I am the forest. You do not hold sway here, child.'

With that the vine holding Linwood's sword whipped round and pointed the tip at his throat. It was suspended in this fashion for a moment and Linwood scowled at it, the faces of all those he had killed with it flashing in his mind. Then the sword drew back, spun at the hilt and with terrifying speed, the vine propelled the blade point first at Riark's chest. It impacted with such force that the wood there rent open and the sword was driven in to the hilt. Riark smiled and the vine was sucked back into the earth. He reached out with his hand and withdrew the sword then tossed it at Linwood's feet.

'An honour to meet you, Lord Linwood, Duke of Stragglers' Drift and Crinan. I look forward to meeting you again under friendlier circumstances.'

The Dryads turned and dived into the trees. All was silent aside from the sound of Linwood's heavy, rapid breathing.

He scrambled to his feet and retrieved his sword, only to find it bent at the middle. He tossed it aside in disgust.

'Riark!' he hollered, 'Riark.'

Only the sound of leaves in the wind and an owl hooting greeted his ears.

Linwood stumbled towards the nearest tree with an arm wrapped around his torso, cradling his ribs. He hauled the shield from his back and smashed it repeatedly into the tree.

'Your men have retreated so quickly?' a voice came from above him. Linwood looked up and saw Riark's head emerging half way up the trunk.

Linwood staggered back and pointed up at him.

'You unhorsed me, unprovoked, in retaliation for crimes I did not even know had been perpetrated. You break my sword and steal my dignity. You are a creature I cannot best nor kill. Come down and face me.'

Riark's head disappeared inside the trunk, but, making Linwood jump, he stepped out from behind the tree, once more cloaked and hunched, clutching the yew staff. He walked over to where Linwood's sword lay and taking it up in his gnarly hands, he bent it back into shape so perfectly, it was impossible to tell it had ever been distorted.

He held it out in open hands and Linwood retrieved it, never taking his eyes from Riark's face.

'Shall we begin again?' said Riark, satisfied that he had conveyed his mastery of all that went on in the forest.

Linwood coughed.

'Do you have a boon to ask of me, Lord Linwood?' said Riark, softly.

Linwood nodded and then spoke,

'Aye. I am building this road so that my people may pass through your forest to our home in the south.'

'Such a road would be possible, but nigh impossible for you to traverse without stations on the route,' said Riark. 'These I will not allow. The north and the south are already cleared of the trees. The waist of this land must remain as untainted forest. I will not allow my realm to diminish any further. I might permit a road around the coast, if more trees are allowed to grow north of our borders in return.'

Linwood thought this unsatisfactory and the road far too long.

'Tell me, Riark, what will you do if Lady Isobel persists with building the road on the route I have already approved?' He thought he knew the answer but also knew his duty.

Riark's face was not visible beneath the hood and when his voice came, it was deep and once more rumbled up from the deep.

'When mites infest a plant, the only hope for the plant is to kill the mites. You can see this will be of no difficulty for us,' said Riark. 'Don't be a fool.'

'I have plans that depend upon this road,' Linwood replied.

'Make new plans,' said Riark and stepped into the tree.

Linwood sheathed his sword and walked back along the road. He met her riding back, and she nearly rode him into the dirt. She saw him at the last moment, diverted into the trees and circled back around. She was wide-eyed and sweating.

'Cousin, are you unhurt?' she winced, seeing that he cradled his ribs.

He nodded.

'Send word to all the sites to withdraw from the forest and make camp to the north. All construction stops for now.'

Riark watched them go and, satisfied, set out for his next destination through the soil. He decided not to trouble Lord Aldwyn as of yet, given that he had not set foot within the forest, but sent Nayr to watch the encampments of the Hinterland.

Riark stepped out of an apple tree and onto a courtyard of stone. He looked about him. The courtyard was encircled by low buildings and beyond them a high wall with steps running to the summit. Riark stepped forward and his companions also exited the tree. Cries went up from a group of people who had been gathered outside what may have been a temple on the north wall and a guard with a crossbow levelled it at them from the wall, calling out,

'Call to the guards! Intruders!'

Riark held up his hands in a peaceful gesture and strode through the Folly streets, heading for the Maw Keep.

Chapter Fifteen

Cathryn was woken by a call to the guards. She was barely into a pair of leather breeches when an urgent rap sounded through her oaken door, restrained and clearly wanting to be louder were it not for her station. She slipped a calico shirt over her head and tied back her hair as she marched upon the door. The face of the guard on the other side was grave.

'My lady, the peninsula has been breached by intruders.'

She frowned, continuing to tidy her hair.

'Intruders?'

Ailsa bustled up behind her, careful to keep out of view from the door and began to gather up Cathryn's weapons and armour while also attending to her own.

The queen of the Combined People met the king of the Dryads halfway down the sloping road between the the Maw Keep and the wall surrounding the lower planes, a stretch of road enclosed by thin stone walls. Cathryn's entourage planted themselves in a line barring the way, shields raised and spears poised, but a mere look at the intruders told them any attack would be useless.

Cathryn turned back to her aide.

'I want archers with flaming arrows atop these walls. Seal all the gates on all possible escape routes.'

Ailsa nodded and set off at a jog, breaking into a run only when she was out of sight.

Cathryn pushed her way through the line of her men and watched Riark lead his people towards her. She recognised him as a Dryad from the tales of old, but even if she had never heard the name, she still would have made a well-reckoned guess as to the nature of this creature; his appearance told all that was needed to make such a judgement.

She said nothing, but stood with her hands clasped in front of her, waiting to see how the situation would unfold. In her mind she extrapolated what would happen if she were to order attacks upon these creatures in particular ways. She found it hard to imagine anything but fire would be a credible remedy to this threat - if it was indeed a threat.

Riark's face became clear as he approached, serene but nearly featureless – his nose, eyes, mouth and ears merely hinted at by gentle contours in the wood. She detected power in his stance and his being, but not aggression.

The group of Dryads came to a halt and Riark bowed. As much as Cathryn wanted to wait, she knew she had to assert her authority and speak first. Her first instinct was to make a challenge regarding the breaching of her walls.

'May I offer assistance?' she said, her hands still gently clasped.

Riark straightened up and his mouth became more defined. It splintered open when he spoke and Cathryn could see green fronds of flesh within the tear.

'Perhaps,' he said, and his voice spoke of wet soil and damp chalk; of mulched leaves washed into a stream by the rain.

'Perhaps we can offer assistance. Perhaps we might just take counsel together,' he said.

For a moment he looked as though he were struggling with something, perhaps a troublesome word or elusive concept.

'I should also offer apology; for the manner of my arrival. Our customs are not the same and my choices were limited. I am Riark and in your tongue, you would style me as king of the Dryads. All forests are my domain, but I take root within the Impassable Forest which straddles this continent. I would have sent word or come to your gate if I had the means, but we travel through the trees and there are none outside these walls. I would speak with the ruler of mankind,' he said, and it sounded as though water was welling in his throat; many a nearby human felt a shiver run up his or her spine.

A voice came from behind Cathryn.

'They appeared through an apple tree in a courtyard down on the plains, Your Majesty.'

Her estimation of the threat de-escalated somewhat in her mind even as she nodded, all the time considering how to proceed.

'I am Queen Cathryn of the Combined People. I bid you welcome and accept your apologies, King Riark.'

She kept her hands clasped and did not turn as she went on,

'Captain of the guard, dismiss the men. Send word to the archers to stand down and tell my aide to meet us on the road back to the Maw Keep.'

A few orders were barked and the bulk of the troops filtered back to their posts leaving Cathryn with only her personal guard.

Riark bowed lower this time and she could hear his body creaking and the green flesh tendrils between his calves and thighs became taut.

'I can arrange quarters for you and your people,' said Cathryn, but Riark shook his head.

'We begin to feel drained when we are away from the soil for too long. Walking these stone streets is tantamount to throwing a fish upon the bank,' he croaked.

Cathryn smiled and walked towards him, gesturing for him to turn and walk back in the direction from which he had come.

'I know of an orchard not far from here where we can sit. Are you in need of food or wine?' she asked as she fell in beside him.

Riark slowly shook his head as though it were for the first time. From beside him and up so close, Cathryn could see quite clearly the grain of his wooden skin and detect the wet aroma that surrounded him. He stood a full foot taller than her and seemed broad across the chest. In some ways, she thought, he reminded her of Lachlan.

'We do not eat nor drink as you do. As you can probably see, Dryads and animals have little in common.'

Cathryn led the party left along a narrower side street that, after half a mile, began to widen out and leave buildings behind, replaced by fenced fields. The orchard was up ahead and Cathryn left her guard upon the road when she walked towards the apple trees. Riark bade the Dryads wait as well, though they did step onto the soil, breathing deep in an unconscious approximation of relief.

Cathryn settled cross-legged upon the grass and after a moment regarding her, Riark mimicked.

'Better?' she asked, watching incredulous as roots struck out from where his legs met the ground, driving into the soil. His face cracked into a smile.

'The fish is back in water,' he nodded, once again with that creaking and drunken heaviness.

She smiled politely and folded her arms not only against the cold but to conceal an adrenaline tremor.

'What brings you to the Folly?' she asked.

Riark sat up straighter than a human would find comfortable, and it made Cathryn's back complain watching him.

'Over the past centuries there has been equilibrium in the forest. Your people have been mostly absent for a long, long time though I knew of your continuing existence here and elsewhere.'

'There has always been deforestation to a certain extent, but this was part of the natural order of things. There are many of your kind who show deference to the forest; a few in the Hinterland and the whores of the Drift even bring us offerings.' He smiled weakly at this and Cathryn sensed that such offerings were akin to murderers sending gifts to his victim's family.

'The deforestation in the north of this continent has been unacceptable of late. As I appear to you now, when we roam abroad, we are beyond destruction, but should our Mother Trees be felled, then we are lost from the forests of this world. Lord Linwood and his road-building have caused such destruction and loss of my kind that I am forced to stand forward and intervene. I have warned him in no uncertain terms to desist. I come to you with a somewhat cooler disposition and, I hope, you can see I offer you respect. I come to ask that all work on the road stops for now. We can, perhaps, discuss a way of connecting your lands, but a route straight through is, to me, cause for war. And, I might add, that is a war in which your kind would not fare well.'

Cathryn's face contorted and settled into a painful frown.

'Linwood has made much progress with his road?' she said softly.

'He has.' Then, realising, 'You were unaware?'

Cathryn shook her head, looking at the grass swaying to Riark's right. She wondered whether divulging anything to this creature would be wise.

'Since we defeated Awgren, I have had concerns that Lord Linwood means to seize this continent for himself. I had heard of his plans for a road, but knew not how far it had progressed. I gave the Impassable Forest royal protection and named it a crime for any to touch it. It seems I was correct about Linwood. I sent a loyal ally, Lord Aldwyn, to govern the Hinterland in order to place a barrier between Linwood's lands in Crinan and the forest. This is troubling news, indeed.'

A new thought troubled her, and she looked up at Riark's face, finding it difficult to fix his gaze given that his eyes had no pupils and no iris for a marker.

'You have my assurance, the Combined People do not approve of such works, and I apologise for the actions of one of my lords. Or one who *was* one of my lords. I name him a traitor and assure you I will not let his treachery go unpunished. Order will be restored.'

Riark nodded and a green tendril at the back of his neck tensed then snapped. Cathryn shuddered, but Riark did not react, save to look quizzically at her. She dismissed her reaction with a wave of her hand, and he spoke up.

'My people are at your disposal. We can be back in the Drift in a moment. Would you have us seize this Linwood or convey a message?'

Cathryn sat straighter, clasping her hands together in her lap.

'You would be willing to act as an envoy?'

Riark's smile was patient.

'I will convey a message.' The queen's cheeks reddened as she realised she had done her guest a discourtesy. Riark either paid no heed or did not notice her reaction as he continued, 'and if necessary, I will act on your behalf.'

Cathryn mused for a time, turning each option over in her mind and weighing up the likely outcomes.

She sighed and did something to which she was not accustomed – she opened up to Riark.

'Linwood presents me with a dilemma,' she admitted. He cocked his head and waited for her to continue, which, after a sigh, she did.

'Throughout my entire reign and for the last centuries, the Combined People have focused all their intent on reclaiming our homelands and defeating Awgren. I must admit I dreamed of viewing lush green lands from up there…' she pointed up at the Maw Keep, '…after years of recovery. I've been picturing shining new cities and smooth, straight roads; farms, sapling forests and peace.' She smiled ruefully. Riark's face did not shift or alter.

'It is not the way,' he said. 'If an enemy is overcome, humans always turn upon one another. You united to address a threat to your people and your lands. That threat is gone, and now your people will decide upon a new threat. Your Lord Linwood thinks of you as the threat to his domination over his own lands, life and people. You in turn will view him as a threat to stability in your pre-existing realm. It is and always was exhausting to us.'

He waved a hand towards the nearest visible curtain wall.

'This…your Folly, it all came from the same problem. Even before Awgren, your peoples were separated into countries for no reason other than someone decided to plant a flag or maintain a border. It is in your nature.'

'And not in yours?'

Riark swept back the tendrils of his mane behind his ears, and it seemed so human a gesture from one so alien that it surprised the queen.

'It was in my nature when I was a man. Still in my nature when I was reborn as a sapling. The tendencies of our old lives fade as the years and centuries grow and die.' He smiled and before she could remark on his comments, he ploughed on.

'The Dryad nation is not territorial in the same way. We do not conquer. We are the trees, wherever they may be. We have no ranks or titles or property.'

'And yet you style yourself King?'

'Only in this form,' he smiled. 'We have no language in other forms. I am not of a noble bloodline - we don't have bloodlines at all. I suppose I am the voice of the forest. All hear my voice, though not all obey. I interpret the beating heart of the woodlands and act in accordance with their wishes, I suppose.'

He crackled a laugh.

'I had not given it much thought at all. With us, much is just…known. It is hard to understand for your kind.'

'So there are no contenders for your crown then?' said Cathryn.

'It is not in our nature to contend. I was not born to my role nor did I vie for it. I became it. It is possible for me to be killed if another desired it. I suppose if one can defeat the living voice of the forest, that Dryad would speak for it anew. But it is not in our nature. We have no fierce instinct to survive as we get older; we simply grow and sometimes overshadow one another. And yet, we have worth and I would not have my people destroyed.'

They sat in silence for a time, but before long a question grew in Cathryn's mind, and it was not long before she felt she could not resist asking.

'Forgive me, but I cannot ask this without the anticipation of bitterness seeping into my voice.'

Riark cocked his head once more.

'Awgren rose up and destroyed my homelands - killed my people. We have been fighting ever since. How came the forest to be untouched? Did you have no impulse to step in and assist? Why have we never spoken before?'

Riark bowed his head and twirled a blade of grass around the crook formed by his little finger.

'You must understand that we have no concern for…foreign policy. We look to ourselves and enjoy merely existing. We do not share priorities. We watch you live and die during the time it takes us to contemplate one aspect of our own lives. There is a natural order to existence; cycles of life, suffering, predation and death. We do not stalk out and interfere with others. I would not stop a dark lord crushing a people any more than I would deny a fox his rabbit. Does it make any sense? I have lived as a man and died. All mammals die. There is no sense in interfering.'

Cathryn sighed and hung her head, knowing full well that she should be conveying a more steadfast outlook and that she was giving away far too much. She tilted her head and looked at him sideways. Riark seemed to hear her thoughts.

'We are not a competing nation nor am I an opposing king,' he said. 'Without us, you cannot live. We make the air you breathe and we grow wherever we grow. Territory means very little to our saplings. You have Mother Trees sown throughout your lands.'

She straightened up and looked at him.

'Can I be frank?'

Riark nodded, 'You have my word that nothing you say will reach the ears of another.'

'I have no personal desire to dominate this continent. I am content to have things as they were during our absence from the southern half of this continent. I know that my husband and other lords feel the same. We have a good life and enough of everything we need. I would be happy enough watching the lands flourish again from the Maw Keep or simply spending time with my family away in the Isles.'

'Then why do you not do so?'

'Because of Lord Linwood and the minority like him who still have visions of grandeur even after they have seen all wealth and power laid low. He would reclaim his own lands and, I fear, even that would not be enough to satisfy him.'

'Let him take back his lands then?' suggested Riark.

'How long before his eyes turn towards the Folly or the Isles? Even if they never did, there will be others we have yet to meet. Lord Aldwyn discovered a new continent and who knows what lurks there. What new power might attempt to recapture these lands and attempt to destroy my people?'

Riark tried to hide a smile.

'What amuses you?' she said.

'You think there are no trees on the South Continent?' was his reply. 'We know something of all the lands of this world, Queen.'

Cathryn opened her mouth to answer, but the implications of this new knowledge overwhelmed her and she remained silent, looking at him.

'I will not lie – your appearance has overturned much of my thinking.' She paused. 'You have much knowledge that would be of value to me and to my kind.'

Riark nodded in acknowledgement.

'Perhaps it has been for the best that I have revealed my people to you, after all. I feared there would be a war between us that you could not win. I would be willing to share my understanding, if we can come to an agreement regarding the treatment of every tree, every copse and every forest. Perhaps sign a treaty, if it suits you?' he mused.

Cathryn nodded once, slowly.

'I believe that could be to the benefit of all. What would you ask of us? I for one would hope we could share knowledge.' She refrained from mentioning mutual defence, waiting for the Dryad to respond.

'I understand the need for timber, but wish to end deforestation. Until now, some of my people have died needlessly so that one of yours could sit on a fine chair or perhaps their corpses are built into your siege engines. That is bad enough, but only the people in the Hinterland had any respect with regard to sustaining that from which they took.'

'The Hinterland?'

Riark nodded.

'One man in particular showed great deference even as he wreaked destruction, planting a tree for every tree he took. He used every part of those he felled so that nothing was wasted. It's the best end that a felled tree could expect, but it has been some time since I have seen him about his work,' he said.

'The surviving men of the Hinterland have been sent home with Lord Aldwyn. They should be there now,' said Queen Cathryn.

'That would explain much. Not long ago I sensed the woodcutter's presence in the forest once again and found him beneath our boughs,' Riark said, his voice creaking. He closed his eyes and tendrils of root emerged from his body, thrusting decisively into the soil.

He frowned as he opened his eyes once more.

'The Hinterland has been ravaged by those who remained of Awgren's minions. Homes and fields burn. Your Lord Aldwyn is doing what he can and has defeated your enemies there.'

Cathryn felt her heart palpitate at the mention of Aldwyn. A smile crept onto Riark's face.

'The woodcutter is very near to his fleeing family now. They travel with refugees from the Hinterland and the shipwrecked crew from one of your vessels. Perhaps they will be reunited soon.'

'You know all this?' she said.

'We are anywhere there is a tree at one time or another,' he replied.

She thought momentarily and words sprang from her lips.

'Would the trees know anything of Lord Lachlan?'

Riark shook his head and the vines of his mane flicked back and forth.

'Not as of yet. The eyes of the forest have not looked for him.'

Cathryn nodded and looked up to the Maw Gate. She felt overwhelmed, as though she was attempting to solve a puzzle that kept extending itself beyond solution. She was beginning to understand Lachlan's desire to flee. But no, she wasn't like him and even considering it strengthened her. She straightened up and looked Riark in the eye.

'We will put an end to the destruction of your forests, King Riark, if you will help me to secure peace in these lands and safeguard them while they recover, acting as watchers on our behalf? Your forest can spread and extend all the way down to the Folly as far as I am concerned, as weregild for all your losses.'

Riark thought for a moment and began to nod slowly.

'What would you have us do?'

'If you could send word of Lord Lachlan if you hear anything of him, I would appreciate it. I would have you inform Lord Aldwyn of our treaty and tell him to return to Oystercatcher Bay. I will meet him there and together we will set sail to deal with Lord Linwood.'

'And how will I vouch for your orders, Queen?' creaked Riark.

Cathryn thought for a moment and said,

'Ask him if he has heard any mermaids sing, as they once did outside the Folly walls.'

Chapter Sixteen

In the north of the forest, Lord Linwood and Lady Isobel had ordered the retreat, and all of his people were either out of the forest or were travelling to do so.

To the south only the refugees and Morrick were still in the forest. The woodcutter ran westward in the sinister, dim light under the canopy.

This is no use.

His foot snarled under an up-thrust loop of root. He yelped and threw out his hands automatically. They delved deep into the mud and a sharp pain shot through Morrick's right palm. Upon raising his hand, he saw blood was flowing and mingling with the slick dirt where the flint had lacerated his skin. He stayed on his knees, looked at his hand for a moment then up at the trees. A gust of wind made them sway sideways, but in his irritation, Morrick took it as an amused shrug of the shoulders as though the forest was suppressing a laugh. He cursed and regained his feet, but any impulse to continue onwards had been replaced by rage. He roared his frustration into the sky until all the breath was gone from his lungs then paced a tight circle in the tall undergrowth as the birds twittered uselessly above him.

'Fuck!' he exalted and leant against the tree. As his heart slowed, he could hear better and the babble of a brook sounded not far off to the west. He shoved off from the tree against which he had been leaning and stalked in the direction of the sound, hoping to quench his thirst.

Even under his dark cloud the brook, with bluebells growing upon the far

178

bank, was a welcome sight. A cluster of midges balled above the surface water pooling on the rocks nearest him and he walked a little south to kneel at the water's edge. He sipped from his cupped hands and enjoyed the cool sensation in his throat.

A twig snapped behind him and the sound of feet squelching in the mud made him turn fast, fumbling for the hatchet on his belt as he did so.

A Dryad stood behind him at a distance of some feet away, hands unclenched and hanging by its wooden hips. A further two Dryads were in the process of emerging from a willow a little further back.

Morrick did not try to speak, but fell back on his hands, which plunged into the brook and slipped away from under him on the mossy pebbles. He called out and his head and shoulders slipped back into the water. Morrick thrashed about, trying to get some sort of purchase and after a moment, he managed to throw his arms around a larger stone and kneel in the middle of the brook. The Dryads moved to the water edge.

Morrick began to slide, painlessly in the moment, on his knees across the brook towards the far side.

'Well met,' he stuttered.

The Dryads inclined their heads and as one, offered but one slow, solemn nod by way of an answer.

The lead Dryad's face seemed to contort and a mouth appeared violently on its face as though it had been rent open by the stroke of an axe. Its voice was choked and lacked finesse of approximation when it emerged from that inexpert slash.

'King Riark has spoken with your queen. All who wander the forest are in violation of the law, both ours and that of your people. The punishment for violation is destruction.'

All three Dryads nodded once more, meagre sunlight dancing across their faces. They did nothing more and seemed to be awaiting a reply, but before Morrick could give them what they wanted, a new voice chimed from behind him, deeper than the babble of the brook, but similar as though it had struck off on a new, deeper course.

'Those who were already in the forest were to be given time to leave.

Besides, this man knew not of the command and I will vouch for him. Speak with Riark. He has an interest in this human.'

Morrick started and turned towards the voice.

A shimmering figure stood beside him in the water, but began only at the waist in the shallow water - a sure impossibility as far as the woodcutter could see. The figure was translucent and seemed to be supplied by the water of the brook, which seemed to course upwards and over it. The water rushed over the Naiad's shoulders and down across insubstantial and intangible breasts before continuing its original path downstream. It was as though she was a ghost standing upon the bed of the brook, and the water had given her shape by filling the void of her presence, rather than breaking against her. The Naiad's face was utterly featureless, but Morrick could distinguish blue eyes beneath the churning surface.

The Dryads did not exchange any obvious communication, but Morrick saw tendrils of roots curling together around their feet as they nodded, their eyes moving between the Naiad and himself in the eerie silence. Their heads did not move at all and he was caught in the midst of a forbidding staring match.

'Very well,' said the lead Dryad, 'See that he does not part your company until he has left the trees.'

The Naiad rose taller in the water, gliding upwards and changing the note of the waterfall that fell from her shoulders and brow.

'Do not forget that this is a shared domain, people of the trees. The trees may cluster hereabouts, but the rivers sate their thirsts. No harm will come to this man, if he leaves my company or otherwise.'

The Dryads looked down as all of their roots thrust deeper. Morrick thought their faces became drawn momentarily and then recovered. After a few moments, the lead Dryad nodded.

'Riark takes no issue and will seek you both out in time. He has business with the woodcutter.'

They tarried there no longer. The Dryads turned and sunk back into the trunk of the willow, then were no more.

For Morrick, still sitting in the stream leaning back on his hands like some sort of dishevelled crab, the spell holding him in place now broke. He found his feet and stumbled up to the bank. Once there he felt torn between getting away from this creature in the water and backing up to the very trees from which the Dryads had appeared.

The figure in the water turned its face towards him and regarded him silently. He stared back for a moment, but was unnerved by the nothingness in the Naiad's face. She tilted her head and when she spoke, her words chimed with the babble of the stream.

'Do you know me?' she asked, quiet and curious. Morrick thought she sounded like a child. Despite a feeling of familiarity for which he could not account, he shook his head slowly.

'Unless I am mistaken, we have not met before,' he said. 'Am I mistaken?'

The Naiad's laugh tinkled and her form sank back into the water until only her head and shoulders were visible. She said no more on it. Morrick began to shiver and as she noticed, the Naiad flowed towards him.

'I need to build a fire to get warm and dry my clothes. Night is drawing in,' he said.

The Naiad said nothing. Her head bobbed above the surface of the stream looking somewhat like a curious seal in the ocean. Just as Morrick was about to bid her farewell and to attempt to move on, she spoke.

'What brings you to the forest?' she said in that same curious tone.

'My home is…' he started, but the Naiad interrupted.

'I know who you are and where you made your home. I wish to know why you are in the forest and travelling into the west, away from your home.'

Morrick frowned.

'I've returned home from the war and found my home has been attacked by Devised. I believe my wife and three children fled into the woods, for they were not among the fallen.'

The Naiad disappeared beneath the water in a sudden motion and the water frothed, bubbling to the bank. To Morrick's eye, it appeared to rear up and thrash down on itself for a moment before once again the Naiad emerged. She walked towards the bank until her whole shimmering, translucent form was standing before him. Morrick's eyes widened as he saw little fish swimming within her torso then escaping down through her legs and on into the stream. She stepped up onto the grassy bank and placed her hands on Morrick's shoulders. He took a sharp intake of breath at the stream's chill as it ran through his body.

'A group did pass this way.'

Morrick locked eyes with the suspended blue marbles, spinning in the churning surface of the Naiad's face and thought he saw pity in them.

'Were my…?'

The Naiad pulled him close and he gasped again as he felt his chest and face sink beneath the surface of her form. He turned his face aside as the water filled his nose and mouth. He sputtered and coughed, but she made no apology.

'Your wife and two sons were with her. All unhurt,' she said. Morrick could feel her pull him close as she spoke, trying to offer comfort but without the form that could provide it. Her words kindled understanding of the gesture and he froze.

'And my baby?'

The Naiad held him tighter.

'Do you not know me?' she said.

Morrick drew back and in so doing, once more caught his foot and ended up on his rump in the dirt. He looked up at the Naiad, but she drew closer and crouched down to him.

'Father,' was all she said and all he could do was stare back at her, understanding little and believing less. He struggled to find a reply, but could think of nothing to say. What was happening? Could it be true? It couldn't and yet, that feeling of familiarity…

'I don't understand,' he said.

'Nor do I, in full,' she said. 'I was your daughter in my last life, Morrick. Not so anymore, I think. And yet when I saw the one who sired me chasing through the trees, some sense of loyalty stirred in me.'

'Your last life?' asked Morrick.

The Naiad paused.

Morrick got to his knees and pushed himself back up to his feet.

'If what you say is true and my family are fleeing in the woods, we must catch up with them. How far behind am I?'

A brow emerged and somehow darkened the Naiad's face.

'I will not assist you in this matter. She does not deserve your loyalty or mine.'

'She's my wife and your mother. What…' but Morrick stopped short and stood aghast at the realisation he had accepted the Naiad was indeed his daughter. He was caught between a fierce desire to press on, the need to dry out and a sudden need to be with this strange, yet beautiful creature. He reached out for her and ran his fingertips gently across the surface of the pool of her cheeks. He perceived that she was smiling and a cold hand gripped his heart.

'What is all this?' he whispered. 'What happened to you?'

The Naiad nuzzled against his hand then drew away and offered a hand.

'It matters not,' she said and her voice was sad and low. Her chill hand caressed his cheek, and she looked deep into his eyes so that he was held in thrall.

'Already I begin to forget what I was and what I have seen. I fear you will be disappointed at the end of your journey, but I can no longer tell why. I have only the sense of it.'

She pulled him close and once more he felt the curious sensation of being drawn beneath the boundary of her body. Wonder mingled with the sense that he was saying a last goodbye to the baby daughter he had never had the chance to know.

Finally she released him and stepped back, looking down to where her feet should have stood on the bed of the stream.

'My kind are aware of many things wherever water flows, seeps and sleeps. Riark is coming now. I will leave you for now, Father. I hope that in time we will see each other again. I have secured you safe passage, for now at the least, and having seen you in this life, I will not now forget you.'

Before ever Morrick had the chance to reply her form dropped away into the water and was swept downstream. Morrick was left standing dripping on the bank with only birdsong and the babble of the brook to accompany him.

Sighing and feeling too exhausted to spend any more time thinking about what had passed, Morrick turned towards the south west and set off again through the trees at a light jog. Tired though he was, the exertion kept his mind clear from ruminating on what had befallen Rowan, Callum, Declan and his baby daughter. His damp clothes clung to his skin and he wondered how far he would have to run before they were dry again and if that would be before the cold of night began to chill him to the bone.

Morrick ran with his eyes down, watching his ever more unsteady footing and so he did not immediately notice when the confusion of the trees gave way into a glade. A few paces in, he looked up and stopped sharp at the change of the light.

Seated upon a boulder in the centre of the glade was a figure cloaked in leaves with a long tendril beard. His skin was rough as bark, and he frowned under mossy brows. At first glance, Morrick thought the bearded figure was holding a staff, but later as they spoke, he realised that the hand and the staff were one. A tall crown of spindles pulsed upwards from the figure's head. The figure beckoned with one hand and, after but a moment's hesitation, Morrick approached. He folded his arms across his chest as he did so, straightening his back as he walked. His heart rate quickened.

He stopped a few yards away from the figure, which merely stayed hunched on the rock and stared at him.

'Do you know who I am?' it creaked.

Morrick nodded slowly.

'King Riark of the Dryads,' he said, marvelling at how many nobles had been in his proximity over the previous weeks.

The figure nodded once slowly in return. It looked an awkward, jerky motion at first and then, as though its head had somehow detached, the movement became fluid and more animal.

'Riark of the Dryads,' the Dryad confirmed. 'You wonder what business we might have together?'

Morrick nodded then steeled himself.

'I do, but I have pressing business myself. My wife and children are not so very far ahead of me heading for the coast, or so I believe. I must intercept them before they move beyond my reach.'

Riark tilted his head.

'You are concerned for your family, of course. I am able to speak to them on your behalf, should you wish it. My kind travel faster than you can imagine. I am as I appear, but much more.'

Morrick took a step forward.

'If you could tell them that Morrick is alive and close behind them. And enquire after their health, situation and intentions? And bid them wait for me at the coast?' Then he added as an afterthought, propriety remembered, 'If you please, Sire.'

Riark stood up fast in a movement that his elderly appearance made seem unlikely.

'I will do so and then return. Perhaps then we can set your mind at ease and take leisure over other matters, though perhaps leisure is the wrong word, considering the gravity of the situation.'

The cloak of leaves shuddered as though caught by a gust of wind then fell to the ground, but as it did so, Riark's form diminished and seemed to draw into the staff in his hand. Then the hand was gone and the staff began to shrink as though sucked into the ground. Within a second there was no sign of the Dryad. Morrick paced back and forth across the glade, his heart beating fast and his mind whirling. He could not rest with such a flurry of thoughts in his mind.

Time wore on and he began to shiver, but considering who could appear at any time, he thought it best not to burn any wood. Instead he took off each item of clothing and wrung it out to get it just as dry as he could manage. That done, he stole Riark's seat upon the boulder. The sun was directly above him - he closed his eyes and shaded them with his arm.

Morrick awoke with a pain in his back and shoulder. He groaned as he shifted onto his elbows and sat up. Riark was standing in the glade before him. He seemed to have taken root and stood straight with his head bowed, the beard and his hair sweeping the ground like a willow. His arms hung down and the fingers had grown so long that their tips were obscured by the long grass. He raised his head, and the fingers drew back to manlike proportions.

'I have conveyed your message,' said Riark.

'Are they safe?' said Morrick shifting so that he was perched on the very edge of the rock. 'Are they well?'

Riark nodded.

'Your wife tells me your sons are well enough. But a malady has fallen over your wife. She grieves the loss of your daughter. She would not speak to me of you and did not acknowledge your survival. The group she is with are heading for the coast, just as you thought. I am sure your sons wish you well and anticipate your arrival when the time comes.' Riark was about to continue, but saw that Morrick was frowning deeply.

'She would not speak of me? For why?' he asked, his voice low.

'I know not,' said Riark, 'All will become clear, no doubt.'

Morrick sensed that there was more to be said but that the Dryad was holding back. He spent a few more minutes asking pressing questions but it became apparent Riark would say no more. Morrick was weighing up whether to honour his word and stay or commence his journey, when Riark drew in close and sat beside him on the rock.

'Though we have never met, I have long known of you and your kin,' said Riark. 'I have watched you boy and man, cutting down trees in my realm where it meets yours. You have killed Dryads in your time, woodcutter; hewn down their Mother Trees so that their spirits were cut loose and their souls died.'

To Morrick, the words sounded horrifying.

'I am dreadful sorry,' he said, 'I had no notion of it. I hope you know it to be true that I always paid the Forest a great respect, planting one for every one I felled. It does not sound as though it would ever replace your loss, but it was well intentioned none the less. Timber and woodcraft has long been my life; carving it, shaping it and making use of it; building from it. I am heartfelt sorry,' he repeated.

Riark tilted his head again in the way Morrick had seen before, as though curious.

'You were not to know, and it's not our way to tell. There is a fate for all things and nature requires consumption and rebirth,' he said. 'There has been much debate over the centuries as to whether man's consumption has been disproportionate but I have resigned myself to our losses over the years and held my people at bay from acting, though it has not been easily achievable when dealing with our younger folk. But times are changing and my control, though still full for now, may wane.

'It is for this reason that I come to you now; for counsel from one I know to be a man considerate of both his own needs and that of the forest. And a man of war, so it seems.'

'Reluctantly. I did not go by choice,' said Morrick.

'Tell me,' said Riark.

'There's not a great deal to tell. I can't be sure of how long ago, but I lived by the Forest edge and made my living there. My wife, Rowan, was newly pregnant with our third child who I have found of late was a daughter. Awgren's Devised came to take the latest load of timber from us, and the overseer gathered all the people in the village together to tell us all the menfolk of a certain age would go to war. Thank the Forest that my boys were too young. If we'd resisted they'd have killed our families and so all of us that were to go bade farewell and were marched off south, taking what provision we could. We were outfitted in a barracks near the mountains. As the weeks wore on, we heard that the queen of the Combined People and Lord of the Isles had marched an army out of the Folly gates and landed two more on the south and west coasts, all marching inland. We heard tell the battles did not go well for Awgren and that mankind had mastered war in new ways he could not so easily counter by weight of numbers. We were thrown into battle after battle and though the cause was not just, I am proud of all we accomplished together to survive, though I was not glad to hurt my own kind.

'Many of us survived. We fought long and hard and were bloodied for it. Then the last battle when the Combined People won through and I thought, in my foolishness, that all would be righted and I could return to my family in peace. As it is, they burned the Devised who surrendered, and I was given the brand you see now across my face. Rather than be allowed straight home,

I've been conscripted into yet another army, the one that now sits in my old home under the command of Lord Aldwyn. To be fair to him, he seems a good enough man, but my dreams of freedom and peace seem to have been naïve. My home is likely burned to ash and my family flee. And you say my wife will not speak of me…'

Riark sat quietly and showed no signs of movement as he perched upon the log. Morrick kept flitting his eyes back to Riark, his peripheral vision shifting every so often in its perception of him as an old man of bark, then a discarded branch laying against the log, then a manlike figure once again.

Eventually, Riark animated once more and turned to him.

'What think you will happen now with your people?'

'My people? They are killed or scattered and our homes burned or occupied.'

'Not simply your village; your people, your kind?'

'Humans?' Morrick balked at the notion that they were all one.

'In all honesty, I cannot now tell. There are peaceable parts to the world, so I hear, but given how I have been treated so far, I'm not sure I would want to live there. And the lords and ladies have already started fighting amongst themselves. I begin to think we were better under Awgren,' he said and felt ashamed for saying so.

'Do you know of Lord Linwood and the road into the forest?'

'I know Linwood. He branded me. And Lord Aldwyn told me of his plans. For my part, I believe the lord and queen will take Linwood in hand and leave your forest alone.'

'And yet they will pass on in a blink of an eye,' said Riark, 'replaced by their children and their children's children. How long before another sees the value of the forest?'

'Who can say?' said Morrick.

The two of them sat in silent contemplation for a while then Morrick articulated all he had been thinking.

'What are Dryads?' he asked, as simply as he wondered.

Riark threw back his head and looked up at the stars which were now beginning to appear in the new night.

'That will take some time to tell.'

The king of the Dryads stood and reached out a hand towards Morrick to help him to his feet.

'We will walk together while you are in my realm. You will be safe, and perhaps we can be of use to one another.'

Chapter Seventeen

Belman had known a fair few brothels in his time but not many that had been the site of such obvious carnage.

The Whoreswood had an ethereal quality, at the same time dank, dark and luminous. The trees were old, twisted, black and close-packed, yet paths wound their way around them and the way was lit by small candle-lamps hung in the lower branches of the trees.

At first this was all Lachlan, Hadwyn and Belman could see besides the usual sights in woodland, but within minutes, when behind them all they could see were trees they had already passed, with no glimpse of the outside world, they came across their first dead man. It was Hadwyn who caught sight of him in the brush, off to the side of the path, lantern light shining white on his pale flesh.

'Over here,' he hissed. Lachlan and Belman followed, and the three men stood looking down at the fallen soldier. He had been dead a few days, as far as they could tell. He was partly eaten, and his empty eye sockets stared up into the trees. If he had been carrying anything, his body had been robbed of it. Here was an empty vessel frozen in the last memory of a painful death, all too apparent from the gaping wound in his left side and a smaller wound in the neck.

'What do you make of it?' asked Belman to nobody in particular.

'I think the ladies of the wood are not to be trifled with,' said Hadwyn. Lachlan said nothing, merely thinking that the ladies must be a sight to behold if being with them could cost so much.

'Do you know much of them?' asked Belman, shifting nervously from foot to foot, 'We are only three, after all.'

Hadwyn smiled and tousled his hair.

'I have finally seen everything! The great Lord Belman, slayer of Devised, who stood nigh at hand watching my back in the midst of our enemies, quakes now in fear at the doorstep of prostitutes.'

'Not prostitutes,' replied Lachlan, fast and low. 'At least, not *just* prostitutes.'

He walked back to the path, looking all about him for signs of movement.

'I should have paid more heed to my tutors,' muttered Belman.

'More heed? You paid any heed?' laughed Hadwyn.

They once again followed the path lit by the lanterns.

'Did you at least hear of the Partisans of Crinan?' asked Lachlan, not turning back.

Belman and Hadwyn exchanged a look as they walked behind him. Much of the humour seemed to be leaving Lachlan the deeper they went into the Whoreswood; the two men were feeling a darkening of tone within their company.

'The fighting clans?'

'Indeed, the fighting clans. What do you know?'

Belman thought for a moment.

'That they rose up against the last king of Crinan and travelled the wild places in secret, striking where he was weakest; a law unto themselves.'

'True enough. And when Awgren came out of the wastes, a law unto themselves they may have been, but the Partisans rallied together and fought by skirmish against him. When King Abernath sounded the retreat, the Partisans protected the rear as the armies fled south. When they reached the Maw Gate, the Partisan men packed their women and children into their wagons, sent them on to safety, but stayed to fight with sword, knife and fist, whip and garrotte against the Creatures of the Devising. They refused to retreat even after the bravest warriors of the three kingdoms left the battle. Even the king of Tayne retreated into the Folly before the Partisans' last stand was done.

'The gates closed, not to open again for many centuries, and the Partisans' charred bones were ground into the surface of the road to the Maw Gate.'

Lord Lachlan stopped and turned, brooding, to look at Belman and Hadwyn.

'We owe our lives and our victory to the ancestors of the people who live within this wood. I want you to carry that with you.'

'Aye, my lord,' said Belman. He hesitated and then went on, 'So how do we come to be calling them whores?'

Lachlan turned and carried on walking.

'The womenfolk who survived have made their choices over the years, and who are we to judge? But it is clear that they are still a people not to be trifled with and the price to engage their services could well be the highest, as our friend back there would attest.'

With that he would say no more and they travelled on in silence into the glow of the lanterns, feeling ever more watched.

A bell rang out at head height just off the path, and Lachlan jumped. As he did so, his feet became tangled, and he flailed about to regain his balance. Looking down he saw that he had unwittingly kicked a tripwire.

'They know we're coming now, it seems,' said Hadwyn. Belman half drew his sword, but Lachlan shook his head.

'We proceed with caution, but do not act threatening. These are still my people, after all.'

'*Your* people, are we?' A woman stepped out from behind the tree even as the bell still rang out amongst the branches. She lifted a horn to her lips and blew. A great blast issued forth, and Lachlan knew that her people were warned. The woman dropped the horn.

'I don't know your faces,' she said, standing beneath a lantern. Lachlan's eyes began to adjust. The woman stood taller than he. She wore a leather corset that displayed her ample bosom, across which were tattooed tally marks, criss-crossing black lines counting some unknown score.

Fallen foes or lovers? wondered Hadwyn.

She wore leather breeches and boots that came up to mid-thigh. Her woollen coat hung to her ankles, and it had a high collar that framed her long, pale neck. Her jaw was sharp and her nose somewhat upturned. Her skin was pale, Lachlan supposed, from a life sheltered under the trees. Her hair was long but stacked in elaborate patterns, pinned, tied and plaited, coursing in places and taut in others. She carried no obvious weaponry, but a crossbow was leant against the tree next to a small, round, targe shield. She spoke again, confident,

'I know not your face and yet I am one of your people?'

Lachlan bowed his head.

'You have caught me unawares with my tongue unguarded, lady,' he said.

She laughed.

'There are worse things than a man with an unguarded tongue.'

'A married man with an unguarded tongue?' Hadwyn ventured, smirking.

'I've not known *that* to be a barrier, in truth,' she said.

'Do you have business with my ladies?'

'I may do. To whom do I speak?' said Lachlan.

'Think it's only right that those who come a-knocking put names to faces first. I don't know how it is under your roof, friend.'

'These are not whores to take lightly,' whispered Belman.

'Nor is it polite to speak hushed and secret,' the woman warned, planting her hands on her hips. Lachlan could not tell if the gesture was meant to be alluring or threatening. He decided both, and a stirring in his groin confirmed at least half of the assertion.

'We've travelled out of the south, lady. We are on serious business, and I'd rather not discuss it on the path.'

From behind the woman by the bell tree, another six drew close, though these wore their arms openly. All were tall and easy on the eye, having chosen their apparel with both appeal and armour in mind. They looked like a grim band, and Lachlan saw in them the resolve of the Partisans in the tales he learned as a boy. Nevertheless, he knew to be cautious, as the ladies had a fearsome reputation for brutal retribution and swift justice as they deemed it.

The lady turned to consult with the newcomers then delivered her decision.

'As you're speaking half-frankly and you're all strapping lads, we'd be happy to bring you further into our woods. If you're lucky and…' she looked them each up and down, 'maybe if we're lucky too, we can conduct our usual business when the serious stuff is done; if you can best us of course.'

Belman forgot his propriety as prurient interest took hold.

'Best you?'

'Aye.' A blonde woman, coming up from behind the first, grinned. 'None lies with a lady of the Whoreswood lest he can best her in combat and steal her honour.'

The bell tree woman's face cracked into a smile.

'But never fear; you'll be bested when we wrestle betwixt the sheets. Prove your manhood or lose it. Win our hearts on the battlefield and willingly lose the battle in the bed.'

Lachlan's cheeks flushed, and the other two men exchanged a look with raised eyebrows and barely suppressed smiles.

The band traipsed on after the women as they cut across country, abandoning the lantern-lit path to hurry through the grass, between bushes and darting between the trees until more distant light appeared ahead.

Lachlan spied the sides of what appeared at first to be wagons but soon became clearer as wooden caravans. Since he was young he had been told stories of these folk, and he was a little disappointed to find that these appeared to be plain, oiled wood with no designs. He watched the fearsome women who walked in front of him and lamented the fact that in this realm he and Cathryn commanded, function had negated beauty in many ways. Once more he felt that familiar ice-hand wrapped around his heart and wondered for what they had been fighting all these centuries – a world devoid of individuality and character?

A glade was encircled with these wagons, their entrances pointing towards the centre of the circle where a bonfire was burning. Horses wandered just outside the circle and animals wandered here and there. Each caravan's porch was stacked with plates, bowls, bottles, weapons and was lit by a lantern. At the foot of its steps, a few yards away, a ring of benches formed an inner circle so that upon them one might sit and stare into the flames in the middle of the wide space.

The women trooped on and filed away to their caravans, but the lady from the bell tree addressed Lachlan and his companions.

'We are a little early for tonight's contest, so there is some time to talk if you have other business, travellers from the south. I must warn you that my mother is not well, but we will do her the courtesy of talking in her caravan.'

'Do you have no menfolk about?' said Belman, scanning the camp.

'Our brothers and sons go out in the world. It would not be good for business to have them around.' She gave a wry smile. 'Who knows about our fathers? They could be any man who passes this way by night and triumphs in the contest.'

Belman raised his eyebrows, whistled and the bell tree woman led them across the circle and towards a caravan.

'My name is Habit,' she said, the words tossed back over her shoulder, enjoying the certain knowledge that the eyes of the men behind her were following the exaggerated sway of her hips.

Upon reaching the caravan she ascended the steps and rapped three times on the door.

'Ella,' she called.

There was a shuffling inside and then bolts were drawn back on the door. Moans came from inside and though Belman's ears initially pricked up, it soon became apparent they were of pain or discomfort, not pleasure. A young girl pushed the door open, and after an exchange of words, she nodded and ducked out to allow the newcomers entry. Habit ushered Lachlan in first, and he entered the dim light of the caravan. Ahead of him stood a wide bunk, and the air smelled foul. A woman thrashed and moaned on the bed, covered by a thin grey blanket. Her head was shaved and her frame was thin and frail. Her face contorted as she turned and made eye contact with Lachlan, but still her limbs flailed.

'Good evening, madam,' said Lachlan, feeling he wanted to look anywhere but into her eyes, yet doing so anyway. Hadwyn and Belman followed his lead, but after a few moments, Hadwyn said, 'There is little space for five, Brother. Belman and I will wait outside if the lady approves?'

Habit shot them a knowing look and showed them out, pulling the door closed behind them so the room was lit only by candles.

She moved over to her mother's side and picked up a bowl. Carefully she began to feed her using a narrow wooden spoon. She never took her eyes from her mother as she spoke.

'This man travels from the south and says he may have business with us, Mother.'

Now she looked to Lachlan.

'You have an unusual bearing and have the look of a man from the Isles. I've been with a few in my time, but not many. Still, they were memorable. Your apparel is less…militant than folk wear in the Drift.'

'You see much, lady,' said Lachlan.

'And now you are under my mother's roof, perhaps you can tell us who you are.'

'First I must tell you what I know of your people.'

'G'ahead, sir.' Her eyes blazed with curiosity.

'I know that the Partisans of Crinan were free folk and under the sway of no man. I know that when Awgren rose, they fought hard to withstand his might and paid a great cost. I know that in the end, the Partisans who had been deemed traitors came to be some of the most loyal to mankind.'

'Kind words.'

'But do they still apply?'

Habit's mother spluttered and food ran down her chin. Habit reached for a rag and wiped it away. She stroked her mother's hair.

'Enough for now?' she smiled at her.

'This is our family's curse – one in two of the daughters in my mother's line are struck down with the Daughter's Blight. It's said even those who first came to these shores were thus afflicted.'

Habit fixed Lachlan with her gaze, candlelight dancing across her face.

'Much is passed down in the blood. Though of course it would be a lie to say that those who survived remained entirely unchanged, but still, much about us endures.'

'And what of your honour? Can I trust to your word?'

'Question it, and I'll question your need for blood in your veins, sir,' she snarled.

Lachlan smiled and raised both open hands to pacify her.

'I will take you into my confidence if I can trust your word and hold you to it,' he said.

'You've my word and that of my mother.'

Lachlan took a deep breath and instantly regretted it. The smell in the caravan was oppressive; it spoke of incontinence and illness. But he had experienced much worse on the battlefield and worse still in the tents of healing after battles.

'I am Lord Lachlan of the Isles,' he said, 'and I believe the realm to once more be in peril.' He worried that he sounded over-pompous in his attempt to sound more lordly than was his custom, but Habit showed no signs of discomfort.

Habit narrowed her eyes as she scrutinised his face and re-crossed her legs.

'Lord Lachlan?' she squinted at him.

'The same,' he replied. 'Consort of Queen Cathryn and fresh from victory in the south.'

'So we'd heard. The soldiers newly returned are full of stories of the glory of the queen and her lords. But what proof that you are the man himself?'

'My seal and my word. The men outside are Lord Hadwyn, my brother and Lord Belman, one of my generals.'

Habit scratched her temple and swept loose strands of hair behind her ears.

'And what would bring you gents north, if this be true. The warm, wet wiles of the Whoreswood? I think not.'

Lachlan was about to answer, but Habit reached up to fetch a bottle down from a shelf.

'Wine?' she asked.

'I wouldn't turn it down,' he replied.

'Why you speak so fancy? What's wrong with a simple yes?' she scolded, laughing. 'Keep your graces for your lady-missus, lord.' She handed him a goblet and returned to her seat.

'What would Queen Cathryn make of her husband skulking around with Partisans and whores?'

'The queen trusts my judgement and knows all too well she owes her realm to your ancestors. But I'd like to think even Queen Cathryn is not beyond a little jealousy at seeing her husband associating with one as comely and pleasing to the eye as yourself.'

'Oh is that the case? Be mindful now or I'll be facing off against ye in the circle before the moon is full tonight. Never had me a Lord of the Isles before. Lord of the Drift maybe.'

'Linwood?' Lachlan near spat out his first mouthful of wine, and Habit's face lit up as she grinned.

'Jealous? Or just not into sloppy seconds, lord,' she teased.

'What do you make of the man?'

Habit lifted her cup to her mother's lips and poured a bead of wine into her mouth.

'Just for the taste. She does not drink well. Not so easy to swallow water or wine these days.'

The woman on the bunk flicked her face away to the wall and back again, staring at Lachlan imploringly, he judged, though he could not discern her desire.

'Thank you for taking me into your home, madam,' he said, feeling the words sounded artificial. He could not feel less comfortable in the presence of this woman and yet she was one of his subjects and of a bold line, for sure. Perhaps in his youth he would have dismissed her, but Cathryn's influence on him was marked.

She made no reply, but her arm flailed out towards him and he took her hand, stroking the back of it with her thumb.

When he looked up, Habit appeared serious. He did not release her mother's hand.

'Lord Linwood? He's harsh and cold. Single-minded. Runs the Drift so that all have enough and if it comes to defending what they's got, they can do it. Doesn't bandy much with us, except to meet his manly needs where his mistresses ain't cutting it,' she said. 'What do you want to know?'

'You know of the road building?'

'Aye, all round here do. And the new villages he's building. Not with his own hands, of course.'

Lachlan marvelled that he had not heard of it in the Isles. There must been some loyalty for the man if no word had escaped his lands. No tyrant inspires so much fear that nobody rebels.

'I've reason to believe he may turn against the Combined People, against the queen and I. To sunder what was brought together.'

Habit shrugged.

'We always stood apart as you know, lord. May be truth in it. Whoever is content with their lot? Awgren is gone, so why should Linwood not want what's his.'

'The queen and I have already granted him his old lands and made him a duke so he can self-govern. But I fear that will not be enough. For my part, I wish nothing more than to restore peace to our lands and return to my home in the Isles. But being ruler means planting hedges against those who would bring future discord. You understand? I am here to judge the peril – I know he has already concealed his true intentions.'

Habit shrugged again.

'I could not speak any sense of what Lord Linwood wants. But I know the people here are loyal to you both, so who knows how it would turn should weapons be drawn. I would tread careful, my lord. I would say the rulers in the Folly have been too distant, and I would not think it uncommon that many think the Drift should rule itself; that times have moved on.'

Lachlan nodded, thinking he probably agreed and that perhaps Cathryn stood alone on this issue.

A bell chimed. Then another of a different note. And another. One for each caravan in the clearing.

Habit stood up.

'Time for the contest. Come…will you watch or take part, lord?'

Lachlan did not answer. He followed Habit out into the clearing. He saw that a woman stood by each of their caravans, ringing bells. The benches around the bonfire were filling with men in varying attire of varying age from young boy to old man. Belman and Hadwyn were already on the bench in front of him, and Lachlan joined them.

The bells continued to ring as more men gathered, first sitting on the benches and when they were full, standing behind them or sitting before them on the grass.

Habit fetched her bell and went to stand before her own caravan. Lachlan could hear bells ringing from the distance and wondered how many such glades there were within the Whoreswood.

The bells stopped ringing.

The Partisan women entered the circle and stood with their backs to the bonfire, singing and dancing around it. The men watched, enthralled, and Lachlan found himself evaluating the women, deciding who he would bed given the chance and the freedom to do so.

A woman stood forward and walked the circle alone, making eye contact with some from every bench.

'Who stands forth to steal my warrior honour?' she cried and drew two knives.

There was jostling on some benches, fuelled by drink perhaps, and there was awed hush over others, but within a second three men were on their feet.

'Sister!' cried the woman, and Habit plucked a knife from her belt at the small of her back and tossed it to the woman. She in turn strode towards the men and handed each of them a knife.

'Last man standing,' she said quietly and seated herself in one of their places. The men either side of her shuffled up to give her space.

The three men formed a triangle, facing each other. Two of them were similarly attired in the military garb of Stragglers' Drift, brawny men and tall. The third was in finer clothing, though not fine as such. He did not adopt a fighting stance, but his eyes were keen and flitted between the two soldiers.

One soldier, bearded, burst forward, roaring at his comrade who settled his weight into a comfortable stance to receive him. The bearded soldier checked his charge and darted sideways at the man in fine clothes, who dodged aside. Lachlan's saw the man grab the soldier's wrist as he moved out of the way.

Fast, he thought.

And he did not stop there; the man in fine clothes twirled low and slashed once at the other soldier's belly, though as a threat not an attack. The soldier jumped backwards and exchanged a glance with his bearded comrade. They seemed to evaluate the threat and together they ganged up on him. The man in fine clothes was swift on his feet and dextrous. He darted, stabbed and slashed. He grabbed limbs and dealt many wounds that bled on the soldiers' arms. But, ere long, the bearded man seized him from behind, clamping his arms to his sides. The other soldier drove his knife into the man's throat, but then, like a scorpion strikes, he shoved the dying man backwards so the bearded soldier was off-balance. As he staggered, the other soldier advanced, kicked him in the shin and seized his beard. The bearded soldier slashed upwards and hewed the blade across the other soldier's wrist. Lachlan winced and the crowd let out a gasp as the blood began to pour. The wounded man struck out with his left and caught the bearded man's face. He buried his knife in his eye and the big man fell back, joining the other dying man on the grass. Then, staggering at first, the last man standing also fell in the grass.

The girl stood from the bench.

'My honour is intact tonight it seems and yet I keep my fee!' she shouted. 'Clumsy fighters and unworthy, but I thank them for the coins.'

A round of reluctant applause started as she returned to her sisters and colleagues by the fire.

Habit stood forward.

'Have we all turned coward, or does any man stand forward to steal my warrior honour?' she cried, taking out a knife and retrieving her other one from the bearded man's eye.

Lachlan stood and strode out.

'My lord!' called Hadwyn.

'No, my lord,' shouted Belman and got to his feet.

'Sit down,' said Lachlan.

Habit strode forward, threatening Lachlan with the point of one knife.

'No man may sit once he has presented the challenge!'

'That man does not present the challenge.'

'He does,' said Belman.

'You'll have to kill each other, you fool!' hissed Hadwyn.

'It is done!' said Habit. 'You will both fight for the privilege of fighting me.'

Others may well have planned on standing, but at this outburst, all were stilled. Hadwyn shifted in his seat but rather than stand he called out,

'This is Lord Lachlan, Lord of the Isles and ruler of these lands. You will do as he bids!'

A gasp went up and even shouts of recognition, for many of the men were recently returned from the war themselves. Cries of support arose, but Habit shouted them all down.

'*No* man is lord in the Whoreswood while the contest plays out! You will fight, or I will muster the ladies and all will be killed. If you are indeed lords, you will honour this place of worship.'

Lachlan sighed.

'Very well. Belman, you have my thanks and my apology.' He walked into the space between the bench and the fire then turned back to his friend who stood, baffled and conflicted before him – his attempt to save his lord having now turned sour.

Lachlan drew his sword and reluctantly, Belman mirrored him.

'I'm sorry, my lord.'

Lachlan shook his head and waved the other man's concerns away.

'Must it be to the death?' he asked Habit.

'Nay, to defeat,' she said and with that Lachlan felt the weight lift.

'Very well!' he said and ran towards Belman. Belman steadied himself and watched the lord's shoulders, knowing from experience that watching the eyes or the sword could mislead. He lifted his sword, and Lachlan brought his blade down upon it. It scraped off Belman's weapon to the right, leaving the general free to whip his arm round and immediately strike at Lachlan's side. Lachlan brought his blade to the vertical, parried and pushed back so Belman was off-balance. Belman wheeled away and, recovered, stepped forward slashing right and left, his arm longing to stab, but his mind demanding he hold back. Lachlan expertly parried every blow and came at his friend with a flurry of blows so fast and so powerful, so ingrained in his muscles, that it took everything Belman had to repel him. When they reached the edge of the ring, men began to scramble out of the way and Belman side-stepped. Anticipating the need, Lachlan darted left twice and seized Belman's right arm. He heaved down on it as he brought his knee up and drove it into Belman's thigh, once, twice and a third time. Belman cried out and his leg collapsed from under him.

Lachlan threw his blade aside and punched Belman with an uppercut to the jaw. Belman, his mouth hanging open, was sent sprawling onto his back missing three teeth and with blood coursing over his lips.

Lachlan retrieved his sword and turned to Habit.

'Come forth,' he demanded, out of breath but full of menace. His blood was up and his eyes wild. His body was remembering recent war, and he reminded himself not to kill the woman or all would be lost in this endeavour.

He marched forward and she took up a fighting stance. She darted this way and that with needle strikes and slashes while Lachlan merely evaded. He took a brief moment of respite to sheath his sword then went on, approaching her with palms open and his shoulders stooped, his weight on the balls of his feet. When next she came at him he swept her right hand away, swept her left and head-butted her in the bridge of her nose. She cried out and fell back. He stormed forward and kicked the knife out of her right hand. She rolled to stab him with the left but he darted back and she over-extended. He stepped in and landed a heavy blow in her ribs with his boot. Her whole body lifted and then dropped on her front. He bent down and forced the weapon from her hand then hauled her to her feet.

'You have lost your warrior honour,' he said and swept her up into his arms then carried her to her caravan. He set her down and, panting and holding her side, she ducked inside and closed the door behind them.

'You are some fighter, my lord,' she said, clearly in pain.

'And you have lost no honour in losing to me,' he said.

'I have, and I will regain it now by stealing your strength from you,' she breathed, trying to straighten up. Lachlan hoped he had not broken any of her ribs.

'Nay, lady. You will regain it by offering the support of your people to me when I call on it. In return, I will grant you sovereign status to rule yourself and new lands, if you desire them, in the Isles, the Old Continent or the South.'

Habit sat back down upon her bunk, scowling at him.

'You not want me?'

'It would not be politic to admit it were it so.' He smiled and his eyes twinkled.

Chapter Eighteen

Linwood mounted his horse and thundered back towards his seat at Stragglers' End, silent and brooding on what had passed.

He mused on his encounter with Riark and strove with himself, unable to decide whether he should feel cowed by the other's might or ashamed for his own lack of boldness. His cheeks reddened as he thought of how powerless he had been before the king of the Dryads and he indulged idle fantasies of how he might have acted, driving back the Dryad with the might of his will and the strength of his resolve. But as the hours passed, he came to some peace with the notion that there was nothing he could have done – Riark had the mastery and it seemed, in truth, that all his plans would come to nothing. For what could he or his forces do against such a foe?

And yet Crinan lay tantalisingly to the south and greatly did Linwood desire to forge a new kingdom for himself, stretching from the rainy northern shores of Stragglers' Drift to the Folly away in the bright sunlight of the south.

He had spent most of his years training for battle, dreaming of the day when he could come into his own. To have an interloper cast his dreams into the sea was beyond his imagining.

He would not accept it.

As he and his retinue drew closer to home, he could see the Whoreswood come into view and hear the bells of the evening summons carried chiming on the wind. The trees' intricate shapes gained new clarity as the road swept around the wood and curved back towards the gate.

He halted his men when they were within a stone's throw of the treeline. Linwood dismounted and walked under the canopy, eyeing the trunks with new suspicion. He laid his open palm against the bark and looked up into the leaves that swayed and rustled above him, competing with the sound of bells now closer.

He stepped further in until he was obscured and then, looking about him, he drew his sword and set about hacking at the trunk of the nearest oak. He hefted his blade three times, chipping at the bark then stopped, awaiting some unknown reaction from a supernatural assailant he had only lately discovered.

But nothing happened.

Linwood set about the tree once more then turned on another then another, grunting and sweating with his labour but leaving scarce markings upon them by which they would remember him. They patiently endured, as was their way.

He sheathed his notched sword and surveyed the damage with frustration. If the Dryad was made of such stuff, he would indeed give battle in vain, thought Linwood.

He heard hooves on the road and started back towards it. A voice called out to him, and Linwood quickened his pace, trying to disguise his rapid breathing.

When he emerged he saw that a rider attired in the uniform of his guard at Stragglers' End was mingling with his retinue.

'Your Grace.' The man bowed his head and dismounted so as to meet the duke on a level.

'What news?' replied Linwood and climbed up into his saddle.

The man was forced to look up at him.

'We have word that Lord Lachlan is abroad in the Drift.'

The noise that Linwood issued did not resemble words, and he gathered himself before speaking again.

'How have I not heard of this? In force? How is it I am just hearing of it now? For what purpose is he here?' He rattled off the questions and his men felt alarmed at the seeming panic in one usually so unflappable.

'I know not all the answers, Your Grace, but I have heard word less than an hour ago that Lord Lachlan is even now attending the contest within the Whoreswood. And rumour has been heard these past few days, of visitors in Redbranch bringing tidings from the south.'

Linwood looked towards the trees and took a tighter grip on the reins.

Am I ever to be vexed now?

'Very well,' he said finally. 'You return to the gate. Issue standing orders to allow no one to leave Stragglers' End and none enter without giving a full account of themselves. Have riders sent to all settlements, to the defences at Strewn Men Bay and to Lady Isobel asking for report whilst urging caution. Tell them what you know. And get a regiment to report to me here. Go.'

The man bowed low, hurried for his horse and spurred it back to the gate at great haste.

Linwood turned to the captains who led the company that travelled with him, some twenty men.

'Your orders are of the utmost importance, Captain. Form a perimeter around the Whoreswood. Nobody goes in or out, lest I send word myself. I *will* send word in due course. Understood?'

'Understood, Your Grace.'

Before he left, one of his men called out to him.

'But if Lord Lachlan should come and counteract your orders?'

Linwood had been about to ride off but instead rode up to the man and, quick and brutal, he drew his notched sword and slew the man at his feet, hacking into his neck. The horses nearby whinnied and grew unsettled. A cry went up from the surrounding men.

'Does anyone else need to know what to do should *any* man question my orders on my own land? Let it be known that King Linwood commands in the united realm of New Crinan, whether north or south of the forest. The Combined People are no more.'

A lieutenant began hollering orders and the men obeyed without further hesitation. Linwood watched them do his bidding for a while then rode up the road towards the gate of Stragglers' End.

He arrived to find the great oak doors closed against him and a guard of five blocking his way with pikes lowered.

'Who goes there?' one of the men shouted.

'King Linwood of New Crinan, lord of these lands and master of this keep. Stand aside.'

A pause.

'Step forward into the lamplight, Your Grace, if it be so,' said the voice.

Linwood was heartened to see his orders had been heeded so quickly and did as was asked of him.

'Apologies, Your Grace,' said the gate sergeant. 'I was told to challenge all.'

'Keep it up. No exceptions,' said Linwood. 'But you will address me as Sire. All of the lands belonging to Crinan are renewed, and the House of Linwood sits upon the throne. Spread the word amongst the men and send word for my council to assemble immediately in the throne room.'

It had been many long months since Linwood had been home to Stragglers' End and he returned to it now with fresh scars and perhaps a harder heart than when he left. There was no cheering as he entered, rather his folk bowed or drew back when they saw that he was coming.

The curtain wall of Stragglers' End was of stone, not over tall and crudely assembled, but its parapets extended out so that the footholds afforded by gaps in the stone could not be used to an assailant's advantage. The streets inside were narrow, lined with huts and lodges. The central keep was encircled by another stone wall and within were vast parade grounds and barracks, forges and stables, armouries and prisons. Nothing grew within the walls, not even a single flower. Instead, tunnels led out to walled farmlands off to the west. Linwood's horse picked its way between his people as they walked the muddy streets. As word passed quicker than he could, the crowds thinned as he neared the keep.

Linwood barrelled through the keep towards his throne room, built in long anticipation of greater importance for his house. There was a long table running down the centre of the room upon which maps were strewn. The room was manned by the castellan, Willard.

'Lord Linwood, my congratulations on your victorious return.'

Linwood sighed at having to repeat himself.

'Issue a royal decree, Willard. I have taken the throne of Crinan and claim both the old lands and the new as part of my realm. Stragglers' Drift and Crinan secede from the Combined People and are now to be known as New Crinan. Send word to all in the new kingdom. And muster for war.'

Willard clasped and unclasped his hands, shifting nervously.

'Yes, Sire,' he said. 'Long live the king.'

With that he turned and was gone. Linwood advanced on the table and ran his eyes over the various maps depicting the defences around his borders, the numbers of the garrisons at all the settlements and the progress of the road. Ere long, Willard returned and Linwood beckoned him over.

'Are these made afresh?' Linwood demanded.

'This very day, Sire, to account for your returning armies.'

'Good. Very good. The Council is assembling shortly. I must away to my quarters, but will return shortly. Have riders ready for when the Council finishes its business. We will have troop movements to make.'

Willard nodded in affirmation, but tarried.

'Sire, have you heard word of Lord Lachlan?'

Linwood nodded, not taking his eyes from the parchment before him.

'I have heard that he even now is encircled within the Whoreswood. What do we know of his numbers?'

'It is said by those that returned from the summons early that Lord Lachlan, Lord Hadwyn and his general, Lord Belman are with the whores, Sire. There have been no sightings of any larger force within our borders.'

'What is the old devil up to?' said Linwood. He brushed past Willard and marched off towards his own quarters where, in anticipation of his needs, serving girls were waiting. He took food and wine, but declined the warm water of the bath that had been drawn for him. He did, however, exchange his sword before returning to council.

He found his commanders, the castellan, high sheriffs and chancellor assembled in the throne room. They stood to greet him and bowed their heads. He took up his seat upon the throne, though it was largely impractical to do so, as it was set upon a dais at some distance from the table and required that he raise his voice to be properly heard. Nevertheless, there he sat and received reports of how things stood within the Drift and then, having declared his intentions once more to secede from the Combined People, he set out about a new tack.

'As you all know, our people have been toiling to create a road and new settlements in the forest. There has been a challenge to our authority to do so and I have met with one who claims to be king of a people within the forest. They are mighty in strength and declare that if we set foot in the forest, they will pour open war upon us.'

'We have men in the forest yet, at the farther encampments. What of them?' said General Oakwood.

'I have ordered all our forces and all our people to leave the bounds of the forest. They assemble at the brink under the command of Lady Isobel,' said Linwood. 'Therefore our work and aims are hindered greatly for now. I seek your counsel.'

There was silence for a moment then Oakwood spoke up again.

'Obviously we can supply our ports at Oystercatcher Bay and deploy from our ships, but I would judge that for a united realm, a united land mass would be necessary. And to have an open border with the forest against the people within…it invites division and war, surely, Sire? Who are these people, Sire?'

'I know not, for sure. I have met with one identified to me as King Riark of a people who dwell therein. I saw with my own eyes that they are a hardy folk with armour well beyond our own. I fear our weapons will do little against them. In truth, they are more fearsome than any creature Awgren devised.'

He stroked his chin and looked at the chancellor.

'Tell me, Adair. What store do we have of food, timber and weapons? Can we wage war as we are, coming only of late from battle in the south?'

'We have weapons enough to arm our people twice over and great store of both food and timber, Sire,' said Chancellor Adair.

The talk went on for nigh on an hour and during this time, Linwood considered telling his lords the full truth of his encounter within the forest, and yet when he made to speak, the words seemed ridiculous to him. Loyal though he thought them to be, he was not convinced that they would not think him mad for speaking of his parley with a man of the trees.

'I've made my decision. All settlements must be put on alert. General Oakwood, I want the defences at Strewn Men Bay bolstered and an army left in reserve at Stragglers' End. The rest of our forces will march upon the forest at first light. Send word to your captains, and see that everything is set in motion. But spread the word that this Riark is a lieutenant of Awgren – it will lend the task greater gravity, but also give hope that our opponents can be defeated.'

Linwood stood and moved to the head of the table, clasping it by the edges and regarding each man in turn.

'You have all heard, I am sure, that Lord Lachlan is in the Whoreswood even as we speak. I have no doubt that, as he comes by stealth and unannounced, he means us harm. I have spoken openly of the new realm and as such, he must be taken forthwith. The castellan and his men will attend me and together we will roust out this foreign lord and see what he has to say.'

Ere long, Linwood and Willard were moving out of the keep with a company of thirty armed men. They passed into the winding streets of Stragglers' End, amidst the throng of peasants, trudging through the mire churned up by their feet as well as the hooves and paws of their animals. They moved through at a smart pace heedless of those in their path, heading straight for the postern gate that led into the Whoreswood. Few men amongst them were unaware of the gate and the path through the woods beyond, as it was the custom amongst Linwood's folk to test their mettle against the whores in order to gain manhood.

Linwood pushed open the door and found he was standing in a bare half circle of ground before the path started into the trees. The first lantern could be seen off in the distance around the first bend. He stepped into the Whoreswood and Willard followed on with his company.

As they walked forward, Linwood consciously paced out in front, unease growing within him. At first he could not identify the feeling then, after much cogitation, he recognised it as the same stirrings caused by his encounter with the king of the Dryads. He once more felt diminished and inadequate, requiring so many men to combat so few. While the realisation did not suit his palate, he knew it would be foolish to underestimate Lachlan. Though he might be a vulnerable interloper and an obstacle to be surmounted before he could fully assert his new rights as king, Linwood had witnessed the man do battle. He had never seen one so strong, so aware and so blood-thirsty amidst the throng. The Lord of the Isles was an educated man, quick on his feet and swift with his blade. He could endure blows near as well as he could give them out and nothing fazed him in the slightest. The more Linwood thought on the man he was soon to waylay and possibly arrest, the greater the unrest in his heart and ever darker grew his mood.

He gripped the hilt of his sword as he walked and his other hand was clasped into a tense fist. In defiance against his doubts, he walked as upright as he could, whipping up his courage as he had once done when new to battle and afraid.

Linwood passed a lantern and the bells, which had fallen silent while he was in council, could be heard again. Linwood stopped, feeling certain that in the noise there lay a signal. He turned to Willard.

'We must hurry,' he said and set off at a run.

Linwood began to give thought to how he would approach the search of the many camps throughout the wood. The ladies of the Whoreswood were not easily intimidated, as he knew well, and he was far from certain that they would grant him entry to their caravans, nor give him any information he requested.

Only time will tell, he thought.

Ere long the bells were ringing out all around them, and Linwood ordered his men to fan out to find who was ringing them, but to no avail. They stormed along the lantern-lit paths and in time came to the first camp. There was no one to be seen. Linwood went from one empty caravan to the next, finding the doors unlocked and signs of hasty retreat.

'What do you make of it?' asked Willard.

'Lord Lachlan has been making mischief it seems. Come; let us press on to the next one.'

So they went on throughout the evening, roaming from camp to camp, finding nobody except his men returning from the contest. These he questioned hard for details and added them to the search party.

Hours passed, and Linwood grew impatient. There were hundreds of women within the Whoreswood and hundreds of their male relations, always out of sight. It was of great concern to him that they had drawn off to their hiding places; the wood was so great that he had very little chance of finding them.

Linwood was very near to calling off the search when Lord Lachlan, Lord Hadwyn and Lord Belman stepped out from the trees and made themselves known.

'You take a strange road to pay a visit,' said Linwood, folding his arms across his chest. 'I had heard there were foreigners marauding across my lands unannounced and find it is the Lord of the Isles and his kin.'

He directed no attention to Hadwyn and Belman, barely acknowledging their presence.

'I think you know full well why I have come, Linwood,' said Lachlan, his voice laced with malice and yet just under control. 'Shall we take counsel together in your keep?' he said.

Linwood was all too conscious of his men's eyes upon him and at last, was compelled to speak transparently.

'The king of New Crinan will receive the Lord of the Isles, but not to receive counsel.'

Belman took a step forward, but Hadwyn seized his arm.

'Awgren is but lately thrown down and yet treason is abroad so soon,' said Hadwyn. 'Do not be a fool, Linwood.'

Lachlan walked towards Linwood and it took the younger man all he had not to step aside or falter in the face of the Lord of the Isles, in whom wrath now burned so greatly that his face was afire with it.

'You have made your intentions quite clear. I strip you of your rank, title and lands in the name of Queen Cathryn of the Combined People.' He kept his eyes locked on Linwood but raised his voice so all could hear.

'Let it be known that Lachlan, Lord of the Isles, and Queen Cathryn declare this man traitor. Let anyone who is loyal to the queen who led you to victory against Awgren, take up arms if any should prevent my companions and I from taking our leave.'

Lachlan turned on his heel and walked back towards Hadwyn and Belman. The men nearby stood with weapons drawn, looking from one to the other. Linwood dropped his hand to his sword.

'Seize them,' he said and shot a look at Willard.

'SEIZE THEM!' Willard roared and after only a moment's hesitation, the castellan's men betrayed their hearts and ran forward.

No sooner had they done so but arrows began to fly, and the first three men fell with shafts quivering in their necks. The men behind them checked their progress and looked from Lachlan to Willard to Linwood.

'I said seize them,' hissed Linwood, anger rising up in him. He drew his sword, but an arrow zipped from the darkness and stuck between his feet.

Lachlan stood between his friends and turned to Linwood.

'Go home, traitor and make your plans. The queen and I will be coming for you. And let all of you here now spread the word that those who are true of heart should rally to my call when it comes.'

With that, all three men disappeared into the darkness between the trunks of the trees and all was silent.

Linwood stood breathing heavily upon the path, sword still in hand. His men stood about him uncertain what to do for the best.

He marched them back the way they had come and as he passed through the postern gate, he ordered it locked and guarded. Safe within his fortress, Linwood gave thought to what he could do about the lord he sought to usurp, who lingered now within his borders.

And then the answer came to him.

'Willard,' he said, seizing the older man by the shoulders.

'We must have that forest swarming with soldiers at great haste. I want all the whores cleared out and Lord Lachlan brought before me.'

Before long Willard had emptied Stragglers' End of all its troops, and they marauded through the woods killing all in their path, moving from camp to camp.

Habit heard word of the massacre before the soldiers reached her own home, and Lachlan's company helped her rally her people. Men appeared from beneath the trees, and they took turns carrying Habit's mother as they made a hasty retreat, abandoning the caravans.

The sound of tramping boots and screams from those who had fallen behind soon reached their ears.

'This is hopeless,' cried Belman as they ran through the woods.

Lachlan despaired, knowing their plight was grave indeed.

He felt Habit's cold fingers interlace with his own as they fled before Linwood's troops.

'They'll pay for this, my lord,' she said. 'Come, follow me.'

Guided only by lamplight, Habit led her people and Lachlan's company through the woods. The ground began to rise up before them, and Hadwyn stumbled due to the unanticipated incline, yet his brother was there to catch and steady him before they rushed on. Midway up the slope they came to an outcrop of rock. On the grass surrounding it were standing stones some ten foot high. Habit ran across the rock plateau and slipped between two large boulders. Had he not been holding her hand, she would have soon been lost to sight as it seemed that the boulders' positions formed a maze. Now it was Lachlan's turn to stumble. He steadied himself against a rock, and looking down, he saw that steps had been cut into the earth beneath his feet.

'Follow,' said Habit, 'but watch your footing. Pass the word to your kin.'

Lachlan did so and followed on with a lighter feeling in his heart, marvelling at how oblivious one could be to the hidden wonders of one's own realm.

The steps ran on, twisting and straightening out as the tunnel sloped downwards. Lanterns were set along the way, and the noise of voices and tools could be heard in the far distance.

'What is this place?' asked Lachlan.

'Our menfolk need someplace to live and something to keep them occupied,' said Habit, turning back with a coy smile.

'We have crude halls, but much in store. We can hide out here for a time until the danger is past.

'Tell me, are there tunnels leading into Stragglers' End?' asked Lachlan.

Habit turned and smiled.

'Are you ready to become a Partisan?'

She led him onward.

Chapter Nineteen

Rowan, like her husband, had never before seen the ocean. She thought of it more and more as they walked, and the prospect of going to sea grew ever more likely.

Captain Lynch never tired of answering her questions. He told her of his boyhood years in the Folly working on the docks; he spoke of how his father was often at sea and how, when he was seven, he too had gone aboard his father's vessel, the Gannet. For many years he had learned seamanship while the Gannet travelled back and forth between the Folly to the Isles to the Drift, ferrying goods and timber. The blackened, dead coasts of Tayne and Crinan were so familiar to him that he could trace the route in his imagination if he closed his eyes.

'It's how I get to sleep when the sleep's hard to come by.' He smiled. 'I lie back with my eyes shut and make the voyage from the Sea Gate at the Folly all the way to Narra on the Butterfly Isle then across to Strewn Men Bay where the Stragglers would come out to us by barge so we need not risk the rocks. 'Cept in my dreams, my father still stands beside me as he can surely do no more,' he would say, wistful and sad.

Rowan's heart yearned for Lynch at those times when he opened his heart to her and she would take his hand in her own, enjoying the rough feel of his skin. His was a world completely foreign to her. She knew of unforgiving soil, toil and cold water under the watchful eye of a harsh occupying force, but not the romance of the sea or the far-off pine forests of the Isles or the majestic architecture of the Folly. When Rowan found sleep hard to come by, she dreamt of a little cottage in the shelter of tall snow-capped mountains near a river that ran down to the sea. On other nights, she thought of passing through the Sea Gate and entering the long canal to the Folly docks before wandering about there, seeing all the splendour and power of a bygone age—escorted of course, by Captain Lynch.

Riark's visit had done nothing to soften her heart towards Morrick, and she concealed it from all others. The Dryad had told her how her husband was near at hand, but conveyed nothing of the circumstances. Morrick entered her thoughts often, but now he was but a ragged figure of torment to her. She thought of his unshorn face, dirty and bedraggled, with small, black eyes staring out at her. He bore the tokens of Awgren and had been his right hand, she saw now. She had been the same, she knew. But now *she* saw the light.

Morrick travelled with Riark, learning of the forest and feeling his spirit renew in the Dryad's calming, age-old presence, yet Rowan imagined her husband tearing on behind her like a slavering dog, and the thought hurried her pace.

She remained unaware that Lord Aldwyn had liberated the Hinterland and, having received the promised visit from Riark, was even now marching back towards the coast under Queen Cathryn's direction, ready to sail to deal with Lord Linwood.

Rowan understood only that she was pursued by the husband who had abandoned her, leading to the loss of both her daughter due to his inaction and her home to the Devised. So she struggled on, often in bleak silence, and she thought ever more of new lands and their ways, seeking escape from her current troubles. As she gathered her strength, she took some mastery of her thoughts and rather than dwelling on the loss of her daughter, she looked to the cleanliness of her sons and the health of Captain Lynch, spending many an hour walking beside him and holding his hand.

Days passed and finally they reached the southwest border of the forest, nigh to the northern shore of Oystercatcher Bay. Here, Lynch hoped, they would find the Combined People had established a foothold where the refugees could find food and shelter before making any weightier decisions about the future - if victory had been achieved.

'If not?' Rowan would ask him.

'We'll see,' was his only reply.

Sure enough, one cold morning when the frozen grass snapped beneath her feet, Rowan emerged from the Impassable Forest and looked down the slopes towards the ocean, shining silver in the early sun, its ragged waves dancing across the horizon. She looked south along the curve of Oystercatcher Bay, hemmed in with wooden palisades which defended against any attack from the land. Great ships were hove-to out in the bay, their sails drawn up, but still beautiful to Rowan's eyes. Declan and Callum ran to her side, and she wrapped her arms around them, tears streaming down her cold cheeks. She hugged them close and they marvelled at the view, both secretly wondering if the folk down there would have any news of their father.

By now Lynch was much healed and though far from fighting fit, he was capable of walking unsupported. Straightening up, he stood before the refugees.

'Listen up, now. We don't know the lie of the land down there. Perhaps the war wages on, perhaps we've won and perhaps we've lost. We don't know how they'll respond to you folk, so it's best I present myself as in charge of this little band till we clear things up. All agreed?'

Those who would have proudly contested such a suggestion weeks before had no energy to quarrel now and so the people of the Hinterland trailed behind Captain Lynch and his crew as they walked down to the gate in the palisade.

Rowan drew nigh to him from behind and saw his head incline. His pace slowed somewhat.

'What's wrong?' she asked.

'What makes you think anything is wrong?' he replied.

'You always slow up when you're thinking. And tilt your head,' she whispered back. He huffed a little and issued a little laugh.

'You know me well, ma'am. There are more folk on the gate than I expected - many more.'

'And what of it?' she pressed, but Lynch had no answer for her. Wearily they made their way to the gate.

Not far behind them, Morrick was lying nestled in the crook of an oak's roots, lying on a bed of moss.

He woke when hands, forming from the bark beneath him, gently rocked and stirred him. He yawned, stretched and sat up.

The low leafy boughs made a low ceiling above him through which shafts of light illuminated the grass. Morrick rubbed his eyes, and he took in the beauty of his surroundings. He felt remarkably at peace, certain that he would be reunited with his family soon. He got to his feet and knelt by the stream they had been following, cupping ice water and sipping it before it could escape through his fingers.

'Are you hungry?'

Riark's voice came from behind him, and Morrick turned to see the Dryad's body form as he stepped out of the oak. He shook off loose bark and tilted his head inquisitively.

Morrick nodded.

Riark waved his hand towards the roots of the tree, and Morrick saw a parcel of large leaves. Folding them back, he found a selection of fruits, berries and roots laid out for him. His heart sank a little, wishing for meat and bread and yet, a little later seated upon the banks of the stream, he was surprised at how satisfying a meal Riark had prepared.

'It seems a man can live quite well in the Forest,' he admitted, reaching for more water from the stream.

Riark did not seem to react. Indeed he once again resembled a young tree as he stood straight and tall, vines whipping about him in the strong breeze.

Morrick left him to it and walked a little further upstream. He stripped down to bathe in the water then returned to find Riark had scarce moved at all.

'Shall we head on?'

Faster than could be perceived, Riark shifted from his treelike state to an animated creature once more. He nodded slowly and strode ahead through the trees. Morrick trotted to catch up.

'Tell me, what do you expect to happen next, Woodcutter?'

'Next?'

Riark did not repeat the question, looking resolutely ahead.

Morrick reached down and picked up a fallen branch, using it as a staff.

'I'll find my family,' he said.

'And then?' asked Riark.

'And then go home,' said Morrick.

Riark laid a hand on Morrick's shoulder.

'I've some respect for you, Woodcutter. You are different to the men in the north.'

Morrick did not reply, sensing there was more to come. Sure enough, Riark continued,

'You have experience in war and have survived to come home to your family even when others did not. You've even come to lead what is left of your people then thrown aside a potentially comfortable life of power under your new rulers in order to chase down your family.'

Morrick said nothing.

'Times are changing for all of us. Mankind has always relied on building and taking resources from the world to a great degree, but of late things have shifted out of balance. There may come a point very soon when I need to rally the forest against the men in the north. It would be of use to me to have someone at my side that both respects the forest and can understand the ways of mankind, yet without being loyal to their masters.'

'Are you making me an offer?' asked Morrick as he drew closer.

Riark's face cracked into a smile.

'Perhaps you and your family could come and live within the forest. We would establish a home for you here and all your needs would be met. In return, I would seek you out for counsel as and when it is needed.'

Morrick stopped and met Riark's eyes, not entirely sure how to respond. His mind was caught on returning to a home that no longer existed and yet there was a wide world now open to him. Could he really commit his family to the forest with these strange creatures?

'What of my people?' he ventured.

'They would be welcome also, if they will live in a manner I deem acceptable.'

'You'd grant the people of the Hinterland a home under your protection away from the Combined People?' Morrick ran his fingers across the scarred flesh of his face.

'If they will live in harmony with the forest and not exploit it,' said Riark.

They walked on, deep in conversation. Morrick opened his heart to the king of the Dryads, voicing his concerns and, in return, learning what he could of their ways. Riark told him much of what had passed between him, the queen and Lord Linwood.

In the bright morning light, they reached the edge of the forest and Morrick stepped out from under the trees. He looked down once more upon Oystercatcher Bay and the palisade that surrounded it.

'Have you thought on my offer?' said Riark.

'I have, but I need to speak to my family and my people. Wherever we decide to make our home, I will always be grateful for your assistance these past days and, if you can reach me, I am always happy to offer what counsel I may even if I am no longer under your protection.'

Riark bowed. He looked out from the brow of the hill at the plains rolling down towards the Blade Mountains and out across the ocean in the direction of the distant Isles. Morrick thought that he looked as though he was trying to remember something.

After a time Riark nodded.

'If you should decide to take shelter with us, just re-enter the forest and word will find me. I will set the watch.'

With that, Riark walked to the trunk of the nearest tree, sank into the thickest of its roots and was gone.

Morrick counted the ships in the bay and gave up at thirty. It seemed there would be more people down there than before. He adjusted his belt, slipping his axe into its loop and set off down the slope towards the gate at a jog.

When Morrick had set out from here many days before, Lord Linwood's men had manned the gate, but now he saw Lord Aldwyn's uniforms. It seemed that not only had the queen's fleet arrived from the Folly, but Lord Aldwyn had returned to the bay in the time it had taken for him to take the longer road back.

Morrick slowed his pace and approached the closed gate.

'Who goes there?' shouted one of the guards.

'A servant of Lord Aldwyn,' called Morrick, conscious that his heritage might not stand him in good stead with these men. He had spent very little time amongst Aldwyn's folk on the journey and was unsure of their feelings towards him. He drew nearer to the gate and attempted to shift the length of his hair across his face without drawing attention, hoping to hide the scarring caused by Linwood's brand.

'Name?' demanded the guard.

'Morrick. I am one of his captains,' he said, though unsure of his continued status.

'Why come you from the woods?' said the guard.

'I marched with Lord Aldwyn to the Hinterland and was separated from him there. I returned under the cover of the trees. May I pass in? I have urgent business.'

'What kind of business?' asked the other guard, stepping closer and barring the way.

Morrick faltered momentarily before replying.

'I am a captain of the Hinterland. My family escaped the burning there, and they were headed here in hope of their salvation. Have they passed by this gate, sir?'

He gripped the collar of his filthy shirt as he talked so as to prevent fidgeting and the betrayal of his unsteady nerves.

The guards exchanged a look.

'The Hinterland?' said the first guard and both men stepped closer.

'Aye that's right. I was one of the conscripts.'

'Is that what you're calling yourselves now, is it?' said the man.

They loomed in with weapons in their hands. Morrick backed off a step, his foot sinking in the black mud and slipping slightly. His balance was off. He held out his hands to steady himself.

'Sirs, I have no quarrel with you nor did I ever.'

'Oh no? I suppose not, as I do not ride a horse; I hear tell 'twas the cavalry you boys thrust your pikes at, to great effect.'

The first guard, who was the larger of the two, seized Morrick by the arm and the second grabbed the other side when the woodcutter wheeled back trying to loosen the first man's grip.

'Off me!' he roared and began to exert all the strength that he could through his arms.

The larger guard thrust a gloved hand at Morrick's face, and he flinched in anticipation of the blow, but it never landed. Instead the leather swept aside his hair and the mark of Awgren was exposed for all to see.

'Devised scum,' the guard hissed, and the other spat in his face.

'We were pardoned,' Morrick growled and the first guard leered at him, moving so close their foreheads were touching. Morrick could feel hot droplets of breath spattering his skin.

'Not fuckin' pardoned by me, boy.'

The second guard punched him in the gut, and the air rushed out of him so that he doubled up. The same man seized his hair and yanked him over. As he did so, the larger guard relinquished his grip and dealt him another blow to his lower back – Morrick's kidneys quivered and he felt a sharp pain there. He cried out, but kept his feet, slipping and sliding below him though they were.

The guards thrust him into the mud then returned to the gate.

'Open up!' the larger man called, and Morrick looked up in surprise.

'Go find your litter. May you fare no better within than without, traitor scum,' said the guard and stood back in his original position, huffing and blowing as he tried to regain his breath.

The pain in his stomach and back was immense, but Morrick was keen to get inside before the guards changed their minds and decided to make sport of him once more. He was coated on his entire right side in the thick black mud, which reeked of a thousand years of defilement by the Creatures of the Devising. He pushed his hands deep within the muck and forced himself up to his knees then staggered through the open gates. He turned aside only to speak a few words to the guards.

'We did not fight by choice.'

'Do any of us?' snarled the smaller guard and shoved the gates closed behind him.

There had been considerable change since Morrick had first passed this way many days before. Guards were posted all along the palisade. In addition to the original huts which served as barracks and guard rooms, Morrick could now see rows of tents which were reminiscent of many a battlefield camp. The pathways between the tents had been strewn with sawdust to give better footing.

Soldiers gathered around small fires or paraded. Folk moved about with baskets of food or carrying loads.

Morrick ducked between tents when he had the chance and smeared some of the mud across his face to better disguise his brand; his hair was now too clotted with sludge to be of any use. He found a patch of sawdust to sit upon for a few moments while he pulled himself together and while the pain dulled. All the time he looked about him for a sight of a familiar face, but saw nobody he knew.

Once he had adequately recovered, Morrick began to wander the lanes in search of his family, all the time whispering their names to himself.

'Rowan. Declan. Callum. Rowan. Declan. Callum.'

There were many soldiers and though they cast their eyes towards him, they saw only a homeless vagabond who wandered the camp covered in reek, and he thought it best to avoid them in case of another violent reaction.

He pulled his cloak tight about him as he walked, glancing furtively from behind his hair. At length he saw a man who was clothed in such a way that Morrick thought he him a civillian. He was crouched on his haunches tending a cooking pot, and he appeared to have his family with him; a wife and a little girl.

Morrick approached openly but with caution. They became aware of him when he came close and the father started then got to his feet.

'Good morrow to you,' he said. His tone was cautious and Morrick could not blame him.

'Good morrow,' Morrick replied. 'I am sorry to disturb you and yours.'

The man was looking him up and down.

'You've fallen? My wife fell yesterday.'

Morrick shifted his eyes to her, and her cheeks reddened, but she gave a little smile.

'Arse over tit, I went. Came up looking blacker than the dead of night,' she said.

Her husband chuckled, stirring oats into the water in the pot. He caught Morrick looking.

'Have you eaten? You look famished.'

'I haven't yet today, but I couldn't take what store you have, sir,' said Morrick.

'Nonsense. Besides, it all comes from the same stores, and you've as much right as do we. Take a pew and we'll get you warmed up. Dry your cloak by the fire if it suits you.'

Morrick was in no hurry to reveal the garb below in case it gave him away. He wrapped his cloak about him and seated himself on a hewn log, thinking of Riark as he did so and feeling a little guilty. Nevertheless, he was tired, and he took the chance to be seated while he could get it.

The man handed him a bowl of the porridge, and Morrick tucked in as fast as decorum allowed. He had finished the bowl before the man had finished serving his family.

'My name is Morrick.'

'Flynn, Nadia and this is my daughter, Cathryn.'

'Like the queen,' said Morrick gravely, but shot the little girl a smile, and she beamed back at him before setting about her morning meal.

'Like the queen,' said Nadia. 'How come you to be here, Morrick? I don't recognise the accent.'

Morrick made a show of scraping out his bowl while he thought of a suitable reply. Who knew how these people would react to any story he told?

'I came with Lord Aldwyn to advise on the Hinterland. I was a woodcutter with many men in my employ and latterly a captain of men. My passion has always been carving.'

'From whereabouts?' asked Flynn, frowning. 'I recognise the accent.'

'I'm from the Isles,' lied Morrick. 'Have you heard of Iona?'

'I have. I'm surprised you know how to speak, let alone have an accent, given how few people live there.'

'You've been?'

'Never in life!' said Flynn. 'Think one such as I could afford such a voyage? But believe it or not, the Isles do get mentioned in the Folly! The Taynish do have schools!' He raised his eyebrow in a playful challenge. Morrick realised that even between the friendlier parts of the Combined People, there was some rivalry. He smiled.

'I hear the education is first-rate down that way. What brings you up here?'

'I squire for one of the queen's captains – we came up with the royal fleet.'

'Where are Lord Linwood's folk?' said Morrick. 'They were manning the palisade when first I came through.'

Flynn shook his head.

'No sooner is the world rid of one dark lord but another rises up, so it seems. The word is Lord Linwood is raising rebellion. No sooner had Lord Aldwyn disappeared, but he marched his folk right back and rousted Linwood's folk back to their ships. It's said he had word from the Folly that Linwood has turned. Aldwyn's encamped now at the shore. You'll know that surely - if you came with him?' Flynn's tone changed.

There was a moment of silence, and Morrick thought the time had come to ask.

'I've heard survivors from the Hinterland came this way?'

Flynn looked up and was about to reply, but Nadia cut in.

'Whole gaggle of them came through in custody of a sea captain named Lynch. Turns out that was just a ruse! Begging at the door they were, as though we owed them a thing.'

'How they've the guts to show their faces.' Flynn was shaking his head in disgust. 'If I was them I'd have turned tail and hid in the forest.'

'I heard Lord Aldwyn pardoned them with the blessing of the queen?'

'Aye, he did so, but there's scarce a one among the rest of us who understands why. Sure enough, they were forced into service, but they've had a thousand years to rebel or send word and have we heard a thing?'

Morrick said nothing, as nothing came to mind which he could show as proof to the contrary. The feeling was uncomfortable.

'Lord Linwood had the right idea, branding their menfolk,' said Nadia. 'I'd have executed them and taken their land as weregild.'

Morrick said nothing.

'Anyhow, enough of that. Much brighter things to talk of on a fine morning such as this,' said Nadia, but Morrick made no reply nor feigned a smile.

After a time, he ventured.

'Were there women and children amongst the beggars?'

'Aye there were some,' said Flynn. 'Most of them are camped out down by the shore now waiting to be taken off with the duke. Was made quite clear to them they're not welcome here in the queen's camp. There's talk of re-settling them on the South Continent, amongst the small folk at any rate. Madness in my view - who knows who they'll fall in with next!'

Morrick stood and wrapped his cloak about him.

'You have my thanks for the food and the company.'

With that, he took the edge of his cloak and wiped away the mud from his brand. It took a moment to register on the family's faces, but when it did there was an obvious tussle between disgust and common decency, embarrassed at their words and yet at the same time, believing them true.

'Where are the refugees?' asked Morrick.

'Down by the shore,' said Flynn quietly.

Morrick bowed low and turned towards the ocean.

Chapter Twenty

Morrick followed the sawdust-strewn paths, ever watchful for glimpses of the ocean. As he walked, his now exposed face drew ever more comment and attention. In short time a small band of malcontents followed on behind him grumbling and muttering.

'Where you headed traitor?' cried a woman.

Something struck him in the side of the head, and a small stone was lost in the mud ahead of him. He made no attempt to check his pace or to hurry. Instead he walked on in silence and boiled in fury.

He could see Lord Aldwyn's banner flapping in the wind above the command tent, but when he first saw standing guards posted either side of what was fast becoming the widest path, he noted that the soldiers were wearing the queen's livery.

As he approached the first of the guards, the crowd behind him halted and dispersed.

His shadow stretched out before him as the morning sun rose behind him. He cut a desperate figure, swaddled in bloody, muddied cloth, his face scarred and branded, his hair and beard grown wild and with muck dripping from it.

He was not far from Aldwyn's banner when he saw a face he recognised disappear down a path to the right – Garrick. He gasped aloud and broke into a sprint.

'Garrick!'

Aldwyn heard the cry and though the voice was familiar, he thought little of it. He was somewhat preoccupied.

Cathryn paced back and forth across the tent. She paused only to seize her goblet from a table before draining it clean then resumed pacing. Aldwyn made pains to ensure that her goblet was full before she attempted to return to it.

'Will you not be seated?' he said eventually.

She glared at him then drained her goblet once more. She stood before him, hands on hips and rage in her eyes. He was beginning to regret asking after Lord Lachlan.

'Cathryn, please,' he chided, and though her pose was resolute, she blinked and seemed to come out of her reverie.

'Oh, it's too much to dwell on.' She sank down into the chair next to him, slouching for a moment before adopting a more regal pose lest somebody should enter.

'What was he thinking?' she asked.

'You know Lachlan better than I. Can you not guess?' he said quietly, drinking from his own cup only to form a barrier between himself and the queen.

She is magnificent, he thought as he watched her battle with herself.

'It's unlordly!' she protested.

'Was he ever lordly?'

'Do not stab at me, Aldwyn.'

'I did not mean to scold you, Cathryn, but you did not marry Lachlan for his table manners. He has the strongest bloodline, the strongest arm and…'

She raised her eyebrows at him.

'The strongest seed,' he finished and looked away.

'Quite,' she conceded.

'He was ever the hunter, and in truth, did you not know he yearned to be away and living wild again?'

She returned to her goblet.

'May I speak freely, Cathryn?'

She tutted at him.

'Enough of that. None of that between us in private,' she snapped, 'speak as you will. Otherwise why speak at all?'

Before he could say more, Ailsa coughed and stepped into the tent carrying rolled-up parchment which she set upon the table therein.

'Do you need anything more, Your Majesty?' she asked.

'No. Thank you, Ailsa. Please see to it that we are not disturbed until I send word.'

Ailsa bowed and ducked out. Aldwyn thought that from the narrow angle his view afforded him, the woman had a curious smile on her face.

What's afoot? he thought.

'You were saying?' she tapped her goblet against the arm of her chair, eyes everywhere but on him.

'Perhaps you should forgive him this indiscretion. He has been long cooped up at the Folly whilst his heart was elsewhere. He has served his purpose politically and given you heirs. He has stood by your side and been perhaps your closest ally. And besides, it seems that if he has gone for the reasons we believe, he may yet do us some good. Linwood is now declared traitor and with any hope, Lachlan is at hand to cast his own eye across the man's works. Good yet may come of this and, after all, the people believe he is gone by your leave.'

She stared at the floor for a time and then looked upon him with a softer expression on her face.

'How can you always speak so fairly about one who supplanted you?' she said in a hushed voice so that the guards outside might not hear.

He smiled.

'It was ever my lot to make you happy, Your Majesty.'

'Not so.' She raised her eyebrows. 'You would have made me far happier by not sustaining your wounds.'

'Do not jest,' said Aldwyn, her words paining him. Now he left his chair and walked idly about the tent, partly unsheathing and sheathing a dagger or feeling a length of cloth; whatever his wayward fingers touched he toyed with.

'What if he does not return?' he said finally.

'What of it?' said Cathryn then as though catching on to Aldwyn's meaning, 'There's no use thinking about that, my love.'

He wheeled at her use of the word, aghast. She appeared caught off-guard and could not help but laugh.

'Planning the coming days has taken a somewhat unexpected turn.' She smiled. 'Perhaps we should look at the maps?'

'Cathryn…couldn't we?'

'Couldn't we what?'

'Perhaps we could try for a while…'

'It'd be no good. As things are,' she said. 'Come – the maps.' She stretched them out across the table and made a show of examining them.

Aldwyn felt heat in his cheeks and a curious feeling in his chest, as though his heart was physically trying to reach out to her. He longed to tell her how much he loved her; that now they were older, and she had her heirs, there was no reason to keep up the charade - that they could finally be together.

As though she could read his mind, she looked up.

'It's no use, Aldwyn. It would not do to have a consort whose queen had been bedded by another. It would not do. Oh that we could…' she started but her voice trembled and she cut off that line of talk and turned back to the map.

'I've left holding regiments at the Folly, but otherwise we have our full force available. 'How soon till you can put to sea?' she asked, prone above the maps.

Aldwyn was breathing hard, longing for her and furious at her as well. She waited, knowing the turmoil he was facing and appreciating his attempts to subdue it.

That, she thought, was the very quality which would have made him a far better consort than Lachlan could ever have been.

Finally, Aldwyn swallowed his ardour, clasped his hands behind his back and joined her at the table.

'I would say by the end of tomorrow we could set sail for Strewn Men Bay. Do you think we can stand against him, considering his troops made up the bulk of your army?' he said.

'I would rather stand against him now than wait till his plans come to fruition. We should not land at Strewn Men Bay. It's where he will be expecting us and his defences are usually the strongest there.'

Aldwyn sighed.

'Has it really come to this?'

'It was always going to come to this, and we were naïve not to realise it. We should be grateful we held together long enough to overthrow Awgren. I will never forget that it was by Linwood's might this was achieved, but as grateful as I am and as willing as I would be to leave him to his own designs, he cannot be allowed to think that I will not thwart any attempts he makes at conquering our lands. Our people turned from that path a long time ago, and we are still ill-equipped to be masters of the world. I rule over realms dedicated to destroying evil, and I will not sit back and let a man grow in power in such a way that it is inevitable he too will turn to darkness.'

She thrust a finger at the map.

'We sail north then stand way out to sea and land at Seal Bay, further to the west than he will expect. We will march straight to Stragglers' End and take the man in hand whilst he is yet unaware how much we know. Agreed?'

Aldwyn shot her a smile.

'Let us take a while to think over the particulars. We must consider how he will react and what we are hoping to achieve? Will we really attempt to slaughter those very men who just fought for you at the Field of the Scarlet Grass?'

Cathryn fetched a bottle of wine and refilled their goblets.

'We have a long night ahead of us, it seems,' she said.

'Mind out!' said a soldier as Morrick knocked in to him as he ran by. He paid no heed and careered onwards, picking between guy ropes and darting around the tents before him.

As he rounded the last tent in a row, he could see an older man walking slowly with a bundle of firewood towards the ocean.

'Garrick!' he called again.

The man looked back over his shoulder, but there was no recognition in his face.

And why should there be, thought Morrick. He resembled his former self in very few ways these days. He ran forward, letting fly his cloak so that it billowed out behind him. Garrick walked towards him, craning forward to scrutinise the approaching face.

As Morrick reached him the old man's eyes filled with tears and shaking hands grasped at Morrick's face. Now it was the woodcutter's turn to be taken aback. He shrank back from the touch, and the light died in Garrick's eyes.

'I thought you were my son.' His voice was shaking and higher than usual. 'I thought you were my son. My son.'

Morrick grasped at his shoulders to steady him.

'I'm sorry, Garrick. I didn't think. It's Morrick. You remember?' Garrick's eyes narrowed as he searched his features.

'Morrick?'

His face drained of colour, but Morrick was oblivious.

'Some of us survived,' he said. 'Where's Rowan?'

'We know…the rest are serving Lord Aldwyn.'

'Where's Rowan?'

'They marched in yesterday morning.'

'Garrick!' Morrick shook the old man by the shoulders. 'Where's my family?' he shouted. All around him people turned and stared.

Garrick shook off Morrick's hands and reached up to run his fingers across the T scorched into his face. Morrick winced as he made contact.

'She's camped not far from here. Down there,' he continued and pointed seaward, 'but you shouldn't go.'

'Why? What are you saying?'

'Your daughter.'

Morrick waved away his concern.

'I know of my daughter already.' He set off at a jog.

'That's not all!' Garrick cried after him, but Morrick was determined not to let anything else get in his way.

He ran by more and more familiar faces, his heart growing lighter. And then he saw Callum and Declan seated by a small fire.

Wary of the lesson he had learned with Garrick, Morrick checked his pace and approached them slowly. Morrick had lost count of the months since last he had seen his boys, and they seemed to have grown immeasurably since. Callum in particular looked leaner and ganglier; a youth rather than a boy. Tears began to stream down Morrick's cheeks as he drew closer and, at last, they noticed him. They reacted with fright, and Callum jumped to his feet.

'No, no, no,' Morrick said softly. 'It's me. Me.'

The little one saw the truth first and ran over, wrapping his arms around Morrick's waist. Callum was a beat behind, encircling his father around his shoulders.

'You're a man,' Morrick found himself saying. 'A man now!'

The three of them were in danger of collapsing into the mud so Morrick staggered them over to the fire where the ground was dry. There, they embraced and cried for a time, each of them trying to talk and tell of everything that had befallen them since they had parted. Eventually Morrick managed to surface and asked,

'Where's your mother?'

At this Declan merely blurted, 'She's on the beach with Captain Lynch!'

And at the same time, Callum said, 'We feared you were dead.'

Morrick frowned and looked into Callum's eyes.

'I know, Son, but I'm home now. Everything will be all right.'

Callum said nothing, simply sat down by the fire.

'Captain Lynch?' Morrick asked his youngest son, cradling his face. The boy was ill-prepared for deceit and his eyes shone with fear.

'Who is Captain Lynch?'

'A sailor from the Folly,' murmured Callum. 'He rescued us.'

'Then he has my thanks. Which way?'

He set off running in the direction Declan pointed, and very soon the mud gave way to a narrow fringe of grass which, in turn, became sandbanks. The wide silver expanse of the ocean stretched out ahead of him as he ran. The sand gave way under him as it sloped and he dropped in increments as he moved forward until he was on the flat of the beach where the sand was strewn with lines of seaweed and dotted with rocks. Oystercatchers ran to and fro in the shallows, the black and white of their plumage standing out against the water, and the bright orange of their bills dipping down into the sand.

He turned on the spot and spied figures away south along the beach. Exhausted though he was, Morrick ran, unclasping his cloak so that it fell behind him and was forgotten. The figures drew ever nearer and he lowered his head to gain speed.

He fell several times, each time bursting up again and powering on.

Then he discerned that the two figures walking towards him were holding hands, and nausea began to swim in his belly. He slowed to a walk and eventually stood still, waiting for them to reach him.

The figure on the right walked with a sway of the hips, and her hair billowed westward in the wind. Once more tears ran down his cheeks at the sight of her alive and well. But who was this man holding her hand? He was broad and tall, dressed in the style Morrick had seen aboard ship. A sword hung at his side.

The energy drained out of him, and unable to breathe properly, he sank down to sit in the sand. He took up great handfuls of it and let it escape into the air with the wind.

'Good morning,' called the man as the couple drew near.

Morrick made no reply. They drew so close to him that the mark on his face became visible to them.

Rowan threw away Lynch's hand and leant in closer, eyes wide. She had to be sure.

'Are you from the Hinterland?' she asked, still not believing.

He looked up at her, and she felt as though she would become stuck in the mire of his deep, doleful eyes as they peered pitifully up at her.

She shrank back from him and began to run back the way she had come.

'Rowan!' called Lynch. Morrick stood and ran after her, still without saying a word.

'You there!' called Lynch and set off after him. Still Morrick made no reply. He caught up with her in just a few steps and seized her by the arm.

'Rowan…' The word came out as a croak.

'No.'

'What?'

'No.' She strained and tried to pull away from his grasp.

Suddenly Lynch was on him and pulling at his shoulders.

'Get off her!'

'Rowan, don't you know me?' Morrick cried. 'Rowan?'

He shoved at Lynch's chest and roared, 'She's my wife!'

Lynch seized hold of Morrick's wrist and looked for Rowan's reaction, but she had covered her face with her hands and was yet again running, filled with guilt and loathing, happiness, relief and horror.

'Let go of me,' snarled Morrick and when Lynch did not relinquish his hold, Morrick swung his right fist into Lynch's face. His wounds not yet fully healed, the captain crumpled onto his back in the sand, and Morrick kicked him hard to deaden his leg before launching himself up the beach, calling after Rowan.

She had no idea where she was going, only that she was not ready to confront him yet, or this spectre that looked like him. She lost her footing and sprawled with her face in the sand. The next she knew there was a great weight upon her and heavy breath on her neck. She cried out with tears and snot streaming down her face, mixing with the sand. Congealed gritty streams wet her skin.

'Rowan,' he breathed between gritted teeth, 'what are you doing?'

'Monster,' she snarled then shouted aloud, 'Monster!'

Morrick's head jerked back in surprise.

'What are you saying? I survived. We made it through together.'

She roared and tried to throw him off, but his weight was too great and his grasp too tight. But then Lynch was upon him, and a heavy boot crunched into his exposed ribs, once, twice, three times. All the air escaped him, and he immediately rolled away and nursed his side, lying in the sand sobbing.

'Don't!' called Rowan. 'Jacob, please.'

And that was all it took for Morrick to understand. Perhaps it was the use of his first name or just her inflection.

'Rowan,' he breathed, barely audible as he lay on his side next to her in the sand. She stared back into his eyes, the shimmering sea behind her. They were closer than they had been in months and further apart than it was possible for two humans to be.

'I fought for you through a dozen battles.'

'I know,' she whispered.

His voice rose to a tearful scream as he replied, 'I've killed for you, I've been wounded and branded, travelled half the world in the company of strangers, chased you through the Forest all the way from the Hinterland. You've been in my every thought; the face I see every time I blink; the name on my lips. You were all that gave me courage to stand when those around me were quailing!'

'I know,' she said, louder and defiant.

'The baby?' he asked.

Her face contorted and she twisted as she lay.

She muttered something.

'What?'

She said nothing.

'What?' he said.

'YOU MURDERED HER!' she roared. 'YOU LEFT US! YOU ABANDONED US! YOU WEREN'T THERE, AND THEY CAME, AND SHE DIED! IT'S ALL BURNED AWAY!'

And then Captain Lynch reached down and scooped her up in his arms.

'The lady's made herself clear and so have I,' said the captain, stern but calm.

'She's my wife,' Morrick repeated. He was caught in disbelief, still cradling his fractured ribs. Lynch turned away and began to walk back down the beach.

Morrick cried out as he shifted onto all fours then, giving everything in him, he sprinted forward.

'ROWAN.'

The cry split the morning air and those back in the camp stopped going about their business at the sound. The wading birds took to the skies as one.

He thundered towards Rowan, pain rippling across his ribcage and sand flying out behind him, hearing only the crashing of the waves to his left.

Lynch dropped Rowan on to her feet and stood to meet him, drawing his sword. Morrick hooked out his axe and raised it high, charging with his eyes wide and a scream issuing from his mouth.

Their weapons met and he swung down, hooking Lynch's sword out of his hand. He was about to deal a blow to his neck when Rowan, screaming, smashed into him with her shoulder and drove him down into the sand, scratching at his face and pummelling him.

And yet still Morrick tried to stand. Still he tried to speak kind words to her.

In Morrick, she saw the man she loved, but she was overwhelmed by her pain and knew that to accept she still loved him was to become open once more to all that she was denying. Here beside her, in Jacob Lynch, was a man who had taken her away from the pain and was offering her a new life.

What was this thing that cowered before her whispering lies and false promises? A shadow of a former hope? She ripped at its skin and tried to silence it. Yet it was too strong and tried to regain its feet.

Captain Lynch kicked Morrick in the ribs once more.

'Stay down!' he roared, retrieving his sword from the sand. 'Stay down.'

Morrick could not hear anything except Rowan's shrieks and the pounding of his blood as it pulsed through his veins. He cried out as once more the boot smashed into the fragile bones in his side and then there was heat and stabbing pain in his right shoulder blade. His right arm gave beneath him. Warm blood coursed over his back and down his arm.

Rowan screamed and tore away from him then, almost as an afterthought, she shouted in defiance, her cheeks wet with salt water, 'You are dead to me, servant of Awgren! Traitor! Not a man, not a father, not a husband. Murderer of babes!' She spat the words and her spittle drained into his wide eyes and gaping mouth as he fought for each painful breath. Then she ran back towards the camp.

Lynch paused for a moment and sheathed his sword, shaking his head.

'Stay down.' he said before going after his woman.

Morrick lay in the blood-soaked sand, pained and weeping. He lay there even as the waves lapped within inches of his face. He watched her go. He watched as her hair blew to the west while her screams faded from his hearing.

Chapter Twenty-One

The Folly's courtrooms were large and decorated with many ornate carvings of wood and stone. Lord Aldwyn had once presided over trials there until he had departed on his expedition into the far south. Now, so many years later, Aldwyn once more held sway over a trial, but in a cold campaign tent.

'Give an account of yourself, Captain Lynch,' he said.

'Your Grace,' Lynch stood with his hands clasped together at his waist and bowed his head in deference. 'As you are aware, I have guided the survivors from the Hinterland to this camp in order that they may remain safe and as such, I have taken them under my protection. In particular, earlier today, I was escorting Rowan along the beach when we were approached by a man bearing the mark of Awgren across his face. I judged from the lady's reaction that he was her husband, returned from the war. She made it abundantly clear that she wished to be left in peace.'

'She did, Your Grace, go so far as to run from him, but he pursued her and assaulted her at two separate junctures whilst she attempted to make her escape. He also assaulted me.'

'The conflict escalated so that I feared for the lady's safety as he was displaying considerable aggression and was armed. As such, I engaged him and pierced his shoulder with my blade in an attempt to end the assault.'

'You maintain then, that you were defending the lady?' said Aldwyn.

'I do, sir. I could have ended him upon the sand had I wished to do so, but dealt him only such a wound as would render him incapable of continuing his assault.'

Lynch bowed once more, deeper this time from the waist as though to signify the end of his account.

Lord Aldwyn scrutinised his face, drumming his fingers on the arm of his chair. He considered all that he knew of Morrick, of his family and his desperation to reach them; of how he had left his own service in pursuit of them.

'Tell me, Captain. How came you to be upon the beach with the lady, Rowan?'

Lynch stared back unblinking.

'I was escorting the lady on her walk.'

'Pure chivalry then?' Aldwyn asked. The corner of his mouth hitched into a wry smile.

Lynch coughed and cleared his throat.

'There has been a developing attachment between myself and the lady over the past weeks, Your Grace. We believed her husband to be dead and in any case, the lady has no desire to remain married to a traitor.'

'I must say, Captain, that my impression of the man is that he is intelligent, devoted to his family and his people, regardless of personal cost. Indeed, you were not to know before meeting his lady wife that I had, whilst in the south, pardoned those from the Hinterland and accepted them as my own folk.'

There was silence in the tent between the two men.

'No, Your Grace and I, of course, acknowledge your decree. The matter at hand concerned only the safety of the lady, and she is resolved on the matter. In truth, our attachment now runs deep and we had hoped to sail for the Isles to make a life there.'

'She will not speak to her husband?'

Aldwyn sighed and held up his hand before Lynch could answer.

'No, do not go on. It is not my place to meddle in the personal affairs of the people in my charge. It is however within my remit to judge them on their crimes. You strike me as an honest man. Those amongst your crew and those who know of you of old, speak well of you. You appear to have sustained injury yourself and I believe that this was no attempt at murder or wounding out of malice, that instead you deemed the action necessary.'

He stood and Lynch straightened up.

'As such, I will not be pursuing this matter further. But I advise you that before we sail in the morning, you and your crew and anyone else that wishes to come with you, should present themselves aboard my ship, the Nightingale. You may also report the findings of your failed exploratory mission.'

'The men of the Hinterland will remain posted here with the appointed garrison until such time that I release them. I will see that Morrick remains here also.'

'You will not approach Morrick, nor send others to do so. And I advise that Rowan speaks with him ere any final decision is made.'

Lynch bowed once more.

'My thanks, Your Grace. I will do your bidding and make the case to the lady, though I cannot guarantee she will acquiesce.'

'Very well, you are dismissed, Captain. And well done on your efforts to cross these lands with so many at your heels.'

Captain Lynch bowed low once more, turned on his praised heels and departed, leaving Aldwyn to muse on the situation. At length, he decided to find the woodcutter and so threw a fur cloak about him and set off into the camp, bidding his guard to stay behind.

He tramped through the mud towards that part of the camp which lay closest to the beach. The main path was guarded by two of the branded soldiers. They stood to attention as he passed by and he nodded to them in due course, mindful that he wished them to feel as though they belonged in his army. Walking the paths of the camp was heartening and the cause of despondence all at once; reunited families in their reveries could not restrain their happiness, which rankled the despondent women and children who sat alone by their fires, mourning those that they finally knew had died in the intervening months.

'Your Grace,' called Garrick. Aldwyn turned and saw the older man emerge from a tent and beckon him over.

The woodcutter lay on a cot, covered by a blanket. His shoulder was bandaged but the cuts inflicted upon his face and arms by Rowan were exposed and raw. He was staring up at the inside of the tent, but shifted his gaze to Lord Aldwyn when he heard him enter.

The duke moved to the foot of the cot and folded his arms across his chest. Morrick met his stare, but he said nothing, breathing hard. After a moment, the woodcutter rolled on to his side.

Garrick excused himself and the two men were left alone.

Aldwyn ran his eyes across the man's form and saw before him not the woodcutter, but himself, long ago injured in battle, in the days before it became apparent to Cathryn that he could no longer father children and was thus no longer a suitor. He remembered unsuccessfully attempting to shield himself from that certainty as he was stretched on a cot not dissimilar to the one on which Morrick now lay. He too had lain on his side and stared at the canvas, seeing the distant future, spurned and alone.

He felt for the man, and he thought that in some small measure he understood his pain. He too had gone to great lengths for his lady and found that it all had come to naught but heartbreak. He *still* went to great lengths for his lady.

The wind picked up and the canvas on the seaward side pressed in towards them.

Without saying a thing, Aldwyn moved behind Morrick and rested a hand on his shoulder, then departed with never a word exchanged between them.

Morrick lay in silence, his arm draped over his eyes to shut out the light that shone through the tent. He thought of the days of his earlier life in the Hinterland with his wife and children. He thought of the long, terrible, forced march on an empty stomach, of the deeds he had felt compelled to do and for whom? The Dark Lord he had never met and of whom he heard only rumour? He had killed his own kind and rallied his people to perpetrate that killing in the most brutal and efficient way possible. He and his men had stood resolute, spearing down the horses of the Combined People, ever watchful of the Devised creatures at their back.

And when finally the darkness was overthrown and his greatest hopes were achieved? All had disintegrated before his eyes. The Hinterland as he knew it was all but gone, and it was clear that his pardon was nothing but words on parchment. There could be no life for the branded men, and how would their families be treated if they returned with them to the Isles or the Folly? Surely then the soldiers of the Hinterland would need to live apart as an unclean people, or they would, by necessity, be forced to abandon their families and serve once more against their will in an army, again with little allegiance. All his old dreams of shining saviours hidden behind the tall Maw Gate or off on the Isles in the west were gone.

Where can I go now? Who will have me?

He supposed he could travel to the Isles and start a small life on some isolated scrap of land, if the lords of the Combined People would allow it. And yet the idea filled him with apathy. What would be the point? The point without his sons and without Rowan?

Rowan.

The memory of her was ever with him, laughing with him as he took her in his arms, her face contorted with rage as though she was an animal, kissing his neck as they made love, clawing at his flesh as she called him a monster. Morrick could not reconcile the two women.

What had she gone through while he was away and was he, in truth, responsible? He did not know and the question plagued him as he lay prone, unwilling to move, nor eat nor drink, though Garrick and others attended him regularly. He drifted in and out of uneasy sleep, ensuring that when he woke, he did not stir, as though by doing so he was protected from the hurt, much like a man who had drank too much ale the night before might shelter in his bed to avoid the worst of the morning's hangover.

The night passed, and preparations were made for the fleets to set sail for the invasion of Stragglers' Drift. It had been decided that only a small flotilla was to bear away to the Isles with the wounded and the refugees, before heading to the Drift with reinforcements as well as supplies.

Captain Lynch jumped from a rowing boat into the cold surf, followed by the oarsmen. Together the sailors hauled the boat upon the sand. Lynch thanked them and was assured it was not a trouble. He set off up the beach and the sand coated his boots as he walked. The preparations had all been made and he felt reasonably content that he had done all that was possible. He was far from certain how Rowan would react with the news of his latest audience with Lord Aldwyn and had avoided returning to speak with her as long as he could.

He found her in a position not dissimilar to that of Morrick. Callum and Declan were nowhere to be seen and she was tucked up in a cot, wrapped in fur and cocooned in memories.

Lynch coughed to get her attention as he pushed into the tent. She looked back over her shoulder at him.

'Where have you been?' she asked, turning back away from him.

'I have had messages to run and preparations to make,' he said. Relations between them had become cold since their encounter with Morrick on the beach. The lady's mood, ever changeable, had darkened since that day, and the Captain felt as though he had fallen from favour.

'Are you well, my love?' he said quietly and came to sit by her. She grunted in reply.

'Rowan?'

She made no reply yet again. He sighed and, resting his elbows on his knees, he bent forward and rubbed at his eyes.

'Will you not speak to me, Rowan?'

Lynch did his best to disguise any annoyance or weariness in his voice, so that it came out as artificially light amid the heavy atmosphere in the tent. Rowan could hear the attempt and it enraged her further.

She was angry. She was hurt. She was guilty. She yearned for Morrick and hated him. She yearned for Lynch and blamed him. She blamed herself for so much and yet when this conclusion drew near, her mind would not allow it and instead, unbidden, her thoughts turned to anger. Instead of accepting her part in events, she wallowed deeper in the unquiet tomb of her pain.

Lynch sighed and moved off, but she rolled and caught his trailing hand. She frowned at him.

'You want me to stay?'

The frown intensified.

'Do you?'

She nodded once, and as he sat, she rolled away again, but kept hold of his hand so that it draped across her shoulder. She released it, and he stroked the downy hair at the nape of her neck where it was too fine to be bound tight into the band above it. She shifted slightly, enjoying the sensation.

They sat this way for many minutes.

'I've been to speak to Lord Aldwyn aboard his flagship,' said the captain, continuing to stroke her with the tips of his fingers.

She made no reply.

'Are you awake?'

She nodded slightly.

'I've been to speak with Lord Aldwyn about your people.'

'And?' she whispered, and Lynch could hear the sadness in the solitary word.

'The pardon holds, but we've seen ourselves how well the commoners feel about it. There'll be no home for you and yours in the settlements of the Isles or at the Folly. The Hinterland is being abandoned for the time being.'

'I would not return there anyway,' Rowan mumbled, thinking of the fast-flowing Whiteflow and her daughter's face beneath it.

'Aldwyn is instructed to keep the Hinterland men in his service until this war is done. The queen is reluctant to let them walk free in her other lands until loyalty is assured. As for the rest of you, you do have your freedom to go where you please.'

Rowan sat up and fixed Lynch's gaze.

'So our great and noble queen is happy to cast us outside to fend for ourselves as beggars and no doubt thieves when needs must? Perhaps Awgren was not so bad - at least we kept our homes. How long before your comrades start raping and murdering our girls?' she snapped.

Now Lynch frowned and was less able to disguise his reaction. He barked back at her,

'Are you always so ungrateful, woman? I begin to wonder now, when I see how you look at me so; one who is trying to aid you, whether you do not look at your husband with those same eyes and with similar injustice.'

She made to slap him, but he caught her wrist.

'Restrain yourself, Rowan. I know you are hurting, but this will not do!' She tugged to get her arm away and he released her.

'I am bound to sail with Lord Aldwyn, and I cannot take you with me into battle,' he said.

Rowan glared at him.

'So you are done with us?' she said.

Lynch stood and stepped outside to take some air, returning once he had mastered his own temper.

'I have a great affection for you, Rowan, and I have thought of nothing but taking you and yours to safety over these past weeks. And of late, I have thought that we might find a life together.'

He stared down at her. She seemed to him to be an animal with its hackles standing on end, ready to receive him in a fury of talons and teeth. Doubt rose in him, and he was relieved it had done so before any formal ties had been made between them.

'I have secured berths for all the Hinterland refugees aboard the ships bound for the Isles. There is land enough there for you to build new homes and start again away from this place. I will come to join you when war is done and the duke grants me leave.'

At this Rowan felt her anger abate somewhat.

'The queen would allow it?' she said, thinking of her cottage by the sea.

'Aye, she will. You can start anew, away from the judgement of bitter eyes and in time, maybe in the time of your grandchildren, the memories of the betrayal of your ancestors and your menfolk will fade.'

Rowan looked down to her lap, nodding. Lynch saw a tear roll down her pale cheek. He went once more to sit beside her.

'What are you thinking?' he said.

She shook her head and buried his face in the fur that covered his shoulder. She would say no more.

Lynch wrapped his arms around her, and he wrestled between guilt and relief, feeling certain that Rowan would go forth, and he would be released from his recently implied commitments to her.

'What of your sons? Will they come with you?'

She pushed away from him.

'What do you mean? Surely they are not bound into service?'

Lynch shook his head.

'Nay, but will they willingly leave their father?'

'After all he has put us through?'

Tense silence. Lynch eventually broke it.

'Sons do not always see things with their mother's eyes. They still have great love for Morrick,' he cautioned. 'They do not see events as do you. They believe he did no more than he was compelled to do and, in all honesty, lady, there is some truth in that.'

'*What?*' she said.

'I know that were I in your husband's place, I would have gone to war just as he did. What choice would I have, knowing I had a wife and children to protect?'

'You don't understand,' she said, almost a shriek. She lay down once more and rolled onto her side away from him.

'I'll speak with the boys and glean what I can from them.'

Lynch stood and as Rowan made no reply, simply lying there with her shoulders heaving up and down under the blanket, he departed. As he made his way through the lanes to his own tent, he breathed out a loud, heart-heavy sigh into the biting wind.

'We can't just leave him again,' insisted Callum. He had been standing over her and now folded his arms. Rowan stood and loomed over him.

'We never left him. He abandoned us and now it's time you see your father for the man he truly is!'

'He never wanted to go! He didn't want to leave us! I saw him weeping the last time he left. I saw *you* weeping to see him go. It wasn't until he showed up,' he pointed at Captain Lynch, 'that you started talking ill of Father!'

Declan's arms were folded too, but he was digging his nails into his upper arms and backed as far into a corner of the tent as the canvas allowed. Lynch thought the boy was near to tears.

'What gives you the right to speak to me in such a way, you ungrateful boy?' spat Rowan and she *was* crying.

Lynch felt a near irresistible urge to escape. He felt for the woman, but all the more now he was coming to believe that perhaps he had judged the woodcutter harshly – following his heart rather than his head.

'I'm not ungrateful!' shouted the boy. 'But I won't leave Father after he's been through so much for us!'

'You have no choice!' hollered Rowan. Her voice was raucous and ragged. It seemed to tear the air around them, and Lynch was compelled to step forward to intervene before things escalated further.

'The boy will have to decide for himself, Rowan.'

'No!' she shrieked, 'No, I won't lose another one! Not on account of him!'

Callum stood resolute, arms folded across his chest and his face a mask. Lynch clutched Rowan to him, and his eyes made a desperate appeal to the boy.

'It's not that I don't love you, Mother, but I cannot forsake my father. He belongs with us.'

'He left us! He left us to those savages and we are one the fewer for it!'

'Father didn't kill the baby,' snapped Callum, 'you did!'

Rowan pushed both palms into Lynch's chest with such force that she broke his hold on her, and he fell back a step. She snarled as she sprang forward and dealt Callum a heavy blow across his face with such speed and ferocity that he fell down. He made no sound, just stared up at her with accusing eyes as she stood panting over him.

'Go to him then. Go and be damned!' She turned and taking Declan's hand, she tore out of the tent and through the partially struck camp.

Lynch shook his head and reached down a hand. Callum looked as though he might not take it for a moment, and Lynch was about to withdraw when the boy's fingers curled around his wrist. The captain hauled him to his feet.

'Do you not see that she is quite mad?' asked the boy.

Lynch said nothing, but took off his hat, swept back his hair and replaced it. The two of them exchanged a glance.

'Go seek for your father, Callum, and wish him well from me. Please send him my regrets. It was never my intent to hurt or malign an honest man.'

Callum nodded.

'I will, and I know it. I appreciate all you did for us. Even if things have turned out badly for our family, it could have ended far worse without your aid.'

With that Lynch withdrew and sought for Rowan. He found her on the beach with her arm around Declan, waiting for a boat to take them to a ship, along with Garrick, Acorna and the rest of the refugees.

Lynch tousled the boy's hair, but Declan did not look up. His chest was heaving and the captain could hear him sob. He turned his attention to Rowan, whose eyes were red and puffy. Her pale cheeks had come up in red blotches and in her face he saw little of the beauty he had come to admire over the past weeks.

'I will keep an eye out for Callum when I can, my love,' he said, hoping the last did not sound as false as it felt. 'I will see him returned to you in due course, fate permitting. Do not harden your heart against him.'

Rowan's weeping eyes looked out to sea, but she rested her cheek on his shoulder.

'We're to be put down on the Butterfly Isle, so they say.'

'I heard as much,' said Lynch. 'There's good land there and woodland as well. You'll be able to make a life.'

She said nothing but slung her other arm around him.

The time came and without further discourse, Rowan led Declan to the boat and Lynch, solemn and still, watched as they were rowed out towards the flotilla in the bay.

He made his way up the beach, picking his way between the slippery rocks and across the slippery seaweed, with the sound of the waves in his ears and salt air in every breath.

Callum reached the tent where his father had been recovering to find that it was empty and devoid of all possessions, save for his father's axe. He lifted it and turned it in his hands, knowing that Morrick would never abandon it in his right mind. In alarm, he ran for the palisade gate and there questioned the guard.

'A branded man passed through some time ago. What of it?'

'Which way did he go?' asked Callum and followed the guard's gesture in the direction of the treeline. He set off after him at a run.

Riark was perched high upon Mount Greenwood in the midst of the forest when he sensed that the woodcutter had already re-entered his realm. He dispersed into the matter of the growing mountain and travelled deep into the soil, arriving in a birch tree not far from where Morrick had been last seen. He concentrated his being and the leaves whispered to him. Once more he travelled into the soil and, stepping out of the bark of an oak, he found Morrick.

The woodcutter was hanging by the neck from one of the lower branches, his skin blue and his eyes bulging, the light fading from within them.

Riark thrust his limbs into the trunk of the tree and his essence swelled the branch around which Morrick's belt was tied. It expanded with such force that the leather broke and the woodcutter's body fell to the ground.

Riark spread his open hands across the woodcutter's face and focused all his thought into feeling the very molecules of the woodcutter's skin. He slipped his own between them and the two creatures began to merge. His sap seeped into the woodcutter's veins, mingling with the blood that cooled as it lay still within them. Riark grew within the woodcutter, pulsing through his cells and his organs, his thought coursing into the flesh. Near done, but not quite, Riark took the woodcutter into his arms and beneath him his form began to shift; where moments before, an approximation of a man had tended the human cadaver, now Riark appeared as a great stallion with a mane of moss and hide of interlocking oak leaves. Morrick was across his back and yet part of it, too.

Callum burst into the clearing just as Riark bore the woodcutter away, but the Dryad checked his pace and extended roots into the ground for a moment. Without a glance backwards, he galloped into the forest at a pace unmatched by any animal that walked the land.

Riark's form intermingled with the woodcutter's as they travelled. Morrick's body writhed and contorted, as though something was fighting to depart it and yet was prevented from so doing.

Callum cried out as he saw his father carried away and broke into a run, but another such steed as he had just beheld leaped from an ash tree up ahead. Nayr sat astride it.

Callum came to a halt with eyes wide as Nayr extended a hand towards him.

Chapter Twenty-Two

The combined fleet of Queen Cathryn and Lord Aldwyn departed Oystercatcher Bay and sailed for the Drift.

Cathryn retired to her cabin as soon as they were at open sea and insisted that Ailsa share a bottle with her. Her aide had private concerns about the queen's increased intake, but thought better of expressing them. As predicted, one bottle turned into two and two turned into three. Ailsa was grateful that the ship had a limited supply.

Lord Aldwyn stayed on deck for much of that first day and often took a turn at the wheel, while Lynch set about forgetting the business of the last few weeks and trying to make a good impression on his commander in the hope that he might soon command a vessel of his own.

Rowan and Declan passed their first afternoon at sea overcome with sickness of both stomach and mood. They sailed westward for their new home in the Isles, but a great sadness was upon them, and they cowered below decks together to seek what comfort they could in each other's arms.

Morrick awoke to find himself hemmed in by wood. He thrashed about and
felt as though his limbs were moving through slime. His brain told him his
knuckles scraped against the wood, yet it was not so.

I'm in a coffin, he thought and tried to beat upon it, screaming silently as
he imagined his mouth and lungs filling with fluid.

The tunnels beneath the Whoreswood stretched far out in many directions,
with entrances concealed in rock outcrops and copses all around the area. Under
Stragglers' End itself, the tunnels widened into caverns and halls, crudely
fashioned and supported with beams of timber, hewn centuries before.

Habit clutched a flaming torch and held it aloft as she guided the way.
Behind her came Lachlan, Hadwyn and Belman, then her own people. Two
young men dragged Habit's mother along on a bier.

'I've lost all notion of time,' said Hadwyn and his voice echoed up and
down the tunnels, competing with the sound of their feet.

'That's all time is,' said Habit, 'a notion. See how you fare just as well
without it?'

Lachlan looked back over his shoulder at his brother's features in the torch
light. He smiled.

'We've arrived,' said Habit.

The party found themselves in a cavern taller than most and widening out
on either side of the tunnel. Beds were made up around the walls, with wicker
partitions separating each small area from the next. A circle of benches stood
off to their left. Lachlan noticed the walls were of chalk and that moisture ran
down them, dripping to form pools upon the floor.

Habit's mother was drawn up to one of the beds, and the two men lifted
her as gently as was possible to lay her upon the furs atop it, propping her up
so that she could see the room. Men began to emerge from the shadows at the
base of the far walls of the cavern and began to congregate about them.

'Well met, brothers,' said Habit. 'Best you put on your shirts and shine up
your armour. We have many a noble visitor this day.'

'Oh aye?' said a short, fair man who stepped out from the crowd.

Habit saw him and gave a little shriek of excitement. She hurried over to embrace him, her height making him look all the shorter. Lachlan wondered for a moment if he was her lover, but the look of the embrace suggested siblings. She stepped back and waved a hand towards the three southern nobles.

'Lachlan, Lord of the Isles. Lord Hadwyn, Steward of the Isles. Lord Belman, General of the Isles.'

'Did they take a wrong turn?' said the fair-haired man, but even as he smiled he bowed low. Lachlan returned the gesture.

'Many a wrong turn,' he replied, 'and I am in need of your assistance.'

'What would the Lord of the Isles ask of the likes of us?' said the man.

'Your name, sir?'

'Sir!' the man laughed. 'William. Her brother.'

'William,' said Lachlan, 'I've come to see whether the Partisans still honour the line of Tayne.'

'They do,' interrupted Habit. 'So say I, and I is the only one that has say.'

She turned to her brother.

'We need word sent to the four winds to gather both our strength of numbers and to find out what support there is for the queen of the Combined People. Linwood has seceded and declared war.'

A murmur grew up amongst the crowd. It heartened Lachlan and his allies. He nodded, held up his hands and thanked them.

'Might we prevail upon your generosity here until I can muster enough troops to move in the open against him?'

Habit nodded.

'Beacon Hall is, as of yet, unoccupied.'

Belman started forward.

'Beacon Hall? Surely…'

'Straight out of legend,' said William. 'Ancient seat of the long-forgotten natives hereabouts. Our people found it during their tunnelling under the Drift.'

'The northern kings are nothing but a fairy story,' said Hadwyn. 'There was never any proof that men lived north of the forest before the Combined People were forced into exile.'

'Proof enough if Beacon Hall truly exists!' said Lachlan, ending the conversation. 'Lead on and indeed, send word and find out what numbers can be gathered. Bring all who are loyal to Beacon Hall.'

Outside the gate of Stragglers' End, Linwood's army had formed up on the east road. When all were assembled the lord appeared, resplendent in full armour, and rode to the head of the column. He set out towards the forest and the march began.

They advanced on throughout the night and into the next day, resting only when necessary and only for as long as was required to prevent men from dropping out of the march. Outriders gathered more men from the surrounding villages, and all who saw them marvelled at the spectacle of thousands of armed troops as they trudged ever eastward.

Linwood raised his fist and halted the line. His captains gathered about him and he gave his orders with no embellishments and no fuss.

'I want encampments from coast to coast, each just within sight of the next. Say, half a mile out from the treeline. The watch must be maintained at all times both to the front and to the rear. I will advance to Lady Isobel's position. The outermost camps will light signal fires when in position and the next camp will do the same when ready. When I, at the central camp, see lights in the north and the south, we will strike. Understood?'

Grim men and women nodded then spurred their horses and rode away.

And so while Lachlan's spies delved into the hearts of his people, Linwood's soldiers fanned out across the northern border of the forest, and as they reached their given positions they made camp. Days passed. Linwood's people took up their positions, while Lachlan and Habit gathered what strength they could in the ancient caverns of Beacon Hall.

Linwood spent his days as was his custom; he rose before dawn and bathed. He donned his full armour, regardless of the likelihood of combat, and then visited his sentries. He led a morning briefing of the captains and received reports from up and down the line. After briefing, he sat at the board to breakfast alone, supping on warm beer and picking at slivers of his cheese. His stomach full, he took to a square prepared for his own use where he would spar with the best fighters in his retinue while his captains paraded the men elsewhere; after all, he did not want them to see any weakness in his art.

Normally he would ride out in the evening, but one day after the northern camp's beacon was lit, he was preparing to mount when a runner came to tell him that the southern beacon too was aflame.

Linwood checked his progress, one foot in the stirrup then nodded before hauling himself up.

'Send word to the captains. Prepare the archers and on my mark, send out the advance parties.'

Ere long Linwood set his horn to his lips and let out five long blasts. For a hundred miles to the north and a hundred to the south, the call was taken up and the air rang with the sound of horns.

Up and down the line, companies of men bearing torches marched forward and made for the trees where the forest bordered Stragglers' Drift. Linwood took himself alone to a high place and there he watched and waited. Lady Isobel came to join him after a time and stayed silent beside him until she could hold her tongue no longer.

'Do you believe we can withstand them if they come? We know not their numbers or their true strength? And we have Lachlan at our back,' she said, respectful and cautious, yet determined to be heard.

Linwood turned and smiled, but his eyes were cold, and she felt her skin prickle.

'I will not be dictated to in my own land. Not by Lachlan, nor by a talking man of the forest, regardless of his strength. The Creatures of the Devising and Awgren himself fell before the might of King Linwood and the Stragglers. We shall see how the Dryads fare.'

With that he let out a long solitary blast on his horn and once again it was echoed from coast to coast.

Let them burn, he thought. *Let them burn and see who is mighty when the ashes are taken up by the wind and dumped in the seas.*

The advance parties broke into a run and when they reached the treeline they set all about them aflame with their torches. Once as much as was alight as they could manage, they hurled the brands far into the darkness to kindle the undergrowth. Once the torches were thrown, they ran back towards the camps, huffing and blowing but daring not to look back, for rumour was growing amongst them about what lurked beneath the dark boughs – something terrible that could not be killed by anything but flame.

Linwood watched as the darkening sky filled with smoke as the fires took hold. A wall of flame rose high, consuming grass, root, trunk, branch and leaf. Animals ran before the flames ever into the depths of the woods, and Linwood's men retreated unscathed. They took formation, turned and watched as the forest began to burn.

Linwood bade his horse come about and sent orders for dinner to be set upon the board.

Encased within the trunk of a wide black oak, Morrick began to sense he was not in a coffin. It was as though he was suspended in honey, upright and unseeing. When he beat upon the wood now, he realised that there was no sensation in his hands, merely the anticipation of contact, and yet he knew that wood was before him and around him. When he breathed, there was no intake of breath into actual lungs. He was remembering breathing and imagining the sensation. His mind hurled left and right, up and down, seemingly confined within his skull, but as time wore on (and he knew not how much) the sensation of being trapped began to lessen. He knew it not, but his body was dissolving around him even as his spirit fought to move it as it once had. For every realisation of what he was becoming, a little less the corporeal sensation became.

Emotions fired and raged within him, and at times it was as though he occupied his memories bodily and yet after a time, he would see them for what they were. He felt as though a billion parts of him were arcing around a billion obstacles and his essence began to flow up and down, to expand and contract. He felt life flowing through him and contentment with it. There was no hunger or thirst. Even his emotions were but approximations and yet they remained compelling. He was haunted by faces and impulses; to love, to fight, to run and hide. He struggled less and less until his spirit settled and was content to flow up and around the tree until it filled every leaf, root and twig. Yet when he reached the tips of the roots he shrank back and remained within the black oak, though he knew not why. There was no sight or touch, merely thought and being. Images of his old life plagued him.

Time and again he would strive to move his body, though by now he knew that what had once been flesh and bone had now dissipated within the tree.

Then he was not alone. On a day when a breeze stirred his branches with a chillness that curled his leaves, he felt a presence with him. He knew her at once and yet could not place her. She was soothing and coursed through him.

Daughter, he thought.

The presence remained for a time then drained out through his roots.

Daughter, he thought again, then dwelt on it no more.

He began to hear others, although hear was not quite correct. He began to know others. To know what they knew, but as understanding not as information. He also began to feel sudden losses as the forest diminished. He sensed the burning of the trees in the north.

'Father.'

He could not hear as he had done as a human, yet the words were spoken and his spirit heard. Someone stood on the outside of this wall of wood, this upright coffin in which he had found such peace.

Morrick swam forward through the trunk of the tree as he had once done through the Whiteflow. He concentrated hard and imagined his hands were extending out before him, visualising it. He felt his open palms reach the inside of the bark and imagined himself with substance until he sank to where the roots emerged above the soil, never relinquishing his hands' touch of the bark. He stepped forward and met resistance. He exerted all his being and forced onward until his hands breached the exterior of the tree.

Callum looked across the glade at the foot of Mount Greenwood towards the black oak. He jumped to his feet, but at the sight of two clawing hands of bark thrusting out from within it, he spluttered and fell back against a tree. Chips of bark dropped from the hands as they kept moving towards him and long black arms became visible. Callum's hands rose to his face and clasped his open mouth, but a reassuring hand took a hold of his shoulder and Riark was there beside him.

'Fear not,' he creaked as he swayed, 'he will know you.'

Morrick felt drained as he expended all that he had into escaping the bounds of the tree. His arms were now full formed, and he stepped forward so that one gnarled foot burst forth. He hooked the other out and dropped his arms back so that he could exert pressure on the trunk and prise the rest of his body into the light. His long torso of black polished wood, armoured in scales of bark, arched out of the trunk followed slowly, by his face and head.

Callum saw a roaring, screaming mask form from the tree, and in a whipping motion, it swept forward. A few moments more and a creature in the shape of a man stood before Callum and the king of the Dryads. It stood some six-feet tall and its bark was living armour, wrapped in tight intricate patterns around him, layering up before their eyes as though it were being carved from a block. Bands of thin wood rose and fell until the figure resembled a carved statue of some decorated god, adorned in the finest armour. The face, however, was of dark polished wood and deep within the sink holes of the eyes, white stars shone out. There was no mouth and to begin with, the head was smooth. Then long, tangled ivy, black and curling, burst through the wood of his head and grew until its ends swayed and tickled the grass.

This thing before him was breathing, Callum could see that and yet there were no orifices though which it could take breath.

He thinks he's breathing, Callum thought. *He doesn't know.*

The creature that had once been his father raised his head in a familiar way and smiled. At least, the surface of the wood hitched up as would cheeks and jowls if a mouth had moved. The effect was unnerving, and Callum shivered. As though he realised what he lacked, Morrick whipped his head back and forth until a ragged mouth burst open, as though he had screamed through lips which had been sewn together.

It was monstrous and Callum was afraid, despite Riark's warning.

'He looks as he feels,' said the Dryad, leaning to whisper in the boy's ear, 'but you need not be afraid. He will know you.'

Morrick stepped forward and loud cracking sounds signalled the first bending of his imagined knees.

'Son,' he said in the hiss of steaming water. Flecks of green foam shot out of his mouth and bubbled around his lips.

'Father,' said Callum, shrinking behind Riark.

Morrick's fingers groped at his neck, feeling for the noose.

'You died – as you wished,' said Riark.

Morrick's white eyes turned on him, and Callum had the impression of intense fury.

'You deny me even death?' he roared, his volume completely unrestrained and unbelievable to Callum. Birds rose up from all around to make their escape. Callum closed his eyes then took a deep breath and stepped forward.

'They saved you, Father. I came after you, but was too late. I couldn't leave.'

Morrick's head turned slowly, and he regarded his son.

'Your sister was here. With me.'

Callum was puzzled. He looked up at Riark who shook his head.

'Now is not the time,' he said. The king of the Dryads turned back to Morrick.

'The woodcutter is dead, but his spirit endures. You are of the forest now, more so than you ever were. And though now you still feel the pain of your passing and carry with you the memories of your life, the more time you spend within the trees, the less you will feel and the less you will remember.' Riark smiled. 'You will have peace.'

The Dryad that was once Morrick looked from Riark to Callum and back.

'My son?'

Riark nodded yet again.

'He may stay with you if he wishes or our people will guide him back out of the forest.'

'I want to stay with you,' blurted Callum.

Morrick stared at him then down at his own hands, turning them before him as though trying to take their measure.

'Who am I?' he said, cracking and creaking as the wood around his lips softened and split.

'You're my father,' said Callum.

'You had a name. I forget it. You were the woodcutter,' said Riark.

Morrick leant back against the black oak and his shoulder blades absorbed back into the trunk. To Callum his father looked as though he had been whittled from a living branch, he was so much a part of the tree and yet still in the form of man.

'I was a woodcutter and now I am of the wood.'

'Of the oak,' said Riark.

The Dryad that was Morrick smiled, and Callum laughed uneasily, surprising himself. Riark turned to him, inclining his head.

'That's what his name means. Morrick. It means of the oak,' Callum explained. 'He told me so before he went to war.'

Riark locked eyes with Morrick.

'Of the dark oak.'

And Morrick nodded.

He remembered all that he had forgotten as a human now that he was no longer constrained by a brain. He knew every word he had heard or spoken, remembered all he had seen.

'Yet it will all go, of that I can assure you,' said Riark, 'the more time you spend with the trees.'

'Will the hate subside?' asked the Dryad that had been Morrick.

Callum sensed heat coming from him, and indeed, steam rose from the cracks in his bark. Ivy thrashed and danced around him.

'It will,' said Riark.

Morrick was quiet for a time.

'I do not wish to forget the hate. I need it.'

Riark shook his head.

'For what? No, but I do need you to remember some things. I made you an offer; that you could reside with us if I could take counsel with you. You are new-born to the forest and retain all that you knew. At a time when war is being waged upon us, your insight will be invaluable.'

Riark turned and walked towards the slopes of Mount Greenwood. Before him the wood parted into a doorway. Callum and the Dryad that was Morrick walked through into the green twilight of the king's halls. He strode towards his bower across many miles while they spoke.

'The humans have set the forest ablaze. Very soon the flames will engulf Mother Trees and so, as I promised to both the child of the linden dell and his queen, I must act.'

'What will you do?' asked Callum, kneeling to drink from a narrow stream that broke the green carpet of the floor.

'What will *we* do?' said a voice. Callum saw a woman form amongst the water and spat a mouthful back into the steam. She tinkled a laugh, and her flowing hair washed down behind her till it rejoined the water. Fish swam up her and a weed flailed within one of her legs.

Morrick offered Callum a hand and helped him to his feet.

'Your sister…' he said.

Callum's eyes widened, and the Naiad stepped forward to embrace him, drenching him as she did so. She laughed again, and he stepped back, not sure what to think or feel. He fell down upon the bank and rubbed his eyes.

'Bracken?' he said. 'I wonder when I will wake.'

'I was Bracken. Now I am Whiteflow.'

Morrick and the Naiad sat down beside Callum. Riark stood off a little way, regarding the reunited family with curiosity.

'I seek your father's advice,' said Riark. 'He knows their ways better than most. He has been a soldier and he has fought the men who now encroach on my realm.'

Callum looked to his father in anticipation, but Morrick did not seem to respond.

'Dark Oak?' asked Riark.

Morrick looked up.

'What would you have me tell you?' he asked and, for the first time, he extended his fingers so they burrowed like worms into the soil. Riark watched him with amusement as a mother might watch a child attempting to crawl.

'If I respond with force, will he stop the onslaught?' asked Riark.

Dark Oak pondered for a time whilst all the while the Naiad, Riark and Callum watched him.

'Linwood has designs on the whole continent. He wants his road. And from what you have told me, you have shamed him. He is not a man who will be slighted. I believe he will let the forest burn if he can. You must destroy him if the forest is to survive,' he said, and when he had concluded, his fingers shrank back to their usual size and he trailed the tips in the stream, feeling again the pain of the branding he had suffered at the man's hand. Callum looked on in horror as the wood of his father's cheek splintered until an approximation of the brand was etched thereon.

Riark turned to Whiteflow.

'Will the Naiads assist us in quenching the fire's thirst?'

'We will,' she said in her shrill voice. 'I suspect the Sylphs will assist as well. The smoke pollutes the skies beyond their tolerance.'

She turned to Callum.

'The whole northern border is ablaze. Streams dry up and smoke fills the air.'

Riark nodded and walked onwards towards his bower, underneath the splendid branches of his elm.

'You are too weak to come with us. Rest here with your children and when this business is done, I will set a place apart for your boy.'

With that, Riark dived into the trunk of his Mother Tree and was gone. Morrick stayed a respectful distance back from the elm, but Callum went on into the bower and nestled into a bowl of the tree, pulling his cloak about him.

The Naiad turned to Morrick.

'Dark Oak,' she said and advanced upon him. Morrick knew not why, but he wrapped his arms around her. She was drawn up into him and he knew her mind utterly.

To Callum's eyes, his father seemed to become inanimate when the Naiad entered him. It was not until she dripped out of his fingers and the ends of his hair and formed again, lying like a cat curled at his feet, that his father moved once again.

Dark Oak reached out to Callum, beckoning him over.

'Tell me. What do you think of the world?'

'How do you mean?' said the boy.

'I thought so little of it that I left it,' said Dark Oak, 'or tried to do so. Do you think it is a good place? Are you happy?'

Callum thought for a while.

'I think it's neither good nor bad, that bad things happen and so do good.'

'And what causes the bad things?' said Dark Oak.

'Humans,' said Whiteflow, and they both turned their eyes upon Callum.

Chapter Twenty-Three

Life, in Linwood's experience, was relentless; it kept coming at you and it was your task to strike, parry or evade as appropriate. Some men remained where they stood, turning frantic circles in the dark as fate approached, parrying shadow-feints and fighting foes that emerged from the mist, but Linwood believed in running head on towards what sought you and in giving it no quarter.

And yet as he sat in his command tent and the forest burned, he doubted himself. He doubted the course upon which he had set his people. He knew not whether he should have acted with more caution and yet, he had moved in haste— gone forward with an act that could not be undone, and so now he must wait.

For what good would it be, to turn tail and depart for Stragglers' End if the fires did not stop Riark and his people, if they decided to make a stand? Linwood had spent his whole life at war fighting not only the humans of the Hinterland, but the Creatures of the Devising – many of which were huge and hideous, powerful to an extreme; he had been battered and scarred as he hunted them; and yet he had never met an enemy like Riark, who emanated such tangible and justifiable arrogance it could cause him to doubt himself, an experienced man of war.

And while perhaps Aldwyn and Cathryn had one another, while Lachlan could debate his concerns with his friend and brother, Linwood was utterly alone, just as he had always been. He brooded in his chair, and the only counsellor he would ever heed was the voice in his mind.

He mulled over tens of options, weighing up the risks and benefits then hurling the scale away when considering the importance of his honour; honour that far outweighed all risk to himself and his people.

He did not sleep, but thought throughout the night, though his eyelids were heavy.

His reverie was interrupted by a great shouting from many voices, pitched with panic and growing ever louder. His castellan, Willard, burst into the command tent.

'Sire!' was all he said before disappearing again. Linwood rose slowly despite the obvious need for haste and found his hands were shaking. His chest felt tight as he marched out into the night.

His tent opened onto the main road to the forest, and he passed hurriedly along it, tucking his thumbs behind his belt so that the tremor in his hands was under control, he made for the crest of the road where the grass plains rolled down towards the treeline. The ridge was manned by every bowman that could be gathered and as many regular soldiers as could be found bows. The rise and fall of their outlines glowed in the light of the bonfires by which they kept warm.

Linwood looked down over the incline of the slope and knew, finally, that he had made a mistake.

Behind a tract of bare black poles shrouded in smoke, the forest was ablaze but the flames, moving faster than a man can run, were the least of it. Towers of grey smoke reached hundreds of feet up into the air, glowing orange deep within the body of the cloud, its outer edges curling back towards the armies of mankind with the wind. The smoke blotted out the sky all across the continent. Linwood looked at the sheer scale of what he had done and was overawed by it. He marvelled at the power of the fire and was afraid, knowing that it was far beyond his control.

And yet he had not seen what concerned his castellan, not until the man seized him by the shoulder and pointed.

'In the cloud!'

Linwood looked and narrowed his eyes, unsure of what he was seeing.

High above the trees, just visible in the moonlight and the glow of the fire, the smoke was beginning to whirl and funnel as though it were forming an unsupported river flowing across the sky. Then, his mind finally adjusting, he saw that like the images he had imagined in clouds as a child, the smoke had in many places taken on the form of gargantuan figures, dancing high above them and it was the grace of their movements that guided the smoke into the suspended river.

Linwood said nothing, his mouth hanging open.

'What are they?' asked Willard, but Linwood could give no answer and before he could think of anything to say, as though his appearance on the hillside had been noted by faraway watchers, the onslaught began.

The river of smoke changed its course and with all the speed of a hurricane, the Sylphs cast it down upon Linwood's armies so that the men were as pebbles pinned by the weight of a waterfall. The hillside was choked, and all about him cries and shouts changed to retching coughs and spluttering. Linwood could see nothing and blundered with arms outstretched this way and that as he hacked his lungs up. His foot caught and someone shouldered into him so that Linwood crashed down upon his side, his feet still ensnared between the legs of a dead man.

He tried to call out, but he could not breathe let alone make a coherent sound.

Then as quick as it came upon them, the smoke wheeled away up into the sky forming a churning grey mountain that retained its shape and yet continued to flow upward thousands of feet in the air where at its peak a great cloud erupted and spread across the skies far above. Linwood coughed until his lungs were raw and scrabbled to his feet, as did his men. Many had succumbed to the smoke, and Linwood looked upon the fallen in horror.

They had yet to draw their weapons and yet men were dying.

He stared up at the cloud, unfeasibly high above him then his eyes fell upon the forest.

It was no longer aflame.

Blackened skeletons of trees, partially burned trunks and the unhurt woods beyond were now islands in a shallow lake which seemed to be washing outwards and towards him. Distant though they were, Linwood was certain that he could see the shape of women moving in the water, seemingly urging it onwards like mothers following behind young children taking their first steps.

'Rally the men,' Linwood said. The words were husky and choked so he cleared his throat and called again.

'RALLY THE MEN!'

About him his army came to some semblance of order as they heeded the orders of the captains that remained, and discipline returned to their ranks. The lessened army reformed either side of him and waited.

Dawn approached, but a great storm was gathering overhead which limited the light. Linwood saw the first of the Dryads emerge from the smouldering forest under the darkening sky. Rain began to fall as the Dryads charged.

They burst forth from the treeline as thunder boomed in the clouds above. The Dryads came on in their thousands; the raging elm and the flash of the lancing silver birch. The marauding willows swept their cat-o'-nine-tail manes and lashed leafy tendrils in a mad frenzy. These and many besides.

The line of men did not quite falter, but it wavered – a ripple ran down it. Lightning shimmered across their armour and Linwood was reminded, absurdly in such a moment, of fish darting just below the surface of the little rivers of his homeland.

Beneath Mount Greenwood all was quiet.

Callum sat in Riark's bower in the shade of the Mother Tree. Dark Oak peered at him and Callum thought his father was weighing something up. Callum looked back in return. In his father he saw none of the beauty of Riark or the other Dryads who had wandered the woods while Callum had awaited his father's awakening. Instead he saw the gnarled, blackened woods of horror-filled fairy tales when he looked at what Morrick had become, this Dark Oak.

'You look cold,' said Dark Oak, and Callum jumped at the sound. He laughed and flashed a humourless smile, nodding fast. Cold sweat beaded on the skin of his brow.

'I am cold,' he said.

'We should build a fire,' said Whiteflow, and Dark Oak shot her a look then returned his gaze to Callum, the white stars of his eyes fixing him with their cold stare.

Callum shivered, and shadows seemed to draw in around them.

'A fire? But...'

'I won't take offence,' Dark Oak creaked.

So Callum nodded and set about gathering fallen wood and kindling. Dark Oak began to build the fire and beckoned Callum to come and sit by him.

'Archers! The archers! Now!' called Willard and along the line the many archers set flaming arrows to their strings. Needing no order, they began to fire high into the air so that the flames arced upwards and fell amongst the horde of Dryads as it rampaged towards them. The arrows found their marks but with no nerves to feel the impact or brain to process the pain, the Dryads did not hesitate for a second.

Still the archers fired arrow after arrow, but Linwood's spirits sank when he saw that his preparations had been for nothing. The Dryads burned and yet they did not die, for what ran at the army of men was but tree shaped in form by spirit and only the death of a Mother Tree could end its Dryad. Now the Dryads who had been hit were flaming brands come to life.

The distance closed, and Linwood knew that his time had come. He called for his horse and sitting proud and high upon it, he called out to his captains and his men alike, though he had no words with which to kindle their courage.

'Throw down your bows and stand your ground!' he roared, and he rode back behind the lines. Men took up their tall shields and interlocked them so that they formed a long wall, their swords held high in readiness.

The Dryads hit the shield wall like a herd of buffalo hits a grass plain. Men were trampled beneath their weight or hurled high into the air as the Dryads careered on through the ranks. The men roared and screamed as they fought, but their enemies moved swiftly and silently amongst them as though they were roots slowly cracking the earth or outstretched branches gradually depriving a flower of light. They overwhelmed Linwood's armies, and it seemed to him that they were moving in a wedge towards him, driving a path through his men. Most of the Stragglers stood their ground, but those who did were turned aside or killed. Where swords and axes struck home they broke against the solid wood or stuck fast in it.

Linwood had seen many a battle in his day and had never led from the rear, and yet he could not bring himself to spur his horse onwards to take the fight to his foe. He sat high above the heads of his army, and he saw Riark, king of the Dryads bear down upon him. The Dryad had grown in size to twice the height of a man and rode a steed which resembled a great horse, and yet seemed to be composed only of living roots and thorns. His attire was a mockery of Linwood's own armour, matching it in shape and style, yet of wood not steel. The vines which flowed from the crown of Riark's head flowed out behind him and yet, like a ring of standing stones emerging from dense undergrowth, a tall crown rose up from his head. There was no emotion in the Dryad's face as its eyes fell upon Linwood, but the steed wheeled without a sound and set its head down as it galloped towards him.

Linwood's body shook all over, but he cried out and dug his spurs into his mount's flank. The beast sprang forward and the two kings hurtled straight for one another.

Between them, the Dryads swept a channel through the army of men, no longer making any attempt to kill them, only to restrain them and hold them back. Their efforts left a channel of bare ground between Linwood and Riark as they closed the distance. Linwood drew his sword and held it aloft, ready to strike out as they met and then, as though he was not bound by the laws of the earth as man understands them, Riark and his steed stopped dead, their forms merging until finally there was only Riark standing straight and tall before him. All this transpired in the split second before Linwood reached him and, as it had before in Riark's presence, Linwood's horse reared and threw its rider.

Linwood fell heavily and was coated in thick mud, his bones broken and his mind utterly aghast with fear. He had provoked this spectacle, it seemed, only so that he could be thrown down in dismay. Linwood wept as he raised his face from the filth and though he tried to roll onto his back or stand, he could not. Root tentacles burst from the ground and seized him around the wrists, ankles and neck, pulling him deeper into the mud. He writhed and kicked as Morrick had done while he hung by the neck, nearing death.

Riark did not seem to move as he looked down upon Linwood's contorting, drowning form. Linwood's eyes were wide but saw nothing as he sank deeper, pulled ever downward, inch by inch, while the mud of his kingdom filled his lungs. Riark was a towering elm, the dark sky all around him and lightning forking down from the great cloud of smoke above. The Sylphs loomed in the air above him, crowding round and the Naiads swam up out of the mud sending a little wave all about them so that Linwood's form bobbed upon it like driftwood on the seashore. They flowed over the burning Dryads to extinguish the flames, leaving them to guard their king even as their charred forms steamed.

Finally Riark's tentacle roots released their grip, and Linwood lay dead and drowned with Stragglers' Drift filling his lungs.

Riark surveyed the balking army that by now had all turned to face him, swords still in their hands and yet rooted to the spot, their many voices enmeshed and indistinguishable as they cried out in fear.

'Silence,' Riark roared. 'Here lies your dead duke. Gone is your allegiance to him. He has led you on a path of folly, and he has paid dearly, as have many of your comrades. Throw down your arms now and seek your homes. Enter not my realm again, and do not dare make war with us lest you all end your days lying face-down in the very earth itself,' he concluded. His voice was terrible and when he was done the words echoed up and down the slopes competing with the furious storm.

The Sylphs dissipated into the air, and the Naiads drained back into the soil, as did the waters which had welled up from within the forest.

Riark began to diminish in stature as he was left alone in the centre of a ring his Dryads were still maintaining, though the men all about were sheathing their weapons and made no move against them.

His approximation of Linwood's armour melded back into his body and the tall crown receded. The men looked on as the armoured giant dwindled into the form of an old man, cloaked in leaves with a beard of moss. He began to walk slowly back towards the forest and one by one the Dryads fell in behind him.

Riark was satisfied that his aim had been met and his oath fulfilled. He knew that none of the men there present would ever dare stand against his kind nor enter the forest.

But as he walked, a curious sensation began to resonate throughout him; a sensation he could not register and yet, it was vaguely familiar from his previous life. In a moment of blind panic, he realised that somehow he was in pain and that the sensation was heat; ever growing, scorching, burning heat.

Callum looked on in horror as Dark Oak stepped into the fire, but his father seemed not to be in pain. Soon he was all ablaze, and Callum shrank back, calling out to Whiteflow.

'Put him out! Put him out!'

The Naiad stepped to Callum's side and wrapped a cold, watery arm about his shoulders.

'Fear not,' she said.

Dark Oak stepped down from the fire and looked to Callum's eyes to be a man aflame. He bowed low to his son, turned and ran towards Riark's Mother Tree. He thrust his arms towards the ancient and beautiful elm, and scores of flaming tendrils were flung around it; they stretched up into the branches setting the leaves aflame. They seized the tree and, like a burning boa constrictor, Dark Oak wrapped his form around the trunk. The tree kindled, and the flames turned white as the heat intensified. The elm burned as the fire leaped up all over the tree. Dark Oak drew back his right arm, and Callum saw that his hand shifted form into that of the head of a monstrous axe. Dark Oak hewed at the trunk of Riark's Mother Tree and the ground shook beneath Callum's feet. Dark Oak struck again and again and again, carving a great rent in the trunk of the elm. Dark Oak squeezed his burning head and torso inside and the elm was aflame inside and out.

Callum shrank back from the Naiad as Dark Oak melded into the wood of the Mother Tree, taking the fire inside its very being, and there he strove with Riark's spirit, blasting it with heat and enraging the molecules of the tree so that fire ripped up and down the blackened elm.

Hundreds of miles north, Riark threw out his arms, looking down at his form as it glowed like a coal within a fire. The Dryads about him looked on, and all present realised what was happening too late. They set off at a terrible pace towards the forest, and Riark was left wheeling and shrieking amidst the terrified army of men who looked on at him, uncomprehending.

Riark's body burst into an intense white flame that rippled over and engulfed him. He thrust deep roots down into the ground, and his legs melded together into a narrow trunk which widened and grew so that he appeared to be a burning hybrid of man and tree. The flames inside his very soul drove him insane as he burned and the vines of his mane whipped out in all directions like whips of lava. The bark of his skin blackened and he screamed so hard that his pit of a mouth split right round his head. He blackened and shrivelled, glowing deep inside as the flames began to shrink and there upon the hillside, Riark fell to ash, which dispersed in the dying winds of the storm.

The men of Stragglers' Drift knew not what to think. They were leaderless and without purpose, but all felt a keen desire to put distance between themselves and the forest. So without a word of direction they turned towards their homes and hurried away. Where all had been noise and light, blood and death, now all was silent. The storm clouds drew back and the smoke billowed ever upwards until it was lost in the heavens. The waters receded and all was still.

Deep in the heart of Mount Greenwood, Dark Oak turned his back on the flaming pyre that had been Riark's Mother Tree. Smoke poured up and out the living mountain, as though it were a volcano and the slopes began to crack and fall.

Callum shrunk away.

'I…' He could not find the words to express his confusion and with Dark Oak looming towards him with a curious motion reminiscent of a sidewinder, he gave up - merely rooting to the spot and awaiting his fate.

Dying wood crashed down through the smoke and shards of debris cut his face. Callum fell to the ground and cried out when a branch crushed his lower leg.

The cry was so high and pained that Dark Oak paused as he moved, remembering the cries of his children when they were but new-born. He looked down upon one of them now, writhing in agony, and felt his father's duty.

'Fear not, Son,' he said and reached down to pick up the boy and cradle him in his arms. He marched on towards his own Mother Tree as Greenwood smashed to the left and right of him, before and behind. His gaze was unwaveringly forward and Callum looked up at his father's face, fearful and not knowing whether it should be so.

Once they were clear of the falling debris, Dark Oak laid Callum upon the grass and the Naiad that was his sister dripped from Dark Oak's fingers and took form, reposed on the grass beside him.

Dark Oak crouched to one knee and caressed his face. The touch was ragged and left splinters as would new, shorn timber and Callum winced, but Dark Oak did not react.

'All will be well now,' the Dryad soothed and with that he raised his right arm. Callum had only an instant to register that he was in danger before Dark Oak thrust it forward. The Dryad's wooden fingers splayed and smashed through Callum's chest with terrible force. Callum's eyes widened, and the blood vessels in them popped as the shock of the impact drove him into the ground. His limbs flailed as Dark Oak used both hands to prise back and snap ribs so that they jutted painfully up through his chest. Callum lapsed into unconsciousness and Dark Oak took gentle but firm hold of his heart until the boy was dead. His fingers became one with the flesh and his sap oozed into the veins.

The blood was slick on the black timber of Dark Oak's body as he hauled the carcass onto his shoulder, and he marched on towards the glade where his Mother Tree grew. Beside it and yet just far enough away that the leaves did not block out the light, grew a magnificent red maple. Dark Oak came to a standstill, lowered his head and stared out from under his furrowed brow. The soles of his feet drove deep into the soil as roots and entangled with those of the maple. Dark Oak imagined his desire and it was so.

With a rending crash the wide trunk of the young maple ripped open vertically down the centre exposing a newly formed void within. He walked slowly forward and as though he were the orchestrator of a new ceremony, he forced Callum's ruined body into the trunk of the tree, and the wood closed in around his son.

Dark Oak turned to his daughter.

'There is much to be done. Gather the Council.'

She seeped away into the soil, and Dark Oak was left alone in the forest, the acrid smell of Riark's charred Mother Tree filling the air.

He looked at his own Mother Tree, the great black oak, feeling the desire to be one with the forest, knowing that the longer he spent in his actual form, the less he would remember and the less he would feel.

But Dark Oak was not prepared to forget and his anger knew no bounds. He waited for those that he knew would surely be coming.

Chapter Twenty-Four

Beacon Hall was delved deep in the earth between Stragglers' End and the forest. It could be reached only by a series of vertical shafts which ran from the outer tunnels up to the surface and by the single opening where the tunnelling Partisans had broken through by accident.

Lachlan had shunned the great throne room for a series of small caves that had once stood as guard houses near the base of the shafts. The messengers returned one at a time bringing with them a scattering of able-bodied men. Though it heartened him that so many had heeded his summons, even bowing their heads to him with smiles upon their lips, their numbers were too few. By Lachlan's estimation his force could not stand against even a few companies of the well-trained and well-armoured armies of Lord Linwood.

Yet before the muster was completed the messengers from the east dropped down from the shafts and told of the burning of the forest; of how Linwood had taken his whole force to its very edge and the word upon the tongues of many was that the strength of Stragglers' Drift had marched off to contend with a hidden power in the forest that prevented the building of the road. The word Dryad had been thrown around and though Lachlan discounted it, he was uneasy; unease that he saw mirrored in the faces of Hadwyn and Belman.

Not so with Habit, however, and in a moment of serious debate between the men, she laughed so that Belman chastised her.

'Do you think us fools, woman? Laugh not.' He said the words without looking at her and drained his ale when he was done. He looked to his lord and friend as though expecting her to react strongly and hoping one of them would resume the conversation before she had the chance, but their eyes flitted to Habit.

'If ever there was proof that strengthening your arm saps muscle from your brain, it'd be you,' she said. Belman's face reddened and he turned to face her.

'My people spend more time in the woods than out of it and yet you scorn my knowledge, as a man who has only of late come to these lands and has been fortunate enough to be raised between walls and under a roof?' she said.

Belman's first instinct was to lash out with insults but he was conscious of affirming her assessment of him, so he held his tongue and took a different tack.

'I do not scorn your knowledge, but your laughter, which interrupts our discourse. How was I to know your thoughts? If I assumed wrongly that you were mocking us then tell me what amused you so?'

Now it was Lachlan and Hadwyn who were amused, seeing how their comrade struggled to pick his words and sweeten his voice. The lord decided he should come to his aid lest the whore struck again and the matter escalated.

'You think there is truth in these rumours about the tree people?'

Habit nodded.

'Couldn't tell you much though, but we've seen things over the years, some of us. There are legends aplenty.'

'There are legends in the Isles too,' said Hadwyn.

'And the Folly,' said Lachlan, 'but only stories.'

Habit shrugged, dismissing both the suggestion and the importance of the matter.

'Legends come from somewhere. Who among us has time to imagine such things in a world where there are mouths to feed and homes to defend? After seeing Awgren's work, do you doubt the existence of anything?'

To that the men made no reply, but Lachlan thought privately on the day when he and Cathryn struck down Awgren; of how easily Awgren had been defeated when they had finally drawn close to him. Had Awgren not been as tall as a tree, shrouded in shadow and wielding power beyond reckoning? So the legends had grown up over the many years of long exile and yet the man bleeding-out at his feet had resembled, well, a man.

'Giving thought to what stories I've heard in my time, I can remember only that Dryads were said to pass in and out of the trees. That at times those who wander in the woods might hear them speak,' he said.

'Little more from our own stories,' replied Habit, 'but I'll not be ashamed to admit that amongst us, many leave offerings for the Dryads and I count myself in that number.'

'And do they take the offerings?' asked Lachlan, doubtful and also surprised.

'Something does, but probably animals,' she conceded, 'but who knows what the spirits of the trees would desire? It's the gesture. I take comfort in knowing that something watches over the woods of my home.'

As she spoke she twiddled a lock of her long hair around her finger, and Lachlan's heart stirred. It occurred to him that he had judged her harshly in being surprised by her spirituality. Yes, she made her living both with a knife and by lying on her back, yet didn't she go about it with ceremony that lent significance?

Hadwyn was scratching at his cheek.

'You look thoughtful,' said Belman. 'Does it hurt?' He grinned, but Hadwyn continued to stare through him though the scratching ceased.

'Brother?' said Lachlan and again, 'Brother?'

Hadwyn shook his head slightly as the daydream broke.

'Your thoughts?' said Lachlan.

'Just that if the legends are true it might explain why Awgren left the forest alone. He razed the old countries from the Maw Gate to the Hinterland but laid not a finger upon the trees there. I've often wondered why he did not burn his way through and finish off the Stragglers long ago,' Hadwyn replied. 'If there is a power there that was able to resist Awgren when the combined might of Tayne, Crinan and Culrain far surpassed our own now, what hope would Linwood have against it?'

Lachlan frowned, and the desire to convey these thoughts to Cathryn was strong in him. Her duty to the realm above herself rose in his thoughts and kindled the same in him.

'And what would it mean for the rest of us? Would that power be able to distinguish between the face of Lachlan and the face of Linwood?'

'Let's hope so,' said Hadwyn.

'Probably not,' said Habit.

'Why do you say so?' asked Belman.

Habit drew her knife and, fidgeting, passed it from one hand to the other over and over.

'I've never yet seen the weather choose one cause over another, nor a sea that cared whose home was lost when the cliffs crumbled. Ever seen a famine care when people starve? Though we run rampant across the world, we are mere flyspecks to it; we are but fleas on a dog. Perhaps ones such as yourselves are untroubled by lice, but I know if I get bit, I don't personally introduce myself to each and every one I find. I do me damnedest to rid myself of the lot of them.'

Lachlan laughed at the many images her words presented and nodded in agreement.

'True enough. Much depends on the nature of this power then, and we must hope for a good outcome, yet plan for the worst.'

He stood and moved to the entrance to the cavern from where he could see folk moving about in the larger adjacent hall.

'I think,' he said, turning back, 'that it should be clear to all of us that we are never going to match Linwood in numbers, perhaps not even if all the Combined People stood against him. And if he is waging a war that *could* be ascribed to us, then we must move against him now and by subtler means. We came by stealth and survive by stealth. It is perhaps possible that I could lead these people and join his army in secret. From what we hear of those that come in, I believe their hearts to be true. It is their sons and brothers that make up Linwood's force and if they are as loyal to the throne as their relatives would have us believe, there is a chance that I could strive with Linwood and yet win the day when his army abandons him to follow me.'

As soon as it was said, he knew that it was his only course of action, and he descended into a moody resignation. As much as he had enjoyed being free of the trappings of royalty and desired to wander the world; as much as he felt keen disappointment and fear, he was also heartened by a growing comfort from knowing that he was doing as Cathryn would wish and he missed her then, not just for the woman that rode at his side in battle, but for the gentle touch of her hand and a thousand little things that made him love her.

He would do this for her.

Dark Oak's daughter embraced Riark's flaming Mother Tree until the flames went out. The blackened wood hissed and steamed.

She returned to her father's side by the black oak and waited for the Council to reply to her summons.

But the Dryads returned first, stepping out of every tree from all around until the black oak was at the centre of a horde of living wood. Dark Oak sensed no malice from them as he had feared, and he had to remind himself that these beings did not have brains with conditioned responses, they did not fight for survival, but instead simply existed and grew. Now the one who spoke for them and guided their growth was gone, so they sought answers.

Dark Oak signalled for them to follow as he stepped inside his Mother Tree. The spirits of a thousand Dryads joined him and each of them breaching the bark was a penetration, a violation. They felt his discomfort, and he knew their concerns, their desire for peace to simply *be*. The soothing nature of the message and the weight of their numbers pressed down on him and yet his own rage and certainty of injustice was so strong that he held them at bay, able to retain these emotions from a life now ended. The Dryads of the world came to know him and understand him and saw that he too desired to simply exist without strife. They attempted to mingle their own tranquillity with his newer instincts and yet he challenged them, emphasising that all was changed, that mankind had overstepped its bounds and was turning all the wonders of the earth into nothing but resources to be exploited; that though Linwood was dead, others would come; that it was as part of the human psyche to expand and conquer and consume, as it was part of a rabbit's to flee from an eagle or as it was for a tree to grow.

And he filled their being with his understanding that Riark had seen a rose with mites upon it and their battle with Linwood had been nothing but picking them off, as would a gardener. Dark Oak overwhelmed them with vehement force of his wordless argument and the strength of his imperative.

If they removed the mites from the rose, the rose would prosper for a time. But the mites would come again. The forest must continue to grow and mankind be forced to realise that it did not hold dominion of the world.

And, they asked of him, just as Riark had plucked the mite that was Linwood from the rose, so Dark Oak had plucked Riark? Dark Oak told them it was not so. Riark was an old elm overshadowed by a bold new oak. Did their Mother Trees not send out branches to seek the light, heedless of the damage done by depriving those beneath them? So he had overshadowed Riark.

Dark Oak made them know his mind. Made them see that he knew what it was to be human and that now was the time— only now would he retain the knowledge of war and the clear understanding which only a human could have of what must be done.

They would no longer limit themselves to acting like gardeners and pick the mites from the rose. The Dryads would learn to hunt.

All of this in moments. Dark Oak was a lone sapling in a forest of thousands and yet the Dryads' inherent placidity was their undoing, for he used his human emotion to dominate them and by this example, full understanding of his argument came upon them. Now they too felt the desire to dominate and control, but hated the sensation. Yet they realised that if this was the nature of man, there would be no peace; that they could never just exist without molestation.

The Dryads had the long-held but unused power to balance the world and for the first time, they not only knew it but could see that it was necessary.

Even as the Dryads were coming to their realisations, Dark Oak could feel himself becoming more like them. He still felt anger and the desire for revenge and injustice at how he had been treated, but just as people do many years after a long ago hurt, that pain would momentarily fade and he achieved a degree of perspective— the Dryad perspective. It was all still there, but seemingly viewed with hindsight. The long ages of the world and the life of the forest seemed to shrink the significance of the wrongs in his life, the significance of nearly everything. He fought the feeling and knew he had to get out of the black oak. Besides, the longer he spent inside his Mother Tree with them, the more violated he felt and sensing this, they began to move off towards the roots. Dark Oak denied them leave. Before releasing them he instilled in them his desires and designs. He insisted that they take human form and keep it for a time, reminding them that to retain what they currently felt, they would need to remain apart from their Mother Trees as long as was possible.

All at once, the Dryads emerged from the black oak, finally followed by Dark Oak himself.

That screaming mouth once again appeared across his face and he addressed them.

'This will not be necessary for long. Once we have secured our existence, we can go back to how things were, though perhaps maintaining peace will take more involvement from us. Follow me and I will see that the forest thrives and grows. How many did we lose because Riark would not stand? We will never lose another. Not one more.'

No sooner had he finished speaking than his daughter arrived. She soaked into him and he received his summons. He stepped back into the black oak and emerged from the First Tree upon the island of the Council. Samura, queen of the Naiads was there in the shallows of the pool. A moment later, Wern, king of the Oreads formed from the boulder. Mayri, queen of the Sylphs descended from the sky and her form was that of a whipping cloud of smoke.

And he addressed them. Linwood had done much of the work for him. Mayri, having seen the polluting of the skies and Samura, who had seen the little rivers and pools boil up in the north, had already acted to maintain balance. They queried Dark Oak hard on his killing of Riark and he used it against them; though he did not speak, his argument was that Dryads did not act in such a manner and that it was his human desire which drove him on. If they took issue with his actions then they had issue with mankind and thus he, Dark Oak, should use his knowledge, fears and hatred to prevent any such actions in future. He would stand as protector of the forest and chief amongst them.

Wern, though not concerned with contending for power, was less moved by his arguments. After all, what effect could humans have on the earth itself? And indeed, millennia before, the Oreads had once had friendship with the humans of old. Dark Oak was surprised to hear that it was the Oreads who had thrown up the walls of the Folly in the time of the First Cleansing long, long ago, in order to protect the humans. Nevertheless, Dark Oak conveyed a message of consumption, showing how the humans had moved from stone, to bronze, to iron, to black powder and steel; how they delved ever deeper and turned the earth to their uses. Wern was not overly concerned, but Dark Oak showed him visions of the future, where humans swarmed across the world in their millions, consuming ever more until the world's resources were used up.

In time, many days in fact, Dark Oak concluded the debate and withdrew back to his Mother Tree where the Dryads waited.

Dark Oak stepped out into his glade.

'Father…'

A tall, thin Dryad with white bark and a mane of red leaves stepped towards him. To Dark Oak's eyes, it appeared gangly and awkward.

'Son,' he said and try as he might, he could not recall his name.

Callum nodded and the bark at his neck splintered.

'You killed me.'

Dark Oak scrutinised Callum's face, but grew frustrated that he was unable to discern his son's emotional state. It would have been clear to Morrick that Callum was confused and betrayed, but Dark Oak was already beginning to lose his understanding of human emotion.

'I would not be parted from you, my son.'

Callum affected a sigh and looked between Dark Oak and Whiteflow.

'We were family,' she trilled and laid a hand on his shoulder. The water of her body soaked into him and she exerted empathy through his being, conveying images of her death by Rowan's hand in order to save him.

'Parents do what they must to save their children. Our mother killed me to save you. She chose to destroy me and favoured her sons. Dark Oak killed you so that we would never again be parted and so you could join our fight.'

'Our fight?' Callum asked.

'Indeed…' Dark Oak struggled for Callum's name and, eventually, conceded, 'indeed, Red Maple.'

He stalked forward and took hold of his other shoulder, also melding with him. He joined hands with Whiteflow and the three of them shared understanding.

'There is peace to be had if we redress the balance,' said Dark Oak. 'I worked my whole life to do right by my family. I did my duty and did heinous acts to protect you. I hoped for the day when the bright hope would win through; when the good and glorious queen of mankind would sweep in to deliver us, but when they arrived? Worse than before. I was imprisoned, maltreated, conscripted again, beaten and rejected. Every hope I ever had was dashed and mankind once again controls the land. Ever deeper they mine and I know that the forests will dwindle as their industry increases. Soon this continent will be dotted with heaving cities and the forest will be hewn to build them.'

Red Maple looked into the white stars of Dark Oak's eyes and, seeing with new eyes and feeling new priorities, his loyalty won out.

Lachlan's force assembled on the great road and when all were mustered, Belman estimated their numbers at around five hundred. Lachlan, Hadwyn and Belman rode at the head of the column, and Habit walked with her Partisans behind. Flanking them were the armoured guards from the villages who had sent aid. Together they marched towards the forest.

For the first time since arriving in the Drift, Lachlan openly wore the silver crown he had long kept secreted in his pack.

They had passed but a few hours along the road when they came upon the first survivors of Lord Linwood's army. Lachlan's first instinct was to jump down from the saddle and get amongst them to hear what they had to tell, but he thought of Cathryn and how she would have carried herself, all too aware that he needed to appear lordly. And so, he sat atop his mount and remained aloof, dispatching his brother and general to gather what news they could. He leant upon his saddle, his heart beating fast, and Habit moved up beside him.

'Don't look like things have gone so well,' she said.

Lachlan said nothing, but nodded.

Ere long Hadwyn returned and with him came the castellan of Stragglers' End, humbled and apologetic.

'Make your report, Castellan.'

The man bowed his head.

'Lord Linwood has been killed and much of the army has been destroyed. You will think me mad if I say more, Sire.'

'Speak and be judged,' said Lachlan.

The man shifted his weight to his other foot then back again.

'Creatures of the air drove the smoke from the fire down upon us and an army of Dryads invaded the Drift from the trees. They smashed through our lines and their king drowned Lord Linwood in the mud. Their king burned up right in front of us and turned to ash in the wind. I have never seen the like, Sire.' Lachlan saw that the castellan was shaking, and he held up a hand.

'Curious. What did you make of their king burning?' he asked, but it seemed none around him could judge its meaning.

'Where are the Dryads now?' he asked.

'They ran for the forest when their king burned,' said Willard.

Lachlan nodded.

'Linwood has made much mischief, and we must seek an audience with these creatures before we return to Stragglers' End. I…'

'Your Grace!' blurted Willard, and his face reddened. He bowed low.

'My apologies for interrupting you Sire.'

Lachlan dismissed his apologies and urged him to speak.

'The Dryads and the other creatures that I saw in the air and the water, there was no killing them. We didn't take down a single one of them. If they should take against us?'

'He makes a fair point,' said Hadwyn and Lachlan nodded.

'We'll proceed slowly and not form line of battle.'

He turned his attention to Belman.

'General, take a small party of riders ahead to the forest edge, and call out for truce and parley.'

'Aye, my lord,' Belman set off to gather his choice of companions.

Lachlan straightened up in his saddle.

'Men and women of the Drift,' he called, his voice booming out so that the survivors gathered in around him as they walked closer. 'Listen up, now. Linwood committed treason against the realm and has paid with his life. I see that it can be no easy thing to stand and defy one who had led you for so long and to so many victories, and I know that in your hearts you are loyal to the crown. Is it so?'

A resounding 'AYE' rose up from the crowd.

Lachlan nodded, making an effort to survey the whole crowd, making what eye contact he could.

'Then forget the doings of these past days and fall in behind me. Castellan, have your people fall in at the rear of the column,' he said and spurred on his horse.

Belman and his riders disappeared and Lachlan led the column onward at marching pace. He was confident now that his position in the north was secure and was anxious to meet with the Dryads to sue for peace and explain Lord Linwood's betrayal. Even more so, he was anxious to send word to Cathryn for he knew that for the first time in their long marriage, she would be truly proud of him.

But his hopes and confidence dwindled fast when they drew close to the spot where Linwood had been killed.

Horses without riders came galloping past the column, back the way they had come. It did not go unnoticed that they matched the number which departed with Belman.

'Brother...' said Hadwyn, but Lachlan made no reply.

'Onward and with haste!' the Lord of the Isles roared.

They reached the ridge upon which Linwood's army had been assembled and Lachlan looked on with sadness at the dead men all strewn across the dead ground before him, but there was no time to pause and reflect. He led his people onwards, concerned that there was no sign of Belman.

Lachlan halted the column a few hundred yards from the treeline. He addressed Habit, the castellan and the captains of the Drift.

'I will set out for the trees alone,' he said, and no amount of objections from Hadwyn would dissuade him.

And yet before he could set out, the ground began to shake and all around them shoots burst out of the ground, growing fast into young saplings. Bright sunlight shone down upon them and as far as the eye could see a young forest was growing up. Many of the men who had fought the Dryads let their fear overcome them and ran, but the new growth of the forest could not be escaped.

From the old forest, thousands of Dryads burst into view and charged towards Lachlan, Hadwyn and the people of the Drift.

Lachlan jumped down from his saddle, shifted his weight from foot to foot and when the Dryad onslaught was but yards away, he drew his sword. He burst forward, leaving the ranks of his men behind him, yelling out until his hoarse shouts were lost in the noise of the fray.

He sidestepped the whipping branches of a silver birch and disappeared amongst the Dryad ranks. Hadwyn and Habit tarried for mere moments before they had roared their orders and set out after him. They too were lost from sight.

The captains called out instructions, but the soldiers could not be rallied in spirit. The saplings had sprouted up into young trees and now all around a young forest divided Lachlan's army. Men ran in all directions and what battle there had been for a few minutes dissolved into quiet.

When the battle was done, birdsong filled the air and a sweet silence hung over the Drift. Men wandered here and there amongst the trees and ran from the Dryads as they stalked the woods. Satisfied that the men had scattered, the Dryads stepped into the trees and disappeared. All was still but for the sobbing and quiet talk of the survivors who banded together.

The soldiers could not find their captains or the castellan. The Partisans searched here and there, but there was no sign of Habit, and none could find Hadwyn or Belman. Though they called his name, Lachlan did not answer.

William, Habit's brother, wandered the new woods looking for his sister, the missing members of his family and the lords.

He came upon a spot deep in the midst of the forest where the light splatter of blood-spray coloured the grass. As he walked, he found crimson pools in which scraps of leather armour now floated like barren islands. William followed a sodden path of bloodied grass through the woods until he came upon a hawthorn tree which seemed to grow up from a pool of blood and splintered bones. Its trunk was a mess of gore and flaps of skin hung from the branches; it looked to William as though someone had been driven back against it and battered into pulp. He approached the tree slowly, seeing something glint in the noon sun. His feet crunched bone until finally he stopped and, with trembling hands, he plucked Lord Lachlan's silver crown from the berry-laden lower branches of the hawthorn tree.

Chapter Twenty-Five

The cuckoo raid began two days before Lord Linwood fell in battle.

From the depths of the cellars of the Maw Keep, the hidden regiments of Stragglers' Drift tore through the stronghold level by level, killing all that stood in their way. Those of their number who had ingratiated themselves set about the Folly Guards from the side and behind, thrusting knives and hacking at undefended backs just before the two groups engaged.

Their priority was to secure the Maw Keep and thus the Maw Gate, therefore the fighting was most bloody around the doors that led into the rest of the Folly. Linwood's men, heedless of their lord's impending demise, swarmed through the fortress and bloodied the previously unsullied floors.

The battle for the Maw Keep raged on night after night.

Lord Aldwyn stood at the taffrail of his ship, the Nightingale, and surveyed the fleet. Far astern and away in the west, the queen's own vessel led her line of ships and was visible through the rain only by its lights.

A beam of light shone out from the east where Abernath's Lighthouse stood on a patch of bare land on the coast midway up the western edge of the forest.

'Perhaps a week till we make landfall, my lord,' said Captain Lynch, who bounded up the steps from the main deck, taking two steps at a time. Aldwyn nodded. He'd never made the voyage before and looked on with curiosity at the lighthouse.

'It must be a lonely posting,' he said.

Lynch nodded as he came to stand beside him. Unlike Aldwyn he was well accustomed to the sea and felt no need to grasp the rail.

'A welcome escape for many a family man.' Lynch smiled and Aldwyn laughed,

'You speak from experience?'

Lynch raised an eyebrow.

'The woodcutter's wife?' asked Aldwyn.

Lynch tilted his head.

'I may have made an error in judgement there.'

'You had relations?'

Lynch said nothing.

'We are all capable of the odd moral lapse,' said Aldwyn.

'Even the high lords of old Tayne?' said Lynch, still staring out at the light.

Aldwyn said nothing.

'You know of Abernath's Lighthouse?' said Lynch.

'I knew of its existence, but not of its origins.'

'It might not look it, but it was quite the feat at the time. After many of the Crinish were wrecked on the reefs that lie between us now and Strewn Men Bay, they spent years travelling down the coast with materials to build a tower upon which they could set a beacon. They say it has never been out since the day they lit it nigh on a thousand years ago. To think of the journey that stone must have made by narrow coastal path or by sea.' Lynch shook his head.

'None could accuse Linwood and his forefathers of a lack of tenacity,' said Aldwyn, 'but look, the light has just gone out even as we look on! Perhaps legends are not always so accurate.'

Lynch's head snapped back towards the lighthouse and his brow furrowed.

'I've made this journey more times than I could count, and I know many a man who has done the same. Never have I heard of the light being out.'

'Perhaps Linwood anticipates our coming.'

At this Lynch seemed to hearten.

'Maybe so, my lord, and if it is the case, we should extinguish the lights of the fleet and go on our way in darkness. Change course and throw off any pursuers or observers if we can.'

Aldwyn mused on it and nodded.

'Speak with the captain and see if he concurs. If so, have him signal the fleet,' he said, gripping the taffrail so tight that his knuckles whitened. His stomach lurched as the Nightingale crested a wave.

To the east, the lighthouse keeper cried his last as the stones of the tower fell down upon him.

Nine Days Later

Queen Cathryn was awoken by a knock on her cabin door and Ailsa left her cot to answer.

'The captain's compliments, and the queen is requested on deck. We are entering Seal Bay.'

'Very well, send word that the queen will attend shortly.'

Cathryn screwed up her eyes against the screaming headache. Her mouth was dry and when she sat up, her innards churned.

'Not before time.' she said and deflected all of Ailsa's attempts to assist in dressing her. She adorned herself in full armour, unwilling to appear anything less than regal, and proceeded upon deck. Those who saw her dropped to one knee momentarily, and Cathryn passed between them without a word until she found the captain.

'Good morning, Captain,' she said, granting him a courteous moment of eye contact before turning her gaze to the coast.

The sight of the trees crowding the shoreline puzzled her, and she turned back to question the captain, but he was shaking his head.

'The shape of the land tells no lie, and I've been diligent in checking the charts, Your Majesty. This *is* Seal Bay. I've been here many a time, but these…' he waved a hand towards the trees, 'were not here.'

Cathryn and Ailsa advanced upon the rail and, taking up the captain's telescope, the queen glassed the coastline from east to west. The beaches had given way to grass banks, which stretched into plains towards the cities, but now they were hemmed in by forest as far as the eye could see.

'There were no defences here?' said Cathryn, unable to see a soul ashore.

'There were, Your Majesty, a stockade and garrison. Yonder...' He pointed towards a headland now populated by what looked like mature pine trees.

Cathryn handed back the glass, unsure what to think and aware that all eyes were upon her. Was this Riark's doing? Had Linwood enraged him further? If it was so, what had happened to her people here?

'I must know what has happened,' she declared in a quiet and calm voice. 'Take me to the Nightingale. I will speak with Lord Aldwyn.'

The Isles appeared as a low black ridge on the horizon which grew larger as the supply convoy made its excruciatingly slow approach. Rowan had long since lost her wonder at the sea and yearned to set foot upon the island that was to be her home.

Each day she and Declan had spent a while on deck before the cold wind got too much, but now as the shape of the mountains became clear, she fetched up blankets so they could stay even longer. She did not want to miss a single detail, ready to fall in love with these new lands about which she had dreamed ever since she was a girl. Here was where the line of the kings of Culrain now dwelled in their fearsome clans.

The low black ridge became towering peaks in the distance, and a passing sailor she queried told her that those were the mountains on Long Isle which was still some way off.

'Long Isle?' said Rowan and clasped Declan to her. 'That's where the Lord of the Isles comes from!' Her voice was excited, and he cuddled up to her leg.

Between the supply ship and Long Isle were the tiny Horseshoe Isle and Low Isle, now distinguishable in the foreground, the Isles no longer appearing as a single dark entity. The ports of both isles were all on the westward side where they were protected from rougher waters by the natural barriers of the land, yet as they passed between the two small islands, the crew became agitated and soon Rowan saw why. The sea was littered with planks, sail cloth, barrels and other such detritus. It appeared to her that great ships must have been wrecked here and yet she spied what seemed to be thatching from a roof and fencing too bobbing upon the waves.

The coastline was unfamiliar to her but word went round that there were trees now lining the shore where before there had been fields. She saw a lighthouse wrecked on the north coast of the Horseshoe Isle and as the convoy drew closer the crew began to work harder at getting every last knot from the ship.

The cliffs of the Horseshoe Isle loomed towards them with tall pine trees crowning their edges.

The convoy rounded the island and entered the Inner Sea, where the wreckage in the water became ever denser, and Rowan began to panic. What had happened here?

'Mother, what is it?' Declan implored, but Rowan could give no answer. She knew and indeed all aboard knew that something was much amiss.

'Come below,' she said and, ignoring his resistance, Rowan dragged Declan below decks to where they had made their berth.

She cuddled him close to her that night, drawing his face to her chest and only after several anxious hours did she fall asleep.

Rowan woke and all was black – the swinging lanterns with their amber glow had all gone out. She was soaked from head to foot. The ship ducked this way and that. She shivered with cold and reached first for the blanket and then for Declan, but her fingers could not find him. She scrambled about and called his name, but heard no reply. There was a metallic smell in the air.

'Declan,' she screamed. No sounds greeted her bar the creak of wood and the slap of slack ropes against sails.

'Anyone?'

She heard a faint cry. Rowan crawled forward and rounded a makeshift partition. The decks sloshed with fluid and, recognising the smell finally, Rowan knew it was iron – blood. She crawled faster as her heart rate went up.

Some way along the deck a hatch was open to the outside, casting a square of light upon the steps. She got to her feet and picked her way across the deck, steadying herself where she could. The cry came again, and she knew it was him.

'Declan!' She shouted so hard that her throat felt as though it was ripping. Finally she reached the steep steps and crawled up them, too unsteady to walk. The main deck was empty and the sails flapped uselessly above it. Rowan looked all around and could see no one.

'Mother!' a voice shrieked, and she knew it was her son. She ran towards the sound and reached the rail.

There in the water was one of the creatures she had seen before in the Whiteflow, carrying off her baby daughter. That churning figure of sea foam seemed to tread water effortlessly at some distance, its figure feminine and lithe.

Whiteflow looked up at her mother and smiled.

Rowan screamed.

'No!'

Declan too was in the ocean and Whiteflow's arms were wrapped about his chest, somehow holding him just high enough so that his shoulders were clear.

'Give him back,' Rowan shrieked. 'What do you want?'

Perhaps in days gone by Whiteflow would have taunted her mother, but in truth the emotion had faded and now she acted purely because she remembered she had once cared, and that Dark Oak had given her instruction. She vaguely remembered these people and had an academic understanding that some sort of justice was being served, but she knew not how and simply trusted to Dark Oak's plans.

She would act and all would be balanced, then everyone could sleep and things would be as they had before. So he had promised.

She sank into the water and it closed about Declan as she took him down with her. The last that Rowan saw of him was his wide eyes, his last screams turning into gurgled, sputtered chokes.

Rowan leaped over the rail and swam out to where her son had disappeared. She dived deep time and time again, weighed down by her clothes. The cold began to drain her, and she knew as she made one last dive, her eyes unseeing in the dark depths, that she had not the strength to do so again. Strands of hair stuck to her face, and she kicked back up to the surface, gasping and sobbing. She cried out as her flailing arm hit a plank then she grasped onto it. Rowan looked all about her and despaired.

Finally with what little strength remained, she swam back towards the abandoned supply ship and climbed the rungs. She threw herself upon the deck and, her clothes soaked with the blood of the crew, she sobbed into her arm.

Far below her, as she flowed into Declan's lifeless body through his eyes and nose and mouth and ears, Whiteflow felt a vague sense of satisfaction, yet did not really comprehend why.

Cathryn and Aldwyn took a boat ashore with no more men than were needed to row.

Cathryn remained in the boat while Aldwyn and the others jumped into the surf. They hauled the boat up the beach, and Cathryn stepped out, dry, on to the sand.

'Remain with the boat,' she instructed and started for the treeline.

'Aldwyn,' drifted back over her shoulder, and he jogged to catch her up, his sword bouncing against his hip.

They moved in silence under the boughs as the light dimmed.

Cathryn's face showed fury, and her eyes were everywhere. Aldwyn dared not speak given her current mood. He followed on, dutiful and watchful, as she wound her way beneath the canopy. New flowers seemed to spring up about their feet as they walked and Aldwyn marvelled at the peace, broken only by the sound of animals, birds and insects as they went about their survey.

Cathryn stepped up to one of the pines and placed her hand upon it.

'Riark,' she whispered.

There was no reply and no sign of the king of the Dryads.

'Riark,' she called.

Nothing.

They peered into the gloom and saw tight packed trunks into the distance in all directions, little streams coursing around them in places.

Cathryn leant back against the tree, and Aldwyn crossed his arms over his chest as he watched her with mounting concern.

'How do you wish to proceed?' he asked, still watching. She looked down at her feet, breathing hard.

'I know not, but it is clear our forces cannot make headway through such thick woods.'

'Given that they are lately sprung up and we know not how or why, it may not be wise to land troops in any case,' said Aldwyn. She looked up and he saw agreement in her soft, defeated gaze.

'Come. Back to the boat,' she said eventually and they set off.

Six days of sailing close to the shore and the view did not change in theme. Though the land reached out and fell away into coves and bays, the forest was unrelenting. Ere long they rounded the headland into Strewn Men Bay and it was confirmed beyond any doubt that the world was changed. Where fleets had lain at anchor, the queen spied the same detritus that Rowan had witnessed around the Isles. Gone were the ships and come was the forest.

Now even the queen's presence on the deck of the Nightingale could not quieten the crew's opinions. She regarded the coast in silence.

'Your Majesty,' said Aldwyn, conscious of the men's morale. Cathryn descended to her cabin and closed the door behind her.

The evening wore on and the hands were piped to dinner. Aldwyn ate with them and sat beside Captain Lynch. All speculated as to what had happened, in particular what would have become of the Drifts' many towns and strongholds. What of its people? After all, the Stragglers made up the bulk of the queen's army.

There was no singing that night, just more talk. Those who would normally be drunk and skylarking, brooded together instead, mulling over all that they had seen. Some thought they should be away to the Isles or to the Folly. Others thought it only right to make for Stragglers' End. Aldwyn felt it unwise to divide their force, and his heart told him that pushing into the forest was both a necessity and a mistake. After all, what if the Dryads had taken against them? And yet there were people in there, surely? And Lachlan?

The whole crew waited for the queen to reappear, but she did not leave her cabin all that night.

Aldwyn knocked a few times but received no reply and so he took what sleep he could find. In the morning when he returned on deck, he could see various trails of thin smoke off in the woods, such as would be caused by small camp fires. They were few enough and distant from one another, but it stirred the men's hearts that there were still folk abroad.

'Captain,' Cathryn's voice made them all jump, concentrating on the land as they were.

'Your Majesty?' bowed the captain.

Cathryn was once again in her full armour, and Ailsa was attired likewise.

'We know not what has taken place and our supplies will not last forever. I will take a party ashore to glean what answers we can. I will send word as to whether you are to go or stay. Must needs ere long you will away back to the Isles and await instruction, leaving but a single ship to take us off.'

She turned to Lord Aldwyn.

'Would you come with me or stay with the fleet, my lord?' she asked and though her tone was even, her eyes seemed to implore him to understand some hidden meaning.

And so it was that Cathryn and Aldwyn were set down once more upon the shore of the Drift where tall pines blotted out the sky and crow calls froze the spine.

Lynch stayed with a small party to man the boats, and Ailsa argued strongly not to be parted from the queen; only by direct instruction did she reluctantly yield. Cathryn insisted that this was not a matter for strength of arm or numbers – that a power was at work here with which she must take counsel. Ailsa too stayed with the boats.

Together Cathryn and Aldwyn decided upon the direction of the nearest camp fire and, but a man and a woman travelling together, bearing only what they needed to survive, they set off into the forest.

The battle of the Maw Keep was won. The captain of Linwood's men took up residence in Cathryn and Lachlan's quarters, fearful though he was that he would be admonished upon Linwood's return. The guards had never yielded and had been hard pressed for days, yet the Stragglers had won out and all opposition was slain. The victors had barred the gates into the keep and burned the bodies upon the summit of the utmost tower so that all the Folly could see how fared the elite guard of the city.

The captain summoned his lieutenants to feast, and they made their plans to dominate the rest of the city, content that they had ushered in a new era of empire for reinstated Crinan.

Way down to the south of the Maw Keep stood a circular courtyard with an apple tree planted in a bank of earth at its centre. The guards who had been watching it since Riark's appearance had been summoned by the city watch when the first sounds of battle drifted down from the Maw Keep. Now the watch had set a siege upon the fortress and most of the Folly was emptied.

So when the first of the Dryads emerged from the tree, it went unnoticed. One after another followed on until the courtyard was full and it was only when they were forced to step up onto the high wall which surrounded the low buildings that the people thereabouts spied them.

The call went up, but to no avail. The city watch were many, many miles distant and the Dryads marauded through the streets, travelling with terrible speed towards the city watch and the gates to the Maw Keep beyond.

Those who lived close to the immense outer wall of the Folly began to feel the ground shake and as though they were being forced up by great plates under the earth, the walls began to rise up ever higher.

The citizens of the Folly gathered their families and ran from their homes as Oreads rose out of the ground, huge in stature and appearing to heft the mountainous walls upon their broad shoulders. Great grey figures of granite they were; they roared, and their solid facsimiles of muscle flexed as they flung the curtain walls out into the sea, leaving but the ruin of their foundations. The peninsula was once again open to the sea air.

The Oreads' work was not yet complete. They stomped along the foundations, hurling themselves into the now exposed cross-section of wall, causing the greater heights to crash down upon their infallible living bodies of rock.

All about them men, women and children wove this way and that to avoid crumbling buildings while the Oreads continued their destruction.

The Dryads tore on like great spiders, hurling out limbs and vines to tear down all in their path.

The city watch, high upon the slopes, turned and saw the destruction of the walls. They stood aghast, but not for long. The horde of Dryads swarmed through the streets like a tide flowing towards them. The humans stood their ground, but were swept aside by the force of the advance. Those who were not pulled apart and broken by the Dryads ran down to find their families, if they were brave enough, while those who were not cowered under what shelter they could find.

With the Folly walls torn down and its buildings being pulverised one by one, Dark Oak stepped out into the deserted courtyard.

He looked about him and saw that all was to his satisfaction. Red Maple stepped out after him and together they walked towards the canal to the Sea Gate and there, they waited.

The people of the Folly sheltered in the wrecked buildings and realising they were not being hunted down, they did what they could to gather supplies and stores; some of the farmers even ventured out to check their animals and crops.

By the canal, Dark Oak and Red Maple waited still. At dusk their vigilance was rewarded. Whiteflow rose up from the canal between the broken beams of one of the gates, and beside her was another Naiad, boyish in appearance and familiar to all. Whiteflow and the Naiad held their form and stepped up onto the quayside and there, father, daughter and sons soaked into and liaised with one another, united at last.

They separated once more, and Dark Oak set off towards the Maw Keep followed by his children, whose true names he could no longer remember. The streets were largely impassable in the built-up areas, but only to human feet. The Dryads and Naiads made fast progress up the slopes, shifting in form to suit their need, moving ever onward. They drew near to the Maw Keep, and Dark Oak bade his children hold back.

He shot out tendrils of roots into the cracks in the stone arch and heaved. Supporting stone fell away and as it did so he cast out new tendrils, ripping away at the door.

The Stragglers inside had spied the destruction and fled deeper into the keep. Dark Oak strode after them, still retaining his human appearance, clad in black armour and with white eyes shining. The black ivy of his hair dragged along the floor behind him as he cast aside all he overtook as they ran from him. None stood against him, perceiving his rage and might.

Ere long he reached the throne room, and there he once more cast down the doors. Moonlight shone in through the exposed northern face of the room, broken only by the pillars. Linwood's men were gathered around the thrones, and Dark Oak strode towards them. They shrunk back from him as he walked, but he made no move against them.

The surviving Stragglers sidled to safety and ran down into the keep.

While the Dryads pulled the Maw Gate from its hinges, and the humans fled before his people, Dark Oak settled down to sit upon Cathryn's throne.

He looked out to the north and saw that the wastes of the Maw were filling with trees that grew, heedless of the poison the Devised had poured into the soil.

Dark Oak was satisfied, and his children joined him in the throne room.

He spoke,

'Their cities are broken and their roads are dust. They are scattered and divided.'

He tilted his head and listened. The sounds of destruction had come to an end and the human survivors crept away as stealthily as their clumsy forms allowed. He let them go – they were of no concern to him now.

'Let them be as all other living things. They will not build beyond their allotted means. They will not gather in great number. Those who rise will be crushed.'

'Will we not forget? Become idle?' asked Whiteflow.

'Only those who return to the trees and the water,' replied the Naiad that was Declan. He and Whiteflow seated themselves upon benches that looked out upon the Maw. They shimmer in the moonlight. 'If we few stay as we are, we will still remember.'

'We can awaken the forest and the rivers at need,' said Red Maple.

'And we will set the watch.' creaked Dark Oak.

Under that same moon, Rowan stepped down into the ship's boat and struggled with the oars. With some effort, she pushed off and heaving with all her might, she set her mind and will upon reaching land.

I know not where he is, she thought, *but I will not lose my last remaining child.*

And slowly, slowly her little boat splashed towards the stony beaches of the Butterfly Isle.

In the midst of the forest away to the north, the surviving Stragglers and Partisans made what shelter they could, foraging for roots and berries, hunting amongst the trees.

And though their situation was bleak and they knew not what the coming days had in store, Aldwyn and Cathryn huddled together for warmth by their campfire and were secretly content.

THE END.

Thank you for reading the first book in this series!

I would love to keep you updated about my new releases, so if you would like to hear more about my work, please consider signing-up for my Readers' Club at www.jacobsannox.com. I'll also be running giveaways for my members.

It would be fantastic (and much appreciated) if you could leave me a review wherever you bought your copy, as it's one of the best ways for new readers to find out that my books exist!

I hope to hear from you!

Printed in Great Britain
by Amazon